DAMNED IF

A NOVEL

TY DRAGO

CASTLE BRIDGE MEDIA
DENVER, COLORADO, USA

CASTLE BRIDGE MEDIA
Denver, Colorado

Cover photo by John Tyson/Unsplash.
This image has been modified.

ST. DAMNED
©2024 Ty Drago
All rights reserved.

ISBN: 979-8-9895934-8-4

PROLOGUE
Camden, New Jersey—1972

"JESUS H. CHRIST!" OFFICER WILLIAM Shaker exclaimed when he turned and saw them, his heart—already pounding—shifting to turbo. "Where the hell did you two come from?"

The two teenage girls stood shoulder-to-shoulder, awash in his flashlight beam.

It took a second for his shock to pass. Then it took another second, no more, for him to realize that this whole thing was—*wrong*

Terribly wrong.

The girls each wore a stained and tattered wedding dress. One looked to be twelve, maybe thirteen. The other was older, definitely high school age. Both were pretty, or would have been, if not for their sunken eyes, their ashen skin, their slack mouths—and the long deep slashes that had opened up their necks, set into stark relief by the glare. Despite his shock, Shaker remained enough of a cop to infer a thin bladed weapon. A razor, maybe.

Somebody cut their throats...

His first thought was an ambulance. In fact, his hand was halfway to his radio before he realized with mounting horror that there wasn't any blood. Well, that wasn't true. Their drained blood was what had stained their wedding dresses. But, even in the poor light, the stains looked old—very old. More than that, the girls' wounds were puckered and dry, the jagged, blackened flesh standing out starkly in the glare of his flashlight. Suddenly,

Bill Shaker—"Shakey" to his friends—understood with an awful, unnatural certainty that both these girls had died a long time ago, apparently on their wedding days.

He further grasped that the pair of them stood between him and the only exit, their small hands hanging at their sides and their eyes hidden by large silver coins.

Coins for Charon…the ferryman.

Shaker only vaguely remembered the old Greek myth from his school days, but it struck the forefront of his memory now with such force that it felt almost like a physical slap.

These girls are dead.

Holy sweet fuck…they're both actually and truly dead.

"Get out…" he began, waving his gun at them ridiculously, all his weapons training forgotten. His mouth felt dry and his heart kept slamming against his ribcage as if trying to break out. Licking his lips, he regrouped. "Get out of my way!"

Neither girl responded. They didn't even move, making him wonder if they were aware of him at all. This thought actually offered some hope. Maybe, if he could stay calm and keep his peace long enough, they'd wander off and let him out of here.

Then his radio chirped, sounding like a thunderclap in this cold darkness. *"Shakey! I need you! Where the hell are you?"*

With a cry, he fumbled for it, almost dropping his flashlight in the process. When he finally got the damned gadget to his lips, his eyes never leaving the two dead *things* in front of him, his voice came out as an arid, desperate croak. "I'm in the church! The front door opened and I saw this girl. She looked like she was in trouble. So, I followed her in. I followed her *up.* But now there's two of them…and they won't let me leave! Please, man. Help me. I—"

Without warning, the two teenagers blocking the archway stepped aside. They did it smoothly, without so much as a shared glance, as if acting with one mind.

A male figure appeared between them. He didn't come from anywhere. He didn't "step forward." He just—appeared, as if the shadows had simply made him and deposited him there.

Shaker's throat closed and his mind seemed to freeze solid. He didn't even know he'd dropped the radio until he heard it clatter to the dusty floor at his feet.

"They are of me," the figure said, the words seeming both distant and hideously close. *"They are my wives, my congregation, my tools."*

Shaker tried to speak, tried to bark orders, tried to remain a police officer. He still had his flashlight and his gun, after all. But they felt heavy in his hands—so heavy.

"Obey your leaders and submit to them, for they are keeping watch over your souls."

"W—what?" Shaker heard himself say. "Who are you?"

"I am the alpha and the omega," the figure intoned. *"I am the sower who now may reap. I am the shepherd of my flock and the master of my house. I see that now. I see it so clearly. They've waited for me. All of them have waited for so many years. And now, at last, I've come."*

Shaker heard this but made sense of none of it. "Get out of my way, all of you." He demanded, surprised by how steady his voice sounded.

Did the figure grin at him? In the gloom of the archway, still half-hidden behind the dead girls, it was hard to tell. *"Rejoice. In moments, you will join us."*

"The hell I will! Now step aside or I'll shoot!"

"My lambs," the figure said, speaking with the smooth, calm cadence of a parent—or a back alley con man. *"Take him."*

Suddenly, both girls *moved*. It happened so fast that it took Shaker's overtaxed brain a moment to process the change. One instant they were as motionless as statues, and the next they lunged forward, their small hands coming up and reaching for him like claws.

Shaker tried to fire, but they were on him too quickly. Fingers, cold as ice and strong as steel cables, locked around his wrists and arms. With a single squeeze, he felt the bones of his right hand snap, the gun falling from his grasp. Pain, shock, and panic all hit at the same time. He struggled wildly, but the girls held him in place as easily as he might hold a toddler.

Shaker screamed, loud and long.

Meanwhile, the figure in the archway slowly advanced, abandoning the shadows.

And, yes, he *was* grinning.

Wordlessly, one of the girls ripped the flashlight from Shaker's grasp and threw it away. For a moment, its beam danced wildly across the cavernous interior of the church. Then he heard it strike something, the floor or a wall, and wink out.

Shaker tried to scream again; he really did. But the other girl shoved her small fist into his open mouth. Her flesh tasted cold and putrid against his tongue as her hand drove deeper and deeper still, first gagging and then choking him.

His eyes bulged in useless panic as his entire body convulsed.

"The wages of sin are death," the man from the shadows intoned. *"Let me show you..."*

Then Officer Bill Shaker of the Camden, New Jersey Police Department was swallowed by smothering darkness.

CHAPTER 1
Newark, New Jersey—2022

"I'M DR. MIRIAM LAKATOS. I'M here to see Assistant Director Brubaker."

Mia shifted from foot to foot. She didn't like offices. They always felt too sterile, too bright, completely lacking in even subtle intimacy. There were no energies here, none at all—nothing to sense, no spiritual atmosphere whatsoever. It was as if the universe halted at the door. There was a reason why so few hauntings occurred in modern office buildings. Such phenomena were fueled by emotion, by humanity, rather than by deadlines or PowerPoint presentations.

The receptionist, a dour woman in her late fifties, looked Mia up and down and made a face that Mia's mother often labeled "sucking the lemon."

Something about a raven-haired thirty-year-old woman dressed in a long earthy skirt with patchwork pockets and a bohemian flowered blouse evidently didn't sit well with her.

The woman sniffed. "Is the AD expecting you?"

Mia smiled sweetly. "I sincerely hope so."

"One moment." The receptionist's fingers danced across the keyboard in front of her. Then her eyes narrowed, and she peered closer at the screen, as if not quite believing what it showed her. "You seem to have a 10:00 appointment."

"Seem to have?"

Eyes behind pharmacy reading glasses flicked her way, only for a moment. "You have an appointment."

"Hard to believe, isn't it?"

The receptionist sniffed again. "Just a moment. I'll see if she's ready for you." Then she picked up the phone, dialed an extension and, after what sounded like three rings, said, "Assistant Director? I have a Miriam Lakatos here to see you." A pause. "Yes, ma'am." She replaced the phone, looked begrudgingly up at Mia, and announced in the manner of someone conceding defeat, "Through the double doors and down the hall. It's the last door on the right. "

"Thanks. Have a blessed day."

The receptionist blinked. "Um…thank you."

Mia pushed through the glass doors that separated the small waiting area from the suite of offices and conference rooms. Outside each one was mounted a circular, colorful blue and gold plaque bearing an official-looking insignia with the phrases "Department of Justice" along its upper circumference and "Federal Bureau of Investigation" along its lower. In the middle were three words, which Mia took to be the agency's motto. "Fidelity. Bravery. Integrity."

Snobbery, she silently added.

The office space proved as sterile as the waiting room had been. Just commercial carpeting, florescent lights, and walls that alternated between labeled doors and unlabeled framed photographs. Each photo was of a white man of middle years wearing both a professional suit and a professional smile. Prior directors, she supposed.

She passed no one. Saw no one. Nevertheless, she could hear voices behind most of the doors, speaking in hushed tones. More than that, she could feel them all around her, thinking weighty thoughts. Very few smiles. No laughter. This was the New Jersey field office of the FBI, and there was nothing funny about that.

She stopped outside the last door on the right. It looked identical to the rest, faux walnut with a faux brass knob. At eye level it bore the name of its primary occupant: Renee Brubaker, Assistant Director.

Mia knocked lightly.

She expected a "come in," but instead jumped a little when the door opened abruptly.

A man stood there. He was tall and broad-shouldered and wore his suit and tie as if he'd been born into them. His skin was dark, his hair close-cropped, and his eyes coolly intelligent in a way that she'd always found attractive. He didn't smile. "Ms. Lakatos?"

She cleared her throat, a little annoyed that she had to. "Doctor, actually."

"My apologies. Come in, Dr. Lakatos."

He stepped aside, ushering her into a larger than expected corner office with a view of downtown Newark. Through the row of windows, she could see the Passaic River meandering through an urban landscape, with the spires of New York City just visible at the horizon. Between herself and those windows stood a large wooden desk, so uncluttered as to seem almost pristine. The woman seated behind it rose to her feet and smiled. "Dr. Lakatos, I'm Renee Brubaker. That gentleman there is Special Agent Prine." Gray-haired and about the age of the receptionist, Brubaker's suit fit her at least as well as Prine's fit him. She was tall, clearly fit, and evidently unmarried, given the bare ring finger on the left hand she used to indicate the other two people in the room. These were a man and a woman. "Agent Archie Delgado…and this is Special Agent Karen Jessup from the DEA."

What followed was a plethora of somewhat awkward handshakes, at least on Mia's end. She'd never been comfortable with this sort of thing. In fact, the entire experience was too far outside of her wheelhouse for anything like comfort. Then she felt Agent Prine at her shoulder, gesturing with one large long-fingered hand at one of the four chairs that had been set up in a loose circle facing the desk, a very intimate conference setting.

She gratefully took it.

"Dr. Lakatos generously agreed to consult with us on the Arias situation," Brubaker explained to the others.

"Doctor of what?" Jessup asked, eyeing Mia much the way the receptionist had. Jessup looked to be in her forties, maybe ten years Mia's senior. Her sandy blonde hair was pulled back in a tight bun and her face was pinched, her eyes small and blue.

"Parapsychology," Mia replied, bracing herself for the usual reaction.

"Is that really a thing?" This came from the guy on her left. Delgado.

He was the youngest of them, maybe only a year or two out of grad school, or the academy, or both. He had a round, open face, much less pointed than Jessup's and rather less pleasingly symmetrical than Prine's. He also sported a small van dyke, neatly trimmed and midnight black, like his hair.

"It's a branch of psychology," Mia explained. "There aren't many schools that offer it as a graduate degree."

"I'll bet," Jessup said.

"Where'd you go?" Delgado asked.

"University of California Santa Barbara."

Brubaker cleared her throat. "Dr. Lakatos is the author of eight books on subjects relevant to this case. I asked her to be here because of the unusual nature of this investigation."

Jessup uncrossed and recrossed her legs. It struck Mia as a nervous habit. "I guess Mulder and Scully weren't available?"

You're dating yourself, sweetie, Mia thought but didn't say.

Prine, who'd taken the chair on Jessup's other side, smiled sardonically. "Haven't heard that one before."

Ignoring him, Jessup focused on Mia. "So, it's my understanding that you're what…a medium?" There was no missing the emphasis on the last word, which fairly dripped with condescension.

"A medium is a supernatural conduit," Mia replied, trying to keep all inflection out of her voice. People like this thrived on defensiveness. "I'm a paranormal investigator who happens to be psychically sensitive."

"Which means you can…what? Talk to the dead?"

"Mostly it's about impressions, psychic vibrations."

The look Jessup gave her erased any doubt. This was a skeptic, and an aggressive one.

"Look," the assistant director said, blowing out a long sigh. "Doctor Lakatos is here as a subject matter expert, that's all. Karen, I'm going to ask you to put a pin in your incredulity for the purposes of this meeting."

"I'll try," Jessup replied, but with a tone that suggested to Mia that the woman would do anything but.

Frankly, the whole dynamic in here was—interesting. Brubaker clearly held both the reins and the rank. But she'd introduced Karen Jessup as DEA, not FBI like herself and the two men. That seemed to imply some kind of inter-agency cooperation, which even Mia, who had little or no experience with government, had heard was often problematic.

Then the assistant director said something that shoved all these hypotheticals right out of her head. "Now then. Dr. Lakatos, it's my understanding that you are familiar with St. Damien's Lutheran Church in Camden, New Jersey."

The name hit Mia like a bolt of lightning. She actually felt the shock charge down her spine. For a moment, all she could do was stare at Brubaker, her mouth hanging open. Then she glanced at the others in their small circle. Prine looked professionally interested, his face neutral, Delgado was actually grinning, and Jessup wore what could only be described as a dismissive smirk.

Steadying herself, she faced Brubaker again. "Yes, I'm 'familiar' with it. What exactly does that awful place have to do with the FBI?"

"Is it really haunted?" Delgado asked, perhaps speaking out of turn, though his boss—if that's who Brubaker was—didn't seem to mind.

Mia almost laughed. But she held back, not at all sure how sane it would sound.

Calling St. Damien's "haunted" was like calling the Grand Canyon a "hole."

Mia cleared her throat and replied, "It's arguably the most paranormally active site in the country."

"Sounds like a yes," Prine muttered.

"You've been there," Brubaker said, her eyes locked on Mia's. It was a statement, not a question. Brubaker *knew*. Well, of course she did. Mia wouldn't have been invited here without a thorough background check.

Mia swallowed, a reflex. "Once. Five years ago."

The assistant director consulted an open file on her desk. The move struck Mia as very low-tech. In fact, she noticed for the first time that Brubaker *had* no computer, not even a tablet or laptop. That seemed odd for an upper-mucky-muck in the FBI in the twenty-first century. "That was when you were with *The Ghost Finders*?"

"I wasn't 'with' them," Mia said defensively. "They hired me to consult on an episode of their reality TV show."

"Which resulted in the deaths of four people," Jessup noted, a veiled accusation. It was a tone Mia had encountered before—every time, in fact, that someone mentioned St. Damien's.

"And the episode never aired," Brubaker added.

"It was a terrible tragedy," Mia heard herself say.

"Yes, it was," remarked Brubaker with what struck Mia as an odd cadence. "The entire film crew died on site. You were the only survivor. The show was promptly cancelled."

Stevie, Kim, Lyle, and Derrick.

They still haunted her dreams. The whole thing had been a publicity stunt, something her agent had insisted on as a way to boost the sales of Mia's latest—and last—book.

It had also been a *lot* of money.

In hindsight though, she wished to the Goddess that she'd turned it down, money or not.

Unable to speak, Mia simply nodded.

"And you blame it on the church?" Delgado asked.

The four of them went silent, looking at Mia expectantly.

She felt her insides twist.

When Brubaker's invitation had come in, accepting her initial consultation fee without pause or negotiation, Mia had been delighted. It had meant getting out of Staten Island, spending an hour or so talking paranormal activity with a few suits, and collecting a hefty check. A good morning's work.

Of course, she hadn't known the nature of the FBI's interest.

St. Damien's.

She cleared her throat again. Her heart was pounding hard, and she allowed herself a moment to try to steady it. Then she said carefully, "St. Damien's has a well-documented history of negatively affecting people who go there, either by entering the church itself or even spending too much time in close proximity."

"Well-documented?" Jessup remarked. "Where, exactly?"

Mia ignored her. "The entire city block on which it sits is derelict. The residents, for years, suffered from exceptionally high instances of violent insanity that resulted in at least a dozen murders and many suicides. Finally, about twenty years ago, the entire dead-end street…aptly named Bleak Street, unlikely as that sounds, was abandoned. I think it's all property of the City of Camden now. Am I right?"

Brubaker nodded. "But you never answered Agent Delgado's question, Dr. Lakatos. *Do* you blame all this on the church?"

Mia took a deep breath. Then she replied, "Of course, I do."

Jessup uttered a weary sigh. "Come on, Renee! Why are we wasting our time with this nonsense?"

Prine responded before Mia could. "Do you have a better explanation? I read the file and Doctor Lakatos isn't wrong. That whole city block went more or less stark raving mad."

Jessup waved the comment away. "I read the file, too. I also looked at a survey of the land. Do you know what's at the end of that dead-end street? A swamp. Wetlands right off the Delaware River. Basically, it's been a chemical dumping ground for every industrial polluter north of Philadelphia for the past hundred years. Decades of shit contaminated the ground water, poisoning the residents. *That's* what accounts for the terrible things that have happened on Bleak Street. And they *were* terrible. There's no denying that. But nobody with an ounce of rationality would blame some old church."

"Is that true, Doctor?" Brubaker asked. "Is the localgroundwater contaminated?"

"The levels of certain heavy metals and pesticides are higher than average," Mia admitted. "But they're not high enough to account for all the carnage, and certainly not high enough to have affected the crew of *The Ghost Finders* after only two hours of shooting. I assume Bleak Street, like the rest of Camden, uses city water. I doubt there's a well in the whole county. So, if the water supply *is* contaminated, wouldn't it affect a broader swath of the population? This is just one block-long street we're talking about. I've never heard of a contamination issue that localized, have you? Believe me… it's not the water."

"Then what is it?" Jessup demanded, leaning forward in her chair as if she and Mia were on opposite sides of an interrogation table. "What drives a whole street crazy? What exactly do you think is *in* that church? Ghosts? Satan? The Jersey fucking Devil?"

Instead of answering, Mia asked, "I'm sorry. Why are you here?"

The DEA agent blinked and sat back, saying nothing. Still seated behind her desk, Brubaker replied, "This investigation has been deemed a cooperative effort between the bureau and DEA. The nature of the case calls for a cross-jurisdictional approach."

"I understood about half of that," Mia said flatly.

Delgado chuckled again. From his place beside Jessup, Prine smiled that smile.

Mia continued, "But all that doesn't matter. *I'm* here because somebody in this room, presumably you, Ms. Brubaker, thinks my expertise is relevant. So far, all I've been asked are questions about one of the nastiest places on Earth, and my answers seem to be upsetting Agent Jessup here."

Beside her, Jessup glowered.

Mia ignored it. "How about if we start over? What *is* this case and what does it have to do with St. Damien's?"

"We can't comment on an active investigation," Jessup said stonily.

But then Prine said to Brubaker, "AD, I suggest we tell her."

"So, do I," Delgado agreed.

Mia looked from one to the other of them. Then she faced Brubaker, who eyed her thoughtfully before saying, "All right. Prine, why don't you read her in."

"It's *my* case," Jessup interjected. "If anybody breaks protocol, it should be me."

"Prine brought in the tip. You wouldn't be here if not for him. Matt, why don't you take point."

Prine nodded. "AD, may I see the file?"

Brubaker drew a folder from one of her desk drawers and slid it over to him. As she did, Mia noticed that the folder was red, blood red. For some reason, that rather harmless fact sent another chill down her spine.

I shouldn't be here. This whole thing has a shitty vibe. I should get up and leave.

But she didn't.

Prine took the folder and selected a sheet of paper from it. This he handed to Mia, having to reach past Jessup to do so, eliciting yet another scowl from the DEA agent. Wordlessly, Mia accepted the sheet and looked at it. It was a digital printout of a grainy photo. It showed a man's face. Forties. Latino. Dark eyes, heavy features, and a mouth that looked like it hadn't smiled in a hundred years.

Prine said, "That's Andres Arias, a native of Columbia. He runs the Arias cartel and is responsible for roughly half of the cocaine, heroine, and raw coca that's smuggled into this country every year. He's personally accountable for at least sixty murders, more than a dozen of them children under the age of twelve. He rules a huge drug organization through terror and the constant threat of horrific violence. He routinely kills the families of his rivals, or even those he deems *might* be rivals. Basically, he's one of the most dangerous men on the planet."

"Oh," was all Mia could think to say. The face in the picture, obviously a mug shot of some kind, looked normal enough. But then, what did she know? "Where does St. Damien's enter into it?"

"Arias is coming here, to the U.S.," Prine replied. "Specifically, he's going to Camden, to Bleak Street."

"Why?" Mia asked. "When?"

It was Jessup who answered her, cutting off Prine. "Today." She checked her watch. "In less than eleven hours. A private jet. The DEA monitors his movements closely, and we think he'll be landing at Trenton-Mercer Airport around nine o'clock tonight."

"Then shouldn't you be waiting there to…I don't know…arrest him or something?" Mia asked, handing the photo back to Prine.

Prine said, "I'm afraid it's not that simple. Arias is dangerous, but he's also richer than Midas and extremely well connected. Legally, we can't touch him unless we get direct evidence that he's in the country to commit a federal crime, such as conspiring with domestic criminal syndicates to broaden his influence in the drug market in the U.S."

Delgado piped in. "Which is exactly why he's here."

"Or so we think," Jessup corrected. "We don't expect him to stay more than twenty-four hours. He's here specifically to attend a summit of sorts between himself and a half-dozen mob bosses from up and down the east coast. It's a rare opportunity, all but unheard of, and it gives us our first and probably only shot at making an arrest."

"And this summit is going to be…where?" Mia asked. "Please don't tell me these guys are meeting at the *church*?"

"No," Prine said. "I have an informant in one of the domestic syndicates. According to him, the summit is being held in what used to be Fairlanes, an abandoned bowling alley across the street from St. Damien's."

Jessup added, "Making your 'haunted church' the best and really only vantage point from which to surveil."

As Mia absorbed this, Prine handed her two more sheets of paper from Brubaker's file. The first showed a wide, squat, single story structure with a large, half-ruined bowling pin affixed to its front façade. The building's windows were all boarded up, its exterior paint, once bright with color, faded and peeling. "That's the bowling alley," he explained.

"I recognize it," Mia said. Then she looked at the second photo—and her breath caught.

St. Damien's was a "neighborhood" church made in the gothic revival style. Two large arched doors, both heavy wood, had been clearly padlocked, a fact evident even at this distance. But, aside from that small concession to security, the place looked—well, "normal" was not a word Mia would ever use in the same sentence as St. Damien's. Well-maintained? In good repair? That seemed closer. No signs of graffiti. No broken stained glass. No indications of vandalism of any kind.

All of which posed an obvious question.

Who was maintaining it, *who* repairing it? After almost eighty years, St. Damien's still held court at the end of a block-long street of abandoned rowhouses and failed businesses. Bleak Street had been lower income in its heyday. But now, after ten years of absolute neglect, it was nothing but a ghost town. No pun intended.

Its houses, once places where working people raised families, were now falling apart, their copper piping and porcelain fixtures long since scavenged. Most of their window glass had been shattered and colorful messages covered nearly every exterior surface. One of them Mia remembered well from her visit there five years ago. In large, balloon-ish letters that looked to have been painted by a skilled hand, it read: *Too hot for Hell!*

Yet for all that, the church itself remained untouched.

And she knew why.

"There have to be other places you can do this," she said, speaking directly to Brubaker, appealing to the authority in the room.

The assistant director didn't reply, though Jessup did. "There aren't."

"Can't you listen to a bug from anywhere in its range? One of the empty rowhouses maybe?"

Clearing his throat, Delgado explained. "We don't use 'bugs,' anymore. These days, we have tech that can see and hear through walls. It's much more secure and virtually impossible to detect. But it requires a clear line of sight. The way the church and the bowling alley are aligned, relative to each other, makes it the only option. The houses and businesses on the same side of the street as Fairlanes are too close to cover a building that large, and the ones on the same side as the church are too oblique."

"It's St. Damien's or nowhere," Jessup concluded.

Mia watched all of them nod. If nothing else, the four agreed on that single factor.

She dropped the photos on the desk and sat back. "Then, for sanity's sake, make it nowhere."

"We can't miss this opportunity," Brubaker said, sounding oddly apologetic.

"For Christ's sake, it's just an abandoned building!" Jessup exclaimed. "We're not talking about ancient Indian burial ground. Yes, I know what happened there. Everybody does. But I've looked up the place's history. It was built less than a century ago on a half-acre of backfilled swampland. It's a 1940s neighborhood church, not Dracula's castle!"

"Ever been there?" Mia asked her.

"I've been in places *like* it!" the other woman shot back. "Plenty of them. Look I don't know exactly what went wrong with that TV crew you signed up with, but we've got a once-in-a-lifetime opportunity to nail one of the nastiest bastards in the world…the *living* world, and I'll be damned if I'm going to miss that chance because I'm afraid of a spooky old church!"

"What exactly are the dangers here, in your opinion, Dr. Lakatos?" This came from Prine and, at least to Mia's ears, it sounded like a serious question.

So, she answered it seriously. "Some paranormal places are like batteries. Only instead of electricity, they collect and store negative energy, sending it out again almost like radiation. These sites can affect anyone who comes close, sometimes in pretty terrible ways."

"Is that what you think St. Damien's is?" Brubaker asked. She sounded, as Prine had, as if she really wanted to know. "A battery?"

Mia shook her head. "St. Damien's is something much worse. Negative energy is just that…energy. It can be dangerous, but it has no purpose, no malicious intent. St. Damien's, on the other hand, is *hungry*. There's a… consciousness…there that deliberately preyed on the minds of the people who used to live on Bleak Street, and that will directly attack absolutely anyone who sets foot in its walls."

"'Attack,'" Jessup echoed, more than a little derisively. "You're claiming it's *alive?*"

"If anything, that church is the polar opposite of 'alive,'" Mia replied.

"Renee, I'm sorry," the DEA agent said to the assistant director with something close to a groan. "I've been as patient as I know how. But time is incredibly short. We need to get down to Camden and set up shop before Arias and the other attendees show up for their summit. If we get spotted, the whole thing goes up in smoke!"

"Of course," Brubaker replied. She turned to Mia. "Is there any way we can protect ourselves?"

Mia blinked. That was a very intelligent question, and not the kind of thing she would have expected to be asked by an assistant director of the FBI. Locking eyes with Brubaker, she sensed something she hadn't before. There was a darkness to the woman, not in any way that she, herself, was evil—but more as if she'd been *touched* by evil.

Have you been there? she wondered but didn't ask. Some instinct told her Brubaker wouldn't appreciate the question.

"That's difficult to say," Mia finally replied. "With most places like this, I'd recommend a cleansing."

"A cleansing?" Delgado asked as if tasting the word. "Is that like an exorcism?"

"An exorcism is a Catholic right intended to remove a demon that's possessing a human host. A cleansing is more like an investigation."

Prine said, "I don't follow."

Mia relaxed a little. This, at least, was familiar territory for her, having explained the concept in lectures, blog posts, and interviews dozens of times. "Not all hauntings are the same. A residual haunting is a kind of psychic recording that's made when something traumatic or horrific happens in a particular location. The site "replays" the event, over and over, but without sentience or intent. I've witnessed several of these firsthand. They can be scary, but they're harmless.

"An intelligent haunting is altogether different. In such a case, there is always one or more conscious entities at work, usually a decedent who has failed to move on. A cleansing is an effort to find out exactly why this entity is either lingering or trapped, thereby releasing them to whatever destiny awaits them in the next life."

Jessup issued an eyeroll so over-the-top that it was nearly audible. Mia, who had dealt with skeptics her entire life, starting with her mother, had to begrudgingly admire it.

Sitting beside the woman, Prine looked thoughtful. So did Brubaker.

Delgado asked, "What about poltergeists or…I don't know…the devil or something? Does that ever really happen?"

"Poltergeist activity usually isn't a haunting and has nothing to do with the dead. It's overwhelmingly linked to a living person, usually a troubled adolescent with a subconscious gift for psychokinesis. As for demonic presences…" Mia hesitated. "Well, I've investigated more than a hundred sites of reported paranormal activity and, while I've never encountered anything that I would label a non-human entity, good or evil, St. Damien's came the closest…by far."

"Why?" Brubaker asked.

"There's a truly terrible presence in that place. It's sentient, predatory, and extremely violent."

"Sounds demonic to me," Delgado muttered.

"Except the presence is that of a very human decedent."

Jessup said, "You're talking about Jonah Ray Barton."

The words drove a spike between Mia's eyes. She almost screamed, "Don't say his name!" as if Barton were indeed a devil who could be invoked. Certainly, he was the closest that Mia had ever encountered.

"We know the story," Brubaker said gently.

"Do you?" Mia asked her.

"Who doesn't?" Prine replied. "Barton is one of the country's most infamous serial killers."

Mia shook her head. "I'm not talking about the murders he committed as a living man. I'm talking about the lives he took *after* he died. Do you know about that…about how it started?"

Jessup groaned again.

The others, for a long moment, didn't respond. Finally, leaning forward in her desk chair, Assistant Director Brubaker suggested, her voice sounding dry. "Why don't you enlighten us, Dr. Lakatos?"

And so, with no small amount of trepidation—*this is old, sour Earth I'm treading on*—she did.

CHAPTER 2
Camden, New Jersey—1972

"410, WE HAVE A 10-16 at St. Damien's Lutheran Church on Bleak Street. What's your 10-20?"

"Dispatch, this is 410. We're currently headed east on York Street. Will reroute."

"Roger that, 410. Use caution."

"Always."

Officer David Mulberry looked over at his partner. Bill Shaker raised his eyebrows, which were crazy, bushy things, and flipped on the rooftop lights. "No siren," Shakey said in his gravely voice.

"Okay."

Mulberry turned the patrol car left at the next corner, heading toward the northernmost part of the city. Around them, dawn light was only just brightening the October sky and the regiments of rowhouses, blocks and blocks of them, stood dark and quiet. Everyone was asleep at this hour. It was probably the safest these streets ever got.

"Bleak Street," Shakey said. "That's your old stompin' ground, right?"

"I grew up around the corner, on Byron," Mulberry replied.

"Ever been to St. Damien's?"

"No. That's Lutheran. My folks were Baptists."

Shakey grinned. "You're all just pagans to us Catholic folks, my friend."

Mulberry chuckled, turning left again. His hands were tight on the wheel—though, if asked, he couldn't have said why. This was just a 10-16, a domestic problem, one of the vaguest of the city's police codes. Most times, this kind of thing turned out to be a drunk locked out of his house or a kid playing drums at some crazy hour. Anything more than that would have elicited a different code. True, Tonya in Dispatch had told him to "use caution." But she always said that, even if the call was about a cat that got stuck in the sewer.

A block later, he turned right onto Bleak Street.

As a kid, he'd spent a lot of time on this block-long, dead-end street; the lack of thru-traffic made it a great place for football and such. Back then, folks filled it nearly end to end, sitting on stoops, working on cars, swapping gossip, talking, laughing, living. But this morning, it was like driving through a cemetery where the markers were all two-story attached houses of clapboard or weathered brick. True, it was early. But, while that might account for the quiet, it didn't explain the almost palpable sense of *dread*. It seemed to flood the sidewalks like fog rolling in off the Delaware River.

"Am I crazy?" Shakey asked in an uncharacteristically low whisper. "Or is it...colder here. I'm rolling up the window."

"Okay," Mulberry replied, slowing the car almost without realizing it. He was tempted, very tempted, to tell Shakey to shut off the roof lights—and he was suddenly insanely glad they hadn't hit the siren. Something, some bile-filled pit in the middle of his stomach, insisted that drawing attention on *this* street at *this* time was a really bad idea.

"There's the church," Shakey said. He sounded—well, shaky.

St. Damien's stood right across the street from Fairlanes Bowling. As a teenager always on the edge of trouble, David Mulberry had wasted many an hour in that place, smoking and sneaking beers and occasionally scoring a joint. He'd even lost his virginity in the men's room to Missy Rogan, who was now married with kids and living somewhere across the river in Pennsylvania.

Had Missy been a Lutheran? Had she attended St. Damien's?

Why does that matter? Why am I so fucking spooked? It's just a 10-16! Use caution.

The church, like everything else on the street, seemed eerily quiet as he pulled over to the curb just ten steps from the big front doors. After killing the engine and lights, he and Shakey just sat there for most of a minute.

"Do we knock on the front door or go around to the parsonage?" Shakey finally asked.

"At this hour, I'm thinking parsonage," Mulberry replied.

"Yeah. Good. Me, too. You ready?"

"Yeah," Mulberry said. He opened his door.

"Whoa, partner. We haven't called it in."

"Oh. Right."

Shakey picked up the radio mike, clicked it twice, cleared his throat, and said, "Dispatch. Um…this is 410. Have arrived at the 10-16 and are now going to investigate the parsonage. Over."

Tonya replied at once. It was weirdly comforting to hear her voice, though Mulberry couldn't help feeling as if she were talking to them from another planet instead of the station less than a mile away. *Roger that, 410. You boys be careful.*

"Roger. Out." Shakey put down the mike and looked balefully at Mulberry. "Partner, I don't know why, but every nerve ending I got is shooting off fireworks."

"I know. Me, too. Let's do it."

They exited the car together and followed the walkway that led around the north end of the church. As they did, Mulberry kept his right hand on the butt of his service revolver. Shakey, walking beside him, repeatedly glanced up at the belltower, which stood three stories high at the church's southwest corner.

"See something?" Mulberry asked him.

"No. Uh…I'm not sure. For a second, I thought—"

"Partner!" Mulberry snapped as the parsonage entrance came into view. "We got a wide-open door!"

Both men drew their guns.

The parsonage sat adjacent to the rear of the church, connected to it by a twenty-foot long, glass-enclosed breezeway that, even in the breaking dawn, looked as dark as a mine tunnel. While Mulberry had never been inside this particular abode, he'd always imagined it to be a cozy place, since the only people who lived there were Reverend Barton and his cook, Fabron.

But right now, with its door swung wide open and with a breeze blowing off the river that stank of decay, the parsonage seemed anything but cozy. Instead, to Mulberry's jangled nerves, it looked like a dead animal with a gaping wound in its center mass.

Jesus! Get a hold of yourself! We don't even know what we've got here!

Except, I do.

Somehow…I do.

And I don't want to go in there and find out I'm right.

"We should call for backup," Shakey said. To Mulberry, it sounded like the best idea in the world. So, signaling for his partner to hold position, he took the boxy radio from his belt and lifted it to his lips. "Dispatch, this is 410 requesting backup."

The only reply was a whine of static.

Shakey said, "We might be out of range. Try again."

Mulberry did. The radio, a fairly new addition to the Camden PD's standard issue, crackled, whined again, and then a voice said, very faintly, *"The last enemy to be destroyed…is death."*

"Dispatch? Tonya? Do you copy?"

But all he got was that voice once more, so whisper soft that Mulberry's neck hairs prickled.

"For if you live according to the flesh, you will die…"

"Christ," Shakey groaned. "What *is* that?"

"Picking up some Bible-thumper station, maybe?" Mulberry guessed.

"Let's go back to the car. Call from there."

And Mulberry wanted to. Right now, he'd never wanted anything more in his life. But that parsonage door was wide open and, while Mulberry had hardly ever even spoken to Reverend Barton, the situation suggested—hell, *screamed*—that he and old Fabron might be in trouble.

Grow a pair and do your goddamned job!

So, he said to Shakey, "You go. I'm heading inside. Put your radio on channel one and stay in constant contact." He looked over at his partner. "Okay?"

"You sure, man?"

"Yeah."

"It's not procedure."

Mulberry tried for a smile and failed miserably. "It's just a 10-16, right?"

"Right. Okay."

Despite all his protestations, Shakey turned and headed back to the street like a man escaping the jaws of a lion. Mulberry watched him for a moment with bitter envy. Then, steeling himself, he faced the parsonage and started moving forward again, slowly, as if through a dream. Beyond the open doorway, he could discern almost nothing. No lights, no shadows. Just a rectangular black hole.

Reaching the edge of the open door, he pressed himself against the brickwork and listened furiously. He could hear a ticking clock, but anything else was lost in the wind's intermittent wail. "Police!" he called. "Reverend Barton! Mr. Avatard! Can anyone hear me?"

He got back nothing, a very *loud* nothing.

"This. Is. The. Police!" he declared again, emphasizing every word. "I'm coming inside! I am armed! If you have a weapon, drop it now and hold up your empty hands!"

He hesitated a moment later, lifting the radio to his lips, "Shakey, you with me?"

"Right here, partner. I'm at the car, but I'm having a hard time reaching dispatch. I keep getting that same religious station."

Mulberry's mouth, already dry, went positively arid. "That's not supposed to happen, man," he said into the radio. "Frequencies and shit."

"I know. But that's what I got. Want me to keep trying or…" Shakey's words trailed off, though Mulberry knew the rest of that sentence.

"Stay there. Keep trying. I'm going in."

"Watch your back."

That's supposed to be your job, Mulberry thought but didn't say.

He drew his flashlight and flicked it on. Then, moving slowly and deliberately, he rounded the door jam and slipped into the parsonage.

With the gun in one hand and the flashlight in the other, Mulberry scanned the room. It was a parlor, small but clean. A heavy wooden clock ticked loudly on one wall. A small black and white TV occupied a stand in the corner, its rabbit ears extended up and outward like the antennae on an insect. There was a couch, old but in good shape, and an armchair that looked older and in less repair. The coffee table between them was walnut and pristine and the rug was a thick shag, either green or blue. It was hard to tell in the darkness.

To the left, an archway led presumably to the bedrooms and, to the right stood a small galley kitchen with a closed door that Mulberry guessed opened into the breezeway and the church beyond.

Is it still called a "breezeway" if it's enclosed? he suddenly wondered. Only to follow that up immediately with, *Who gives a shit?*

That was when he saw the blood.

Later, it would occur to him in his grief that he initially missed it because there was so *much* of it. It covered the parlor's back wall and the floor beside a small upright piano so completely that, at first, he mistook it for more shadows. But then he noticed how his flashlight beam seemed to reflect dully back at him, indicating something liquid, and a second or two later his mind caught up.

"Shakey?" he called, his hand trembling as he worked the radio. Someday, cops might be issued a more sensible solution for juggling gun, flashlight, and communications, but that sure as hell wasn't today.

For a moment, he heard nothing, just more of that weird, whiney static. But then his partner said, *"I'm here."*

"I've got blood! I need you to get in here!"

"What? Yeah."

"Shakey? Do you hear me, man? I've got blood, buckets of it! Move your ass!"

"Okay, partner. Okay."

"Did you manage to call for backup?"

There was a very long pause, so long that Mulberry thought one of their radios had conked out. But then Shakey replied, *"Still can't get through. But Dave, the front door just opened. And I think I see—"*

"What? Shakey?"

But then his radio *screamed,* delivering a high-pitched, electronic shriek so loud that it seemed to drive nails into Mulberry's head. Cursing, he fumbled for the volume knob, dropping his flashlight, but not his gun, in the process. The light hit the carpet, bounced, and rolled under the couch.

"Goddamn it!" He yanked the radio from his belt, the screaming setting his teeth on edge. His thumb fumbled with the volume. It was up, all the way up, though he couldn't remember setting it that high. Shakey certainly hadn't been that loud just now; in fact, Mulberry had needed to strain to hear him.

So, what the hell just happened?

And where's my fucking flashlight?

He tried to glance around the parlor but, without his flashlight he was functionally blind. So, with another curse, he dropped to one knee, kept his gun up, and felt under the couch with his free hand. The move cost him maybe ten seconds, but they were a *long* ten seconds, and at any moment he half-expected to grab something besides his flashlight, maybe something cold and dead and slick with blood.

Or maybe, some part of his traitorous mind suggested, *the something will grab you.*

But then his fingers closed around the familiar cool metal and Mulberry breathed a shuddering sigh of relief.

It's just a 10-16.

Except we're way past that now, aren't we?

"Shakey? What's your twenty?"

His radio crackled but there was no answer.

Mulberry straightened, once again sweeping the room with his flashlight. There was something in the middle of the small dining table over by the galley kitchen, but a big flowerpot blocked the way, casting it into deep shadow. Swallowing dryly, Mulberry shifted his beam to the piano—and the blood.

Slowly, his heart hammering, he stepped toward it, skirting around the knee-high coffee table.

"Shakey! Goddamn it, where are you?"

But, instead of his partner, he heard that other voice, thick with whiny static, *"No, I tell you; but unless you repent, you will all likewise perish!"*

That almost did it. Duty or no duty, Mulberry almost cut and ran. But then, as he cleared the couch and reached the edge of that pool of dark liquid that stained the rug and the wall, his foot connected with something heavy.

Heavy—but at the same time soft and yielding.

He'd been a cop in Camden long enough to know a body when he felt one.

With a gasp, he pointed his flashlight down, where it splashed hideously across a cooling corpse. It appeared to be wearing clerical garb, dark slacks and a dark shirt, with one of those telltale stiff square collars at the throat. Except that was as far as it went. Though it took Mulberry's brain interminable seconds to process what his eyes showed him, he eventually realized that the body at his feet was headless—just a ragged, bloated stump for a neck and nothing else.

Mulberry made a sound halfway between a curse and a moan. He nearly dropped the flashlight again, and only managed to hang onto it because the idea of being left in the dark with this mangled cadaver was too horrifying to accept.

Slowly, or at least it seemed slowly, his mind started working again.

This had to be Reverend Barton, his headless body the source of the blood that had flooded this corner of the room. Training and procedures flashed through Mulberry's mind. Checking for a pulse was laughable, of course. But checking for ID might be prudent. Maybe the reverend, if this *was* him, carried a wallet.

But that would mean turning him over to get to his back pockets.

Besides, where's the head? Where's the man's goddamned head?

With a stab of insight that turned him arctic cold, Mulberry recalled the *something* on the dinette table. That was only a few steps away from here and, now that he was across the room, the flowerpot would no longer be in the way.

Except I don't want to look! I really don't!

His disloyal arm came up anyway, the beam surprisingly steady as it found the table, with its four wooden, straight-back chairs nestled close around it.

And there, staring back at him, mouth agape, was the head of Jonah Ray Barton.

That's when Mulberry finally felt it *give*. Whatever strand of courage or sense of responsibility had brought him this far snapped like the thread it was. Suddenly, he needed to get out, craved it, wouldn't wait another second. He whirled around, ready to all but throw himself across the room and out the open doorway, back into the slowly brightening dawn.

Except the door wasn't open anymore.

It was shut.

Mulberry screamed. He couldn't remember the last time he'd done that. But he did it now.

"Shakey!" he cried, his voice cracking. "I need you! Where the hell are you?"

A part of him didn't honestly expect to get a reply, just more static or another fucking Bible verse. But his partner answered instantly, *"I'm in the church, man! The front door opened and I saw this girl. She looked like she was in trouble. So, I followed her in. I followed her up. But now there's two of them…and they won't let me leave! Please, man. Help me. I—""*

"Where are you? Shakey!"

This time, only static came back, shrieking again, crazy loud ike before.

As before, Mulberry fumbled for the radio's volume, only to drop it. It bounced off the headless corpse and tumbled end over end, coming to land in the pool of blood.

Mulberry forgot it and ran for the door.

It was locked. He pulled at the knob, but it wouldn't budge. He slammed his shoulder against it. But, like most exterior doors, the hinges were on the wrong side for that move to have any effect. Mulberry, his eyes bulging almost as badly as those in Barton's lifeless, bodyless head, pounded his fists on it. Then he turned his attention to the windows that stood on either side. Through them, he could see the graveyard beside the church and, beyond it, the Delaware River and the skyline of Philadelphia. So close. So many miles away.

But, if I can see all that, how is it so goddamned dark in here?

He hurried to the nearest window, fully prepared to break or, if necessary, shoot his way through the glass, anything to get out of here.

Then he saw the figures, six of them, standing in a row just a few yards from the front door, blocking the walkway back to the street. For a long moment, Mulberry simply stared at them, uncomprehending.

Girls. Teenage girls, all of them wearing white dresses.

And all of them clearly dead.

Corpses in wedding gowns…

Each of their faces was blank and each of their throats had been slit wide open, almost like a second mouth. Each girl's skin was ashen, her lips parted and her jaw slack. And instead of eyes, each had gleaming silver circles that it took him a minute to identify.

Coins. They had coins for eyes, or maybe *over* their eyes, like in that old English tradition he'd heard about in school.

Then he remembered Shakey and thought, *He's in the church!*

Mulberry headed for the kitchen more quickly than was probably smart. He considered going back for his radio, fishing it out of the deadman's blood and wiping it off on his uniform shirt. But that lasted all of a half-second. He was *done* with this room, done with its decapitated body on the floor by the piano and its disembodied head atop the dinette table like a centerpiece. His partner, his friend, was in the church proper. So that was where he needed to go.

Then, as he reached the galley kitchen and the door to the breezeway, he spotted the second body.

It stopped him cold with one hand on the knob.

Mulberry had never met Fabron Avatard. But this had to be him. He lay on his back, same as the reverend, but Mulberry could tell at a glance that the cook hadn't died the same way. For one, the man's head was still firmly attached. For another, the flashlight beam illuminated multiple stab wounds in his face and neck—especially the neck.

Someone had chopped off Barton's head and cut his cook's throat.

No, not just cut his throat…whoever did this dug it out, obliterated it. Rage…

I have to call this in.

It was a ridiculous notion, given that his radio was soaked in blood and wasn't working in any case. What he really had to do was find Shakey, get them both out, return to the cruiser, and drive away. Then, and *only* then, would Mulberry make that call.

Dragging his eyes away from this last horror, he turned the knob and pushed into the breezeway. It was dark in here as well, despite the windows on both sides. The incongruity was such that he had to stop, if only for a moment, and try to understand what he was—or more to the point, *wasn't*—seeing.

The outside world *was* there. The sun hadn't fully risen, but he could clearly see that the night had ended. Yet, none of that illumination made it past the glass, none of it shone on even an inch of the floor under his feet. Though he dared not do so, Mulberry knew on a level deep in his lizard brain that, were he to shut off his flashlight, he wouldn't be able to see his hand in front of his face, light outside the windows be damned.

It was impossible, insane.

And yet he was looking at it, which implied that either the impossible was really happening or *he* was insane.

Right now, he couldn't have said which option offered less appeal.

Again, he considered shooting through the glass, shattering it and escaping over a carpet of shards. Then, if Shakey was truly in the church, Mulberry could get to the car and summon help. It made perfect sense.

Except for the girls.

This time there were twice as many. He felt pretty sure that six of them were the same girls from outside the parsonage, except now they'd apparently brought "friends." Like before, they stood in lines outside both sets of windows. And they were staring at him, their mouths slack and their throats cut, almost as if begging him to shoot the glass, begging him to hit them in the process.

"What the fuck?!" Mulberry screamed at the top of his voice. Then he turned and ran full tilt toward the heavy wooden door that stood at the far end of the breezeway, and which presumably led into St. Damien's Lutheran Church.

He half-expected to find it locked, but he didn't. The latch lifted easily and the door opened with a push, though it squeaked loudly on ornate hinges of blackened iron. Inside, he found himself in a large open space, his flashlight illuminating what he took to be the back of the church, at least a dozen feet behind and to the left of the altar.

The first thing that struck him, and with no small relief, was that in here there was more light. Not a lot, mind you, but just enough to finally let him see beyond what the narrow beam of his flashlight could show him. Ahead, past the marble altar, the church opened up, with the nave and its dozens of pews extending toward the front of the church before being swallowed by deep shadow. To the left was a raised pulpit, complete with railing and lectern, from which Reverend Barton no doubt sermonized—or used to. To the right stood a small space with a large, sculpted marble baptismal font.

"Shakey!" he called. His voice bounced off the high, buttressed ceiling, booming almost like thunder. Trembling, his gun lowered and forgotten, he skirted the altar and ran down the center aisle, scanning left and right for some movement in the gloom, some sign of his missing partner.

What he saw instead stopped him in his tracks.

Girls lay on the pews, perhaps as many as a dozen of them. Each was on her back, her arms folded across a bosom draped in blood-smeared white satin. They ranged in age from maybe twelve to seventeen, and they each had coins on their eyes. Like the ones outside, they had all been butchered, their throats cut wide open.

For an interminable moment, Mulberry just stood there, his own mouth hanging open and his own eyes so wide they hurt.

I've got to get out of here! If I stay another second, my mind's gonna crack like an egg!

But where was Shakey?

"So, I followed her in. I followed her up."

Mulberry raised his eyes, not to the distant ceiling but to the loft above the church entrance, where the choir or maybe the organ player would be stationed during regular service.

Bill Shaker stood there, just beyond the railing, flanked by two dead, be-gowned and be-coined girls. Except, unlike the ones outside and the ones on the pews, these girls were moving. They had a hold of the man, gripping his arms with small ashen hands. Though struggling wildly, and bigger and heavier than the both of them combined, Shakey seemed utterly pinned and miles *past* scared.

Worst of all, Mulberry saw that one of the girls' fists was shoved deep into his partner's throat.

"Shakey!" he exclaimed, pointing his pistol at the girls. Except he wouldn't shoot, he didn't dare, not with the pair of them closed around his partner like that. Instead, he shouted, "Let him go! Let him go right fucking now!"

But the girls either didn't hear or ignored him. Their eyes—completely hidden by silver coins like the rest—nevertheless seemed wholly fixed on their prisoner, their prey.

Shakey stared down, his whole body convulsing, his eyes flashing with helpless panic.

Mulberry looked frantically around the nave, forcing himself to disregard the other girls, all of whom remained prone on their respective pews. He tried to spot a way up to the choir loft, but the shadows were impossibly thick. It was almost as if they were alive and purposefully hiding what he needed to see.

I'm going crazy!

Then he saw it, a narrow, unlabeled archway just behind the last pew.

He started that way.

"Behold, I will corrupt your seed, and spread dung upon your faces."

Mulberry froze, his gun still in his hand, his eyes still focused on the archway that led, or rather he *guessed* led, up to the loft and his desperate partner.

He wanted to keep going, but his legs wouldn't move. Not another step. Instead, his whole body turned toward that new voice, drawn as if by a magnet.

"Submit yourselves for the Lord's sake!"

Reverend Jonah Ray Barton stood there, just three feet away. Mulberry gaped at him, unable to speak, barely able to process what he was seeing. The preacher regarded him with eyes that glowed an eerie, inhuman blood red—not a living man's eyes at all. But nothing like a dead person's stare, either. He wasn't an especially big man, thin in the shoulders and lean. But his visage was arresting, his angled, smooth-shaven face featuring an oddly hooked nose and a widow's peek so long and sharp that it might seem able to cut you.

In one hand, Barton held what looked like an open straight razor, the sort that Mulberry's father used to use before the cancer took him. It had a fancy pearl handle and a four-inch stainless-steel blade that gleamed in the meager light that tried to come through the rows of stained-glass windows on either side of them.

Barton raised his head, gazing up at the choir loft. As he did, Mulberry saw the red jagged line across his throat where his head had been severed from his body—the same head that had now, somehow, been reattached.

"It's so easy," he whispered, as if marveling. *"I will it and they do it. So easy. My congregation. My..."* He seemed to take a moment to search for the right word. *"...Forever Congregation."*

Then he grinned, his teeth crooked and yellow, and called, *"Make him fly, my lovely brides! Make the sinner fly!"*

That seemed to snap Mulberry out of whatever trance had seized him. With a fresh cry, he spun around and stared upward. He was just in time to watch the two girls, acting as if with a single mind, pool their strength and effortlessly lift Shakey off his feet—

—and toss him, without ceremony, over the choir railing.

Bill Shaker, the fist finally removed from his throat, screamed as he dropped fifteen feet, his arms and legs flailing uselessly. An instant later, he connected head-first with the church's unyielding slatted wood floor, landing with a snap and crunch as terrible as they were final, not ten feet from where Mulberry stood. There he lay, his neck bent unnaturally, his body broken, and blood spilling freely from his ears, nose, mouth, and eyes, squeezed out from the impact.

At the same instant, as if summoned by a bell, the girls on the pews sat up together, the coins still over their eyes. Then, as Mulberry stared, his mind shutting down, calling it quits, getting the hell out of Dodge, every single girl began speaking, though their slack mouths never moved.

"The wages of sin are death. The wages of sin are death. The wages of sin are death. The wages of sin are death..."

CHAPTER 3
Newark, New Jersey—2022

MIA FINISHED HER STORY. FOR a long moment, the four agents in the room simply stared at her.

Finally, in a nervous tone that belied her words, Jessup demanded, "I have to ask how it is you know all that. It wasn't in any report I've ever read."

"I spoke with Mulberry," Mia replied flatly.

"Did you?" Brubaker asked. "When was this?"

"Five years ago, not long after the *Ghost Finders* tragedy. It wasn't an interview. I had no intention of publishing anything at that point. I just… needed to understand more about the church."

"He had to have been an old man," Delgado remarked.

"He was thirty-four when he stepped into that parsonage. He was seventy-nine when we talked. I heard he passed away last year."

"And *that* was the story he told?" Jessup asked, sounding incredulous.

"Yes."

Wordlessly, Delgado crossed himself, which seemed an odd gesture for an FBI agent to make, even a devout one, while in a meeting with his boss. But nobody commented on it. Finally, he asked in a small voice, "Were any arrests ever made?"

Before Mia could answer, Brubaker did. "There was an arrest for Barton, but the man took his own life in his cell before he could be arraigned."

"What about the cop?" Delgado asked, sounding uneasy. "The one who died."

"The Camden Police Department generated a lot of paperwork regarding St. Damien's back then," Brubaker replied. "That's understandable given the number of bodies found. I've read most of it and I remember coming across Shaker's name, but his death was ruled a suicide."

"It wasn't a suicide," Mia told her.

"According to Mulberry," Jessup remarked.

"You don't believe his story?" Prine asked the DEA agent.

"Of course, I don't," she said, sounding genuinely surprised. "Do *you*?"

"What happened to him?" Delgado asked Mia. "Mulberry, I mean."

She replied, "When his dispatcher didn't hear from them, she called backup on her own. They found Mulberry's unconscious body at the curb outside the church. He was hospitalized and regained his wits the following day, but nobody really believed most of his account. The official conclusion was that he'd tragically witnessed his partner's suicide, hadn't been able to handle it, and had escaped into some kind of twisted ghost story to explain his failure to get to Shaker in time."

"Sounds plausible to me," remarked Jessup.

Mia ignored her. "But he stuck to his guns, and it cost him his career. After being released from the hospital, he never went back to police work."

None of them commented on that.

Finally, Delgado remarked, "Um…but I thought Mulberry lost it *inside* St. Damien's."

"That's how he tells it."

"Then how did he get out into the street?"

Mia shrugged. "I have my theories, but no one knows for sure. He doesn't have any memory of escaping the church."

"How about the cook?" Prine asked. "Fabron, wasn't it? I remember the name from the file, but not the details. What was his story?"

Mia found herself glancing at Brubaker. Clearly, the assistant director had researched the site. Maybe *she* should be the one answering her agents' questions. But Brubaker said nothing, her face passive, which Mia took for permission to proceed.

"Fabron Avatard," she told Prine. "A French-Canadian. He and his wife Dominique had worked for the Bartons since well before Jonah was born, Fabron as the chef and Dominique as housekeeper and maid to Jonah's mother."

"Barton had servants?" Delgado asked.

"The Bartons were among the original settlers of New Jersey. In fact, for generations, they tended to think of themselves as New Jersey royalty. It was a heritage that Jonah Ray Barton took very seriously by all accounts. The irony is that, when his parents died, he sold the family's shipping businesses, went to seminary school, returned to Camden and built his church on a portion of his family's land. All of Bleak Street originally belonged to the Bartons. It was a fact that he regularly reminded his congregation of at Sunday services."

"None of that is in any file I've read," Jessup said, eyeing Mia as if this little history lesson were somehow suspicious. "How did you find all this out?"

"I told you," Mia replied, keeping her tone light. "After the tragedy with *The Ghost Finders*, I spent some time researching St. Damien's past and police reports aren't always the best place to look."

"There's something I don't get," Delgado said. He sounded a little steadier now. "The Saint Damien *I* know wasn't canonized until sometime around 2010. But the file says Barton built this church in the 1940s. Besides, he was Lutheran, right? Do Lutherans even *have* saints?"

Mia replied, "Well first off, yes, some Lutheran churches are named for recognized saints. But you've got the wrong St. Damien. You're thinking of St. Damien of Molokai. Barton originally named his church after Saints Cosmas and Damian, two Arabic physicians and martyrs who died in the third century. Barton shortened it only a few years after the church opened. No one knows why. It may simply have been a way to make the name of the church more pronounceable. In any case, it's worth noting that he was a Lutheran in name only. Barton came to consider himself and his church independent of any doctrine but his own. Classic megalomania."

"Interesting," said Brubaker. "But where does Fabron come into it?"

"Dominique, Fabron's wife, died quite young. Pneumonia or something like that, I think. Afterward, her husband remained with the family. Even when the parents eventually passed away, and their only child opened his church and moved into the parsonage, Fabron moved with him. He was sixty-six when Jonah Ray Barton made him his last victim."

"The cook was Barton's last murder?" Delgado asked.

"That much *is* in the report," Brubaker said. "This was in 1972, of course, before DNA evidence. But skin was dug out from under Fabron's fingernails, suggesting he put up a fight. Also, the wounds on his face and neck matched the straight razor found on Barton's person, the same straight razor that he used on his other victims."

Delgado looked a little green.

"I read that too," Jessup said. "There was even a profiler's analysis, which was rare back then. The attack on the cook suggested…well… savagery. Avatard's throat wasn't just cut, it had been hacked apart. He died very hard."

"If I remember the file correctly," Prine remarked. "Barton murdered Fabron and then later that night he was killed himself."

"Yes," Mia replied. "By the father of one of his victims."

"How many were there?" Delgado asked, sounding like he didn't really want to know the answer. Apparently, unlike his colleagues, *he* hadn't read the file.

"Twenty-seven," Prine replied. "Twenty-seven girls. Add Fabron that brings Barton's kill count to twenty-eight. More than Dalmer but less than Gacy or Bundy."

"Jesus…" Delgado muttered.

Brubaker said, "For almost thirty years, Jonah Ray Barton preyed on adolescent girls from in and around the neighborhood. As I understand it, the bodies found in the cellar all wore cheap, mail-order wedding dresses, and were in various states of decomposition. Many were just skeletons, which made it hard to determine who they were…or had been. Eventually though, all but a few were identified as locals who were thought to have run away some years before Barton's death."

"And no one suspected him?" Prine asked.

"Apparently not," Brubaker replied. "Not all of the victims were from among his parishioners, of course. But no. Until his crimes were revealed, no one connected Barton with any of the 'missing women.' From what I understand, he routinely held prayer vigils for their safe return."

"Sweet Jesus," Delgado muttered.

Prine shook his head. "It's incredible. Twenty-seven girls spread out across close to three decades…and nobody knew a thing."

And he wasn't finished, Mia pointedly didn't add.

"But I'm confused," Prine said. "Barton was…white, wasn't he? I mean…a 'royal family of New Jersey' is going to be white."

"Yes, he was."

"And he was accepted by the local residents of an entirely black neighborhood." He made this a statement, not a question.

"More than accepted," Brubaker told him. "Based on the interviews in the file, Jonah Ray Barton was beloved by his parishioners. Exposure of his crimes devastated them, in no small part because most of his victims were daughters of the very families he ministered to."

"But he didn't bury them," Prine said. "There's a graveyard on the property, isn't there?"

This one Mia answered. "Yes, one that isn't visible from the street. And no, he didn't bury a single one…though I understand he, himself, is interred there, along with much of the rest of the Barton clan."

"So," Brubaker said, sitting back in her chair and steepling her fingers. "You're suggesting that Barton is the 'sentience' that haunts St. Damien's, and that his haunting began on the very night he was murdered."

"Alleged haunting!" Jessup corrected. "If we're going to keep on with this farce, can you give me that much at least?" When none of them responded to her, she fidgeted in her chair, uncrossing and recrossing her legs again.

"It happens more often than you'd think," Mia replied. "Especially with as strong and dark a spirit as his."

Jessup rolled her eyes again. "So, you're suggesting if we set up our stakeout in the church, that…what? The ghost reverend and his army of teenagers will come after us?"

Mia regarded the woman coolly. She met her share of skeptics. In her field it was pretty much an occupational hazard. But this woman seemed exceptionally *passionate* about it.

It reminded Mia of her mother.

Though she knew from experience that it was a mistake, she said, "It must be hard, walking through life with such a narrow viewpoint."

"Excuse me?" Jessup said sharply. "You come in here and tell us this ghost story, and we're supposed to just take you at your word? Listen *doctor,* I live in the real world, where murders and suicides happen all the time without there having to be some kind of Edgar Allen Poe bullshit going on!"

Mia looked from her to Brubaker and back again. Jessup was fuming. Beside her, Prine appeared uncomfortable, or maybe "socially awkward" would be a better description. For his part, Delgado wore the tiniest of smiles, as though the whole confrontation were somehow funny.

Mia really, really did not want to be here. Let Jessup and the rest of them believe what they wanted. She'd told them what happened to Bill Shaker. She'd warned them about St. Damien's, and about what they'd face if they went inside. What was it to her if they didn't listen?

And what if they go there, despite me? What if they get killed?

What if they end up worse than killed?

Her eyes fell on the Tiffany lamp that stood on Brubaker's desk. Mia, of course, wouldn't really know—but it *seemed* an unusual piece for a government office. Brass appointments and a domed multi-colored shade that reminded her unpleasantly of the stained-glass windows that adorned St. Damien's. Five years ago, those windows had all been unbroken, pristine even, despite decades of abandonment. Based on Prine's photos, that was still the case.

Of course, it is. He's still there.

"Agent Jessup," she said. "Watch the lamp."

"What?"

"The lamp on Assistant Director Brubaker's desk. Watch it."

"What for?"

"Indulge me." Then, after a moment, Mia added, "Please."

With an impatient sigh, Jessup shifted back around in her chair, facing forward. "Fine," she stated. "I'm watching it. What am I supposed to—"

Mia pushed.

It was a lot, but she took what she needed and sent it down the line.

The lamp lit up.

"Whoa!" Delgado exclaimed. At the same time, Jessup sat back, startled, and Prine actually jumped out of his chair. Only Brubaker took it in something like stride. She studied the lamp for several seconds before reaching out and lifting it up. But the only thing under it was bare desktop and, except for its power cord, it wasn't connected to anything.

"Cute gimmick," Jessup remarked, trying to sound dismissive. But then she swallowed, as if her mouth had suddenly gone dry.

"Unplug it," Mia said, maintaining her focus on the lamp. "Quick. I can't keep this up too long."

Jessup glared at her. "What? Why?"

But Brubaker didn't hesitate. She rose from her chair, rolled it out of the way, and wordlessly pulled the lamp's power cord from the wall outlet.

The lamp stayed lit.

"That's…wild," Delgado said, grinning a weird, sort of awe-struck grin.

"Energy surrounds us," Mia explained. "Just because you don't see it doesn't mean it isn't there. And energy can be redirected."

Brubaker asked. "Is that what you're doing?"

Mia nodded.

"It's a parlor trick!" Jessup insisted. She stood and snatched the lamp off Brubaker's desk. Mia expected Brubaker to admonish her, but the assistant director simply resumed her seat and watched, her face impassive. Jessup turned the lamp over, her fingers running along its metal neck and up under the Tiffany glass shade. "There has to be a battery…and she's got some kind of remote control or something!" Mia couldn't tell if she was trying to convince the others or herself.

"It's an antique," Brubaker said. "I found it at a flea market years ago. All it does is plug into the wall."

Feeling sweat sting her brow, Mia relaxed and sat back.

The lamp winked out.

"I'm not buying it," Jessup declared, sounding more emphatic than angry. "What is this, some kind of hazing thing? A childish prank on the DEA agent? A little inter-agency fun?"

"We're the FBI, Agent Jessup," Prine said with what looked like a genuine deadpan. "We don't *have* fun."

With a grunt of disgust, Jessup put the lamp back down on the desk—a bit harder, Mia thought, than was necessary. "Do it again," she told Mia.

"No."

"Ha!" the woman barked. "Why not?"

"Four reasons," Mia replied wearily. "First, I'm not an organ-grinder's monkey. Second, it's hard to do and very tiring. I haven't tried it in a while, and I guess I'm out of practice. And third, something tells me I could do it a hundred times and you wouldn't believe it."

"You're right," Jessup told her. "Because it's fucking impossible!"

"You said four reasons," Prine remarked. "That's only three."

"The fourth reason is that there aren't anymore handy power sources to drain."

"What?" Delgado asked.

Mia sighed. "I can't create EM radiation. But I can borrow it from one device and send it to another. In this case, to light that lamp…just for a minute or two…I had to take the energy from all four of your cell phones."

What followed was an almost comical, twenty-first century scramble into pockets and purses by everyone in the room. Well, everyone except Mia. Mia didn't have a cell phone. She hadn't owned one for five years, not since her one and only trip to St. Damien's.

Delgado was the first to produce his, one of the brand new iPhones. "It's dead," he announced, looking at the others with what Mia could only label wonderment. "The battery's completely drained!"

"Mine, too," Prine reported, working the button of his Samsung *Something-or-Other*. "It won't even turn on."

Brubaker just shook her head, a broad smile playing on her lips as she looked at her device.

Jessup glared at her phone, as if outraged that the cell phone would betray her like this, as if the device were in obvious "cahoots."

They all regarded Mia with nearly identical expressions, ones that mixed astonishment and awe with something almost akin to fear. It was a look she'd gotten many times in her career and it always struck her as the look Puritans might have given a "witch" they were about to hang.

"Agent Jessup's partly right," Mia told them. "It *is* a parlor trick, insofar as it honestly has no useful, real-world application. I'm able to psychically move electricity around a little bit. Growing up, my father called this kind of thing *vrăjituri*, which is an old Romany word for "spells." He saw no harm in them, but whenever my mother caught me doing it, I'd get a lecture, and sometimes a spanking."

"Magic," Jessup said in a tone that wasn't quite an accusation. "So, you're what now…a sorceress?"

Mia shrugged. "Well, I'm a practicing wiccan, so label it however you like. I was only hoping to make a point."

"What point?" Brubaker asked.

"That there are more things in Heaven and Earth than are dreamt of in Agent Jessup's philosophy," Mia replied.

"The point's made as far as I'm concerned," Brubaker said. "Agent Prine?"

"I'm convinced."

"Delgado?"

"Hands down!" the young man said, offering Mia a grin.

Jessup looked from one to the other of them, glowering. Finally, she threw up her hands and dropped back into her chair. "All right. Fine. Let's assume that Dr. Lakatos' ability to turn a lamp on with her mind is somehow proof that a church in Camden is haunted. Sounds like a serious disconnect to me, but whatever. Does that mean we should abandon the operation, let the single most wanted man in the Western Hemisphere just slip in and out of the country without repercussions?"

"Dr. Lakatos," Brubaker said. "How unsafe is St. Damien's?"

Mia didn't hesitate. "*Very*. Going into that place, day or night, is dangerous in the extreme. The simple truth is that I've visited more than a hundred paranormal sites in my career. Most are completely benign. A few carry some small degree of risk. But St. Damien's is in a class all by itself. The veil is thin there, maybe thinner than anywhere else in the country. Worse, that thinning is under the control of the darkest spirit I've ever encountered."

"Which means…what?" Prine asked. "That the church will get into our heads, make us kill each other and then commit suicide? Isn't that what happened to the residents before Bleak Street was eventually abandoned?"

"It is," Mia said. "But that's not what'll happen to you if you go *inside*. If you do that, then Barton will hunt you down and add you to his… congregation."

"This is completely crazy," Jessup muttered.

Brubaker said, "Let's assume for the moment that it's not. Let's assume that it's simply another risk factor of this operation, one that needs to be mitigated before we go in." She paused, as if waiting for someone to either agree or argue. When no one did, she turned to Mia. "What's the best thing we can do to protect ourselves?"

Mia replied, "Don't go within a mile of that place."

Brubaker nodded, as if she'd anticipated this answer. "Assuming that isn't an option. What's the *second* best thing?"

Mia shrugged. "I suppose you could try bringing someone along to bless the place. A priest, rabbi, or reverend. But that presupposes that Barton will be impressed by such a show of theological authority."

"You don't think he will?"

"No, I don't. I think you're going to set foot in that church and find yourselves attacked almost immediately."

"By brides with coins on their eyes?" Jessup asked with what Mia supposed was sarcasm.

Mia fixed her with a level gaze. "By them. And by others, including Officer Shaker. But really by Barton. Everything that happens in that church is controlled by that single entity."

Jessup looked at Brubaker as if expecting the other woman to burst out laughing, revealing this whole thing to be an elaborate prank. When she didn't, when no one did, the DEA agent sat back, visibly exasperated.

Delgado uttered a nervous laugh. "If a blessing won't work…how about an exorcism?"

"As I said, exorcism is a Catholic rite intended to dispel demons," Mia replied patiently. "Jonah Ray Barton isn't a demon. He's a powerful, sentient entity, a psychic predator. He hunts any soul…or mind, if you prefer…that enters his sphere of influence."

"Why?" This came from Prine. "I mean, what's the point? What's his endgame?"

The question was interesting. In all these years, Mia had never really thought of paranormal entities as having "endgames."

"Well…" she said thoughtfully. "I suppose he would want to…" She had to scrounge for the right word. "…conscript you."

"Conscript?" Prine asked.

"It's the only way I can think to explain it. Barton died in 1972, having killed his cook and more than two dozen teenage girls over the course of his tenure at St. Damien's. Then, after he was himself beheaded, he somehow… took command of them. Perhaps their murdered souls were already trapped in the church. That's actually pretty common. But Barton's taken it a step further. By some means, he's made those innocent, murdered spirits his weapons. He uses them, likely unwillingly, to kill others and add to his… army. I'm not sure about an 'endgame,' but Barton clearly wants to increase his power, and the only way he can do that is by taking more lives…by ensnaring and dominating more souls."

Brubaker seemed to take a few moments to digest this. "And you're suggesting that, if our team goes in, Barton will try to do the same to them."

The assistant director's attitude was surprising. Prine and Delgado's too, for that matter. Given Mia's experience with law enforcement, she would have expected them to be disbelieving, if not openly hostile toward her, despite having invited her to consult on this case. True, this was her first time having been approached by the FBI, or any other federal agency for that matter. So, maybe some were more open-minded than others.

"You mentioned a 'cleansing' earlier," Brubaker said. "Is that an option here?"

"Cleansing takes time. Research. It's necessary to understand what's tying the entity on this plane of existence. In some cases, it's guilt or shame. But that isn't Barton. Nothing that's happened since 1972 suggests a soul driven by self-recrimination. Quite the opposite. That leaves anger, resentment, hatred, fear. But I really don't think it's any of them, either."

Brubaker nodded. "Then what *do* you think drives him?"

"I don't know enough about him to say."

Brubaker sat back in her chair. "Let me be frank, Dr. Lakatos. I want you to accompany my team to St. Damien's."

What Mia felt in that instant was almost like an electric shock. "What? No!"

Brubaker was unfazed. "If you do, perhaps you can garner enough information to attempt a cleansing. In any event, maybe you can keep him busy while my people do what they need to do."

Keep him busy? You mean tell him jokes or do a soft shoe?

"Listen to me," Mia said, trying hard to keep the terror, the near *panic*, out of her voice. "I came here today at your invitation to consult, not to participate. And frankly, if I'd known you were talking about St. Damien's of all places, I wouldn't have done even that much."

"I can understand your reluctance, doctor," the assistant director said with what seemed like practiced calm. Around her, the other three had gone graveyard quiet. "But *you* need to understand what's at stake here. We are close…*so* close…to capturing one of the most wanted men on the planet. This is a one-time opportunity. Andres Arias is a monster, at least as bad as what you believe lurks inside that church. He has to be stopped, and you have to help us stop him."

It was a good speech, and it left Mia trembling.

"Can you legally compel me to go along?" she asked in a small voice.

Brubaker looked uncomfortable. "Of course not. And I wouldn't try. I'm simply appealing to your—"

Mia stood. "Then there is nothing, *nothing* on Earth, that would get me back into that church. I don't care if you put a gun to my head. I won't do it."

And, without a further glance at any of them, she started for the door.

"Dr. Lakatos!" Brubaker called.

Mia ignored her. She had one hand on the knob before she hesitated and, with no small effort, looked back. Delgado and Prine had both turned in their chairs to follow her with their eyes. Each wore an expression of dismay, as did the assistant director behind her desk. Only Karen Jessup's gaze was elsewhere, her expression neutral.

Clearing her throat again, Mia said, "I leave you with just this. Don't go there. Don't go anywhere near there. Nothing's worse than what Barton will do to you. Do you know what the title of the episode of *Ghost Finders* would have been called, had it ever aired? It's kind of a nickname that the church has well earned."

When none of them replied, she told them anyway.

"St. Damned."

CHAPTER 4
Staten Island, New York—2022

"I'M SO PROUD OF YOU, peach."

It was something Mia's father used to say. He'd used it when she'd first showed him the *vrăjitură* she could cast. She'd managed to drain the batteries in one toy to power another that had no batteries installed in it at all. She'd been eight years old at the time and couldn't have said how she'd even known she could manage it. But she had—though the effort exhausted her.

"I'm so proud of you, peach."

Her mother hadn't shared that sentiment. Later on, after her father left for work, Mia had been savagely lectured, and what she had done called "evil."

The incident marked the first time that Mia had understood the schism between her parents—and how, despite living together for so many years, they were not friends.

Of course, that had all been before he'd died.

Dad, I miss you.

It long ago became her mantra, her prayer. And she used it now as she made her way home.

These days, "home" meant a studio apartment on Staten Island, not far from the Bayonne Bridge. It was her third year in this tiny place, having been forced to break her lease at her much larger Manhattan two-bedroom when money got tight. Her mother called it "God's justice." Mia's agent called it, "a bad patch." Her former publisher called it, "a shift in the market due to some unfortunate press."

Mia called it, "St. Damien's."

"Hey Cheever," she muttered to the small tabby cat who met her at the door. He weaved in-between her legs, purring in a way that, to the untrained, might seem affectionate. But it was really impatience—and hunger. So, moving as though on autopilot, Mia slipped into her miniscule kitchen and dumped some kibble in the little fucker's bowl.

Then she walked the four feet to her bed and dropped wearily onto her back.

She felt like crying, or maybe screaming, or most likely both.

That goddamned church!

She'd first heard of it eight years ago, right before earning her PhD. At the time, she'd only half-believed the stories. Up until then, no paranormal investigation, at least no serious one, had been conducted at the site and almost everything attached to it smacked of tabloid nonsense and local lore, melodrama at its worst. For quite some time, she'd considered going there herself, on her own dime, and seeing if there was any truth to the lurid rumors. But something else always got in the way: a legitimate cleansing, a book deadline, a blog tour, and she never got around to it.

Until five years ago, that is, when *The Ghost Finders* had called.

Since that single, awful night, St. Damien's had definitely haunted her, if not Barton's ghost than the "ghost of his ghost," biting away at her reputation a little at a time until she found herself—

—well, here.

The phone in her kitchen, a landline, rang softly, its ringer having been set as low as possible. She always did that. Lyled sounds weren't her friend. It was one of the reasons she no longer carried a cell phone.

One of them.

With a sigh, she rose from the bed and checked the small screen that showed the caller id.

Mia's sigh became a groan.

Then, with an almost physical jolt, she remembered what day it was, and her groan grew deeper and even more despairing.

For a moment, she considered not answering, instead just letting the call go to voicemail to be returned a little later, after some wine. But she knew from bitter experience that procrastination wouldn't help her case. She'd screwed up and she needed to face it, own it, and hope the repercussions weren't too terrible.

Pasting on a smile, she lifted the receiver, put it to her ear and said, "Happy birthday, Mom!"

"Thank you, darling. Honestly, though, I was expecting a call before now."

Mia glanced at the clock beside her bed. Like most of the things in this tiny space, furniture included, it was second-hand. But the clock, at least, wasn't a concession to her recent financial straits. Even back when her books had sold and she'd been welcomed as a lecturer at the more progressive liberal arts colleges, she'd still bought almost everything from consignment shops, yard sales, or antique dealers. Mia liked things that had "lived," that had "born witness," things she could *feel* when she handled them. It wasn't clairvoyance, at least not in any meaningful way. But it was pleasant and comforting—usually.

The clock was one of these, a 1970's era flip-number plug-in that, when she handled it, always made her sense its history, one filled with children, family, and love.

And right now, it was informing her that it was not yet noon.

Goddess, what a rough morning.

"I told you," she said into the phone, struggling to keep the irritation out of her voice. "I had that meeting in Newark."

Her mother's tone changed on a dime as it often did. *"That's right! The FBI! How did it go? Did they hire you?"*

"It was just a consultation, Mom. Nothing long-term."

"Are you sure? Nothing would make a better birthday present than to see my only child gainfully employed."

It was an old song, but not the oldest. "Sorry. It wasn't any kind of an interview. They had some questions for me about an investigation they're doing."

"They're not investigating you, are they?" From anyone else, Mia would have taken this as a joke. But, from Gail Lakatos, she knew better.

"Of course not. It's related to a site I worked a while back. I can't give you the details."

"I see. Well, then I guess I'll have to expect something else in the birthday present department. I'm not looking for much. I realize your money's still tight."

"Mom—"

"Oh, I know! You can come to church on Sunday, and we'll call it even!"

And *that* was the oldest song.

"How about lunch instead," Mia suggested. "My treat. We could go to that place you like in Soho. What is it? Bernard's?"

"Bernard's won't Save you, darling."

Mia could actually hear the capital S in "save."

"Mom, can we not—"

"I know. You're sick of hearing it and I'm sick of saying it. But I have to keep trying. You're my only child and you're on the wrong path."

"I'm on Dad's path," Mia said, and she regretted the words the minute they were out.

"Your father was a Christian, despite his…bad habits."

And it was true, sort of. Alexander Lakatos had been raised in the Greek Orthodox church. Yet at the same time, the Romanian immigrant had grown up at his mother's knee, learning the Old Ways. As a girl, Mia had found herself drawn to her father's tales about life in Romania and their family's culture of mysticism, despite her very American and *very* Christian mother's efforts to keep her focused on traditional western religion. The result had been fights between her parents, so many that young Mia had often wondered why they'd married at all. Their song had been a sad one, and always the same. Gail didn't respect Alexander's heritage. Alexander refused to renounce his commitment to "pagan rites."

They never divorced. Neither of them believed in such a thing. So, instead they persisted in a bitter, loveless marriage until Alexander, on an otherwise random winter night, crossed a busy street on his way to a local indie bookstore when he was hit and killed by an Amazon delivery van. Mia had been nineteen at the time and his death had all but broken her.

Her father hadn't lived long enough to see, as he'd often vocally dreamed, his only child earn her doctorate. It was a fate that Mia's mother had attributed at the time to "God's punishment of a chronic sinner."

That one comment had stopped mother and daughter from speaking for more than five years and had irrevocably severed any connection Mia felt to Christianity.

"Mom," she said, carefully and deliberately. "I called to wish you a happy birthday. If you intend to turn it into yet another round of 'Repent or Burn in Hell,' I'm going to hang up."

There was silence on the other end for a long while. Mia waited. Finally, in a tone that mimicked her own in terms of care and deliberation, Gail Lakatos said, *"First of all, Miriam, you didn't call me. I called you. And second, I can't stop trying. I won't. You know that."*

"Then stop trying for now. I've had a difficult morning."

"The meeting in Newark didn't go well?"

"Not really."

"But you will get paid for your time, won't you? Do you need money?"

"I'll invoice them. I'm sure I'll be paid what I'm owed. It was just...a little more confrontational than I expected."

"I'm sorry, Darling."

"It's not important. So? Bernard's on Sunday?"

"I suppose that would be fine." Then, with false casualness, her mother added, *"Could you pick me up at the church, maybe?"*

Mia sighed. "I suppose so. But I won't go in. I wouldn't want to...I don't know...burst into flames or anything."

"That's not funny, Miriam."

"It's a little funny. Okay, Mom. I love you but I have to go. Happy birthday and see you on Sunday."

She ended the call—feeling, as she often did after such conversations, worse than when she'd answered it. So, instead of forcing herself to scrounge up some lunch from her mostly bare larder, she decided to shut her eyes, just for a moment. This was something she'd been doing a lot lately and it troubled her. She was barely over thirty but napped most days like an old woman.

Like my mother.

She hoped, prayed to the Goddess even, that there would be no dreams.

They came anyway. Of course, they did. So much had been dredged up during that morning's meeting. So much fear. So much pain. So much—failure.

St. Damned.

In the dreams, which were disjointed and incoherent, Mia saw them all again, Stevie, Derrick, Lyle, and Kim—just flashes of faces twisted in terror, open mouthed in silent screams. She saw herself, or rather her hands, desperately trying to work a cell phone that repaid her efforts by *shrieking* at her. She saw blood, smelled it even, though she'd heard you couldn't really smell or taste things in a dream. She could feel her heart pounding as she sought an escape, only to find herself surrounded by *his* people. People but *not* people. Souls. Trapped. Enslaved. So much despair. So much horror. They looked at her, somehow seeing her despite the coins on their eyes. They reached for her, not because they wanted to, but because *he* made them. They were *his*. His congregation. His army. His toys.

Barton.

Mia saw, yet again, Derrick's body fall from the belltower, tumbling down the ladder and landing with a dull, sickening crunch on the floor at her feet—

—only to then be standing there a moment later, straddling his own corpse, still wearing the same clothes he'd just died in.

Mia shot awake, not quite sitting up but close to it. There was sweat on her brow and her breath came in labored gasps. She heard a noise, somewhat removed but insistent. Had that woken her or had her mind simply fled the dream as it often did? Either way, she was grateful.

Then the sound and its meaning finally wormed into her consciousness.

Buzzing. Lyled. Grating.

Someone's downstairs, outside the street door, pressing the buzzer.

With a long sigh, Mia climbed off the bed, padded over to the door and tapped the intercom button. At her feet, Cheever purred contentedly. At least one of them had eaten.

"Yeah?" she asked, still groggy.

"Dr. Lakatos. It's Renee Brubaker. May I come up?"

Mia was fully awake now. "Can I ask what this is about?"

"I can't discuss that on the open street. Please, Dr. Lakatos."

"Yes. Okay."

She knew it was a mistake, already having an inkling of what was coming. But she pressed the buzzer anyway. Soon after, she would wonder why.

She would wonder why *a lot.*

Two minutes and two long, narrow, steep flights of stairs later, Mia answered a gentle knock on her front and only door. She'd spent the last two minutes tidying up as best she could. While not what anyone would label a "slob," she did live alone—well, her and Cheever—and could count on one hand the number of guests she'd welcomed since moving in here three years ago. Just where had her social life gone?

The way of her professional career, she supposed.

With another sigh—sighs, of late, had become her "go-to"—she opened the door.

Mia was immediately struck by how tall the assistant director was. Five ten, at least, fully a head taller than Mia, herself. Brubaker had been seated throughout almost all of their meeting, and the one or two times she had stood, Mia had been too preoccupied with the other goings-on to notice her stature.

"Hello again, Dr. Lakatos. Thank you for seeing me."

Mia met her eyes. "If you're here to try to talk me into going to Camden with your team, then I'm afraid you came all this way for nothing."

Brubaker nodded, as if she'd expected this. "Mind if I come in? Just for a minute."

Mia regarded the older woman. Then she stepped back.

Brubaker's eyes raked the small apartment. Mia waited for some sign of judgment, the way her mother had reacted the one and only time she'd been invited here. But nothing came. Instead, Brubaker noticed Cheever, reached down and scratched the cat behind the ears with what seemed like genuine pleasure. For his part, Cheever purred like a motorboat.

Finally, the assistant director straightened, turned back to Mia, and said, "Derrick Porter was my son."

For a moment, Mia didn't think she'd heard right. But then, as her brain caught up with her ears, she felt herself actually rock back a little, as if that name had *weight* and had struck her.

Derrick.

She'd known the young man for only a few hours, a long-haired, lanky kid just out of college. He'd nevertheless owned a sweet smile and she'd rather enjoyed the clumsy crush he'd had on Kim. She'd liked him, maybe more than Stevie and the others.

Besides, he had courage—and more strength than perhaps anyone I've ever met.

The flashback to the dark dream from which she'd only just awakened was stark and as sharp as a knife, or a razor. Mia looked—gaped, really—at Brubaker, whose own expression remained stoic, though Mia thought she recognized in the woman's eyes the familiar grief of long-ago loss.

"I'm…I'm sorry," Mia stammered. "I had no idea…"

"Nothing to apologize for, Dr. Lakatos."

"Please, call me Mia."

Brubaker nodded. "Then I'm Renee."

"Your name—"

Brubaker cut her off. "His father and I divorced about a year after Derrick's death. I went back to using my maiden name."

"Oh," was all Mia could think to say at first. But then, as seconds passed and she processed the news, she said, "I'm confused. Given what happened to Derrick, how is it you're running an investigation involving St. Damien's? I'd have thought the bureau…" Her words trailed off. She was speaking out of turn and she knew it. Then again, this woman had come to her, uninvited, and dropped this bomb. Brubaker must have anticipated Mia's reaction to the blast.

"It's an operation, not an investigation," Brubaker corrected patiently. "But more to the point, it's not about St. Damien's. It's about Arias and the bowling alley. Believe it or not, no one at the bureau made the connection.

Even the bureau has its blind spots, believe me."

"Then why tell me?"

"Because I need your help."

"You of all people should understand how dangerous that place is," Mia said. "Sending your agents in there…and I'm sorry for how this sounds…is the height of irresponsibility."

"I agree."

Mia blinked. "You do?"

Brubaker nodded, looking thoughtful and grim. "When I asked you to come in to consult with us this morning, I'd hoped you'd have some kind of solution, that something in your experience with that church could somehow…pave the way for us. But you made it very clear how narrow our options are. I shouldn't have asked you to join my team. *That* was the height of irresponsibility, and I don't blame you one bit for leaving the way you did."

"Oh," Mia said again.

"Afterward, I told Karen…Agent Jessup…that we'll have to find another stake-out opportunity. She told me I was being ridiculous and insisted there isn't one. I've known Karen Jessup for four years. We're not exactly friends, but we respect one another. She's absolutely competent and, between you and me, she knows more than a little about loss, herself. But she's opinionated and abrasive. She always has been. On the other hand, she has a well-earned reputation for closing her cases, whatever it takes. And she has a…personal stake…in finally nailing Arias."

"I'm sorry…Renee," said Mia. "But I still don't know why you're telling me all this."

Brubaker sighed. "After I ended the meeting, Karen went to her boss. Half-an-hour later, I got a call from mine. The operation *will* be taking place. Jessup, Prine, and Delgado *will* be going into St. Damien's by five o'clock this afternoon to setup their surveillance of the bowling alley. And 'ghosts' are not to be a consideration."

Mia went cold. "It's going to be a disaster."

"I know. But I can't stop it. Arias is too high a priority, and the interagency politics are too convoluted."

"Can you at least do what you need to do during daylight hours?"

"Would that be safer?"

Mia felt herself shudder involuntarily. "I don't know. Maybe. Probably not. But it's all I can think of."

"And there's no way to…cleanse…the place? You're quite sure about that?"

"We'd have to know a lot more than we do about Jonah Ray Barton."

"I've studied his police file," Brubaker said. "After what happened to Derrick, I had to. The man they arrested for Barton's murder gave a lengthy and detailed confession."

"I was never able to get access to it," Mia admitted.

"Well, I was. The man…John Cooley…told a prison guard that he was seeing things, that Barton kept sending his dead daughter to him, taunting him, torturing him."

"That's horrible," Mia whispered.

"That night he hanged himself."

"That much I *do* know. I've visited the cell."

Brubaker's eyebrows rose. "Have you?"

Mia nodded. "After…what happened with *The Ghost Finders*, I got a little obsessed with St. Damien's for a time. During one of the *many* "interviews" I had with the local police, I all but begged them to let me see the Camden County Jail cell where Cooley died. They eventually relented; more I think to shut me up than anything else. Of course, this was forty-five years after it all happened. But even so, the cell was empty. Apparently, they don't use it much anymore. Prisoners kept there tend to become violent or self-harming. Cooley wasn't the only person to kill themselves in that little box…just the first."

"And what was your impression of it?" Brubaker asked.

Mia looked pointedly at her. "Are you asking if I *sensed* something?"

"Did you?"

"If I say yes, are you going to believe me, Renee?"

"I'm not Karen Jessup, Mia."

"That's not an answer."

"It's the only answer I can give you since I haven't heard what you have to say yet."

Fair enough.

Mia rubbed her face, remembering. "Imagine a bad smell, the lingering odor of something corrupt and unclean. Whatever left that stench may be gone, but its influence…its *memory*…is still in the bricks of the walls and the cement in the floor and ceiling. Let's just say *I* wouldn't want to spend too much time in that cell, and I at least have some defenses."

"What kind of defenses?" Brubaker asked.

"Psychic ones. They're sort of like mental shields against metaphysical attacks."

"Wouldn't these shields protect you in the church?"

Mia laughed, the sound harsh and bitter even to her own ears. "It would be like trying to use a cookie sheet to hold back a tidal wave."

Brubaker looked hard at her but didn't say anything for several seconds. Then, in a very calm voice, she said, "Yet, of all the people who went into St. Damien's for that reality TV show, my son included, you're the only one who came out alive."

It was true, and that truth had poisoned her life for five years.

She looked at the other woman, wondering if Renee Brubaker knew the story. Had she read Mia's statement to the Camden Police? If she had, was this some sort of recrimination? Honestly, Mia wasn't sure she'd blame her if it was.

"I'm so sorry about Derrick," Mia said, meaning every word of it. "He was a brave young man." She tried to say more, but her throat closed up.

Renee nodded, as if she understood, and she probably did. "Not right now…but sometime, I would really like to hear the details about what happened to him and the others." Then she took a deep breath, seemed to center herself, and added, "Now, however, I have four more people who are required to spend a night, or at the very least several hours inside that place."

"Four?" Mia asked.

"I'm going, too."

"You? Do you…I mean, do FBI assistant directors generally go out in the field like that?"

"No, and officially, I won't be there. My presence will stay completely off-the-books. But I can't let Karen and the others face whatever's waiting for them in there without me. I couldn't live with myself if I did."

Mia said urgently, "Call it off, Renee! For God's sake!"

"I can't. It's out of my hands. It's happening with or without me. I'm choosing for it to be with me."

With a groan, Mia turned around and went into what passed for a kitchen in what she'd come to think of as her "living cubical." She took a half-empty bottle of chardonnay from the fridge and poured a generous helping into a glass. Then, as an afterthought, she gestured at Brubaker, holding up the wine.

"No, thank you," the assistant director said, watching from her spot near the door. Mia supposed she should have offered the woman a seat. But these days she kept the sofa-bed open most of the time, and her only other chairs were folding ones that she stored in the closet.

She took a swallow of Chardonnay. Then, gasping, she took another.

Goddess…it's not even noon. I must look like an alcoholic.

Am I sure I'm not?

"I can't cleanse St. Damien's," she finally said. "I don't have what I need to do it."

"You mean you don't know what 'drives' Barton, as you put it."

"Yes."

"Could that be something like a…secret?"

"A secret," Mia echoed.

"I have reason to believe that Jonah Ray Barton carried a secret to his grave, something beyond his murders and depravities."

"What reason?"

"Not yet. First, tell me if you believe discovering that secret would cleanse St. Damien's."

Mia took another big swallow from the wine glass. She knew this was a bad idea, but she couldn't help herself. These past few years, she'd "not been helping herself" quite a bit. If her mother knew just how much wine her heathen daughter went through in a week, she'd have had AA knocking on her door by now—not that AA did that sort of thing.

But, if they *did,* Gail would have had them doing it.

"It's possible," Mia said, her heart suddenly pounding. "I was investigating the home of a wandering spirit…a little girl. It turned out that the only thing keeping her here…the *only* thing…was a lost thimble. I found the thimble and she crossed over. Just like that, the house was clean."

Brubaker actually laughed, though it was a hollow sounding thing. "Reminds me of that old movie, the one where the medium declares at the end 'This house is clean!' I can't remember what it was called."

"*Poltergeist,*'" Mia replied. It had been one of her father's favorites. "And, as I recall, the house turned out to not be clean after all. Just kind of 'Hollywood" clean."

"What about in this case?" the assistant director asked. "Would the cleansing stick or would it be just 'Hollywood" clean?"

Mia offered a shrug. "Ghosts aren't what most people think they are. Being on this plane isn't natural for them…and staying here is an act of will. Every sentient haunting I've encountered has involved a person known to have been particularly strong-willed in some way, whether for good or evil. But even the strongest of them is always anchored by something."

"Like a secret," Brubaker pressed.

"Maybe. *If* Barton *does* have a secret, and *if* it's important enough to him to be his tether to this world…then, yes, that could very well be his anchor. But discovering it wouldn't be enough. The secret would then need to be revealed, loudly and publicly."

"And that would cleanse the church?"

"It could conceivably snap that tether and send him on his way."

She looked over at Brubaker and was surprised to see that the woman had scooped Cheever up in her arms and was cradling him. More than that, the cat was purring. Usually, Cheever only accepted affection on his own terms.

"I don't know the secret," Brubaker admitted. "But I do know something that might help discover it."

"What's that?"

"A bit of…graffiti, something scrawled on Barton's gravestone only a few days after his death."

"Scrawled by who?"

"By his murderer."

Mia had never heard of such a thing.

"That wasn't in any of the press releases."

"I'm not surprised," Brubaker said. "At the time, Bleak Street was already a sideshow. The Camden Police probably didn't want to give the gawkers one more thing to gawk at." Then, after a pause she added, "But it's in the case file, along with Cooley's full confession, which is a scary read. I also have the reports from the officers who took him into custody. Have you seen that material?"

"No," Mia admitted.

"I didn't think so. But do you suppose there could be something in there that would help you?"

"Help me?"

"Unearth Barton's secret. Cleanse St. Damien's."

"You mean *today?* Before your team goes in this evening? That kind of 'lucky break' would border on a miracle!"

"Would it hurt to try? I could recount what I read, and you could tell me what you think. Reasonable?"

Mia hesitated. She didn't want this. She didn't want any of it. But she could *feel* the universe pushing her in a certain direction. "Currents of Fate," she called them. Mia believed in free will, believed in it completely. But she also knew that, sometimes, you were "nudged" along. Sometimes, the Goddess wanted you to be somewhere and do something. You could fight it. You could even beat it. But in doing so, you could lose a piece of yourself.

She drained the wine glass. Then, still trembling a little, she said, "Go ahead."

CHAPTER 5
Camden, New Jersey—1972

"IT'S ABOUT…ABOUT RACHEL, JOHN," Russ stammered. His hands shook and his eyes seemed to be looking everywhere at once. "I saw her, man. *I just saw her!*" This last part came out as a half-sob, so loud that Wanda dropped something in the kitchen. Cooley heard it shatter; the sound making him wince.

"What's happening?" Wanda Cooley cried, coming into the parlor while wrapping a dish towel around what looked like a cut hand. "What's going on, Russ? Do you have news about our girl?"

Russel Saunders, their neighbor and friend for eighteen years, looked from Wanda to her husband and back again. His expression was twisted, his eyes streaming tears. He opened his mouth to reply.

"No," Cooley said. He delivered the word very deliberately, hard and flat as coffin nails. It usually did the trick with most of the kids at school.

Apparently, it worked on Russ, too.

"I…" he began. Then he glanced at Cooley and said, "Nothing, Wanda. No news. Sorry."

"Then what the hell, Russ?" Wanda demanded, crying a little now. "I heard you say Rachel's name!"

"Different Rachel," Cooley replied evenly. Then, without looking at his wife, without daring to, he stood, grabbed his neighbor, and pulled him to his feet. "Russ's having some woman troubles again, that's all," he said. "I'm taking him to Ben's to settle him down over a couple of beers."

"Beer doesn't solve problems, John Cooley."

Cooley was relieved to hear her say that. If Wanda was lecturing, that meant she'd put aside her fear, the fear they'd both been living with for close to three months, the same fear that had just cut her hand and broken whatever it was she'd dropped in the kitchen.

"Maybe not," he said, ushering Russ to the door and still, studiously, not looking at his wife. "But it helps you see them better."

"Like hell," his wife murmured before returning to the kitchen. A moment later, Cooley heard her starting to clean up in there.

"You just cost me supper," he told Russ, who said nothing.

Then they both left the house.

Ben's had been the local watering hole since before John Cooley was born. It was attached to Fairlanes Bowling, both establishments located right across the street from the church. Nobody named "Ben" owned it and, as far as Cooley knew, nobody by that name ever had. Instead, Reece Falwell owned both the lanes and the bar, which made him the flushest man on the street, a fact he liked to put on display every chance he got. Mind you, Falwell still lived on Bleak Street, the anus of Camden's ample ass, so he wasn't all *that* well-to-do.

It was nearly six on a Friday evening, dinner hour, so the crowd wasn't as heavy as it would be later on. Cooley recognized most of the faces the moment he opened the screen door. The night was warm for October, and Darrell, who kept the bar, had the windows open.

"Sit," Cooley ordered, depositing Russ down on a chair at one of the corner tables. Russ, looking small and spent, complied without a word. Then Cooley went to the bar and signalled Darrell for two beers.

"In trouble with Wanda?" Darrell asked as he placed the sweating bottles in front of Cooley.

"Who, us?" Cooley replied with a forced grin. "We're like newlyweds!" Then, leaving Darrell laughing, he took the beers, returned to the table, sat down across from his neighbor, and declared, "Start talking."

Russ nodded, took a long draught from his bottle, and said, "Reverend Barton rang me up a couple of hours ago, just after I got back from the shop, and asked me to come by and replace some bulbs. That's all it was, just bulbs. But you know those lamps in the church, how high up they are. So, I brought my A ladder, the big one. I figured I'd have to find out what kind of bulbs he needed and then hope he kept some around the place. Otherwise, I'd have to drive over to the hardware store.

"But when I got there, the reverend was coming through the basement door with a box in his hands. He gave a quick bless you, put the box down on one of the pews and headed back into the parsonage. I got the feeling he was…I don't know…upset about something. Anyway, I opened the box and there were the right bulbs, easy as that.

"So, I started replacing them. There are four big hanging lamps in there, and each one takes six bulbs. Well, all four had at least one bulb out, so it was a job moving the pews around so that I could get my ladder under them. But I did it, or almost did it. Because, as it turned out, the reverend's box had in it just enough bulbs to do the job, no more…and as I was trying to get the last one screwed in, it slipped, fell all of fifteen feet, and broke.

"I figured at first I'd have to knock on the parsonage door, you know, the one between the church and that glass walkway. But then I remembered how the reverend looked…upset about something. So, I figured I'd just go down into the basement and see if there wasn't another box of bulbs." Russ looked up at Cooley, his beer bottle already half empty. "Ever been down there?" he asked, his voice shaky.

"No," Cooley replied.

"Me, neither. Don't know anybody who ever was. Whatever's down there that needs getting, the reverend always gets it himself…either that or sends Fabio for it."

"Fabron," Cooley corrected.

"Whatever. The French guy."

"French Canadian," Cooley corrected.

"Okay." Russ sighed heavily, tremulously. "Anyway, I went to the basement door. Half-figured it might be locked. It usually is. But it wasn't. Seems Reverend Barton was so distracted about something that he forgot to lock it. So, I opened it and went down the wooden stairs I found there.

"It's big, that basement, and dark like most. But I found a light switch and flipped it. Jesus, I wish I didn't."

"What did you see, Russ?" Cooley asked. He hadn't touched his own beer, and something told him he wouldn't be.

"I saw Rachel. Her and others. Maybe four or five of them. All of them were laid out on the floor on heavy tarps. All of them…oh God, John, I'm sorry…all of them were dead with…with their throats cuts. The stink…well, the stink was just awful!"

For the first time since his neighbor had pounded on his front door, Cooley felt his hands close into fists. His daughter, his youngest, had been gone since mid-summer. Wanda was distraught, but Cooley had always quietly figured that the sixteen-year-old had run off with some boy. It happened all the time, especially in this part of town. So, when Russ had shown up with wild stories about Rachel being dead, a part of Cooley, a big part, had kind of dismissed him out of hand. Russ wasn't the sharpest tool in the shed at the best of times.

But now—

"Did you recognize any of the others?" he asked, feeling his throat tighten.

"I'm pretty sure one of them was Liza Gold. You know her?"

"Yeah," Cooley heard himself say. Liza had gone missing maybe six or seven months ago. Cooley knew her from school but thought maybe Wanda was friendly with her parents from church.

Church.

St. Damien's.

Right across the goddamned street!

"Another one might be that Masterson girl. But she was too messed up, man. Her face was all sunken away."

Of course, it was. Bev Masterson had been gone more than a year. That's a lot of time to decompose.

"Reverend Barton's got 'em down there," Russ whispered over his own empty beer. "He's dressed them all in white and laid 'em out, side by side on those tarps. And the tarps…the tarps are like soiled, you know?"

"Soiled? You mean dirt?" Cooley asked.

"No, man." And, for a moment, Cooley thought his neighbor would vomit. "Like those girls been rolled up for months, falling apart inside those tarps, and part of them…*parts* of them…stuck to it when he unwound them."

"Barton," Cooley said. "You think it was Barton?"

"Who else, man?"

"Fabron, maybe?" Cooley suggested. "Could Fabron have killed my little girl and then Barton just found them and *that's* why he went past you looking so upset?"

Russ blinked. "Didn't think of that. Maybe, I guess. Probably." The man actually looked relieved. "It makes the most sense that Fabio did it. I mean…we all *know* Reverend Barton. The whole street. We all go there on Sunday and listen to him preach! Jesus Christ, John. What's going on? What's it all mean?"

"It means you go home, Russ," Cooley said, keeping his tone as matter-of-fact as he could. "Meanwhile, I'm going to go have a talk with Fabron and the reverend."

Russ licked his lips and, when Cooley slid his own untouched beer over to the man, Russ drank it greedily. Then he declared, wiping his mouth, "We gotta call the cops."

Cooley shook his head. "No," he replied, using that voice of his again, the one he used at work when he wanted people to fall into line. He didn't need to explain. Russ knew as well as anyone on the street what the cops would see: a black man bad-mouthing a white man and a reverend to boot.

Russ looked at him, sweating despite the cool autumn air. "Okay, if you say so. No cops. But…whatcha going to do, John?"

"I don't know yet. Go home."

Then Cooley stood, dropped two bucks on the table for Darrell, and headed for the door. As he did, he felt more than saw the other patrons looking at him. How much they'd heard, Cooley didn't know—and, right now, didn't much care. He wasn't sure what was true. But he intended to find out.

The sun wasn't yet down when he stepped out onto the cracked sidewalk, but the light was fading, casting St. Damien's long shadow across Bleak Street to end almost exactly where Cooley stood. He looked down on it, and something in the shape of it—twisted and distorted in the way of evening shadows—fueled his already burning anger.

If what Russ said turns out to be right...

But Cooley didn't finish that sentence. He couldn't, not yet, not even to himself. He'd been a violent youth, poor and angry about it throughout most of his childhood. But he'd abandoned all that after meeting Wanda. Now, having a family he loved and a career he was proud of had turned him into a peaceful man. At least, that was what he'd believed for the last twenty-five years of his life.

But if Rachel...

He didn't look back as he crossed the quiet road, but he could sense his friends and neighbors watching him through Ben's small windows, Russ no doubt among them. To his right, the sound of crashing pins and laughter rolled out through Fairlanes' open glass doors. But, to his left, Bleak Street, with its two dozen rowhouses on either side from here to the corner, stood empty and still. Cooley got the feeling, vague but persistent, that the night was holding its breath.

He reached St. Damien's front entrance, a pair of heavy wooden doors that, together filled a rounded archway. He found the righthand one standing partly open and wondered if Russ had left it that way when he'd fled first the basement and then the church. If so, then apparently Barton hadn't returned from the parsonage, otherwise he'd surely have closed and locked it. Unlocked doors were rarely seen on Bleak Street.

Cooley pushed his way in. The lights were off, the interior rendered gloomy and uninviting. He'd never considered himself particularly religious. But Wanda *was* and, when their kids had been younger, she'd insisted that everyone not only attend St. Damien's every Sunday but dress up for it. Since his boys had grown up and moved out, that had left only Rachel. And when she'd turned fifteen and declared that she no longer believed in God, Wanda had been heartbroken.

But Cooley, who was considerably less devout than his wife, understood.

Glowering, feeling his fists flexing almost in time with his thundering heart, Cooley moved away from the doors and deeper into the nave. There was no one here, though he spotted Russ's ladder still standing under one of the heavy, hanging light fixtures.

Cooley considered calling for Reverend Barton, but he doubted anyone would hear him from the parsonage. Besides, the part of his brain still doing any real thinking told him it was better to confirm Russ's story before he faced Barton wrapped in all his barely contained anger.

So, wordlessly, he made for the basement door.

The stairway was dark, just as Russ had said, though Cooley could see a single bare-bulbed light shining at the bottom, illuminating what looked like a mostly dirt floor. With a final glance around the empty church, he headed down, mindful of each step, though the stairs didn't creak much at all.

The cellar was big—a sprawling foundational space thick with shadows. The lit bulb seemed the sole source of light and, by it, Cooley could make out boxes of church supplies, everything from King James Bibles to hymnals and altar accessories. Against one wall stood a workbench that didn't seem as if it had been touched in a decade. Various tools, all of the well-worn, manual variety, were piled there without apparent rhyme or reason. An axe, fifty years old if it was a day, stood propped up in one corner, its heavy blade red with rust.

Then a smell hit his nose, rank and putrid. Though he'd never in his life seen the death of anything bigger than a stray cat, some visceral part of his lizard brain reacted instantly. His breath caught and his heart quickened as he slowly turned toward the cellars opposite wall. Heavy cloth tarps, like the sort professional painters used, had been stretched out on the floor, just at the very edge of the circle of light. Atop them lay four girls. Each was on her back, wrapped in what looked like a cheap, strapless wedding dress. And each had coins, silver dollars, resting over her closed eyes.

And one of them, the left-most one, was Rachel.

Cooley wailed. He hadn't intended to, hadn't meant to make any sound at all down here if he could help it. But the sight of his little girl lying dead on that tarp, her arms folded across her bosom and her throat cut wide open, the blood it contained long since gone, had steamrolled right over what remained of his self possession. In his mind's eye, he saw her seven-year-old smile, her one-year-old laugh, her twelve-year-old anger, and her sullen, surly teenage angst. Through it all though, she'd been *his* Rachel, his only daughter, the sun in his sky.

And there she was, dead, her light extinguished.

Snuffed out.

He went to her, dropped to his knees and cradled her head. Tears blinded him, falling on her cold, lifeless face as the coins tumbled from her eyes and landed on the tarp beside him. He didn't bother checking for a pulse; on some level he knew—*knew*—she was beyond hearing him. Her skin was too gray, and the dress she wore, which he'd never before seen, too soaked in her blood. Nevertheless, he begged her to wake up. When she didn't, he simply held her and cried until his entire body shook and he felt as wrung dry like an old rag.

Dear God in Heaven...

What am I going to tell Wanda?

"I'm sorry to see you down here, John," said a voice from the foot of the stairs.

Cooley's head snapped up. With one hand, he wiped the tears from his eyes and looked into the face of the man who stood barely ten feet away. Reverend Jonah Ray Barton was fifty-six years old, ten years Cooley's senior, a white man living and working on a block that was entirely black. That should have made him a pariah, perhaps even a target. But the people of Bleak Street, *good* people, had embraced him almost from the moment he'd built this church. Barton, after all, was from a very old and very rich family in this county. He could have done anything, *been* anything.

But, as Wanda often said, he'd chosen God over money.

Barton wore his familiar black clerical suit, complete with Roman collar. His manner was calm, infuriatingly so, and his hands were behind his back. His eyes were small and set just a little too close together, a feature that had always made him look—shifty—at least in Cooley's opinion, though Wanda believed the man all but walked on water.

"What did you do?" Cooley screamed, holding his dead daughter more tightly to his chest.

Barton didn't reply.

So, Cooley elaborated, "What the fuck did you do to my little girl?" Every word felt like a knife in his gut, their blades ice cold. The horror of it, the *finality* of it, nearly stole the breath from his lungs.

For a long moment, the man didn't speak, didn't move. Then, in a whisper-soft voice he said, "You should thank me, John."

"*Thank you?*" Cooley demanded with a savage, almost feral snarl. "You killed my baby!"

"I sanctified her."

"What? What the hell is that supposed to mean?"

Barton smiled then. He had very yellow teeth, the canines oddly pointed. "I saved her soul, John. I spared her from the sins brought by adulthood. The drugs. The prostitution. The endless, meaningless promiscuity. Now she will dwell forever in the light. But take heart John, she died a woman…"

"What?"

"A married woman," the pastor said. "I made a proper bride of her. After all, fornication outside of wedlock is a sin."

Cooley struggled to process this. "Fornication," he heard himself whisper.

"That's what I meant by 'she died a woman.'"

"You raped my little girl before you cut her throat…all to send her to *God*?" Cooley exclaimed. "Is that what you're telling me, you sick fuck?"

"No, no," Barton said. He drew one hand, his left hand, from behind his back and slowly waggled his forefinger to and fro, a *tsk tsk* gesture that Cooley's mother used to use. "There is no God, John. I don't believe there ever has been. No, the light sweet Rachel dwells in now, the light they *all* dwell in, is entirely mine." Then the smile returned, wider than before, and the madman added, "But to do it, first I had to cut her flesh…and then I had to *know* it."

Cut her flesh and then know it.

That means, after she was dead, he…

It occurred to Cooley briefly, with a sense of clarity that was there and gone in an instant, that Barton was baiting him, saying these things to induce him to react precipitously and out of vengeful rage. But that fleeting clarity vanished like smoke as Cooley put down his poor, dead child's head and jumped to his feet. His face was hot with blood and his fists felt like hammers as he launched himself at the smaller man.

Barton moved with surprising speed, his right hand flashing out from behind his back. Cooley caught a glimpse of something silvery that shone in the light. Then a slash of hot pain cut across his forehead. A second later, blood filled his eyes and he staggered off-course, crashing into some of the boxes, landing in a clumsy, blinded heap.

"And whosoever was not found written in the book of life was cast into the lake of fire!" Barton exclaimed as though standing behind his Sunday pulpit.

Cooley heard the man approaching him and realized that he had to move. But he was upended like a turtle and, every time he tried to leverage himself to his feet, whatever box he put his weight on collapsed, dropping him to the floor again. Meanwhile, Barton's steps drew closer and, as Cooley wiped the curtain of blood from his eyes, he saw the straight razor in the pastor's long-fingered right hand.

Barton intoned, "Then he will say to those on his left, 'Depart from me, you cursed, into the eternal fire prepared for the devil and his angels.'"

Then he raised his blade, his eyes seeming to shine.

Cooley kicked him in the knee.

Barton shrieked in agony. For a second, the pastor swayed and staggered, but then he righted himself and, still clutching the razor though apparently bereft of any further desire to use it, he staggered toward the cellar stairs. He moved slowly, dragging his right leg and groaning in obvious pain. Even so, Barton was hobbling his way up the steps before Cooley could regain his feet.

Then Cooley heard the unmistakable click of an old, sturdy lock being engaged.

"Shit!" he exclaimed, running up the stairs to the closed door, already knowing what he would find.

Barton had locked him in the cellar.

He spent half-a-minute slamming his shoulder uselessly against the stout wood, accomplishing nothing besides mixing sweat with the blood that still ran freely from his slashed forehead, repeatedly blinding him.

Then he remembered the axe.

Pulling off his shirt, he wound it as tightly as he could and tied it around his bleeding forehead. It was certainly no bandage, but at least it stemmed the flow and let him see where he was and what he was doing. Later, he supposed, it would need stitches, but right now that reality felt so far away it might as well have been on the dark side of the moon.

He went back down the steps and turned right, studiously, almost desperately, *not* looking at his dead daughter and those other girls. The man who'd done those things, the *monster* who'd murdered and raped Rachel—Cooley could only pray it really had been in that order—was upstairs right now, probably arming himself anew. Worse, maybe he was calling a lawyer, or even the cops. Barton had money, family money. Maybe he would try to work things so that Cooley, himself, took the blame for those poor girls. True, Russ would refute such a cheap frame job, but this was Camden and everybody knew how *that* would go.

All of which meant Cooley had to get out of here now and find Barton, find him and end him for what he'd done.

He located the axe, still standing in the corner, and picked it up. It was a heavy, sturdy thing, one that reminded him of chopping down a rotted old maple tree in their backyard when he'd been a kid. Holding it felt good, felt *right*, and with it he returned to the stairs.

At the top, he resisted his initial impulse to start hacking away at the heavy planks that made up the meat of the door. Instead, he wracked his brain, trying to remember if there was a deadbolt or simple knob lock at play here. He'd been inside this church a hundred times or more, usually somewhat reluctantly, and he'd surely passed that cellar door that many times on his way to one pew or another. But, before tonight, he'd never tried the knob and couldn't recall how its lock was situated.

One way to find out.

Cooley turned the axe over and brought its boxy backend down hard on the knob. It snapped off instantly and with a satisfying clank. Then, he shoved the spindle all the way in. It resisted a little as the latch caught in the faceplate. But then he heard it crash to the floor of the nave on the other side.

The door itself, however, didn't move.

Might be a deadbolt. Might just be sticking. Again, one way to know.

Cooley shoved his shoulder against the wood.

The door creaked open.

Shit, yeah!

But any celebration he felt was grim as hell, blackened by the memory of what lay behind him in the cellar.

Without so much as a satisfied smile, he surged out into the church proper and, clutching the axe firmly in both hands, headed down the center aisle toward the altar and the door to the parsonage that he knew lay behind it.

The air hung heavily around him, and his every step bounced off the high, vaulted ceiling and the tall, narrow stained-glass windows that flanked the nave. When he reached the altar he noticed a Bible atop it, open to one of the latter pages in the New Testament. That stopped him for a moment—though, if asked, he couldn't have said why. Cooley wasn't all that well read when it came to scripture, but Wanda was, and often liked to recite passages to him when he would much rather she didn't.

There wasn't a lot of light in here; the setting sun had to be close at hand. But there was enough for him to see that a passage on the righthand page had been sharply underlined.

They will suffer the punishment of eternal destruction, away from the presence of the Lord and from the glory of his might.

"Believe it, you mother-fucker," Cooley muttered to himself.

Then he closed the Bible and hurried on his way.

The parsonage door led him into a corridor of glass. This was called a "breezeway," at least according to one of his neighbors, who'd helped install it something like twenty years ago. Before then, "poor" Reverend Barton had been forced to walk outdoors between his home and his church, regardless of the weather.

"Might have caught his death," the neighbor had said.

If only…

Cooley crossed it at a run.

The door at the far end stood wide open, the interior lit. Cooley supposed he should stop and listen. Broken knee or not, Barton still had that razor—hell, and a shotgun, for all Cooley knew. But then he remembered Rachel, *his* Rachel, who had once been a six-year-old who'd cried when she'd lost her favorite hair ribbon, and all thoughts of stopping, pausing, or slowing down so much as a step went right out of his head.

He stormed into the parsonage, a place he'd never visited before, and scanned the small dwelling in the space of a heartbeat. It was modest, modest everything—modest kitchen, modest dining area, modest parlor.

All of it appeared empty.

"Barton!" he heard himself scream. Only the silence replied.

Then Cooley spotted Fabron.

The cook lay on his back on the kitchen floor, just steps away, his sightless eyes on the ceiling, his arms and legs akimbo. And there was blood, a *lot* of blood. Fabron had always been a quiet, unassuming man, devoted to the reverend. He'd often brought homemade soup to those on the street who took sick. Wanda and the rest of St. Damien's congregation had loved him almost as much as Barton, himself.

But now he barely looked human, his throat brutally gouged out, not neatly slit like the girls downstairs.

Not like Rachel.

Another to add to his list, Cooley thought darkly. *The last one.*

"Have you ever been lied to, John?"

Cooley whirled toward the voice, raising the axe.

Jonah Ray Barton stood in an archway on the opposite side of the sitting area, one that presumably led into the bedrooms at the rear of the parsonage. He looked smaller somehow, diminished, though Cooley noticed that the razor was still in his hand.

At the sight of him, Rachel's sweet face flashed through Cooley's mind, at first alive and laughing and then dead and still and with coins for eyes. The images fueled him, like gasoline on a fire.

He found that the axe felt heavy in his hands. But it was a *good* heavy.

"Have you ever been lied to by someone you trusted?" Barton asked. His eyes had a faraway cast, as if he were speaking to the universe, despite having used Cooley's name.

"You killed my baby."

Barton smiled. But it wasn't the wide, toothy grin he'd used in the basement. No, this was a small, almost wistful thing. "I told you. I sanctified her," he corrected without rancor. "She's been spared the pain of this life and is now with me forever, under my protection, an angel in my army."

"You have no army," Cooley said, taking one step closer, then another. At any moment, he expected Barton to turn and run—or limp—away, as he had downstairs. But the man never moved and, if he had any inkling of just how close to his end he was, it didn't show. "You have no time," Cooley told him. "You have nothing."

"Oh, but that's where you're wrong, John." And now the grin *did* widen and his eyes, wide and black as lumps of coal, snapped onto Cooley as if pulled by a magnet. "I have everything. I *am* everything."

Cooley charged, the axe at his shoulder.

At the same time, roaring like something from another world, Jonah Ray Barton did the same, his razor slashing the air between them, lightning quick.

But, as angry as Cooley was—angrier, in fact, than he'd ever been in his life, he wasn't blind. Barton's razor was surely sharp.

But it was small and the axe—the axe *wasn't*.

So, with the man who'd killed his child still two steps away, Cooley swung with everything he had.

The blade wasn't the keenest, but it did the job, catching Barton in the neck, almost exactly between his jawline and his collarbone with a sound like a wet slap. The effect was immediate. Blood, a fountain of it, hit the wall beside him, soaking a nearby standing piano and the carpet beneath it.

Barton staggered, the razor dropping from his grasp. His gaze stared blankly, his mouth moving soundlessly. Then, as Cooley yanked the axe out, sending even more blood gushing, the pastor, the fallen priest, dropped to his knees as if in supplication. For a heartbeat, maybe two, Cooley loomed over him, almost numb with shock. For all his rage, all his determination, John Cooley had never killed a man before, and the reality of it dropped a veil over his every perception. He felt distant, removed, as if he were *watching* this unfold instead of *participating*.

Perpetrating.

Except I haven't killed him, yet. He's still breathing. It isn't done.

So, grasping hold of that thought firmly, he raised the axe to his shoulder again and muttered, "For Rachel."

Meanwhile, Barton's mouth continued to move, though still no words came out.

So, Cooley swung again.

He didn't know what he expected exactly, maybe another deep cut like the first. But perhaps this swing had even more behind it, because the result went further than he would have imagined.

Jonah Ray Barton's head came clean off.

CHAPTER 6
Camden, New Jersey —1972

FOR A LONG TIME, MOST of a minute, Cooley just stood there looking down at the headless corpse at his feet. The strange mental detachment he felt, born perhaps out of the horror of first his daughter's cruel death and now the murder he'd committed, only deepened. He was breathing, he knew that, but where it had moments ago been in great, heaving lungfuls of air, it now came in short, stuttering gasps.

Fucker…

And he suddenly wondered if he was referring to Barton or himself.

Slowly, as if pulled by a string, Cooley turned his head and looked toward the parlor's front windows. Outside, the sun had nearly set, casting an orange hue over everything in the room that seemed weirdly unnatural, *unclean*.

Then his gaze fell upon the severed head, which had landed on its ear beside the sofa.

Though only just separated from its body, it already looked less than human. The skin had gone pasty—*even pastier than usual, for a honkey,* Cooley thought bitterly—the mouth slack and the eyes as empty as the man's soul had been. Cooley stared at the grotesque thing, half-expecting to puke up his last meal. But then he remembered that he and Russ had left the house before supper and, hell, he hadn't even touched his beer back at Ben's. So, he supposed his belly was safely empty.

Besides, what was there to puke about, anyhow? Sure, he'd killed a man, and in a pretty nasty way, truth be told. But who on God's Green Earth would say Jonah Barton hadn't had it coming? Who would look at the four bodies in the cellar, sweet Rachel among them, and call Cooley the monster?

He turned, the axe still in his hand and still dripping blood. He harbored some vague idea about going back through the church and out the way he'd come in. Of course, the parsonage's front door was right there, just a dozen paces away. But reaching it meant skirting around the sofa and stepping over the *thing* that lay on the carpet and, for some reason, Cooley just didn't think he had it in himself to manage that.

So, the church it was.

As he reached the door to the breezeway, giving poor Fabron one last pitying look, he spotted something that stopped him cold. If the kitchen light hadn't been on, its yellow glow surprisingly anemic, he wouldn't have noticed it at all.

The dead man clutched something in his right hand.

Cooley leaned closer, trying to discern what it was. Amazingly, despite what he'd just done, he didn't want to actually touch Fabron's body.

What he saw was a single sheet of paper, folded and wrinkled and colored a faded blue.

With a groan of *something*, disgust maybe, he knelt and gently retrieved it. As he did, he half-expected Fabron's fingers to be board-stiff. Rigor Mortis. But apparently that hadn't set in yet, and the cook's thin-fingered hand opened without complaint. The moment he had the whatever-it-was, Cooley all but jumped to his feet and stepped away, even though he knew he was being ridiculous.

Looking back on the events of that long and terrible night, John Cooley had only one regret, and it had nothing to do with Barton or the axe. No, the only thing he would come to rue, and rue bitterly, was picking up that paper and looking at it.

Because doing so killed him.

But right now, in weary but blissful ignorance, his hands bloody, he slowly and carefully unfolded the single sheet. Then he tilted it toward the light and blinked his eyes, trying to push back the numbness long enough to focus on what it said.

"Holy…shit," he whispered.

"I wish you hadn't seen that, John."

The words hit him like a bolt of icy lightning. He screamed and spun around, still holding the paper but now clutching it against the handle of the axe.

The room stood empty.

Cooley waited, his eyes scanning every shadow. For the first time since leaving the cellar, he felt the throbbing ache of his slashed forehead, like a hammer being struck behind his eyes. Suddenly, he wanted nothing more than to run home, hold his wife, and go straight to bed. In fact, the urge to leave this place was so strong that he considered throwing himself through a window.

But why use a window when there's a door right there?

In fact, he was having a hard time recalling why he'd wanted to go the long way through the church in the first place. Something about not wanting to step over Barton's severed head. But now, if disembodied voices were going to start addressing him by name, maybe the head thing no longer mattered.

That was when he saw Barton.

Not the dead Barton. Not the Barton on the floor in two pieces and an ocean of blood. No, this Barton seemed entirely whole and intact as he stood in the corner near the door. Yet somehow Cooley found that he couldn't see him *completely*, a fact that the fading illumination from the sunset sky couldn't explain. It was as if the man were "part darkness," a walking, moving, talking shadow, as he stepped silently across the carpet and paused beside the couch.

Then, as Cooley gaped, his sanity screaming, Jonah Ray Barton reached down casually and picked up his own head.

He held the grizzly thing by its hair, tilting his own head—his *other* head, the one still attached—to and fro, as if analyzing it carefully. A smile touched his lips that looked rueful, bordering on amused. *"Such a prison is the flesh,"* Cooley heard him say. Then he walked, slowly but purposefully over to the dining area and none-too-gently deposited the head—his head, his *other* head—atop the table, more or less in the center.

Dead center, Cooley thought weirdly.

"So," the Darkness-Man said. He turned to Cooley, who suddenly felt his guts freeze solid. He knew he should run, *needed* to run. But his legs wouldn't budge, not an inch. *"Seems I should thank you, John,"* Barton said, though there was no gratitude in his tone.

Cooley tried to reply but couldn't. His entire body started to shake, and his eyes felt so wide in his skull that he figured they'd pop like squeezed tomatoes at any moment.

"You've set me free," Barton said. *"You've granted me something I never imagined, the chance to finally reap what I have sown. But..."* He raised one finger, looking like a teacher reprimanding a child. *"...you really shouldn't have read that."*

Cooley dragged his eyes away from the Darkness-Man long enough to glance at the sheet of blue paper still clutched in his hand. Somewhere along the line, he'd lowered the axe and now held it in his other fist. It felt heavy and useless.

Barton slowly shook his head. *"Sadly, you can no longer join my Forever Congregation, John. However, I will make you this bargain. You will soon die. But, if you tell no one between now and then what you have learned, then you will be the only one to die. Wanda and your boys will live on, at least for a time, at least until I'm ready to claim them for my flock."*

Cooley stared at him.

Barton smiled again, a tight-lipped, cruel thing. *"Do we have a deal, John?"*

"What?" Cooley said, the word tumbling out. Then he licked his lips and tried again. "What the...fuck...are you?"

Cooley's tight smile split into a wide, wide grin, far wider than a living face could manage. His lips spread until they reached his ears and his yellow teeth seemed to multiply in his head to fill the space. Each tooth was tiny and sharp, like those in the piranha that Cooley and the kids once saw at the Baltimore Aquarium.

"I am the resurrection and the life," Barton intoned, somehow speaking the verse without moving his lips and changing one iota of that monstrous

grin. Then his head fell back and he laughed, his mouth opening impossibly wide, reminding Cooley, with a madman's hilarity, of a Pez dispenser. It was like Barton's entire head split open, his mouth facing the ceiling, his tongue dancing like a snake as he guffawed.

John Cooley felt something *snap* inside his mind.

He turned and ran, still holding both the paper and the axe. He went to the parsonage's front door, no longer looking at the Darkness-Man, No longer considering anything except escape. His hand, the one with the paper, fumbled for the knob, turned it.

Out! I have to get out!

A hand touched his arm.

Cooley shrieked, an animal in mortal panic. Then he looked at the person who had touched him, and his shriek turned into a piteous wail.

It wasn't Barton, as he'd thought—or feared. It was far, far worse.

It was Rachel.

The girl, *his* girl, stood beside him, touching his hand lightly, the way she would rouse him as a small child whenever he fell asleep on the chair before dinner. Except, this Rachel wore no sweet smile. Instead, her mouth was slack, her throat a black gash, and her eyes were coins.

And she wore the same blood-soaked wedding dress as when he'd last seen her.

He married her. He "married" my baby.

Then he cut her throat.

Without warning, words spilled out of his daughter's mouth, though her lips never moved. And, more insanely still, the voice Cooley heard wasn't hers. No, it was *his*, the Darkness-Man's, Barton's. *"I am the shepherd of the Forever Congregation, the general of the Army of the Lord."*

"No!" Cooley exclaimed, throwing off his daughter's touch as if it were flame. Then he tore open the door and staggered out into the deepening twilight. For a moment, he thought he'd fall to his knees, but the idea of doing so with that open doorway at his back scared him into staying upright. He ran to the curb and stared across the street at Fairlanes. It was still noisy over there, noisier maybe than when he'd left. He heard laughter and good-natured shouting mixed in with the crash of bowling pins.

He wanted to go there, wanted it desperately.

But he was standing here, bare-chested, with his shirt tied around his slashed forehead while holding a bloody axe. Maybe worse than all that, he was still clutching the paper in his other hand, the single sheet that would, if the Darkness-Man was to be believed, kill whoever read it.

No. I have to go home.

The thought popped, more or less unbidden, into his head. But, once it did, he saw the sense of it. Go home. See his wife. Tell her—

Nothing. I'll tell Wanda nothing.

This is on me, all of it.

Rachel, I'm sorry.

With those thoughts warring in his mind, Cooley staggered up the empty street. He saw no one, not until he reached his front door. With a final look around, he carefully deposited the axe behind one of the big bushes that flanked his stoop and, under the glow of the porchlight, let himself inside.

He'd been gone an hour, perhaps less. But it felt like a century.

The first thing that struck him was how dimly lit the front room was. Had it always been like this, just wells of shadows mixed in with some low wattage lamps? It reminded him of St. Damien's cellar, which then reminded him of his daughter, all of it threatening to tear down what few mental walls he'd managed to erect during the walk back from the church.

The second thing that struck him was his wife's hand. She'd emerged from the shadows in the direction of the kitchen and delivered a full slap that took him so completely by surprise that it almost knocked him over.

"John Martin Cooley!" she exclaimed. "Where the hell have you been? I've been yelling down the street for you for half-an-hour!"

He rubbed his stinging cheek and said nothing.

"You think I didn't hear?" Wanda exclaimed, shaking her finger in his face. "You think I didn't hear Russ say something about our Rachel! How *dare* you leave this house without telling me what's happened? I'm her mother! I—" Then her eyes finally saw through the haze of her righteous anger, and she saw—really saw—what her husband looked like. She took in his naked chest, his bloodied hands. Then her gaze raked his face and, in a flash, her manner changed. "What—what happened to you? Were you in a fight?"

Cooley stared at her, his wife of twenty-six years, the best friend he'd ever had, and was completely tongue-tied. He didn't even feel the slap anymore. Wanda had slapped him a few times over the course of their life together. It was how she reacted to fear.

I reacted with an axe.

"Wanda…" he heard himself finally say, his wife's name like a prayer on his lips.

"John," she replied. "Please, baby. Tell me what happened…"

He started to cry. The tears came out of nowhere but, at the same time, it seemed as if he'd barely been holding them back. Stunned by this, Wanda pulled him down to her, pressing his filthy, blood-soaked head to her shoulder and wrapping him in her arms.

"Tell me," she whispered.

And he nearly did. He nearly told her all of it, let the poison spill out of him before it consumed him completely. And what a relief it would have been, to share the nightmare with the strongest person he'd ever known.

But then, his face turned away as Wanda held him, Cooley saw something that stifled the confession in his throat.

He saw Rachel.

She stood in the archway to the kitchen, still wearing the soiled white dress from the cellar. Her mouth, as it had been in the parsonage, was slack, her skin ashen.

And her eyes were coins.

The sight of her, the *meaning* of her, hit him like a bucket of cold water. This was the Darkness-Man. This was Barton, reminding Cooley of their bargain. Of course, Cooley had never actually agreed to anything—had, in fact, barely said a word to the *thing* in the parsonage; he couldn't quite bring himself to consider it a "ghost."

But something told him that his acquiescence didn't matter one bit. The bargain had been forced on him. If he said anything to Wanda about what he'd learned, then his wife would also start seeing their poor dead girl with coins on her eyes.

And that, John Cooley would not have.

So, stealing himself, he pulled away. "I'm all right," he said, though he wasn't and never would be again. "Is supper on?"

"What?" she asked, blinking and staring up at him. "Are you crazy? What happened? Why is your shirt around your forehead?"

"Cut myself," he said.

"How?"

He shrugged. "It doesn't matter. The bleeding's stopped," he replied, breaking eye contact. When he looked back at the archway, Rachel, with her slack lifeless mouth and coins for eyes, was gone. Giving his wife a gentle, absent pat on the shoulder, he headed straight into the kitchen, Wanda on his heels.

This was a small space, just a few feet of countertop, some old appliances, and a Formica table that the Cooleys had bought at a flea market fifteen years before. But right now, all he was interested in was the stove. He turned on the gas and took a match from a box of them on a handy shelf and used it to light the burner.

"John. Johnny," Wanda said from somewhere behind him. It almost made him smile. She only ever called him "Johnny" when she was worried about him.

"It's gonna be fine, baby," he replied without turning.

Then he took the blue paper that Fabron had been holding when he'd died, the single sheet that had doomed them both, and touched it to the stove. It caught almost instantly, and Cooley held it up, watching it burn. Without this, he alone knew what the Darkness-Man feared.

And soon, very soon, he figured he'd be gone. Maybe Barton would come himself, or maybe he'd send Rachel. But, either way, Cooley was looking at the end of the road—looking at it hard.

"What was that?" Wanda asked as he dropped the burnt paper into the sink and washed it away as ash.

"Nothing," he replied. "Nothing, at all."

CHAPTER 7
Staten Island, New York—2022

BY THE TIME BRUBAKER HAD finished talking, Mia had refilled her wine glass and sat down on the edge of her bed. Taking a long drink, she looked up at the assistant director.

"That's awful," she said finally.

"Yes, it is."

"And all that's in Cooley's confession?"

Brubaker nodded. "According to the detectives conducting the interrogation, it was the single creepiest confession they'd ever elicited."

"I'll bet," Mia muttered. "And he never told anyone what was on the paper he burned?"

"No."

"He sacrificed himself to try to protect his wife, his neighbors... everybody."

Cheever, who had been snuggled contentedly in Brubaker's arms throughout the assistant director's storytelling, squirmed impatiently. Brubaker bent and placed him gently on the floor, whereupon the cat immediately scampered off toward his food bowl. Cheever needed to eat every thirty minutes or face starvation.

"But is that really *possible?*" Brubaker asked, straightening. "Can a...a ghost...really be that powerful?"

Mia smiled, despite herself, despite everything. "Hard to say out loud, isn't it?"

The return grin was a little sheepish. "Yes, it is. Frankly, if anyone at the bureau heard me say it, I'd be looking at six months of mandatory counseling followed by a career-ending psych eval."

"Yet here you are."

"Yet here I am."

"For your son?"

"For him. For the others. For my team. But you never answered my question. Can a ghost really be that powerful?"

Mia met Brubaker's eyes and held them. "I honestly don't have an answer. There's so much we don't know about how a consciousness continues after death, where it draws energy, nourishment, how it *thinks* at all without a brain, without neurons and synapses. But I've had five years to obsess over this, and…where Jonah Ray Barton is concerned, at least…I have a theory. Do you want to hear it?"

Brubaker nodded wordlessly.

Mia said, "I told you earlier that some places store psychic energy like a battery. Well, I believe that's what happened in St. Damiens. Barton's pretty unique as serial killers go. He went along for a quarter century before his crimes were discovered, always killing in the same place, always hiding the bodies of his victims in the same place. Those murdered girls, their pain and suffering and degradation had decades to *soak* into the walls of that church, staining it more completely than blood ever could. And I believe that Barton, as the author of all that pain, was somehow able to connect to it upon his own death, draw from it, and take immediate command of the souls he'd trapped in there.

"I think, from Officer Mulberry's account, that Barton was as surprised as anyone by the power his new state of being afforded him. But, once he understood what he could do, he reveled in it…and has been reveling in it ever since. In the years after his death, he tapped into that battery, sending negative energy, less focused and less immediate than inside St. Damien's itself, out into the surrounding neighborhood, where it leached off his former parishioners and *twisted* their minds, all to help swell the ranks of his Forever Congregation. I don't know how many of those souls he actually managed to ensnare, but I know for a fact that he's got more than dead girls in his so-called "army."

"I'll tell you something else, too. I think he's still doing it or trying to…which is why that whole street's been deserted for twenty years, why no developer can do anything with it, why the city hasn't even tried to tear anything down. Oh, they don't talk about it. You won't see anything in the local papers about Bleak Street's ghost town and its haunted church. Rather, any proposals to repurpose the area are back-burnered, indefinitely."

Brubaker visibly swallowed, shaking her head as if not quite believing it.

Except, Mia thought. *If you didn't believe it, you wouldn't have come.*

"Renee," she said. "Please listen to me. I understand that this Arias person is awful. I know you and Agent Jessup and the rest want…need… to trap him and get him off the streets. I understand how vital that is. But Jonah Ray Barton is the closest thing to true evil I've ever encountered. He's miles past any typical paranormal activity, any 'haunting.' He's merciless, manipulative, and absolutely sentient. From the minute you walk into that church…hell, from the minute you step onto that street, he's going to know you're there and start coming after you."

"Unless we can figure out his secret," Renee said. "Unless *you* can."

Mia rubbed at her face. As if sensing her discomfort, Cheever temporarily abandoned his bowl of kibble and came over for a leg rub. Absently, Mia reached down and scratched the cat's head. As always, it soothed her—a little. "You mentioned a message," she said finally. "Some kind of graffiti Cooley painted somewhere."

"Not painted," Brubaker corrected. "Etched. Four days after the murder, John Cooley slipped into St. Damien's graveyard and chiselled it onto Barton's grave marker."

"What does it say?"

But Brubaker shook her head. "If you want to know that, you're going to have to come down with me to Camden and see it."

Mia's reaction surprised even herself; she burst out laughing. For a moment, Brubaker just looked at her, perplexed, which only made Mia laugh all the harder. Then, after maybe half-a-minute, she composed herself and said, "Sorry…the way you 'sprung' that on me struck me funny given that I pretty much saw it coming."

"Does that mean you'll do it?" Brubaker asked.

"Do what?"

"Come to Camden and see what Cooley wrote."

"I'm not going into that church," Mia said.

"You don't have to. Just the graveyard."

"That's dangerous enough. Why not just tell me what it says, and I'll see if it makes any sense to me. Why all the games?"

Brubaker sighed wearily. "Call it manipulation born out of desperation. My people and I *are* going into St. Damien's. We *are* going to spend the night in that place. There's nothing either you or I can do to stop that. But if I can get you to help then, maybe there's a chance they'll come out again. So, no. I won't tell you what Cooley wrote. Instead, I'll make you this offer: you come with me to Camden, to that graveyard, and read the words. Then, if you think maybe you can solve whatever kind of riddle this is and cleanse that place, so be it. If not, then you can decide if you want to go home. And, in return, I'll get you a consulting fee in the middle high five figures."

Mia blinked. "High five…" she began, but her words trailed off.

The assistant director shrugged. "This is Andres Arias we're talking about. I have a substantial operating budget and the leeway to use it as I see fit. And, yes, the money is also a manipulation. I need you, both your expertise and your experience. There's no one in the bureau with anything like your skill set. So, let's make it *high* five figures. At least seventy thousand dollars and maybe more, depending on how the situation develops. I…um… know you need the money."

And she did. Mia *did* need the money, badly. If her situation didn't turn around soon, she wouldn't even be able to afford *this* hole in the wall and she'd end up moving into her old bedroom at her mother's house with her tail between her legs.

And poor Cheevers would have to go to the pound. Gail Lakatos was allergic to cats.

But this is St. Damned we're talking about. Remember what happened five years ago!

As if she could forget—ever.

"Mia?" Brubaker asked.

"Yeah."

"May I sit?"

"Sure. Um. There's only the bed. Sorry."

Brubaker lowered herself onto the squeaky, pull-out mattress beside Mia. "Listen to me," she said gently but firmly. "I'm not going to try to tell you what I'm asking isn't dangerous, as you know it is better than I do. And I'm not going to use the standard bureau line of, 'We can protect you,' because against this kind of threat, I'm not sure it's true. But, Mia, I get the feeling you've been running from your memories of that awful place for a long time."

Mia nodded, not quite ready to meet the other woman's eyes.

"Well," Brubaker said. "Maybe this is your chance to stop running. If Barton *is* the predator you make him out to be, then you're the one that got away."

But did *I get away?* Mia wondered. *It cost me so much, including my sleep.*

Aloud, she admitted, "Maybe. So?"

"So, isn't there some part of you that wants another crack at him?"

"You mean like Captain Ahab wanted another crack at Moby Dick?"

Brubaker laughed without humor. "Not a great example."

Except the thing was: Mia *did* want another crack at Jonah Ray Barton. St. Damien's was the most catastrophic failure of her career, of her *life*. And, as a result, four people had died, one of them evidently this woman's son. How much of the fault could be reasonably laid at her feet was perhaps debateable. But that had become cold comfort these past years.

I can't go back there!

Even if my body survives it, my mind won't.

But then she heard her treacherous mouth reply, "Yes. Yes, I do."

Brubaker took her hand. For a moment, Mia started. It had been a long time since anyone had actually touched her, handshakes not withstanding. She couldn't remember her last date, and she and her mother hadn't so much as hugged since Mia was a teenager. But, in this moment, the other woman's hand felt warm, larger and safer than her own. It made her feel younger, younger and protected. She knew it was an illusion, maybe even a manipulation. But the feeling persisted, nonetheless.

"Then come," Brubaker said gently.

"I'm not a hero, Renee," Mia said in a small, sad voice.

"Neither am I."

"All I'm promising is the graveyard."

"I understand."

"No, you don't," Mia told her. "If you did, you wouldn't be asking this of me."

Brubaker didn't reply. Why should she? She'd gotten what she'd come for. Mia was going back to Bleak Street, back to St. Damien's.

But I'm not going inside. Whatever happens, there is no fucking way I'm setting foot in that godforsaken church again!

Aloud she said, "I need to let my neighbor know. She takes care of Cheever whenever I'm away."

"Of course."

Mia gently extracted her hand from Brubaker's and stood. "And, on the way to Camden, I want you to tell me the rest of John Cooley's story."

"Certainly," Brubaker replied. "In fact, I'll do you one better. I have the full Camden police file, including the transcript of his confession out in my car, if you think it'll help."

It won't. Nothing will, not if you're going to go inside St. Damned.

But aloud, she said, "Maybe. Maybe not. But something tells me it'll be worth knowing regardless."

"An intuition?" Brubaker asked wryly.

Mia didn't reply.

CHAPTER 8
Camden, New Jersey—1972

WHEN JOHN COOLEY FINALLY WENT to bed after that longest of nights, he expected nightmares. He expected to snap awake screaming, seeing images of walking dead men, grinning and carrying their own severed heads. But he didn't. In fact, he didn't sleep at all. Instead, he lay there beside Wanda, whose own sleep was clearly fitful, and stared helplessly at his daughter, who stood at the end of the bed wearing that damned wedding dress and with coins on her eyes.

When she'd been small, he'd often imagined her wedding day. In his mind's eye, he'd envisioned Wanda and the boys looking on as he proudly walked her down the aisle—the center aisle of St. Damien's, which transcended mere bitter irony. Seeing her now, dressed in some bloody parody of bridehood, hollowed out what little remained of his already broken heart.

At first, he tried talking to her, but even his whispers, admittedly urgent and not altogether sane, were enough to make Wanda stir and blearily ask what was wrong. Then he tried reaching out to his dead little girl, but she only looked back at him, unmoving—if "looked back at him" was even appropriate, given those goddamned coins.

Finally, around two a.m., he climbed as noiselessly as he could off their squeaky old bed, walked right past Rachel, and slipped out into the parlor.

His daughter didn't follow him. Instead, she was waiting when he got there, standing by the front window. This time, her back was to him, her small, slight frame a silhouette against the streetlight that filtered through the drapes. Outside, Bleak Street remained quiet. No sirens. No voices. Apparently, Barton, Fabron, Rachel, and the rest hadn't been found—yet.

But they would. Cooley was certain of that. He'd left the parsonage door wide open with two corpses inside, one he'd killed and one he hadn't. Before long, someone would see, someone would investigate. Barton, after all, was the neighborhood pastor, respected, even beloved, despite his being a white dude. Wanda certainly revered him. She came home from church every Sunday fairly singing the man's praises.

That thought begat another: who would be holding services *this* Sunday?

The idea roiled around between his ears for a moment and almost— almost—made him laugh, though he knew to do so would be grotesque and, again, not altogether sane.

He approached Rachel, who still had her back to him. She looked so small, so frail, the way she had as a child, before all the angst and attitude. With a hand that shook badly, he reached out to touch her shoulder, wondering if he could, wondering if he *should*.

He did anyway.

She was solid, but not quite *real*. It was hard to wrap his mind around it. There was definite substance, firmer than flesh, colder too. But, at the same time, it seemed spurious, false, as if whatever it was made of could fall apart and disappear in an instant.

"I'm…sorry, baby," Cooley heard himself whisper.

Rachel *moved*. She whipped around with shocking speed, catching his wrist in an iron grip. Her fingers were small and icy, all the blood gone from them. Yet, when Cooley tried to pull free, he found he couldn't. The girl's mouth, slack and black tongued, began speaking as it had before, without so much as a lip twitch. And, again, the voice he heard belonged not to his daughter, but to Jonas Ray Barton.

"It is the glory of God to conceal things. Keep your peace, John Cooley. Carry what you know to the grave. Do otherwise and this hand on your wrist will find your wife's throat. So sayeth the Lord!"

Then, in the blink of an eye, the hand, the girl, and the words were gone, and Cooley found himself alone in the dark parlor.

The next thing he knew, he was seated in his favorite chair, the one furthest from the television that stood beside a small end table with a built-in lamp atop it, perfect for reading. He had no memory of having sat down. But given the chair's proximity to where poor Rachel had been standing, he supposed he must have reached for it subconsciously like a drowning man reaching for a bit of driftwood to keep him afloat.

A part of him supposed he could go to bed. But the idea of lying there beside his wife with Barton's warning ringing in his ears—

No.

So instead, he just sat there, alone in the dark, looking at nothing, listening to nothing, barely even thinking. He didn't notice the passage of time, didn't notice as the sunrise slowly began to beat back the night, didn't notice when a Camden Police cruiser rolled past his house in the direction of St. Damien's, its lights flashing but its siren silent. Then, less than an hour later, he didn't even notice when more cop cars arrived, this time with all the noise and bother that every resident of Bleak Street associated with trouble, rather than help.

And such was how Wanda found him some hours later, his face gaunt and his eyes—well, haunted.

She emerged from their bedroom, hurriedly wrapping herself in her robe. She paused in the parlor when she saw him. "John?" she said.

Slowly, Cooley turned his head and looked at her, loved her, and that love felt like a noose around his neck. "Couldn't sleep," was all he could think of to say.

"Didn't you hear the phone?"

"What? No."

"It was Helen. There are police outside of the church. Reece down at the bowling alley noticed the parsonage door open and called them. Helen says a body's been found. I'm going to get dressed and go down there to see."

"Okay," he said.

"Johnny, why won't you tell me what really happened last night?"

He looked askance. "I *did* tell you. I tripped and cut my head coming out of Ben's. It was bleeding so much that I had to use my shirt to staunch it so I could see to come home. Just a stupid accident. Too many beers."

Too many *lies*.

Wanda, he sensed, hadn't believed him last night, when she'd used Bactine and Band-Aids to close the gash from Barton's razor. And, from the expression on Wanda's face, she clearly didn't believe him now. But then someone knocked on their front door and, with a final, exasperated look thrown his way, Wanda went to answer it.

She didn't return for quite some time.

At one point, Cooley pulled himself up out of the chair and headed upstairs to piss, brush his teeth, and shower. This last he did carefully, not wanting to wet his bandage but doing so anyway. Then he dried off and dressed. Fortunately, it was the weekend, and he wouldn't need to be back at the school until Monday.

Right now, Monday felt a very long time off.

He went down to the kitchen and made coffee. He considered breakfast, but the idea of putting food in his stomach made him almost nauseous. So instead, he poured a big mug of joe and settled himself at the kitchen table to wait.

He felt like a man killing time on death row.

It was almost an hour later, at exactly 7:51—Cooley was watching the clock—when Wanda came in, her footfalls uncharacteristically heavy as they moved through the parlor, paused, and then followed the smell of coffee into the kitchen.

When Cooley looked up from his now cold, half-drunk mug, she was standing in the archway, still in her robe. Her arms were crossed as they were when she was angry, though there were tears in her eyes and a look of utter, bone-crushing dread on her pretty face.

"Reverend Barton's dead, John," she said in a whisper.

He didn't reply.

"Somebody killed him last night. Somebody killed him and Fabron both."

Cooley stared up at her, uncertain of what he should say, what he *could* say. His "bargain" with Barton involved only the blue piece of paper. The madman's other sins had to be fair game, didn't they?

But he wasn't sure. He couldn't be sure.

Wanda must have read something in his hesitant silence because she suddenly surged forward, dropped onto the chair beside his, and grabbed both of his large hands in her small ones. "John, please, tell me what you did."

And her face, her eyes, broke down his flimsy walls. The tears came as they had the night before. Instantly, Wanda pulled him to her ample bosom. Cooley wasn't a man who cried. He'd buried both his parents with barely a tear shed. And yet here he was, sobbing in his wife's arms for the second time in twelve hours.

"Baby," she said, lifting his face and cradling it in her hands. "Did *you* kill them?" She asked this matter-of-factly, though Cooley could tell that her control was wafer thin. Wanda hovered on the edge, just like him. But, unlike him, she was holding it together. If he were honest, she'd always been the stronger of the two of them.

"I killed him," Cooley heard himself say. "But *he* killed Fabron."

Wanda stiffened at this news, but still didn't surrender to the despair that he sensed she was choking on. "Why?" she asked after a long pause.

"Why did he kill Fabron?" Cooley guessed. "I don't know."

Another lie.

Because he absolutely did know.

"No…why did *you* kill Reverend Barton, Johnny?"

This next part was going to bash down even *her* defenses; Cooley understood that. But he told her anyway. He told her because he needed to, and because she needed to know. The street would find out soon enough, and he didn't want his daughter's mother to hear about it from the gossip-mongers. "Because he murdered Rachel."

Wanda gasped and pulled away as if he'd caught fire. "That's not true!"

"It is, baby," Cooley said. Suddenly, he felt stronger, maybe because, at this moment, he knew he had to be. "Russ came across her body last night. I went there and found it for myself." Then he told her all of it, or almost all of it—skipping the part about finding the blue paper and being warned into secrecy by what he could only call Barton's ghost. All that he kept to himself, saying that he'd fled the church right after chopping the reverend's head off.

As he talked, Wanda didn't move. Cooley wasn't even sure she blinked. But she breathed. Oh, she definitely breathed. In fact, the further along he got in his tale, the more her chest heaved. She was fighting hysterics, he supposed, though he'd never in their long life together seen her anywhere close to hysterical.

But if anything could do it, this could, he supposed miserably.

When he'd finished, he sat back in his chair, feeling as empty and limp as a deflated balloon and just looked at her. For her part, Wanda's gaze had slipped into the middle distance and, gradually, her breathing steadied. This behavior, at least, Cooley recognized.

His wife was thinking.

Finally, her eyes locked on his and she said flatly, "You're sick."

He swallowed. "I know it seems that way. But I—"

She cut him off. "No, fool. You're sick sick. Under the weather. Flu maybe. You'll go upstairs, get into bed, and stay there. Bring a book if you want to but the TV stays off. You're sleeping and can't see nobody."

"That won't work," he said. "I was with Russ at the bar last night."

"Not one of those boys is going to give you up and you know it. I'll talk to them, just to be sure. The sick thing is for the cops when they come, and they *will* come."

"Yeah," Cooley said.

But she went on as if she hadn't heard him. "If nothing else, they'll go door to door. 'Canvasing' I think they call it. They'll ask everybody what they saw, if anything. We say nothing. Nothing at all. Are you with me, Johnny?"

Relief hit him so hard he nearly broke again. "I'm always with you, Wanda," he heard himself whisper.

Then she leaned forward and kissed him hard. There wasn't any passion in it, however.

This kiss was more about unity, commitment—and fear.

The day that followed, and the days immediately after that, struck like gut punches, one after the other. Cooley spent most of it upstairs, just as ordered, foregoing their bed in favor of the rocking chair by the window, from which he watched as Bleak Street, and the friends and neighbors he'd known for most of his life, imploded.

The first cop came to the door around late morning. He knocked politely but insistently until Wanda answered. Cooley listened to their exchange from the rocking chair, the words rolling easily up the steps and through the open bedroom door. Yes, Wanda knew Reverend Barton. Yes, she'd learned of his murder from the neighbors. No, she hadn't seen or heard anything. No, she couldn't think of anyone who would want to kill such a beloved and pious man. Her husband? He was upstairs with the flu, sleeping right now. Come back later? Well, the cop could try, but she wouldn't promise anything.

And, just that simply, the man went away.

But Cooley knew he'd be back, or someone would, and soon.

The death of the "sainted" Barton was bad enough, the shock and grief so profoundly shared that Cooley often heard open wailing filter in from the sidewalk where clusters of parishioners gathered to share the latest news. This trickled in slowly as the cops struggled to make sense of the crime and its ever-widening scope.

The initial grief over their precious, lost reverend gradually gave way to the even darker revelations as a third body was taken from the church. This eventually turned out to be a Camden cop, and a rumor circulated that he'd died from throwing himself off the choir loft just after Barton and Fabron were found. His partner, it seemed, had been discovered outside the church, barely conscious and babbling incoherently about girls with coins for eyes.

When Wanda had shared this, Cooley had gone cold, physically cold.

He hadn't told her about seeing Rachel's ghost and had no intention of doing so. The loss of her daughter was bad enough. The idea that Rachel's spirit, if that was what the apparition was, hadn't moved onto, as she kept saying, "Christ's bosom," might be more than even her iron constitution could handle.

Several hours after the first policeman left, close to dinnertime, two of what Cooley had long ago come to think of as "The Church Ladies," showed up at the door. Again, Cooley listened, though this exchange seemed more hushed than the one with the canvasing cop.

Somebody had heard from somebody who'd heard from somebody in the Camden P.D. that even more bodies had been found—a lot more.

Twenty-seven more.

The Church Ladies evidently hadn't yet realized that these newest victims were all girls who had gone missing, not just Rachel but the daughters of others throughout the surrounding neighborhood. So far, they only knew that more cop cars and county morgue vehicles now filled the street and St. Damien's had been completely cordoned off. "Can't get within spitting distance of the place," one of them complained, sounding oddly put-out by it.

After they left, Wanda brought dinner up to him. Cooley had wanted to come downstairs and eat properly, but his wife, looking exhausted and heart-wrenchingly sad, insisted. "We have to keep up appearances. You never know who's going to stop by."

Cooley ate as well as he could. Last night's horrible events, especially the bit *after* he'd chopped Barton's head off, had taken on a surreal, dream-like quality. He'd almost managed to convince himself that he'd suffered a series of hallucinations, no doubt brought on by the horror of what he'd found in the church's basement and the shock of what he'd done about it. He'd even—almost—decided that Rachel's "visits" had been part of that shock.

But then, that night, she came again.

And the night after that.

Each visit was a little different, a little worse. The second time he awoke to find her at the foot of his bed, staring at him from behind her coins. She didn't speak, but she didn't leave either, not until Cooley, in misery, slipped out of bed and went, as he had before, into the living room. Once there, with him sitting in his favorite chair again, Rachel finally said her piece. Except, of course, it wasn't her. The voice was Barton's, quoting obscure Bible verses and insisting that John needed to keep silent about what he knew lest *"sweet Wanda and your handsome boys suffer for your flapping tongue. And don't think of running. If you leave my street, if you even try to, Rachel and others will be on you immediately, day or night. They'll put you down, John...and then they'll go after those you love, all on my say-so."*

The third night, Rachel moved closer, standing right at his bedside, her coin-covered eyes shining in the light from the streetlamps outside their window. *"Time to close your book, John,"* Barton said. *"Time to sluff off this mortal coil. 'When his breath departs, he returns to the earth; on that very day his plans perish.'"*

More Bible shit, though this one Cooley happened to know. It was from Psalms, and Barton was taking it way out of context. As a matter of fact, the more he thought about it, the more Cooley came to an unexpected and important understanding.

Jonah Ray Barton was scared.

Whatever death had turned the human monster into, he still feared something, maybe only one thing.

He feared that blue slip of paper that Cooley had taken from Fabron's dead hand.

And now that the paper was gone, burned, that left only Cooley himself. Barton wanted to silence him, and Rachel's nightly visits were his way of telling Cooley that he had the power to compel it to happen. Cooley knew that as sure as he knew darkness would fall every night.

But the notion of leaving this life, of giving Barton what he so desperately wanted, turned Cooley's ever-present fear into fresh anger. Simmering anger. Impotent anger.

Between a rock and a hard place, that's me.

On the third day, Wanda and a collection on women from the street all went down to the morgue. Apparently, that connection between the bodies in the church cellar and the missing girls had finally been made by someone. When Wanda returned, she wouldn't speak of it to Cooley, not a word. But, from his place by the upstairs window, he heard the wails of grief and horror as mothers and fathers finally learned what their precious Reverend Barton had done to their girls.

Then, on the fourth day, the police returned.

It was a pair of detectives this time, both in plain clothes, both white. Cooley listened from his place by the bedroom window as they introduced themselves as Tyler and Grant. They began by offering their deepest sympathies to Wanda on Rachel's death. Then they asked to speak with her husband.

"He's been sick with the flu all week," Wanda replied. The lie had passed her lips so many times that it'd become rote. A corner of Cooley's heart broke a little every time he heard it. His wife was, or had been, the most truthful person he'd ever known. It was something he'd always loved about her. But now she'd discarded that virtue—and worse, she'd done it for him. "This has been a brutal week for us both," she added, the sob in her voice not needing to be faked. "And poor John's the worse for it, being so sick on top of our terrible loss. I'm guessing you two can appreciate that."

"We can, Mrs. Cooley, which is why we've stayed away this long. But now, I'm afraid we really do need to speak to him." Detective Tyler said this in a manner that seemed cordial but at the same time absolute.

"He's sleeping at the moment," Wanda replied.

"Wake him," Grant said. He sounded somewhat less cordial than his partner.

"I will not. The both of us know full well what happened to our little girl. There's nothing to be gained by bringing him down and dragging him through it again."

"We have a witness who says otherwise," Tyler explained in his oh-so-patient tone. "Now please rouse Mr. Cooley."

There was a pause. Then Wanda said in a tone that Cooley knew only too well. "And what if I don't?" He could picture her, clear as day, facing down the two men, her shoulders back and her chin jutting forward.

"Then we'll do it for you," Grant said flatly.

"Without a warrant?"

"Mrs. Cooley," Tyler said, and this time his patient manner was—less so. "Terrible crimes took place at St. Damien's Lutheran Church, a church I believe you attend."

"Not anymore," Wanda said. "Obviously."

"My point," Tyler continued. "Is that people, not just yourselves but your neighbors and friends, are in terrible grief. We have to understand what happened. It's Camden PD's number one priority, and I think you'll find more than a few 'legal niceties' will be set aside to further our investigation. So, please let us in, otherwise my partner and I will have no choice but to detain you and then go upstairs and do the same to your husband."

Cooley, still listening from the bedroom and feeling like a coward, decided, *Enough.*

He went to the top of the landing, dressed only in boxer shorts and a sleeveless white t-shirt of the variety that Russ so charmingly dubbed "wife-beaters." Then he said, clearing his throat, "I'm John Cooley."

All three of them, gathered together at the open door right at the bottom of the stairs, looked up. Wanda wore an expression of utter horror. "John!" she exclaimed. "You need to be in bed. Your fever spiked again this morning!" How smoothly she said this, as if she believed it as surely as she believed in the sunrise. It was a terrible, guilty thing for him to witness.

"It's down," he reported. "The aspirin finally helped. It's all right, Wanda. I'll talk to them." Then to the cops, he said, "Give me a minute to put something on."

"Take your time, Mr. Cooley," Tyler said. He was taller and thinner than Cooley had pictured, given the man's deep voice. His partner was shorter and a bit thicker in the shoulders. Probably played high school football, though not in Camden. Both were way too white to be local boys.

Cooley pulled on a pair of slacks. Then he traded the "wife-beater" for a simple, blue button down that he often wore to work. Finally, he went into the bathroom, splashed water on his face, brushed his close-cropped hair, and went downstairs.

The four of them sat together in the parlor, with Wanda placing herself protectively beside Cooley on the sofa and the detectives taking the two worn armchairs. Cooley expected his wife to offer them coffee or tea, but she didn't. Apparently, the "protector" in her had trumped the "hostess."

Tyler started by introducing himself and Grant. Then he asked carefully, "How are you feeling?"

"I'm sick," Cooley replied.

"The flu," Grant supposed.

"That…and the fact that my only daughter was murdered."

Both men traded unhappy looks. "Of course," Tyler said. "We're very sorry for your loss."

"Thanks," Cooley replied flatly.

"What happened to your head?" Grant asked.

Cooley absently fingered the bandage above his eyes. Wanda had been tending to it with deliberate care. Even so, he knew he'd wear the scar for the rest of his life, however brief that seemed likely to be.

"Fell," Cooley said.

"You get stitches?" Tyler asked.

Cooley shook his head.

Wanda piped in with, "He should have. I tried to get him to go to the hospital, but of course he wouldn't. Stubborn." She even whipped up a glare to throw Cooley's way, which he considered a nice touch.

"How'd you fall?" Grant asked.

"Does it matter?"

"Not right now," Tyler said.

"Here's something that does matter." This came from Grant, accompanied by a look that Cooley supposed was meant to be intimidating. But that was a high bar these days, set by a girl with coins over her eyes. "Can you account for your whereabouts on the night of Reverend Barton's murder?"

"Went out for drinks with a friend. Came straight home around seven." All this, he and Wanda had practiced in anticipation of this very eventuality.

"That was where?" Tyler asked. He consulted a small leather-bound notebook. "At Ben's?"

Cooley nodded.

"That's attached to Fairlanes Bowling, right across from St. Damien's, right?"

"Right."

"Who were you with?" Grant asked.

"A friend."

"We need his name."

"Why?"

Tyler replied, "To corroborate what you're saying, John. Do you mind if I call you John?"

"Yes, I do."

The detectives shared another pointed look. "We're not the enemy here, Mr. Cooley," Tyler finally said.

"Uh huh."

"Please tell us the name of your friend, Mr. Cooley," Tyler pressed.

"Russel Saunders."

Tyler's face stayed passive. But Grant smirked. Cooley got the feeling he'd just said something foolish. It didn't take a rocket scientist to guess what had happened.

Russ talked.

Wanda must have picked up on it too because Cooley felt her squeeze his hand a little harder.

"We spoke with Mr. Saunders," Grant said. "He says he was doing work in the church that night, went down in the basement to look for light bulbs and came across the bodies of four girls, your daughter among them. He ran out of there and came straight here to tell you about it. Then you and he went to this bar where he spilled the whole story. He then says you went across the street to…what were his exact words, partner?"

"'Have it out with Barton'," Tyler read from his pad.

"Does that sound about right to you, Mr. Cooley?" Grant asked, leaning forward.

Cooley didn't reply.

Tyler said, "Look, we get it. You'd just heard that Barton killed your little girl, and you went over there to confront him. I'm a father, too. I'd probably have done the same thing."

Cooley still didn't reply.

Grant said, "What did you use? The M.E. thinks it was an axe, and a pretty blunt one. Rusty. You must be a strong man."

Wanda gripped Cooley's hand even tighter, almost painfully. He continued not replying.

Grant leaned forward. "After you chopped Barton's head off, where'd you ditch the axe?"

Cooley just stared at the man. The truth was that he hadn't "ditched" the axe anywhere. Wanda had. She'd slipped out of the house before sunup two days ago, taken it from where Cooley had hidden it behind the front shrubbery, wiped it clean, wrapped it in a trash bag and tossed it into the river, walking right past the church in the process.

Cooley should never have let her do it. And he wouldn't have, had he known. But she'd waited until he had one of his fitful bouts of sleep in the living room chair before sneaking out the back.

My Wanda...

Tyler said with a gentleness that sounded about as real as a three-dollar bill, "Why don't you tell us what happened, Mr. Cooley? We can help you."

"Like hell!" Wanda snapped. "I seen how you cops 'help' folks like us!" Her diction always suffered when she was upset, Cooley observed almost absently.

"Mrs. Cooley, we're trying to sort out what happened."

But Wanda was having none of it. For days, she'd been bottling up all of her anger, grief, and terror, and now it burst forth like water from a spent dam. "You want to know what happened? Then let me tell you. A man who was my shepherd, a shepherd to almost everyone on this street, turned out to be the devil in human skin. I loved Jonah Barton. Not in the way I love my husband, nothing like it, but I loved him all the same. I admired him, relied on him, trusted him completely. And he repaid all that by stealing my daughter and killing her. So, now he's dead. Somebody went and took his life from him. Well, I call that person...whoever he or she was...a hero, not a criminal, and certainly not a murderer."

His wife didn't so much as glance at him during this speech, but her hand continued to grip his fiercely. Though it would sound trite to say it out loud to anyone, even her, John Cooley had never felt so loved in his life.

It was a feeling that would strengthen him in the hours ahead.

Grant sat back in the armchair, looking a bit non-plussed. Beside him, Tyler studied Wanda with an expression that Cooley couldn't quite read. Finally, the detective said in a low voice, "I can't even imagine the hell you folks have been through. And, for what it's worth, as things are becoming clearer in this investigation, I think I might agree with you, Mrs. Cooley. But the law is clear. Whoever took Mr. Barton's life...and/or the life of his housekeeper...has to answer for it in a court of law."

"Reverend Barton killed Fabron," Cooley said. The words came out without a moment's thought behind them, and he knew at once they were another mistake.

"Is that right?" Grant asked, leaning forward again." You know that for a fact, do you?"

"It's just what people say," Wanda insisted, still not looking at Cooley.

"Mr. Cooley," Tyler said. "I think you should come with us."

"Am I under arrest?" Cooley asked him.

"No. This would be voluntary…for now."

Wanda's chin stuck out. "Then he ain't going nowhere!"

Cooley said nothing.

Grant's face darkened and he looked about to rise. But Tyler, evidently the senior of the two, touched his shoulder and almost imperceptibly shook his head. Then, addressing Cooley again, he said, "Secrets are hard to keep, especially the bad ones. They get under your skin. They get into your dreams. They *eat* at you, a bite at a time, until you're chewed up and empty. I've seen it, Mr. Cooley. I've seen it more times than I can count. I know the look of a man with a secret like that, one that's feeding on him. And I know there's only one way out of it, and that's to share it."

"I think you both should leave," Wanda insisted. "Like I said, my husband's going nowhere with you."

But Cooley found himself talking right over her. It was something he knew she hated, all the more so given the seriousness of this situation. But he couldn't help it. "You're right, Detective Tyler. But what if the secret can hurt the people you care about? What if it's not about protecting yourself at all? What if it's about protecting them?"

He didn't expect Tyler to have an answer to this. But he did. "Then you *find* a way to tell it, Mr. Cooley. You puzzle out some way to reveal the truth without putting others in jeopardy. One way would be to tell us, right now, what that secret is. Then the four of us can figure out what comes next."

"I want you to leave!" Wanda demanded. She almost jumped to her feet, but this time Cooley squeezed *her* hand, and she kept her peace, though she threw a glare at him that he did his best to ignore.

The detectives didn't move. Instead, they looked expectantly at Cooley, Grant with aggression and Tyler with his false but well-practiced congeniality.

This is some serious Good Cop/Bad Cop bullshit right here, Cooley thought bitterly.

Then something caught his eye, and he looked past the men and at the kitchen doorway.

Rachel stood there, slack mouthed in death, her eyes shining silver. This was the first time he'd seen her in daylight, and it terrified him. Not the apparition, per se. The shock of that had more or less worn off over the last few nights. Instead, it was what her appearance here and now, with late afternoon sunlight streaming in the living room windows, seemed to imply.

He's getting stronger.

She didn't speak; Barton was too smart for that, and he'd chosen the spot well. Positioned as she was, the cops couldn't see her. Not even Wanda could, the line-of-sight was wrong.

Of course. He sent her just for me.

A reminder of our "bargain."

"Well, Mr. Cooley?" Tyler asked, as if he were an actor on cue. "Do you have something to share with us?"

Cooley swallowed. Then he turned to Wanda. "Baby, I want you to go stay with your sister in Philly. I want you to leave today, right now."

She looked at him as though he'd gone insane. He offered up the best smile he could manage, which he could tell wasn't much.

"Promise me," he said.

She blinked, looking utterly confused. "What? Why?"

"Because Barton's coming for me, my love. And I won't let him take you, too."

"Barton," Tyler said. "Jonah Ray Barton?"

"Jesus," Grant muttered. "Cooley, what's going on with you?"

"John…" Wanda began. Then she licked her lips and said, "Reverend Barton's dead, baby."

"Yeah, he is," Cooley replied with a nod. "Even so, he's coming for me. He's scared shitless of what I know. He doesn't care about the girls he murdered. But he cares about *this*."

"About what, Mr. Cooley?" Tyler asked. His eyes had gone wide and both men looked pale with shock.

In the kitchen doorway, Rachel was gone.

But she'll be back.

Moving slowly and deliberately, Cooley stood. Both detectives stood as well, eyeing him as if he were a growling dog. But neither reached inside his jacket for his gun.

"I killed Barton," he told the men. "I killed him because he *needed* killing."

The detectives didn't reply.

So, Cooley went on, "And I'll come with you. I'll confess everything. But there's something I have to do first. Wanda…sweetheart…you are going to your sister's. Promise me."

"Johnny, no…"

"Promise me!" he exclaimed, almost screamed. Wanda, the only one still seated, jumped a little in surprise.

Tyler didn't move, not an inch. But his partner *did*, reaching for his weapon.

In one smooth motion, Cooley drew his father's old revolver, the one he'd kept in his dresser drawer upstairs for almost thirty years, the one he'd tucked into the back of his jeans just before coming down here. This he leveled at both cops. Grant froze, his right hand inside his jacket. Beside him, Tyler raised both palms. "Take it easy, Mr. Cooley," he said. "Nobody else has to get hurt."

Cooley swallowed, screwing up his courage. "I need you both to take out your guns and put them on the floor." He was amazed at how calm and in control he sounded, when the simple truth was he'd never been so scared in his life.

"Cooley," Grant began. "This won't—"

"Do it now," John Cooley said. Then, for emphasis, he drew back the gun's hammer with an audible and very demonstrative *click*.

CHAPTER 9
Camden, New Jersey—1972

OVER THE NEXT FEW MINUTES, Cooley used Grant's handcuffs to shackle the detectives to each other before marching them awkwardly down into the cellar. There, in a space a good deal smaller than its counterpart below St. Damien's and blessedly clear of bodies, Cooley used Tyler's cuffs to fasten them to one of the heavy water pipes.

Throughout it all, Wanda first screamed and then cried. She couldn't understand what her husband was doing and flatly refused to move no matter how many times Cooley told her to go upstairs and pack a bag. For their part, the cops bounced between curses and entreaties, threatening everything from a lifetime in prison to getting shot down like a dog in the street if Cooley didn't forego this insanity.

"I'll call and let them know where you are," he told both men once he had their radios and anything else that he thought might aid with either escape or premature rescue. "I'll turn myself in when I'm done."

"Done what, Cooley?" Grant demanded. "Why are you doing this?"

"I need a little time to send a message."

"What message?" Tyler asked, wincing as he tried to settle himself on the cellar's rough and dusty floor. "To who?"

"A message in a bottle," Cooley replied.

Then, without another word, he left them there.

In the parlor again, he took Wanda by the arm and led her up to their bedroom. There, he pulled one of the suitcases out of the closet and started throwing her clothes into it.

"Stop it!" his wife screamed. "Just stop it and talk to me!"

He ignored her protests, moving as quickly as he could. He didn't know how long it would be before Tyler and Grant were missed and more cars arrived to back them up. He needed to be out of here—now, but he couldn't leave until he was sure Wanda was safely gone from Bleak Street.

So, he did something he hadn't done in their marriage—ever; he took her roughly by the shoulders and gave them a hard shake. "Listen to me," he said, staring her right in the face. His actions were making her angry, he could see it in the blaze of her beautiful eyes. That was good. She *needed* her anger right now. They both did. And, holding onto that knowledge, Cooley jumped off the metaphorical cliff he'd been romancing all week. "Jonah Barton's dead, but he's not gone. He's in that church and he has Rachel, *our* Rachel, somehow…" He struggled for the right word. "…beholden to him. She's been haunting me all week, and something tells me she's not the only one that son of a bitch has on a leash. There were…what? Twenty-seven girls found in that cellar? Twenty-seven! Plus that cop who jumped off the balcony and poor Fabron."

"Rachel…" Wanda echoed, wrapping her lips around the word as if it were new to her. "Haunting you?"

"Yes, baby."

"She's with the Lord!"

"No, she's not. I wish she were, but she's not. *He's* got her and he's using her. But I have a weapon. At least, I think I do. I know something that scares him. It scares him badly. I don't understand why. Compared to his crimes, it seems small, even pointless. But it matters to him, Wanda! It matters *tremendously*."

"What secret, Johnny?" Wanda asked. Her eyes were no longer flashing. Now they glistened with fresh tears.

"If I tell you, he'll kill you, too."

"Wh—at?" she stammered. "What do you mean, he'll kill me…too?"

Cooley swallowed. This would be the hardest part. "Listen," he said again. "If you've ever loved me, you'll go to your sister's and, no matter what happens, you'll stay there. Sell this house if you can. But don't *ever* come back to it. This street is damned, Wanda. The devil's in that church and he's damned it."

"You need help, baby." She said this with a sob but, Cooley sensed, perhaps not complete conviction. Wanda Cooley was a church lady, a Christian believer, and his quite deliberate mention of Satan had pushed her buttons.

"What I need is an hour, just one hour. That's why I locked those two cops in the cellar, and that's why you're leaving this place for good and all. Promise me, Wanda."

"What about you?"

Cooley wondered if he should lie. It might sell this better to her if he did. But looking into her eyes as he was, he found he couldn't. "I'm already dead, baby. Barton can't let me live knowing what I know. But, before he kills me, I'm going to make sure of two things. The first is that you are safe."

"And...and the second?" she asked in a quavering voice.

"Like I told the detectives, I'm going to leave a message in a bottle."

In the end, Wanda left. He wasn't at all sure she would. A part of him feared—and, yes, guiltily hoped—that she would insist on staying by his side. But then he reminded her of their surviving children, their two boys who were off at college. He told her with steely reluctance that *they* needed her to stay alive, and *she* needed them to keep her safe and away from Bleak Street.

So, finally, she went.

As he threw her suitcase in the back of their old Chevy and all but picked her up and placed her behind the wheel, he suspected she was at least partly humoring him. She was scared, certainly, but scared enough to believe in ghosts? Of that, he wasn't so sure. Instead, she might be leaving like this because she simply had no other recourse. She would run to her sister and tell her what had happened, probably planning to return by morning.

But, by then—hopefully— it wouldn't matter.

She hugged him fiercely, and he clung to her. She felt warm and alive, though the kiss she gave him—their last—was tremulous and dry. "I love the hell out of you, John Cooley." It was something they'd said to each other frequently during the early days, before three kids and time had blunted their passion. Hearing it now was both a burn and a balm.

"I love the hell out of you, too, Miss Wanda."

And then she was gone. He watched the car's taillights recede in the deepening twilight, with the rows of adjoined houses on either side of him standing quiet, despite the early hour. Everyone was inside, their doors most likely locked, either grieving in solitude or hiding themselves away from the horror that stood at the end of the street. Cooley couldn't blame them. He wished he could somehow convince them *all* to leave. Let St. Damien's have the whole, empty block. Let Barton starve in a barren hunting ground.

Then he thought miserably, *Alone.*

I'm alone.

He would probably never see Wanda again. The truth of that hurt almost physically. It was all he could do to remain standing, to not surrender to the desire to just collapse right here in the middle of Bleak Street.

But there were things to be done.

He turned then and found himself face-to-face with his daughter's tortured and enslaved spirit. Worse, this time and for the first time, he found she was not alone. There were other girls, dozens of them. They filled the street like a Greek phalanx, all of them looking at him with their seemingly sightless coin-eyes. Every single one wore some form of wedding gown, blood-stained satin draping their small, frail bodies. And each one, like Rachel, had that deep, tell-tale slit under her chin.

"I'm sorry, baby," he said to his dead child.

Rachel didn't, likely *couldn't* respond.

Because that bastard won't let her.

That thought got Cooley moving.

He half-expected Rachel and the other girls to try to stop him as he navigated his way through their ranks, but they didn't. In fact, he wasn't acknowledged at all, not so much as a turn of the head. He passed among them, through them, almost as if *he* were the ghost, invisible and inconsequential.

Then, as he emerged through the rear of their ranks, he saw the cop.

It was a white man, short and stocky. He wore a Camden PD uniform, complete with badge and gun. He was standing in the threshold of Russel

Saunders' house, which was across the street and three doors closer to the bowling alley than Cooley's own. For a moment, Cooley thought it was simply another canvasing officer, this one working later than most.

But then he saw the strange bend to the man's neck and, perhaps more telling, the coins over his eyes, and Cooley's blood ran cold.

Russ.

Russ's house had been his planned next stop once he'd seen Wanda safely away. Until now, his goal had been to borrow the tools he would need for his message in a bottle. But, as he watched the cop with the coin-eyes step silently off the stoop and then just as silently vanish as if mixing with the breeze, Cooley's internal priorities shifted in an instant.

He ran for Russ's open door, his heart in his throat and his breath coming in ragged gasps. He'd known Russ Saunders for close to twenty years and, while the dude wasn't what anybody would call a MENSA candidate, he had a good heart and—aside from his recent, evident admission to the police— had always been a stalwart friend. Cooley didn't know exactly what that ghost-cop had been doing in Russ's house, but his every instinct told him to get there in a hurry.

When he reached the open front door and peered inside, everything looked more or less normal. Russ's house was laid out just like his own, just like every other house on the block. There was a parlor in the front, a small dining room in the middle, and a kitchen in the back. Upstairs, three small bedrooms also ran from the front to the rear of the house. Six rooms and a single bath. But there the similarity to the Cooleys' residence ended.

Russ had lived alone since his wife had abandoned him almost ten years ago. The marriage had been childless, leaving Russ with nothing in his life other than friends and work. As a result, his house lacked "a woman's touch," as Wanda might have put it. There were no family photos, very little of anything on the walls, which had been painted a now pealing eggshell white decades ago and then forgotten. The furniture was mostly second hand. In fact, the only piece of any real value was a large dry bar that Russ kept in one corner of the living room. Behind it, he stocked as many types of liquor as he could afford on his janitor's pay, and Cooley had lost count of how many times he and his friend had sat there, swapping stories and sharing whiskey or tequila.

But now the room stood empty, as did the whole of the first floor.

"Russ?" Cooley called, his voice echoing off the blank walls. He waited, trying to calm his breathing, but no reply came.

He went to the foot of the staircase and peered up. The second floor looked dark, darker than the fading daylight outside could account for. This was a city neighborhood, after all. There were streetlights and other ambient sources of illumination. Even with all your lamps off and your shades drawn, it was hard to find pitch blackness on Bleak Street.

Cooley headed upstairs.

The landing stood empty, the bedroom doors all shut. But the bathroom was wide open, its light on, a feeble yellow glow spilling out onto a threadbare hallway carpet that might once have been blue. Cooley stared at that light, his mouth dry. He knew he would go in, knew he would look around that small space, and knew what he would see. His friend was dead in there, somehow murdered by a coin-eyed cop who was, himself, deceased as of four days ago. Because Cooley had no doubt, none at all, that the policeman he'd seen coming out of this house was the same one who'd thrown himself from the choir loft in St. Damien's on the morning after Cooley had taken Reverend Barton's head from his shoulders. Somehow, Barton had claimed his soul as well, trapping it the way he'd trapped Rachel and those other girls. Wanda would probably label it a "deal with Satan," that is, if she believed it at all.

But Cooley didn't think so.

No, whatever Jonah Ray Barton had become, Cooley felt sure that it was singular, maybe even unique, and that no god or devil had any hand in it. It was an odd thing to be so certain of, but certain he was.

Of course, none of that made him any more interested in checking out Russ's bathroom.

But he did it anyway. He did it because Russel Saunders was his friend, a man who'd had more than his share of bad luck in his life, a man who deserved better than he'd gotten tonight.

Except when Cooley stepped tentatively to the bathroom threshold and looked inside, he didn't find Russ dead.

What he *did* find, however, was worse. Much worse.

To his left was an overflowing hamper and a sink and mirror that hadn't been cleaned in months. To the right stood a toilet, both its cover and seat up, and a big porcelain claw-footed tub. To the latter, Russ had added a makeshift shower stall fashioned of steel piping that rose from the floor and formed a circle at about shoulder height that could be used to hang a shower curtain. In this way, a person could stand in the tub and wash themselves using a handheld shower head that had been screwed into the tub's faucet. The Cooleys had once used a similar contraption, but some time ago Cooley, with Russ' help, had replaced it with a proper, tiled stall, doing most of the work over the course of a long and arduous Memorial Day weekend.

Evidently, Russ had never felt so inclined.

"Oh Jesus…" Cooley heard himself whisper.

Russel Saunders stood upright in his tub, completely naked except for a pair of long, dark red socks. His arms were both up and lashed to the curtain piping with what look like thin wire, the ends twisted cruelly into the flesh of his wrists. On his head was more wire, a lot of it, wound around and around his forehead and cut into jagged points that had chewed into Russ's flesh, sending rivulets of blood down his face to drip obscenely onto his bare, hairless chest. The whole tableau looked bizarrely familiar. Even so, it took Cooley several seconds to make the connection.

His friend had been turned into a makeshift crucified Jesus, complete with crown of thorns.

Russ's head moved. His entire body twitched. His left eye, the only one not blinded by blood from his lacerated scalp, opened and fixed on Cooley.

"John?" he muttered.

Cooley took a step forward. His own body was shaking badly. As he did, he got a closer, clearer look at the inside of the tub—and realized he'd made a mistake. Those weren't red socks Russ was wearing. The skin below his knees had been flayed and the tub around his feet was slick with blood. Thick streams of it were curling their way down the drain.

"John?" Russ muttered again.

"I'm here, man," Cooley heard himself say. "I'll call somebody."

"He done for me, John," his friend said. "He done for me good."

Cooley wavered, trying to decide what to do. Russ was bleeding to death right in front of him. He needed an ambulance. But the nearest phone that Cooley knew about was downstairs in the kitchen, and the idea of leaving his friend strung up like this felt obscene.

I need wire cutters, he thought. *I'll go call for help and then get some wire cutters.*

Then, like a complete idiot, he asked, "Where's your wire cutters?"

Russ didn't reply. He just hung there, his skin going ashen as blood poured freely from his skinless calves.

Cooley had never felt this utterly helpless in his life, not even when he'd been holding Rachel's body in St. Damien's cellar.

"The cellar," he said, answering his own question. "Hang on, man. I got you."

Then he turned and stumbled out of the bathroom. The world seemed to be tilting around him like some kind of carnival funhouse. He felt nauseous, but fought it fiercely, on some vague level convinced that puking in Russ's house would somehow be the worst of insults. He staggered down the stairs and around the corner, making his way to the kitchen.

The phone was on the wall just inside the archway. The room smelled of dirty dishes and rotting food. Cooley picked up the receiver and dialed O for the operator. He expected to hear the customary clicks and then ringing as the connection was made.

Instead, he heard a voice.

Barton's voice.

"Russel has been smote, John. As the scriptures say: 'For the wrongdoer will be paid back for the wrong he has done, and there is no partiality.'"

Cooley supposed he should be frightened. But everything that had happened—everything that had *been* happening since the night he'd killed this man had pretty much squeezed the fear out of him. What it left behind was a kind of impotent rage. "You mother-fucker!" he screamed. "What did he do? What did Russ ever do to you?"

"He went into my cellar. He saw what he shouldn't have seen. You, of all people, should understand. You're also going to die tonight, John...and it's Russel's fault."

Cooley clicked the cradle until he got a dial tone. Then, with a shuddering sigh, he redialed.

But, as before, there was no click and no ring.

Just Barton.

"A pity you can't join my Forever Congregation, John. Sadly, what you know can't be shared, can't be spoken. I won't have it, John. And I won't allow you to live knowing it."

"Fuck you!" Cooley screamed. This time he slammed the receiver down and, just for good measure, ripped the entire treacherous phone from the wall and threw it across the kitchen, where it shattered against Russ' Frigidaire. Then, with his hands balled into fists and sweat stinging his eyes, he went to the cellar door, switched on the light, and made his way down the rickety wooden steps.

In his own house, the cellar was a dusty but organized place; Wanda had seen to that. But this space was crowded with boxes and bags of any and all sorts of detritus, the flotsam and jetsam of a lonely man's life. Cooley impatiently navigated his way through it, the image of Russ' tortured frame fueling his urgency.

He found what he was looking for in a corner near the water heater. Russ kept no workbench, but he *had* tools, plenty of them, and here they were. Most were old and in poor repair, piled into an aged egg crate to which their owner had affixed rope handles, turning it into something akin to a toolbox.

Dropping into a crouch, Cooley fumbled through it, knowing full well how ironic it was for him to be doing so. His plan had been to come here and borrow a pair of tools that he remembered Russ having. But now all that was gone from his head, eclipsed by the need to get back upstairs. Calling for an ambulance was no longer an option, "out the window" as Wanda liked to say; Barton had seen to that. But he could still cut down his friend and—well— maybe find a way to staunch the bleeding.

Then he stumbled across the very tools he'd originally come for.

A mallet and an iron chisel.

For a moment, but only a moment, he stared at them. Then, impatiently, he put them aside and kept digging through the box, throwing useless items away one or two at a time in a desperate hunt for—

Wire cutters. They were small, rusted, and dull, their handles wrapped in red rubber.

He was on his feet in an instant. He half-expected someone to be there, Rachel maybe or one of the other girls or even the cop. But the cellar stairway and the main floor stood empty. He bounded up the stairs to the second floor two at a time and, this go around, he didn't pause for an instant. He simply rounded the corner, ran down the short hall, and turned into the bathroom.

There, he stopped in his tracks.

Russ was free. He stood by the sink, his back turned, still completely naked. Around his wrists were thin slits in his skin, both going almost to the bone. But no blood. The wounds were ragged and ugly, but they weren't bleeding. And his feet—the "red socks" of flayed skin looked the same, except they too seemed to have stopped the relentless draining of Russ' life fluid.

Then, as Russel turned toward him, Cooley saw why.

His friend had coins over his eyes.

Without wanting to, Cooley found himself glancing at the tub.

Russ' body still hung there, now drooping completely as if whatever meager strength he'd had left to hold himself even partly up had drained away—which, of course, was exactly true. While Cooley had been trying to find the wire cutters, his friend and neighbor had bled to death.

He looked back at what he now knew to be Russel's ghost. The apparition was reaching for him, extending two ashen arms tipped with thick, clawing fingers. And his mouth, slack like the girls', like Rachel's, emitted a voice that weirdly reminded Cooley of the PA system at school.

"Your turn, John."

He screamed. Then he ran. He almost tripped down the narrow hallway and very nearly fell down the stairs. But somehow, blinded by panic, he managed to stay upright, crossing the parlor and throwing himself through the still open door and out onto Bleak Street. It was now full dark—though, by the light of the streetlamps, he could see them standing there, waiting for him.

Rachel and the girls.

I need to get to the graveyard, his overtaxed mind screamed, this thought like firecrackers going off in his head. *But I can't. I can't leave the message without the—*

Then he looked down at his hands. In the right one, he held the wire cutter he'd never gotten the chance to use. In the left, by some miracle, were the mallet and chisel. He'd held onto them. He didn't *remember* holding onto them, but he'd done it anyway.

It was a break, the only one he'd gotten since this whole terrible business had started and, most likely, the last he could reasonably expect. But he'd take it.

Oh yes, he would.

Cooley began running down the sidewalk in the direction of Bleak Street's dead-end, toward the marshlands, the river, and the church.

"Where are you going, John?" one of the girls asked. Cooley thought maybe he recognized her from the neighborhood, though he couldn't for the life of him recall her name. Besides, it wasn't her voice he heard but Barton's, always Barton's.

Cooley ignored it, pushed past her, and kept going.

"Where are you going, John?" another asked.

"Where are you going, John?" asked yet another.

Then they were *all* saying it—chanting it, as he weaved his way through their numbers.

Twenty-seven. Twenty-seven of them. Plus that cop. Now, plus Russel. *I've got to stop this...*

He reached the graveyard, his chest heaving. St. Damien's loomed above, a dark and utterly evil edifice, so black that it looked almost like a hole in the world. Going in there would destroy him; he knew that. It would snap what little remained of his reason like a twig in a hurricane.

Fortunately, going inside was not his plan.

He bypassed the main entrance and cut around to the back. The parsonage door was closed, yellow POLICE tape stretched across it.

No one, absolutely no one, was in sight. At this hour, he'd expect to hear the crash of bowling pins and the sounds of laughter floating across the street from Fairlanes. But that place looked completely closed down. Nobody on Bleak Street was doing anything for fun these days, and probably never would again.

St. Damien's graveyard occupied less than a quarter acre behind the parsonage and right at the edge of the marshy ground that gave way to the Delaware River. It wasn't much, just thirty or so granite markers, a few of them in the shapes of crosses. This land, like the land upon which the church itself stood, had belonged to the Barton family for more than three hundred years. The reverend, back when Cooley had still been able to think of him that way, had often recounted the dozen or more of his proud ancestors, his parents included, who were interred there. He called it an honor to share that sacred ground with them, and personally presided over every parishioner's burial there over the past quarter century.

That had included Cooley's mother and father.

Now the land was stained, corrupted by the sins of the man who'd ruled it for so long. Of course, Jonah Ray Barton, himself, wasn't here—not yet. His body still lay in the city morgue. But to do what he intended, Cooley didn't need the man to have been interred. He needed only what he knew was already there, what *had* been for more than a decade.

Barton's gravestone.

It had been the subject of some talk when he'd announced it, *unveiled* it actually, after services one particular Sunday. Cooley had been there to witness it, along with most of the rest of the street. Their reverend had been *so* excited, all smiles, telling everyone that his place as a Barton—as, in fact, the *last* Barton was secure. He would lie beside his progenitors forever, a testament to his great family name.

"American royalty" he'd called it at the time.

While some of their neighbors quietly whispered about the hubris, about what kind of "man of God" would spend so much money and energy just to make sure his gravestone would be exactly as he wanted it, Wanda and some of the other church ladies defended him. "He's got nothing, John," she'd insisted over dinner one night right after the unveiling. "No family. No wife. No children. He's right. The Barton line ends with him. He just wants to make sure they're remembered."

Cooley, not caring much either way, hadn't argued with her.

But now, tonight, as he shoved his way through the creaky iron gate and half-stumbled into the graveyard, he cared about nothing else. He was tired, weary to his soul, but he pushed on. He pushed on because it was almost done, *he* was almost done. After this, whatever happened to him—well, happened. But his message in a bottle would have been sent.

He dropped to his knees before the gravestone. It was a big one, one of the biggest in the yard, with its owner's name etched into it in huge serif letters.

Jonah Ray Barton

There was a birth date. Barton was a Taurus, like him. Cooley didn't know why that should bother him, but it did. Naturally, the death date was blank. Sooner or later, someone might get around to filling it in, though Cooley rather doubted it. Barton's posthumously revealed crimes had killed forever his reputation and his following. There'd be no one to bother with completing the stone under which he would eventually be interred.

So, let me complete it for you.

Cooley raised the mallet and chisel and went to work.

They came as he did it, chipping out each letter in each word. The girls were first, silent and slack-jawed. They were followed by the cop and poor Russ, who stood like a sentinel at the graveyard's only exit. He half-expected them to close in on him, stop him. But they didn't. Maybe Barton was curious.

Cooley hoped so.

Fabron was there as well, the first time Cooley had seen him—at least since the cook's death. Unlike the rest, there were no coins over his eyes. Instead, coins filled his mouth, dozens of them, pushing out both his sunken cheeks and gleaming faintly through his cracked, slightly parted lips.

Barton had *silenced* his former cook, and Cooley could guess why.

Then, finally, just as he was finishing the last word, Barton himself appeared.

The reverend had no coinage dand no slack mouth. Of all of them, he alone seemed truly aware of his surroundings, and might even have passed for alive but for the shadows that seeped out of him, covering the ground around where Cooley knelt, working feverishly with Russ' mallet.

"What are you up to there, John?" Barton asked. *"Not telling tales*

out of church, I hope. Wanda would suffer for that. So would your boys. Oh, I'm aware you sent her away. But we both know, sooner or later, she'll come back. And, if you tell, I'll take her, John. I'll take her and everyone else I can reach. So, let me see what you're doing to my precious stone."

Cooley finished the last stroke and sat back. He was wrung out, his arms as heavy as lead. In the distance, he could hear sirens.

Barton leaned down, bringing his Darkness-Man face close as he read Cooley's work. Cooley wouldn't have thought a ghost could have a smell, but Barton did. Decay. Rot. The stench of death. It reminded him of the church's cellar, of Rachel. He wondered if she was here, in the graveyard with the rest of them. Probably, but he lacked the strength to look for her.

Barton chuckled. Cooley wouldn't have thought ghosts could do that, either. But apparently this one could. *"That's it? All this fuss and bother just to leave something so…mundane? A limerick? A curse? I can't even guess what you were thinking, but clearly I had nothing to worry about when you came in here."*

"Nothing to worry about," Cooley heard himself say.

"Quite so. All right then, John. It sounds as if they're coming for you. The police. They've just turned onto my street, all lights and sound. But don't imagine that means you'll escape me. I can't let you live knowing what you know."

Then he was gone. All of them were gone. In an instant, John Cooley found himself alone in St. Damien's graveyard, staring blankly at the tombstone he'd just defaced.

Moments later, the Camden PD arrived in force.

And Cooley welcomed them.

CHAPTER 10
Camden, New Jersey—2022

MIA CLOSED THE THICK FOLDER with its official looking seal and its long and disturbing story. She'd just finished John Cooley's astonishing confession, given to Camden Police Detectives James Tyler and Harrison Grant fifty years ago. When she glanced to her left, she saw FBI Assistant Director Renee Brubaker behind the wheel of her late model Ford Taurus, a car so non-descript and bare bones that it just *had* to be a bureau vehicle.

"Well?" Brubaker asked.

"Goddess," Mia muttered.

A little to her surprise, Brubaker laughed softly, both her hands firmly on the steering wheel. They were on the New Jersey Turnpike, headed south in the general direction of Philadelphia, a city Mia rather liked. Unfortunately, she knew full well they wouldn't be going that far, instead exiting just on the Jersey side of the Delaware River in the city of Camden, seat of Camden County, and a town about which Mia had less favorable feelings. "If that's Wiccan for 'Jesus Christ!' then that was exactly my reaction when I read it."

"When *did* you read it?"

"In the weeks after Derrick died." The woman said this so matter-of-factly. Nevertheless, Mia's heart went out to her. She couldn't imagine what it must be like to lose a child, much less one who'd died the way Derrick had. "Back then, I wanted answers. Derrick's death was strictly local jurisdiction, of course. But that didn't mean I couldn't poke around during my private hours, and I did. Believe you me, I did. At first, nobody gave me a hard time. I was a grieving mother, after all. But eventually, the director called me and 'suggested' I put it down and find a way to move on. I think the Camden brass reached out to him. They *really* don't like people asking about St. Damien's."

"That much I know," Mia remarked.

"How about you?" Brubaker asked. "Had you read any of that before?"

"No. I knew he'd killed Barton and later himself. But, like I told you, they wouldn't let us see the file."

"Us?"

"Me and *The Ghost Finders*."

Brubaker nodded. "Right. Of course."

"I take it Cooley was arrested at the graveyard?"

"Actually, no. He was only brought in for questioning. Apparently, a neighbor spotted him out on the street after he sent Wanda off and even witnessed him entering Russel Saunders' house. She kept watching and eventually saw him running out again and heading down the street in the direction of the church. It alarmed her, so she called the police."

Mia asked, "When did the actual arrest happen?"

"As soon as he got to the station and revealed what he'd done with Grant and Tyler. The initial charges were two counts of assault on a police officer. But, shortly after that, Saunders' body was found in his bathroom, and they added murder to the list. Cooley waived both a lawyer and his right to remain silent and started talking. Everything was recorded and then transcribed."

Mia hefted the thick folder on her lap. "And after that?"

"He was put in a holding cell in county jail and his arraignment scheduled for the following morning. But that night he hanged himself using a bedsheet."

"Goddess," Mia muttered again.

"Yeah."

The two women were quiet for most of a minute. Finally, Brubaker asked, "You think it was Barton who killed him, don't you?"

"Don't *you*?"

"Honestly, I'm not sure. Look, I'm a believer, I really am…to a point. But can a…ghost or whatever…really be *that* powerful as to reach the mile or more from Bleak Street south to the county jail and…what? Strangle a grown man with a sheet and make it look like suicide? Or was it more like he got into Cooley's head and convinced him to kill himself. Or maybe Cooley did it entirely on his own. In any case, he was silenced."

"Yes, he was," said Mia.

"I have to say, Agent Delgado had a point before. Barton *does* sound like the devil."

Mia shook her head emphatically. "In life, he was a megalomaniacal psychopath who remained a megalomaniacal psychopath after he died. Now, he's an intelligent, sadistic spirit with a ton of power at his fingertips, more than any entity I've ever heard of. But he's not the devil."

The other woman glanced sideways at her. "You sure about that?"

Mia started to reply. But then she remembered Cooley's story and thought better of it.

Maybe "devil" is in the eye of the beholder.

They exited the turnpike, heading along a four-lane secondary road that eventually led them into a low-income neighborhood rife with brick rowhouses and ill-kept streets.

Camden.

The city had been waging a war against poverty for more than a half-century and, as far as Mia could tell, had been losing. But at least on these streets there was life. Children played on the sidewalks. Adults sat on evening stoops talking and laughing, some with small bags of groceries, probably bought at a local corner store.

But all that changed when Brubaker turned them onto Bleak Street.

Here, on this single block that ended with a haunted church across from a dilapidated bowling alley, the homes on either side were almost exclusively boarded up. And those that weren't had clearly been gutted by fire sometime in the past fifty years, their windows broken and bricks blackened. On Bleak Street, no one played. In fact, not a single soul could be seen. And Mia knew why.

Everyone had fled, or died, or killed their entire families and then themselves, all to feed the "Forever Congregation" of Jonah Ray Barton.

The injustice of it was like an open wound. If Barton had been a living man holding such terrible sway over an urban street, the Powers That Be would have rooted him out decades ago. But he *wasn't* a living man, not anymore, and neither the City of Camden nor the State of New Jersey would acknowledge his existence much less address his atrocities.

After all, there was no such thing as ghosts.

Brubaker said, "There's an alley that runs behind the church. It leads to a weedy lot in the back where we can park."

"And this big meeting is supposed to happen tonight?" Mia asked.

"Yes. Sometime past midnight."

"In the bowling alley?"

"Yes."

"Then what makes you think this Arias person doesn't already have the whole street under surveillance, the church and the vacant lot in the back included?"

"Because we're not going into this blind, either. Agent Prine has been carefully monitoring Bleak Street via satellite imaging for the past week, ever since his CI told him about the upcoming summit. Arias' contacts have been observed here on numerous occasions, scoping out the site, preparing the way, so to speak. All their preparations were completed days ago, and everyone involved in the effort is being carefully surveilled. With the summit now so close at hand, they won't risk attracting attention by arriving on site before full dark. As long as we park inconspicuously and are nicely tucked away before then, we should be fine."

Mia uttered a nervous, humorless laugh. "Should be?"

Brubaker said seriously, "If I didn't think I could guarantee your safety, you wouldn't be here."

I'm crazy to be here at all, Mia thought but didn't say. *And so are you.*

"And I guess satellite imaging wouldn't be good enough for what's happening tonight."

Brubaker shook her head. "The technology's good, but it's not that good. To get what we need to finally arrest Arias, we have to be on site."

"Figures," Mia muttered.

Moments later, they came upon the alley and Brubaker turned smoothly into it, the Taurus' wheels crunching on old gravel. They rumbled slowly along, with St. Damien's stony façade on one side and its nearest neighbor's outer wall on the other. Being this close to the church after so many years was—unnerving. So much had happened to her here, none of it good.

Instead of parking behind the church, Brubaker turned into a weedy lot across the alley from it, behind a neighboring row home and well out of view of the street. Two other cars were already parked there. One was a Chevy Malibu and the other a Toyota Camry, both with Jersey plates and neither new-looking.

"We're the last to arrive," Brubaker remarked.

"Is that a surprise?" Mia asked her.

"Not at all. For an operation like this, protocol dictates that all team members be on site at least eight hours before the anticipated event." She said this with easy familiarity, as if quoting from a manual.

"Then we're behind schedule," Mia pointed out, checking the clock on the car's dash. "It's almost seven."

Brubaker offered her a pointed grin. "Well, I had to stop along the way to pick *you* up, didn't I?"

Mia didn't reply.

Brubaker parked beside the Camry and killed the engine. The new silence was punctuated by the distant thrum of traffic and a whistling breeze that blew trash around the lot like tiny tumbleweeds. As Mia watched, the assistant director placed a smart phone against her ear. "I've arrived with Lakatos," she said a moment later. "Are we a 'go' for the graveyard?"

"All clear," someone replied. It sounded like Agent Prine, his voice just loud enough for Mia to catch it.

"Roger that." Then she broke the connection, lowered the cell phone, turned to Mia and said, "Ready?"

No, Mia thought.

"Yes," she said. Then, hastily she added, "Graveyard only."

Brubaker nodded. "Graveyard only."

They climbed out of the car.

With the late spring sun already well into her afternoon descent, the church to their immediate west cast a heavy shadow that swallowed the vacant lot, the Taurus, and the two women who'd just emerged from it. Mia hoped the chill that seemed to permeate that shadow was in her imagination.

Then she saw Brubaker shiver and hug herself a little. "Weird," the assistant director remarked, mostly to herself. "Maybe it's because we're so close to the river."

Mia didn't reply.

"The graveyard's around this way," Brubaker said. And, just like that, the woman was off, marching around the rear of the church.

Mia gave the huge, gray stone edifice one more unhappy and distrustful look. Then she followed.

The graveyard was a sad little patch, just a loose collection of markers interspersed among weeds and high wild grass. There were no trees, just a three-foot wrought iron fence that looked to be falling down in places, probably due to the soft, marshy ground. To Mia, it seemed more pathetic than frightening.

Unlike St. Damien's itself, which frightened her aplenty.

"Which one is Barton's?" she asked.

"I don't know," Brubaker admitted. "I suggest we find it while we still have daylight."

So, they did just that, splitting up by wordless agreement and moving slowly through the squat forest of brush and granite. Many of the stones were so grown over that Mia had to push aside, or even pull out, tall clumps of grass in order to read them. Almost all of the death dates fell between the late 1940s and early 1970s, which she supposed made them parishioners. None of the last names were Barton.

After a few minutes of this, she heard a crunching noise and glanced up to see Karen Jessup marching toward them from the direction of the parsonage. The DEA agent wore a scowl so deep it looked like a permanent fixture. She was dressed in black slacks and a black long sleeve knit top—warm for the weather. A shoulder rig, complete with pistol, was fastened under her left arm pit.

"Renee!" she said in a sharp stage whisper. "You need to come inside!"

"In a minute," the assistant director said, still going from gravestone to gravestone herself. "We're looking for Barton."

"You can't be seen!" the DEA agent insisted.

"And we won't be. We're out of sight of the street and the bowling alley's unoccupied right now anyway. Prine would have warned me off if that weren't the case."

"As far as we're aware, yes," Jessup admitted. "But it's still not smart and you know it."

"Then help us look and we'll be done faster. This is important, Karen."

"The hell it is," Jessup muttered. But she went to work with them, hurriedly moving through the uneven ranks of the dead, her scowl etching itself ever deeper. At one point, she and Mia nearly bumped into each other. But when Mia nodded and said a reasonably polite, "Agent Jessup," she received no reply.

"Here!" Brubaker finally said, not shouting but loud enough for the other two women to stop their efforts and hurry over. Across the Delaware River, the sun was falling behind the Philadelphia skyline. It wasn't twilight, not yet, but it would be soon, and Mia needed to be long gone from here by then.

This sense of urgency fueled her as she all but ran to the assistant director's side. Brubaker had yanked out the weeds that had grown over one of the larger stones. "All these are Bartons," she reported as Mia approached. "I count eight names in the row, but this is the one we want."

Mia looked unhappily down at the marker. It stood not quite three feet tall, arched in the classic way of some granite gravestones, with angels' wings and even a cherub adorning the upper perimeter—a bad joke if there ever was one. But then this stone had been erected here years before Barton's death, when he'd still been a "pillar of the community."

A man of God.

The stone read: "Here lies Jonah Ray Barton, Shepherd of the Lord." Below that were the man's birth date and a hyphen. No one had ever gotten around to adding the rest. That would have cost money that no longer existed, and require respect that was, by then, utterly gone. In its place were chiseled words, all sharp angles and shallow, uneven cuts. They'd been added fifty years ago, and the years had not been kind. Nevertheless, as Mia squatted down and peered closely at them, she found she could read them well enough.

"*This* is Cooley's 'message in a bottle?'" she asked, glancing back up at Brubaker.

The assistant director nodded while Jessup came to stand glumly at her shoulder.

Mia read the words again.

Then she read them a third time.

"All Victims Avenged; Truth Always Raises Demons."

Well…shit, she thought.

CHAPTER 11
Camden, New Jersey—2022

"THAT'S IT?" JESSUP BARKED. "THAT'S the big mystery we need to solve to beat the 'ghost?'" This last she said with air quotes.

Brubaker ignored the comment. Instead, she crouched down beside Mia, the two of them regarding Cooley's message. "Notice anything about it?" she asked, and the eagerness in her voice both surprised and dismayed Mia.

Barton was right, she thought miserably. *It's nothing. John Cooley had been broken by the things he'd done and seen. Anyone would be. This isn't some big clue. It's just a limerick, about as relevant as a fortune cookie with lottery numbers on the back.*

Except...

"What did he do for a living?" Mia heard herself ask.

Behind her, looming a bit, Jessup remarked, "Who? Barton? Seriously?"

But Brubaker got it. "John Cooley was an English teacher. In fact, he was head of the English Department at Camden High School."

Mia nodded as if she'd expected this, which she had—more or less.

"How did you know?" Brubaker asked her.

Mia shrugged. "How many tombstones do you see with a period, much less a correctly used semi-colon? As scared as he was, as grief-stricken, he still got his punctuation right."

Jessup said, "What difference does that make?"

"I'm not sure," Mia admitted.

"Touch it," said Brubaker.

Both Mia and Jessup replied, "What?" at exactly the same time. It might have been funny under very different circumstances.

"Touch it," the assistant director urged. "See if you sense anything."

Mia stared at the woman, but Brubaker's expression was utterly unironic. This wasn't a joke or a prank. It was a legitimate request made by an assistant director of the FBI for a consulting "expert" to attempt to gather information via clairvoyance. Back in the car, Brubaker had described herself as a "believer, a word that, in Mia's experience, a lot of people threw around without really meaning or even entirely understanding it.

But Brubaker's request, delivered so sincerely, implied that in her case it might just be true.

Mia had a modicum of psychic sensitivity, yes. But it was a small gift, less useful than say—a knack with cars or a really good memory. She could, sometimes, get impressions from touching objects, but those impressions were rarely useful. She'd once encountered a twelve-year-old boy who could recite the name, age, and even hometown of the owner of any given item just by running his fingers along it.

Mia had nowhere near that level of ability.

"I don't think…" she began, then stopped herself. She was here, in the most psychically active place she'd ever visited. True, it was negative energy but, for some things, energy was energy and maybe, just maybe, she *could* tap into it, if only a little.

Taking a deep, cleansing breath, Mia reached out with her right hand, annoyed at how it trembled, and rested it atop the stone that marked the burial site of Jonah Ray Barton. The granite was warm under her touch and as rough as sandpaper, pitted by decades of wind coming off the nearby river.

She closed her eyes.

Behind her, Jessup groaned.

"Shut up, Karen," Brubaker said in a sharp whisper.

Mia ignored the brief exchange. If this was going to work at all, she needed to be serene, her mind as open as she could make it, a radio receiver moving slowly through the frequencies of the universe.

Grief.

It struck her like a wave, almost dropping her back onto her butt on the damp ground. Grief and fear and urgency, all things that John Cooley had been feeling as he'd chiseled these words. He'd lost his daughter, his friend, and perhaps some of his mind as well, chipped away by Barton over the last days of his life much in the way he'd chipped at the dead man's headstone. But there was determination here as well, mixed in with the desperation and near panic.

Cooley had been hell-bent on leaving this message in a bottle. It would be his last act, or nearly so, upon this Earth, and he *would* do it. For Wanda. For his sons. For Rachel. For Russ. For all of them.

For a moment, Mia thought that was it. Grief, fear, urgency, and determination. In fact, she nearly said so, except at the last moment she detected something else. It was deep, carefully—perhaps even deliberately—hidden, but she found it.

"Guile," she said.

"What?" Brubaker asked.

It took some effort, but Mia managed to pull her fingers from the stone. "He was scared and he was choked by horror. But, for all that, he knew exactly what he was doing."

"So, what do the words mean?" Jessup demanded.

"I don't know," Mia admitted. "All I can tell you is that they mean *something*. Cooley couldn't reveal to anyone what he knew directly, because doing so would make them targets. So, he did *this* instead, trusting on somebody down the line to see it and figure it out."

Jessup said nothing. To Mia, it seemed like a nice change.

Brubaker took out her cell phone, held it carefully up to the marker and photographed the words, both collectively and, zooming in, individually. She took her time about it, with Mia and Jessup looking on—and, when she'd finished, she stood and said to the DEA agent, "Where are Prine and Delgado?"

"Inside, of course," Jessup replied. "Setting everything up."

"Then maybe Delgado's toys can do something with this. We should head inside."

"Wait a minute!" Mia said, jumping to her feet. "The deal was I look at the gravestone. Well, I have, and I want—"

Brubaker's cell phone chirped. There was no ringtone, just a simple triple beep that, despite her sudden alarm, Mia found very FBI. Without addressing Mia's protest, or even meeting her eyes, the assistant director answered it, taking a moment to engage the speaker phone. "Go ahead, Delgado."

"We've got...a situation in here!" the young agent replied. He sounded alarmed.

No, Mia corrected herself. *He sounds scared.*

"Give me a sit rep," Brubaker said calmly. "What's happening?"

There was a pause on the connection, lengthy, worrisome. Then Delgado muttered, *"Sweet Mary, Mother of God..."*

"Agent Delgado!" Brubaker said, more sharply this time. Mia glanced at Jessup and saw that the DEA agent had paled. Her eyes were fixed on the parsonage and, behind it, the blocky, hulking shape of St. Damien's.

"Sorry. Sorry, AD." Delgado seemed to take a moment to try to calm himself. Mia found that she was wringing her hands, a nervous habit of her mother's that she hadn't even known she'd picked up. It made her wonder how long she'd been doing it unconsciously. *"I just spotted...I mean...one of Arias' men is in the church, by the altar."*

"What?" Brubaker exclaimed. She turned to Jessup. "Call in backup. Right now!"

Jessup nodded and drew her own phone.

Then Delgado said, *"He's not moving. He's not saying anything. And... and...there are coins on his eyes!"*

Mia was running before she even made the decision to do so. One instant she was standing with the others, listening to Delgado, and the next her feet were carrying her out the graveyard, around the front of the parsonage and toward the walkway that would lead her directly into—

What am I doing?!

But she didn't stop. She didn't wait to see if Brubaker and Jessup were following. She heard, or thought she heard, Brubaker call her name. Yet she ignored it. She was going into the last place on Earth she wanted to go, all to help a young man whom she'd met exactly once. It was crazy to the point of suicide.

She'd warned him after all. She'd warned them all repeatedly.

I don't owe these people anything!

And yet she was running to their rescue anyhow.

The church had two main doors, big wooden things, very Gothic revival, that together formed a nine-foot-arch wide enough for two people to walk through abreast. Both doors were currently closed, their wood weathered and their brass knockers and fittings tarnished with age. When Mia reached them and pushed on them, she half-expected/half-hoped to find them locked. But the one on the right opened easily enough, though its hinges complained.

The smell that hit her mixed decades of musty air with a sharper and more immediate stink of sweat. Or maybe it was *fear*. Fear permeated this place, after all. It filled it and stained its every surface, soaking into the floors and walls like linseed oil on wood. The palpability of it, the *realness*, jolted her, throwing her already pounding heart into a full-throttle hammering. She gasped and, for just a moment, couldn't take another step. Her feet seemed to have melted into the threshold, and she couldn't muster the will to move them.

But then something grabbed her arm and pulled her inside.

Mia screamed. It was something she hadn't done in a long while, not since that awful night five years ago. Since then, nothing had scared her, not even a mugging attempt she'd suffered through on Staten Island last February. Beside this church and the *thing* that thrived within its walls, every other threat paled and withered.

St. Damien's door swung closed at her back.

She flailed wildly, kicking and throwing her fists, but whatever had her was impossibly strong. It dragged her several feet into what she knew to be the church's modest vestibule before stopping in the gloom and spinning her around.

Mia, never much of a fighter, nevertheless cocked one fist, trying to decide if she should go for the nose or the throat. Someone had once told her that the throat was a very vulnerable spot, even more so than the crotch. But someone *else* had once assured her that a broken nose stops even the biggest assailant in their tracks.

Of course, both presupposed that whatever had her was human—and living.

"Hold up, Dr. Lakatos!" a deep voice said. "It's me!"

She blinked as her eyes finally got around to adjusting to the darker space. Before her, still clutching both her shoulders, the *something* took shape.

"Agent Prine?" she whispered, the words coming out in a terrified gasp.

"Sorry if I scared you," the tall man said, his dark skin half-lost in the shadows.

"Shit!" Mia exclaimed. "Why did you grab me like that?"

"Because being visible from the street is a bad idea," he told her calmly. "We all need to be coming and going either through the parsonage or the alley exit."

"Delgado called Brubaker," Mia told him. She was having a hard time reconciling his steady demeanor with the fear she'd heard in his colleague's voice. "He said there was an intruder in the church."

Now it was Prine's turn to blink. "He said…what?"

He doesn't know.

"Delgado said it was one of Arias' men, and that he was down by the altar. But—"

Before she could finish, Prine released her, spun around, and drew the pistol from his shoulder holster. "Stay here. Right here." Then he left her, heading deeper into the church, out of the vestibule and into the nave.

Mia stared after him, too shaken to follow. Nervously, she glanced over her shoulder at the church's shut door. The urge to throw it open again and escape back into the fading sunlight was nearly overpowering. After all, hadn't she just passed the "rescue thing" off to a professional? Wouldn't the smart thing be to head back out, go straight to Brubaker's car, and sit there until somebody had the decency to keep their agreement and drive her home?

To hell with this place…

Except she still didn't move. Instead, she kept peering into the darkness that filled the greater part of the church, picturing what she remembered of the nave. The pews on either side, dozens of them, flanked a wide central aisle that led up to a raised dais with an alter atop it. Above the dais stood a twelve-foot-high cross of what had once been gleaming brass, but which had long ago lost its battle with tarnish.

That's where Delgado said the coin-eyed man was standing.

If so, then neither he nor Prine can possibly deal with it.

And what in the name of All That's Holy makes you think you can?

This second voice was her mother's, always so pious, always so negative. Gail Lakatos was the most pessimistic person Mia had ever known, a trait that she'd worked hard to instill in her only child. Fortunately, at the same time and with much more gentle subtlety, her father had been working to instill the opposite.

If you're not standing, you're falling, peach.

It had been one of his favorite axioms.

And Mia thought, *Time to stand.*

She ran into the darkened nave.

It was cooler here than in the vestibule and significantly colder than outside. Also, the gloom was thicker, despite the dozen narrow stained-glass windows set into the side walls—and the one enormous one that filled the front wall above the choir loft. The light from outside, fading though it might be, *should* have been filtering through all that leaded glass, infusing the large space with at least some modicum of ambient light. But there was nothing, just shadows and deeper shadows.

"Archie!" she heard Prine call. "Tell me where you are!"

There was no reply, which was reply aplenty. Mia fished into her purse for what she thought of as her "Doohickey," an admittedly silly name for a handy, multi-function gadget that she'd purchased online. She twisted its single knob to the flashlight feature and shone it in front of her. The illumination it offered was narrow but better than nothing and, by it, she could see Agent Prine, his back to her, moving down the middle of the aisle slowly, his gun held up before him in a professional-looking, two-handed grip. He held a flashlight of his own, though it seemed to be switched off.

As Mia's light washed across him, he turned and looked at her, his eyes wide and his face awash in sweat. "My batteries died," he said in an oddly stunned voice.

Mia nodded. That kind of thing was commonplace at any paranormal site, but doubly so here. She knew from bitter experience that the battery in her own gadget might not last more than a few minutes, a half-hour tops.

Barton's with us, watching us. He's feeding on the energy we're giving him.

Prine motioned for her to give him the Doohickey, but she shook her head. His gun and his training weren't going to help anybody, not in this situation. So instead, she marched up and past him, drawing on a well of courage she'd had no idea was there. He watched her but didn't make any move to restrain her.

From here, she could see the altar. It was large and marble, easily big enough for a person to lie upon. For the moment, at least, it was barren, just a cold slab that reflected the light from her gadget so that it seemed to glow from within.

Beside it, on his knees, was Agent Archie Delgado. And behind him, towering over him, was a large man with short-cropped dark hair and a bushy beard. He stood at least six feet tall and thick at the shoulders. He wore jeans and a black t-shirt that showed off heavily muscled arms covered with tattoos. His forearms were thick enough to make Popeye jealous, and his hands, large and blunt-fingered, where clamped on either side of Delgado's head.

But it was his eyes that truly defined the situation for Mia.

They had silver dollars over them.

The man was facing Mia, his mouth slack and there could be no mistaking the angry red burn around the fellow's neck. His body, she knew—his actual corpse—would be elsewhere in the church, no doubt hanging by a makeshift noose from one of the ceiling rafters.

What she was looking at now was entirely spirit.

But spirit could be strong, very strong. It was a lesson she'd learned up close and personal.

"P—please," Archie whispered. "Help...me..."

"Don't move," Mia said. Then, lifting her eyes to the dead man, she added in a low voice that she hoped sounded authoritative, "Let him go, Barton."

The slack mouth never moved. Even so, words emerged from it. John Cooley had described this nasty little trick in his confession.

And Mia had seen it, herself—five years ago.

"Well, well. Who is this pretty little lamb before me? The prodigal daughter, perhaps?"

Mia felt her insides freeze solid. For several moments, she couldn't even breathe as a sharp visceral stab of terror seemed to collapse her lungs. The man with the coin-eyes watched her, his face impassive. But at the same time, his slack mouth turned upward at the corners in a grotesque parody of the smile.

I shouldn't be here! Oh Goddess, why did I come back to this place?

But then a large hand, warm and alive, touched her shoulder, shaking her out of her paralysis. With a gasp, she glanced over to see Prine at her side, his gun still out and focused on the coin-eyed man. "FBI," he barked in a tone that managed to somehow be both flat and commanding. "Release that agent, step back, and raise your hands above your head. Do it now."

It was an empty threat. Prine's bullets meant nothing here. But the fact that he was making this ultimatum, pointless as it might be, was drawing Barton's attention—and buying her a little time.

"Put your gun down," she told Prine in a tremulous voice. "And get ready to grab Agent Delgado."

"What?" he asked from beside her, sounding almost comically confused. "What are you talking about?"

Moving with shaking hands, Mia again turned the single knob on her Doohickey, selecting its other setting.

Instantly, the light it emitted changed from bright white to a muted violet, with the majority of its electromagnetic output outside the visible spectrum. It didn't illuminate much anymore, just enough to encompass Delgado and the apparition that gripped him.

The coin-eyed man's twisted smile vanished.

"Toys," Barton said through the fellow's slack, lifeless mouth, the single word uttered as an impatient curse.

Mia didn't reply. Instead, she took one step forward and then another, keeping the violet beam focused on the figure's pale face.

"Dr. Lakatos!" Prine warned. "Don't get too close!"

"Get ready to grab Delgado!" she barked again, not daring to look at him.

Another step closer.

The coin-eyed man didn't retreat. Instead, he sort of faded, lost substance, the huge hands that enveloped Delgado's skull becoming translucent.

"Now!" Mia cried.

To his credit, Prine moved instantly, jumping forward, his pistol already holstered, and pulled his fellow agent off the dais in a single, swift movement. At the same time, Mia advanced another step, extending her arm and focusing as much of the beam as possible directly into the apparition's blank face.

The slack mouth uttered a long sigh, a strange thing to hear from something that no longer took in air. And then it was gone.

Mia let go of the breath she only now realized she'd been holding.

Delgado was shaking badly as Prine lowered him onto the front pew with surprising gentleness. There were tears in the younger man's eyes and his nose was bleeding. With a grateful nod, he accepted the handkerchief Prine offered him.

As Mia switched her Doohickey back to flashlight, she heard Prine mutter, "That's... impossible."

"Welcome to my world," she told him without humor.

CHAPTER 12
Camden, New Jersey—2022

BRUBAKER AND JESSUP APPEARED A minute later. Both had their guns out and their flashlights on as they poured through the door that led into the breezeway. Apparently, instead of following Mia around the front of the church, they'd chosen to go through the parsonage. Mia guessed this had been, as Prine had said, to limit visibility from the street. This *was* supposed to be a stakeout, after all.

But the detour had made them both late to the party.

"Agent Prine!" Brubaker snapped. "I've been trying to call you!"

"Cell phones are down, AD," Prine replied without a trace of defensiveness. "Drained batteries."

"That can't be right!" Jessup said as she took in the scene. Mia was on her knees beside Delgado, who sat with his back to the altar, breathing hard and with blood running from both his nostrils. The young man hadn't said a word since the coin-eyed apparition had released him, though he shook as if he were freezing to death. That, Mia knew from experience, was adrenaline. "I checked those batteries myself not an hour ago," Jessup continued. "They had a full charge. All of them."

"I checked, too," Prine agreed with a nod. "Nevertheless, the battery in mine is dead."

"Mine…too," Delgado gasped, looking up.

"What happened?" Brubaker demanded. "Agent Delgado, report."

"I was…attacked, ma'am."

"Attacked? By who?"

Delgado rubbed his face with trembling hands before pushing himself up from the pew and climbing awkwardly to his feet. Mia was frankly impressed. The young man had nearly been killed just now, and by something not of this earth. Yet, here he was, an FBI agent addressing his superior and determined to do so with some dignity. She couldn't help but admire it, though it scared her. She needed to get these people out of here.

But the more time she spent with them, the more obvious it became that they weren't the sort to run—even when they should.

Brubaker stepped back and gave Delgado the time he needed. After a few long moments, the young man steadied himself and, keeping one hand on the altar for support, faced his boss and said, "I was in the choir loft setting up the parabolic mikes when I spotted movement down here by the altar. At first, I figured it was Prine. He'd gone to do an interior perimeter sweep after Jessup headed out through the parsonage to meet you. So, I called him, per procedure."

Prine said, "I was in the basement at the time."

Delgado nodded. "That's what he told me. So, I asked him to meet me in the nave, drew my weapon, and went down the staircase. I discovered this guy…sorry, suspect…standing by the altar. When I identified myself and ordered him to turn around, I recognized him as someone who worked for Arias. I can't remember the name, but his picture and dossier are in the file. I'm sure of it."

"Continue," Brubaker told him. Mia sensed she was impatient, even anxious, but too much of a professional to let it show. "You said something about coins on his eyes?"

For a second or two, Archie Delgado's affected demeanor cracked. His mouth twisted and his eyes squeezed shut. But then he straightened and took a deep breath. "Yeah. He had coins over his eyes. Silver dollars, I think. That's when I called you, but my phone died almost immediately. Like Prine said: battery. Damned thing just went blank, not even enough trickle to display the zero-battery indicator."

"Forget the phone," the assistant director said. "Continue."

"Well…realizing I was on my own, I ordered the guy to show me his hands. When he didn't move or say anything, I approached him. I had my gun out and my flashlight up. But just as I got close, the flashlight died too. The next thing I knew, I was grabbed and forced down to my knees. Christ, he was strong! I tried to bring my gun up, but he was…squeezing my head in his hands. It hurt! I couldn't move. I couldn't even yell. I don't know what happened to my gun."

"It's there," Jessup said, using her flashlight beam to point at the floor by the altar.

"It wouldn't have mattered anyway," Mia remarked.

They all looked at her.

She threw up her hands. "Do I really have to say it?"

"You think Delgado's attacker was a ghost," Brubaker remarked without any discernable sarcasm.

Jessup groaned theatrically.

Then Prine said, "AD, I…I think maybe it *was*."

This time, they all looked at *him*.

Mia expected the man to squirm. He didn't. Instead, he stood there, his face awash in their flashlight beams, looking stolid. "As I said, I was checking the basement. We'd given it a cursory glance when the three of us first arrived, but this was my first opportunity to really search it. While I was down there, I discovered a body."

He said it so matter-of-factly that, for a moment, none of them reacted.

Then Jessup demanded, "A body? Whose body?"

Brubaker and Delgado said nothing.

Prine didn't reply to her question. Instead, he continued his story.

His "report," Mia silently corrected.

"I tried to notify the team. That's when I discovered that my cell phone's battery had drained prematurely. So, I went upstairs, meaning to reconnect with Agent Delgado and hopefully use *his* phone. As I exited the cellar through the doorway under the choir loft, however, I heard the front door open and found Dr. Lakatos entering through the vestibule. I immediately went to her and shut the door, afraid she'd be noticed from the street."

Then, speaking as if he were reciting the latest stock market quotes,

Matthew Prine preceded to describe the confrontation with the coin-eyed man and the "device"—his word—that Mia had used to "drive away"—again his words—Delgado's assailant.

"What exactly do you mean, 'drive away?'" Brubaker asked. "Where did he retreat to?"

"Nowhere that I saw, ma'am. He simply faded from sight."

"A ghost," Jessup said, the word fairly dripping with derision.

"Yes," Prine replied without rancor.

"And you're quite sure of that?" Brubaker asked him.

Prine nodded.

Jessup took an almost accusatory step toward him. "How exactly are you 'quite sure' of that, Agent Prine?"

Prine's answer was delivered with so little emotion that he might have been Vulcan. "Because I saw his face, Agent Jessup. He was the same man whose body I found in the cellar. Delgado's right. He's one of Arias' men. His name's Rojas, I believe."

"So maybe he's got a twin!" Jessup exclaimed. "Did you consider that?"

Prine seemed to take a moment to do so now. "The man I found downstairs had a long scar running from his left eye to his left jawbone. The man who assaulted Delgado had the same scar. I find the notion of twins sharing it…unlikely."

"*More* unlikely than spooks?" Jessup challenged.

Prine considered another moment. "Yes."

"This is insane!" the DEA agent exclaimed. "You do all realize that, right?"

"What was it you used on Archie's attacker?" Brubaker asked Mia.

She held up her Doohickey. It was still on, its flashlight now splashing across the buttressed ceiling high overhead. "It's got a UV setting."

"So why isn't *its* battery drained?" Jessup asked, her eyes narrowing.

Mia replied, "I haven't been in the church long enough. It's the same reason your phone is still working."

Jessup looked anything but convinced.

Meanwhile, Brubaker asked, "A UV setting?"

Mia nodded.

"May I see it?"

Mia handed it to Brubaker, who examined it with a critical eye, experimenting with its single knob. "Where did you get it?"

"Amazon," Mia replied. "Fifteen bucks."

"And *that* chases away ghosts?" This came from Delgado. The young man sounded hopeful, even eager. Mia noticed that his nose had stopped bleeding, though he was still holding the red-stained handkerchief that Prine had lent him.

"In some cases, it can weaken them enough that they can't stay corporeal," Mia replied, choosing her words carefully.

"Can we use UV lamps to protect ourselves?" Brubaker asked.

"We don't have any," Delgado pointed out.

Mia shook her head. "Wouldn't matter much if you did. This isn't like a crucifix to a vampire. Studies have shown that UV light can sometimes inhibit paranormal activity, which is why most experiences occur at night. But it's nowhere close to absolute, and I wouldn't trust it an inch against something as powerful as Jonah Ray Barton."

"But it worked in this case," Prine pointed out.

"Only because that particular spirit was new, his death recent. New spirits are often confused, and their manifestations can be weak or unstable."

"The guy didn't feel anything like weak to me," Delgado remarked, rubbing at his temples.

"That was because Barton already had him and was pouring his will into him. But apparently even that monstrous intent couldn't sufficiently shore up so young a spirit."

"It's something to keep in mind," Brubaker noted.

"Renee!" Jessup exclaimed. The woman was seriously agitated, pacing back and forth. If she'd been sitting, Mia had no doubt she would be crossing and uncrossing her legs. "I can't believe we're even pursuing this! Look, I don't know exactly what happened here. Obviously, Agent Delgado was attacked, but I promise you, his attacker was a living human being, not something out of a *Ghostbusters* movie!"

They all looked at her, Brubaker with something like weariness in her expression, while both Prine and Delgado appeared uncomfortable, as if they were children and their parents were quarreling.

"Then what do you think we should do, Agent Jessup?" Brubaker asked patiently. Mia knew there was some kind of history between these two, something that connected them, something that apparently inspired Renee Brubaker to accept so much—insubordination—from the other woman. True, they worked for different agencies, but that by itself couldn't explain it, not given the disparity in their respective ranks.

"I think," Jessup said, "that, ghost or no ghost, one of Arias' people was here, stationed inside the church when we arrived, hiding in the cellar. This guy surely had a cell phone and just as surely reported our presence. In all likelihood, this entire operation is already blown."

"Not necessarily," Prine said. He took an old-fashioned flip phone from his pocket. "It's a burner. I found this on the body downstairs and the battery is completely drained, just like mine. My guess is Arias put Rojas here simply to keep an eye on the church, not because he expected anything, but as a sensible precaution given the gravity of the summit that's going to take place across the street in a few hours. I'd have done the same thing."

Jessup took the phone from him and looked it over, pushing its various buttons. "Just because it's dead now doesn't mean it was dead an hour ago when the three of us came in here. We could still be blown."

"Do you want to abort, Karen?" Brubaker asked her, and something in the older woman's expression made Mia think this was a test of some sort.

For her own part, Mia couldn't think of a smarter outcome than calling this whole business off.

But Jessup said, "No. Not yet." She turned to Delgado. "How close are we to being fully setup and operational?"

"Very close," Delgado replied, and Mia noticed that he said this with some prideful enthusiasm. He was the tech guy after all, not a field agent like Prine and, presumably, Jessup. Brubaker had brought him onto the team because he had the chops to let them look and listen into the goings-on at the derelict bowling alley across the street without the risk involved in planting on-site microphones and cameras.

There was irony in that, she supposed, given the risk involved for all of them in being *here*.

"I've got the Xaver 800S set up with its sensors focused through four square holes I cut through the big stained-glass window." He pointed up at the choir loft. "The window's about twelve yards from the front of the bowling alley and, according to Prine's informant, the meeting's going to take place in the old bar room in the south corner, which is a little shy of fifteen yards away, well within camera parameters."

"Good," Brubaker and Jessup said together. It was *telling* and, again, might have been funny but wasn't. When the two women looked at each other, Mia noticed that Jessup was the first to lower her gaze. Insubordination aside, it seemed Brubaker remained in charge.

Delgado continued. "Um…I was just about done setting up the parabolic mike. That one needed a bigger hole, but it's calibrated for the distance and sensitive enough to hear through walls. It'll be like we're in the room with them."

"Very good," Brubaker said. "How about the church itself? Where are we with on-site security?"

Mia wasn't quite sure what that even meant, but Delgado didn't miss a beat. "Well, I have wireless motion sensor video cameras setup at every entrance, all tied to my laptop upstairs and linked to my smart watch. If anybody sets foot on the grounds, I'll get notified."

"Were you notified when I came in the front door?" Mia asked him.

He glanced uncomfortably at her, then at his watch. "Um…no," he finally said. "The battery's dead."

"How about inside the church itself?" Jessup asked. "Any cameras in here?"

"Well, no," Delgado admitted. "I mean, that's outside mission parameters." He looked at Brubaker. "Isn't it, AD?"

"Technically, yes," Brubaker replied. "But, under the circumstances, I'm thinking we should broaden those parameters." She faced Mia, "Do these…things…show up on video?"

"To some degree," Mia told her. "But rarely with any real definition."

"Convenient," Jessup muttered.

Mia stiffened. "Is it? How do you figure?"

"No real evidence. No real proof." The challenge was unmistakable, and irritating as hell, given what had just happened.

"There's plenty of 'proof' of the paranormal, Agent Jessup," Mia said. "The problem isn't a lack of evidence. It's a lack of people willing to accept that evidence. Let me guess: everything's faked, the witnesses are lying or delusional, and people like me are charlatans. Am I right?"

"You said it, not me," Jessup replied with a smile so sickly sweet it would have killed a diabetic.

"Enough," Brubaker said. "All right, Karen. You don't want to abort. What *do* you want to do then, given Delgado's attack?"

Jessup looked suddenly uncertain. "This body in the cellar," she said to Prine. "Any ID?"

Prine shook his head. "But, as I reported, I recognized him from the photo in his dossier."

"And you're sure he was dead?"

"He was hanging from the rafters from a length of old wire that had been wound around his neck and looped over one of the joists. I took his pulse as a matter of protocol, but there was no mistaking that he was deceased."

"Which raises the question of who killed him," Jessup said.

"No, it doesn't," Mia remarked.

"Let me guess," the DEA agent said with a groan. "Ghosts."

Mia didn't reply.

"Could it have been suicide?" Jessup asked Prine.

"No," he replied.

"Why not?"

"Because it doesn't fit the facts. The victim is at least two feet off the cellar floor, with no stool, chair, or other support anywhere nearby that he might have kicked away. Also, the ceiling is high down there, higher than you'd think. At least ten feet. He'd have needed a ladder to reach the joist to fasten the wire around it. Yet I didn't see any such thing down there. Based on the on-site evidence, I have to assume murder."

Mia watched as the team went quiet, as if digesting what Prine had said. After maybe a half-minute, Delgado pointed out, "We need to call for backup. There's been a death on the scene."

"That *is* protocol," Brubaker agreed with a nod.

"But doing that ends this operation!" Jessup said emphatically.

"Yes, it does," Brubaker said.

"Good," Mia blurted. "This whole thing was a terrible idea from the start."

Jessup glared daggers at her. "Tell that to Arias' scores of victims!"

"Getting yourself killed won't help them," Mia pointed out.

Jessup threw her hands up in frustration, her flashlight beam bouncing over the dusty pews. She was careful, Mia noted, to keep its beam away from any of the stained-glass windows. Even now, angry and probably more scared than she wanted to admit, Karen Jessup remained too professional to risk the operation by doing anything that might be visible from outside.

Is it fully dark yet? If not, then it has to be close.

Why the hell am I still here?

"Listen," she said to Brubaker. "I did what you wanted. Can you please—"

But Brubaker cut her off. "Prine, how do you see it?"

"We should stay," Prine said without hesitation.

"Really. And your reasons?"

"Arias is coming here, AD. It's the first time he's risked a trip into the U.S. in more than a decade. If we report Roja's death to the Camden P.D., he'll likely get wind of it in minutes and pull out. Then he'll be out of reach again, maybe for good. I realize I'm suggesting a break in protocol…but, in this case, I think the reward justifies the risk."

"I agree," Jessup added.

"Delgado?" Brubaker asked.

The young man squirmed. His eyes flicked over to the altar where he'd been kneeling only minutes ago with a monster's hands clamped around his head. Mia could sense his conflict. He'd already nearly been killed once since stepping into this church. Truth be told, he kind of reminded her of Derrick, Brubaker's son. They'd both been young, smart, and enthusiastic— until Barton had gotten ahold of them. At least Delgado had survived his encounter.

So far.

Finally, Delgado said, "I think we should stay. But I think we need to be smart about it. I've got some spare cameras. I'll set one up in the choir loft that looks down on the nave, full night vision. If something moves down here, we'll know it."

"Agreed," Jessup said. "Then it's settled."

"No," Mia told her, told them all.

They looked at her.

"Dr. Lakatos?" Brubaker asked.

"You talked me into coming down here to look at Barton's gravestone. Well, I did that. I never intended to set foot inside this fucking place, and I have absolutely no intention of staying."

"Fair enough," Brubaker replied without hesitation or rancor. Then she reached into her jacket pocket and pulled out a set of keys. These she handed to Mia. "Take my car and go home. I'll get a ride back with one of my team. But I have to stay here. Thank you for your time and effort."

Mia stared at the keys in her hand. When she looked up again, she found them all regarding her. Jessup's expression was easy to read: unfriendly, maybe even contemptuous. But the rest were a little more opaque. "I know I've said this before," she told them all. "And I know it sounds melodramatic, but it's the truth. If you stay here, you're all going to die."

For a moment, there was no response, not even from Jessup.

Finally, Brubaker replied, "Whatever risks we're taking are to serve our duty and the public trust."

It sounded like something off an FBI recruitment brochure, and Mia nearly said so. But then, instead, she asked, "Renee, what's the battery level on your cell phone?"

Brubaker checked. "It's down to sixty percent," she admitted. "And I had it on full charge in the car."

"Mine's down to twenty percent," Jessup said sourly.

"That's because you spent time in the church before we arrived," Mia told her.

"So what? Equipment problems happen."

"That's how it goes," Mia told them. "By now, I'll bet most if not all of those wireless cameras Agent Delgado set up are drained dry."

"I have a recharging station upstairs," Delgado said. "We can fast-charge the phones. I also have spare batteries for the cameras."

"And what's powering the recharging station?" Mia asked.

Delgado looked from her to Brubaker and back again. "A bank of four lithium-ion batteries, setup in series. They're also running the tech I've got pointed at the bowling alley."

"Any way you can check on *their* power levels?"

"This is ridiculous!" Jessup exclaimed. "Fine, Lakatos. We hear you. The ghosts are sucking at our power!"

"It'll get worse."

"Do we have backup batteries?" Brubaker asked.

Delgado nodded. "Four of them. They're in the trunk of my car, parked across the alley."

"Good. But Dr. Lakatos has a point. Given our equipment failings, whatever the cause, what *are* the battery levels on the power station you've set up in the choir loft?"

Delgado admitted, "With my watch dead, we'll have to go upstairs and check."

"Then let's do that," Brubaker said. "Mia, you've done your part and we've heard your warnings. Please believe me when I say that I'm taking them seriously. But we have a job to do."

Again, Mia looked down at the keys in her hand. She could be gone from here in the next two minutes, driving away from Bleak Street just as quickly as Brubaker's Taurus could safely take her, leaving behind—what?

Barton would claim these people. She knew that as surely as she knew the sun would rise. He'd take them and the next time some unsuspecting skeptic came in here, they'd encounter Brubaker, Prine, Delgado, and Jessup, all with slack mouths and coins on their eyes, the newest members of St. Damien's congregation.

Fuck. She thought. *Fuck. Fuck. Fuck.*

I can't go.

Sure, I can. Renee said it herself. I've delivered my warning. I've done what was asked of me. What happens now won't be my fault.

Of course, wasn't that—or something close to it—what she'd told herself after the last time, when she'd been the only one to leave this church alive.

And it was this woman's son who got me out!

Is he here too, somewhere, with coins on his eyes?

She felt helpless and almost sick with terror as the seconds ticked by and she looked into the faces around her. All of them were professionals, dedicated law enforcement agents. This wasn't a TV show or a publicity grab. This was a serious, even vital operation conceived and executed to take advantage of an opportunity and finally capture a human monster. It was a kind of hunt, one with a dangerous quarry. But how could they have known their chosen hunting ground would have a monster of its own?

Because I told them. I told them and told them and told them.

But would that help her sleep any better when she heard they'd all died here?

Mia trembled. Tears filled her eyes. She felt like vomiting.

Nevertheless, she heard herself mutter, "I'll…I'll stay."

CHAPTER 13
Camden, New Jersey—2022

MIA REMEMBERED THE CHOIR LOFT from her first visit to St. Damien's—though, like the graveyard, the horrors of that day hadn't given her the time to visit it.

It hung over the nave—one might even say "loomed"—throwing its shadow over the rear quarter of the pews. It spanned the full width of the church, though the only way to reach it was via a narrow staircase accessible through an equally narrow door at the back of the nave.

The loft turned out to be a fairly large space, made all the larger by the fact that its own pews—where once boys and girls had sat during Sunday services, waiting for their cue to sing of Christ's glory—had been moved and stacked against the far wall. And, judging from the freshly made tracks on the dusty floor, Mia guessed that Jessup, Delgado, and Prine had done the moving.

One look around made it easy to see why.

The loft was heavy with equipment, especially up near the big stained-glass window, the one that overlooked the church's frontage and the street beyond. From the outside, this was an impressive, ornate mixture of molded iron and colored glass. From the inside, it was all that—but also *huge*. It filled nearly the entirety of the loft's back wall, twenty feet from the open railing that stood opposite and that overlooked the nave. It was from here that Officer William Shaker had been thrown, head-first, to his death.

Mia had to drag her eyes away from the spot.

The moment they all arrived up here, Delgado made a beeline for his equipment. He ran his hands across the various gadgets, some of them free-standing, and others lined up on a six-foot folding table that stood in almost the exact center of the loft. Atop that table were a laptop, what looked like a charging station of some kind, and several other electronic devices, the nature of which Mia couldn't even guess at. As she watched, Delgado deposited his dead phone into one of the slots in the charging station, motioning for the others to do the same. Then he went around the table to the window, where even more exotic gadgetry waited.

"What the holy hell!" he suddenly exclaimed, making Mia jump.

"What is it?" Prine asked, coming forward.

Delgado looked up at him from beside a gadget mounted on a tripod that had four small square sails, each one pressed right up against the big window. The young agent's face seemed, for a moment, as it had downstairs right after the attack. Scared. Uncomprehending.

"What's happened?" Brubaker demanded.

Both she and Prine looked where Delgado was pointing. Mia saw Prine's eyebrows shoot up. "That's…not possible," he said.

"What's not possible?" demanded Jessup. She hurried over there, leaving Mia the only one still standing in the low archway between the stairwell and the choir loft. As they did, Mia felt a chill, ice-cold, roll down her back. This was accompanied by a feeling of *proximity*, of someone or something standing right over her shoulder, the sensation so strong that she gasped and whirled around.

The landing and the stairwell were empty.

For now, she thought, and her stomach clenched.

Behind her, she heard Delgado say defensively, "The glass isn't cut!"

"So, cut it," Jessup said.

"We did," Prine told her. "Archie and I cut the holes at least an hour ago while you were sweeping the parsonage."

"Obviously, you *didn't!*" Jessup shot back.

Mia turned around again in time to see Prine walk over to the long table, select a rectangle of colored glass from atop a short pile of them, and hold it up for the others to see. Brubaker came forward and took it from him. She examined it, then went back to the window and placed it beside a particular leaded frame.

"There has to be an explanation," Jessup muttered, staring at it with her. Even from where she stood, Mia could tell that the rectangular shard and the section of window, behind which one of the tall gadget's four wings was positioned, were a perfect match.

"There is," she heard herself say.

They all looked at her. She was starting to really hate it when they did that.

"Well, don't keep us in suspense," Jessup said.

"The church…" Mia began. She knew full well how this would go over with the team in general, and Agent Karen Jessup in particular. But they needed to know. So, she coughed and tried again. "The church *heals* itself."

Not surprisingly, Jessup groaned. Frankly, at this point, Mia would have been disappointed if she hadn't. The two men just kept staring at her. But Brubaker said, "Can you explain that, Dr. Lakatos?"

Mia shrugged. "Look around. St. Damien's has thirteen stained-glass windows, including that big one there. In the fifty years since it was abandoned, not one pane in any of them has been broken. There's no graffiti on the outside walls, no sign of vandalism of any kind, anywhere. Why do you think that is?"

"Well, it's sure as shit *not* because the building itself is fucking *healing*!" Jessup exclaimed, almost shouting.

"Barton's *will* heals it," Mia explained, knowing how it sounded. Even the most die-hard paranormal investigator balked at such an idea. In all her studies and travels, she had only ever encountered one other place that exhibited that bizarre capability. That had been a castle high in the Carpathian Mountains, another place she'd sworn never to return to. "I don't know if it's illusionary or if he's somehow actually able to repair matter. Either way, he's determined to keep his precious church as pristine as possible."

"Just one more crazy on top of another," Jessup declared.

"Then *you* explain it, Karen," Brubaker suggested. Then she asked Mia, "What can we do about it?"

"Cut new holes and then watch them. It's possible that Barton can't fix them while they're being observed. That fits with the 'illusion' theory. But I can't promise a damned thing."

Delgado blew out a long shuddering sigh. "Okay," he said. "Okay." Then he picked up a small device. "Help me out, will you Matt?"

Prine nodded and carefully moved the winged gadget on its tripod out of the way so Delgado could get to work. The device he'd picked up turned out to be an electric glasscutter of some kind. Mia was half-sure its battery would be dead, just like the phones. But it seemed to work well enough, slicing first one rectangular hole and then another in the stained glass.

Meanwhile, Jessup examined the rest of the equipment with a critical eye. Then she checked her watch. "It's fully dark now. That means we've got about three hours before the summit starts. We need to be completely ready by then."

"We will be," Brubaker promised. "Agent Prine, what's the status of the batteries in our charging station?"

Prine looked. "Forty percent. They were fully charged when we arrived, with enough juice to last days."

Brubaker nodded, as if she'd expected this. "When they get below twenty, I want someone to go out to Archie's car and get two of the four spare batteries. We need to conserve power, but we *cannot* risk running out of it. So, keep an eye on that gauge. Dr. Lakatos, any idea how quickly the batteries will drain?"

Mia shook her head. "It depends."

"On what?" Jessup asked impatiently.

"On whether we're alone up here."

That stopped them all in their tracks. Mia watched as the four of them scanned the choir loft. With the gadgets running there was more light up here than there'd been in the nave. But that didn't mean the shadows weren't deep, plenty deep. Jessup and Brubaker both shined their flashlights into each nook and cranny. After about twenty seconds of this, Jessup's light winked out.

"Shit!" she exclaimed.

"Thirty eight percent," Prine said.

"*Shit!*" Jessup yelled.

"Keep your voice down, Karen," Brubaker admonished. "Stick any drained flashlights in the charging station." She looked at Mia. "Is he here?"

"Probably."

"Watching us?"

"I think so." How easily the words passed her lips, despite the way they turned her insides to jelly.

"If that's true," Jessup said. "Why aren't we surrounded by these girls with coins for eyes?"

"He's taking his time," Mia replied, swallowing. She wished she had some water.

"Playing with us?" Prine asked.

"Something like that."

"Bullshit," Jessup said—though Mia noticed that, for the first time, there seemed less weight behind the woman's denial. Between Delgado's attack, the "regrown" glass, and the draining batteries, even her wall of skepticism had begun to crack.

Just wait, Mia thought dismally.

"Done!" Delgado announced. Then, as he and Prine moved the winged gadget back into place in front of the four freshly cut—or re-cut—holes, he added, "One of us will need to stay up here at all times. Right, Doc?"

Mia nodded.

"What about the motion sensors at the exits?" Prine asked. "What's *their* power level?"

"Crap! I forgot!" Delgado said with a groan. He ran around the table and tapped a few keys on the laptop. This, Mia noticed, was plugged directly into the charging station. If it hadn't been, it too would likely be dead by now.

Drained, she corrected herself. *Don't use the word 'dead.' Not here.*

"They're working," Delgado reported. All three of them. We're good. Levels at a little over fifty percent."

"Can we set up another one overlooking the nave," Brubaker asked.

He nodded. Then he started fishing through a large box beside the laptop. After a few moments, he came up with a fist-sized camera. He took this to the railing, the same railing over which Shaker had done his fatal swan dive and went to work.

"Can I get some water?" Mia asked.

"Yes," Brubaker said. "Good idea. We all should stay hydrated. Prine?"

"It's over there in the corner, ma'am." Prine pointed.

Mia went that way. After a moment, she heard someone follow her, but it wasn't until she found the satchel filled with small bottles of water that she realized it was Karen Jessup.

For a moment, the two women just looked at each other. Then Jessup offered a razor-thin smile and said, "Give me a few and I'll hand them out."

Wordlessly, Mia did so, pulling three of the small bottles from the satchel and putting them into Jessup's waiting hands. With a nod, the DEA agent straightened and turned away, then seemed to rethink it and turned back. "So," she said, that slash of a smile still on her face. "If I were to draw my gun and put a hole in the wall right above your head, the ghosts would just fix it. Is that what you're saying?"

Mia wasn't sure if this was an attempt to intimidate or simply more condescension. Either way, she replied, "More or less."

"How do you know?"

Mia took a couple of water bottles for herself and stood upright, facing Jessup head on. "Because, unlike you, I've been here before," Mia replied evenly. "I've seen evidence of it."

"Eyewitness testimony is notoriously unreliable."

Mia didn't reply.

"You really think Rojas' ghost attacked Delgado?"

"Yes," Mia said. "And so do you."

To her supreme satisfaction, the DEA agent seemed taken aback. "What makes you say that?"

"The fact that you decided to continue with this operation of yours. You don't believe, in your heart of hearts, that Delgado was grabbed by a living man. If you did, if Prine and I are both full of shit about the guy disappearing when I used my UV light on him, then it stands to reason this 'living man' took off and is currently hiding somewhere in the church. But you're not looking for him, are you…this hiding attacker? No, instead you're up here giving me a hard time while pretending to be thirsty."

Jessup's face lost all expression—well, except for the glare. "Do you believe in God, Lakatos?"

The question surprised Mia, who'd just been patting herself on the back for her little bit of deductive reasoning that had so deflated Jessup's attitude. "Why?" she asked, suddenly wary.

"Curious."

"My belief system isn't germane."

"You're a Wiccan. Isn't that what you said?"

"Yes."

"So…do Wiccans believe in God?"

Mia glanced past the woman and saw Brubaker standing by the long table, silently watching them. For some reason, the sight fueled her courage, letting her lock eyes with Jessup again and reply, "If you're thinking of joining, then I'm happy to explain the various Wiccan beliefs. But if this is just another round of 'Mock the Ghost Lady,' I think I'd prefer it if you fucked off. So? Which is it?"

Jessup's face reddened. Then she took a long, measured breath, and said, "There *is* no God, Lakatos. No Heaven. No afterlife. I don't know what the hell happened downstairs, but that's what I believe and you're not going to change my mind."

She stalked off without another word.

Mia uttered a long, slow sigh.

Then, still standing by the satchel in the corner, she screwed the cap off one of the water bottles and drank deeply. The water was room temperature, but it eased her parched throat and, to a much lesser extent, her ragged nerves.

"Can I have one?" Brubaker asked, coming up to stand beside her.

Mia nodded and handed it over. There were plenty more in the satchel.

The assistant director thanked her and drank. "I've asked Delgado to run Cooley's epitaph through his cypher system."

"Cypher system?" Mia asked.

"It's kind of a code breaker. Very hi-tech AI. Don't ask me how it works. I don't have a clue. But I've seen it in action before and it's pretty good. Maybe it'll see something in the message that we don't."

Mia drank some water herself, draining almost half the bottle in the process. The brief confrontation with Jessup had left her mouth Sahara dry. With a sigh, she replied, "I hope so."

"I heard some of what Karen said," Brubaker remarked.

Mia shrugged. Then in a low voice, barely a whisper, she asked, "How did you two become friends?"

"We seem different, do we?"

"Very."

Brubaker's smile was rueful. "We...share a history, but not a professional one. Karen and I met about four years ago...in a support group."

"Support group?"

"Not my story to tell," Brubaker said. "But I'm guessing you'll figure it out eventually. There aren't any flies on you, if you don't mind my saying so."

"I'll take a compliment any day. Thanks."

For a few moments, neither of them said anything. Then, in a voice even quieter than the one Mia had used, Brubaker asked, "Sorry you stayed?"

Mia's reply was both immediate and honest. "Every second."

"You can still go, take my car."

Mia hesitated, tempted. Then she shook her head.

"Why not?" Brubaker asked.

"I couldn't handle the guilt."

"That's actually pretty brave of you."

"I'm not brave," Mia said. "I never have been."

"I watched you run into this church the instant you heard that Delgado might be in danger. Brave isn't a thing you are, Mia. It's a thing you *do*. Besides, we're in more danger from Arias than from any ghost."

"I know you think that, but it isn't true."

Brubaker said, "You don't know Andres Arias."

"And you don't know Jonah Ray Barton," Mia replied. "Here's the thing none of you are getting, not even Delgado...or he'd have been out of here like a shot, mission or no mission. There's more at stake here than your lives. I get that this Arias is a bad dude. Hell, I'm sure he's a full-blown psychopath. But all he can do is kill you. If Barton gets you, you don't just die. You end up one of his 'Forever Congregation.' You end up becoming his eyes, his ears, his hands. You end up trapped here, in St. Damned, with coins on your eyes."

As Brubaker listened, Mia saw the blood drain from her face. Too late, she realized what she'd just done.

"Is Derrick here, Mia?" the mother of a dead son asked in a small voice.

Mia struggled with how to respond. "We haven't seen him, so maybe not."

"Is that what you really think?"

Mia swallowed. Then, reluctantly, she shook her head.

Brubaker put a hand to her mouth. Tears filled her eyes. She let go with a sob, just one, but loud enough for the other three people in the loft to look their way. Prine and Delgado appeared concerned. Jessup scowled.

"I'm sorry," Mia whispered.

Renee nodded. Then, lowering her hand and looking plaintively at Mia, she asked, "Have you ever lost someone?"

"My father, when I was a teenager."

Brubaker processed this news. Then she said, "My parents are both still alive. I never knew my grandparents. Before Derrick, I'd never lost anyone. Does it ever…go away?"

"It gets better," Mia replied as honestly as she could. "But no. It doesn't go away."

"Are you close to your mother?"

It had been an innocent enough question, but it made Mia's insides clench. "Not really. She's a devout Christian and my father and I…weren't. I had the Bible drilled into me from the age of four. The two of them fought about it, and about *me*, all through my childhood. After my dad died, my mom and I fell out for years. We've since made something akin to peace. But it's never been good between us."

"I'm sorry to hear that," Brubaker said.

"Was it good between you and Derrick?"

Brubaker's small, sad smile was almost heartbreaking to look at. "What's the old saying? My son, my moon, my stars?" Then, after a thoughtful pause, she asked, "Will you tell me how it happened? I mean…I know the cause of death and I've read your statement. But most of that was officially discounted by the Camden police."

"Yes," Mia whispered.

"You'll find me much more open to your account of events than they were."

"I know. I'm just not sure I have it in me to tell it."

"Please, Mia. I think I *need* it."

"What's going on?" Jessup demanded. She marched toward them, Prine and Delgado in her wake.

Brubaker turned and looked past her. "Archie, are we all ready?"

Delgado nodded. "Provided we can keep the batteries from uber-draining and the window from…fixing itself again, then yes. All we have to do now is wait."

"Good," the assistant director said. "Because Dr. Lakatos is going to share with us her experiences during her last visit to this site. Isn't that right, Mia?"

Mia looked at her, looked at all of them. Reliving that awful night, one which had poisoned her life ever since, was the absolute last thing she wanted. But maybe, just maybe, the telling would somehow help these people. It might even convince them to leave this place while they still could—*if* they still could.

"Brave isn't a thing you are. It's a thing you do."

"Okay," she said finally. "I'll tell you."

CHAPTER 14
Camden, New Jersey—2017

"DR. LAKATOS! I'M STEVIE DOYLE. I'm the producer and director of *Ghost Finders*. This is Lyle Back and Derrick Porter. Lyle is our cameraman and Derrick does sound. And *here's* the star of our little show, Kimberly Allesbrook!"

Mia shook hands all around. Stevie was a tall, lean man in his early thirties, just a few years older than Mia, herself. His ready smile looked so practiced that she wondered if he might have taken classes in director school. Then she chided herself; she'd been getting *so* cynical lately.

Lyle was a bear of a man in his fifties. Standing maybe five-foot-six, he had a thick neck and an ample gut. His bearing and manner were that of a TV veteran who'd seen it all and done it all and, to him, *Ghost Finders* was nothing more profound than a paycheck. In contrast, Derrick looked like he was barely out of college, lanky, long-haired, fresh-faced and clearly excited to be here.

Mia liked him immediately.

Kimberly, of course, she'd seen on the small screen. Truth be told, Mia rarely watched *The Ghost Finders*, though she did find the show somewhat better than others of its ilk. It didn't fake anything, at least not that anyone had so far been able to prove. It used scientific methods, not gimmicks, and let each site they investigated be the star of the episode, rather than trying to manufacture drama.

Of course, the show's ratings owed more than a little to its host, Kimberly Allesbrook, a statuesque blonde with perfect cheekbones and an hourglass shape.

That shape was currently wrapped up in jeans and a sweater in deference to the cold.

It was a bitter December day in Camden, and a biting, late afternoon wind sluiced off the Delaware River, cutting through Mia's coat almost as if it weren't there. She hugged herself for warmth, annoyed at how the others didn't seem to feel it.

"Welcome to St. Damned, Dr. Lakatos," Kimberly said with a musical, vaguely southern accent. "We're excited to have you aboard!"

"I'm excited to be here," Mia replied by rote. "And please call me Mia."

"Then I'm Kim," the young woman replied with a smile that seemed to have its own wattage. "Have you ever visited this site before?"

Mia shook her head. She'd heard of St. Damien's of course—everyone in the paranormal research community had. But, despite living only two hours north, in New York City, until now neither her schedule nor her inclination had brought her here. *The Ghost Finders* marked her first foray into the world of television, a move that her agent assured her would validate her professional credentials and not sully them.

Standing here, however, looking at the cheesy, tricked out van this bunch had arrived in, Mia wasn't so sure.

Stevie said, "Kim, before going inside, I want to do a couple of quick setup shots out here with you and Dr. Lakatos—"

"Call me Mia. That goes for everyone."

Stevie grinned. "Mia…standing in front of the church. But let's start with a street intro and then swing it around."

"You got it, boss!" Kim declared, offering him a mascara-ed wink as she glided—that really was the only word Mia could conjure to describe the way she moved—toward the cracked sidewalk at the edge of the street.

Bleak Street, Mia thought. *Given the history of this place, that's a little on-the-nose, isn't it?*

At the edge of the gravelly, weed-strewn verge, Kim twirled around like a runway model. The empty street was at her back, a boarded-up bowling alley standing silent vigil across the way, as she smiled and waved the wireless microphone. "Ready when you are, S.D." It took Mia a moment to realize that 'S.D.' were Stevie's initials.

"Lyle, Derrick, can we set up the shot. I don't want to lose the daylight."

"Yep," Lyle said, the word barely more than a grunt.

Derrick, on the other hand, beamed and sprang into action. "You got it, boss!"

Mia watched as the team did what they'd been doing for nearly three full seasons now, conducting their business in a coordinated rhythm that seemed to require few words. Lyle set up a folding opaque screen to block the light from the setting sun, while Derrick fitted Kim with an all but invisible clip-on mike. Then he did the same to Mia, affixing it to the collar of her blouse.

Kim's handheld microphone, Derrick explained to Mia in a conspiratorial whisper, was just a prop. She liked the "drama" of speaking into it.

For some reason, Mia found that funny.

Derrick stepped well out of the shot, fiddling with a small contraption that hung over his shoulder. A set of expensive-looking headphones dangled from this black box, which the young man fitted over his ears. "Give me a sound check, Kim?"

"'Her purse was full of useless trash,'" the young woman said conversationally, which Mia thought sounded better than "'Testing, One, Two, Three.'"

"Good," Derrick declared, offering Stevie a thumbs up. "Now you, Mia."

"Um…" she said, suddenly tongue-tied. "Testing, One, Two, Three?"

Derrick's half-hidden smile turned her cheeks red. Nevertheless, the young man offered another thumbs up. "Sound's ready!" he announced.

At the same time, Lyle moved up the walkway, planted a large professional camera on his broad shoulder, fitted the eyepiece over one half of his face and flipped several switches, apparently going by practiced touch. "We're recording," he reported.

"Places," Stevie said. No one moved, which Mia supposed meant they were already placed where they were meant to be. "Silence. Action in three, two, *one*." He pointed at Kim.

"I'm Kimberly Allesbrook," the blonde woman said in a voice so well modulated it might have been on the evening news. "I'm standing outside the infamous St. Damien's Lutheran Church in Camden, New Jersey. This is our last show of the third season, and it seems only proper that we should close the great year we've had with what some have called the paranormal community's white whale."

Mia, who couldn't recall ever hearing anyone in the community use that heavy-handed Moby Dick aphorism in connection with this or any other site, raised her eyebrows but made no other comment. These people were better than most in their field, but a reality show was still a reality show. So, she supposed she could forgive a little hyperbole.

"Getting here took time and wasn't easy," Kim continued. "The City of Camden is notoriously tight-lipped about this place, and the abandoned street over which it holds sway. The last resident of Bleak Street, which is behind me, left their home in 1977. Since then, all efforts to sell any of the properties have failed and, ultimately, the city bought the entire block up in 1985. Since then, no one has lived here…and nobody has set foot inside this church for forty-five years…no one alive, at least."

"Cut!" Stevie called. "Great!"

"You want a second take?" Kim asked. "I felt like I was a little flat."

"Nope. We don't have the time and you were perfect as always. Let's swing it around."

When Mia had arrived here all of twenty minutes ago, she'd driven the Lexus that she'd bought last year with the advance from her upcoming book. *Ghost Finders* had offered to send a car to pick her up at her Manhattan address, but she'd politely declined. She'd disliked riding for long periods of time with strangers; it was always so hard to think of something to say. So instead, she'd let her onboard NAV system bring her here and had found the entire crew already waiting when she'd pulled up. Stevie had even gone so far as to motion for her to turn around and park partway up the block on the opposite side of the street. She now realized that this had been to keep her shiny silver sedan out of their "street intro."

And, as Lyle, Derrick, and Stevie all rotated themselves around so that the camera faced the church and Kim, smiling, motioned for Mia to join her, she realized something else as well.

Until this moment, she hadn't really *looked* at St. Damien's.

If asked, she couldn't have said why. The intervening minutes had, of course, been busy with introductions and gadgets and direction and motion. But that alone didn't explain why she'd never bothered to so much as glance up at the place that was the focus of this project, and the reason for her hefty paycheck.

No, she hadn't looked because, on some deeply subconscious level, she hadn't *wanted* to.

But now she did—and immediately understood why.

To all outward appearances, St. Damien's was a standard gothic revival neighborhood church. Its entire frontage was layered in gray stone, a common facade over an infrastructure that was almost certainly ordinary wooden framing. The roof was sharply pitched with jet-black shingles, and in the front south corner was a three-story belltower with a squared, decorative parapet at the top. Dominating its street presence, however, was an enormous, ornate, stained-glass window. This started just beside the double front doors and extended upward in a triangle, the tip of which didn't quite reach the eves.

Mia had visited many churches, both in the US and in Europe, and had seen countless stained-glass windows. Some were larger than this one. Some were smaller. Most were older than St. Damien's postwar cornerstone date. Overall, the leaded glass that adorned this neighborhood church was pedestrian.

But now, looking at it, it seemed to morph in her mind. Gone was the standard sharp angled, vaguely abstract depiction of a Christian afterlife. In its place were panes of ornate glass, Mia counted at least forty of them, that seemed to depict sinners in torment. Everything from beatings to flayings to dismemberments were brought to colorful life in those panels, some of the images so detailed and graphic that they made her blood run cold. No such window should adorn what had been originally a house of worship.

And it doesn't adorn this one.

It's just in my head.

And as she thought this, processing it while standing beside the tall, statuesque blonde who hosted this reality TV show, Mia felt St. Damien's look *back* at her.

Mia's father had grown up a showman—what the unwashed might call a gypsy—in his native Romania. He'd had a talent for Tarot and had been uncannily good at fortune telling, at least enough so that he'd been able to help his parents earn a living. But his mother, whom Mia had never met, had been something else altogether if her father's many stories were to be believed. Her name had also been Miriam, and she had been able to find lost things simply by holding the owner's hand. She could predict the gender and general health of a baby still in its mother's womb. And she could "know" someone simply by touching something that belonged to them.

Mia, herself, had inherited a little of that, a very little. She wasn't what anyone would call clairvoyant. But every once in a while, she found herself sensitive to specific vibrations that certain places seemed to transmit like radio waves.

This was like that—times ten.

Mia suddenly felt as though the breath were being squeezed from her lungs. She gasped and then staggered, wiping the smile off Kim's face and causing Stevie to run up and take her arm. Good thing, too, as she might have toppled right over otherwise, so badly was her head spinning.

"Dr. Lakatos? Mia?" Stevie said.

"What's the matter with her?" Kim asked, and Mia noticed on some vague level that she sounded different now, younger, that perhaps there was a girl and not a grown woman behind all that hair and makeup.

"I'm…sorry," Mia heard herself stammer, her voice sounding oddly far away. Her knees buckled again, and this time Derrick came up beside her as well, helping Stevie to keep her upright. She squeezed her eyes shut, blocking out the visage of the church but unable to do the same to the— *energy*—that place was putting out.

"What is it?" Kim asked. Then, more professionally: "Can you tell us what's happening, Dr. Lakatos?"

Mia replied, almost without thinking, "Malice. Hunger. A greedy, bottomless *need.*"

"And you're getting that from St. Damien's?" the woman pressed. "You're getting all that right now?"

"Yes!" Mia exclaimed, nearly screamed.

Then she remembered her father, and one of his stories. Mia's grandmother, who had never gotten past the sixth grade and had never set foot outside her small Romanian village, had nevertheless earned local renown for two things. The first had been her wisdom and knowledge, all either inherited or self-taught, which brought troubled persons to her door from miles around.

The second had been her power.

Miriam Lakatos the Elder had spent her life seeing things that others couldn't, knowing things she'd shouldn't have, and understanding things that, Mia's father once assured his daughter, would have turned any American scientist or theologist's hair white overnight.

And one of the things she'd understood had been how to recognize— and fight—the Evil Eye.

In paranormal circles, there continued to be debate as to what, exactly, the "Evil Eye" was. In the Bible, the Book of Proverbs described a person with an "evil eye" as selfish, greedy, and to be avoided. In Greek and Roman cultures, it was a kind of bad luck curse that befell boastful or prideful people. But to most of Mia's colleagues, and Mia herself when she thought about it at all, "Evil Eye" was simply a colloquial term for negative energy. Some people and some places exuded it, almost always as a product of past trauma or pain.

But *this* was different.

This Evil Eye felt—purposeful, even predatory.

Intelligent.

Mia's father had once shown her a simple gesture, something he'd picked up from his storied mother, a means to ward off the Evil Eye. Even as a child, Mia had found it silly, and had even giggled when he'd first demonstrated the charm, only to have him gently rebuke her.

"This is serious, peach. It's real, and you might need it someday."

Now, with Derrick on one side of her and Stevie on the other, and with Kim looking worriedly on and Lyle presumably filming the whole thing, Mia raised her left hand, spread her index and middle fingers, and placed each on either side of her nose with their tips just below her eyes.

"Give me room," she said, not unkindly, to the men who supported her.

After a moment's confusion, the two stepped back. As they did, Mia noticed that Stevie's eyes were shining with something that looked a bit more like excitement than worry.

Good TV, she thought bitterly.

Then she faced the church again, her fingers pressing almost painfully into her cheekbones, and projected her will. Mia didn't really expect it to work. In the past, those very few times she'd felt the need to use it, the effect had been subtle—likely more about the focus that the facial pressure afforded her than any paranormal aspect.

But, to her surprise, the Evil Eye that was blasting her from St. Damien's receded almost immediately, pulling back like the undertow of a departing wave.

Relieved, though a bit confused and perhaps a little suspicious, Mia blew out a long sigh and straightened up.

The four of them stared at her, all but Lyle, who still held his camera on his shoulder. Mia said weakly, "Sorry about that."

"What happened, Dr. Lakatos?" Kim asked. She held up the fake microphone.

Mia swallowed, unsure of how much she should, or even could, explain. Finally, running a trembling hand over her forehead, sweaty despite the cold, she said, "There's an…energy here. It…it took me a little by surprise."

"A little?" Derrick exclaimed. "Doc, you almost fainted!"

"Derrick," Stevie chided. "Get out of the shot!"

The soundman blinked. Then he visibly gulped and retreated. Mia watched him, still feeling shaken by what she'd just experienced. A moment later, Stevie stepped back as well, holding his hands up at Mia as if willing her to remain standing. Then, he pointed at Kim and declared, "Go!"

Kim turned to Mia and asked again, "What happened, Dr. Lakatos?"

Mia struggled to compose herself. A part of her—a *big* part—wanted to head straight back to her car and drive away. In ten years of paranormal investigation, she had never felt anything like what just came off that church, and it had shaken her to her core. Except, damn it, she had a book coming out and she needed this, needed the attention it would draw. Stevie and his crew might seem callous, using her "episode" to help feed the show's drama. But she understood it. Any self-promoting writer would.

"I…" she began. Then she sighed long and slow, as if pushing something besides air out of herself. "There's an energy here," she said again, a little surprised by how steady her voice sounded. "Something dark and very hungry. It took me by surprise. Sorry."

"No apology necessary," Kim said. "Do you think you're capable of continuing with the investigation?"

That was the million-dollar question, wasn't it? And Mia knew precisely what Stevie and Kim wanted her to say.

So, swallowing a huge mouthful of unease, Mia gave it to them. "I'm not going to tell you there isn't some risk here," she said into Kim's fake microphone. "But I'm prepared to see it through."

"Good for you!" Kim declared, smiling like a pageant winner. "Good for all of us!"

CHAPTER 15
Camden, New Jersey—2017

AS *THE GHOST FINDERS* TEAM, heavy equipment in hand, mounted the short stoop and opened the church's front door, Mia was surprised to find it unlocked. For a moment, she supposed Stevie must have already unlocked it with a key provided by the city. This was certainly possible, since he and his crew had arrived here at least a couple of minutes before Mia had.

But Stevie noticed her looking quizzically at him and, seeming to read her mind, said with a smile that didn't quite reach his eyes, "The door was unlocked. Apparently, it's *always* unlocked."

"You'd think the city would keep it locked tight," Kim remarked. "You know…vandals."

"Yeah," Lyle said. "It ain't a great neighborhood."

"It's not a neighborhood at all," Derrick pointed out. "The whole block's deserted."

"It has been for going on fifty years," Stevie told him. "The city can't afford to demolish the whole street, and they can't *give* the land or the houses away. Believe you me, they've tried."

"What's the problem?" Kim asked him, looking doe-eyed.

"My contact in city hall says no one likes to talk about it. Bleak Street doesn't exist as far as any cop or elected official is concerned. Some nasty shit happened in the first years after Barton died and his murders got discovered, bad enough to convince everybody to abandon their homes and since then no one seems to come anywhere near here. That much I'm sure about. But as to exactly *what* went down, nobody's saying." He cracked the door open just an inch or two. Through the gap, Mia saw only darkness. "But my guy did tell me this much," he added. "Apparently, for a time they tried to keep this place locked up. At first, they used the regular key. But the door kept...unlocking itself by the next morning. So, they switched to installing padlocks on every exit. But every time they did, both the lock and hasp would be gone the next day."

"I call bullshit!" Lyle protested. "Look at the wood. Nobody's screwed anything into *that*...ever. Your man's lying to you."

"Maybe," Stevie replied. "But there's more to it. Apparently, over the years, there's been vandalism reported. Broken stained glass windows. All kinds of "street art" going up on the walls."

"So what?" Lyle said.

"Do you see any of that now?"

They all went silent.

Stevie's grin had a lot behind it. It reminded Mia of being a kid and telling ghost stories under a blanket with her friends. The same mischief, the same excitement, the same undercurrent of dread. "Thing is...nobody's cleaning it up," he said. "Why would they? It's an abandoned church on an abandoned street. You saw the graffiti that's covering some of the old rowhouses, right? But not here."

"What's your point?" Derrick asked. The young man looked nervous.

"My guy claims that the church fixes itself."

"Oh, come on!" Lyle exclaimed.

Stevie laughed, but it was an oddly hollow sound. "Then explain the wood. No drill holes, right? Except, I've *seen* pictures of this place with padlocks on it. Try it yourself. Why don't you scratch your initials in the door, Lyle? And we'll see if the letters are still there when we come back out."

Mia said, "I don't think that's a good idea."

"Neither do I," Kim agreed.

Lyle said nothing. But he didn't move either. He just looked at the door with an uneasy expression.

"Relax, guys!" Stevie said with a laugh that only sounded a little forced. "I told you this place was special. Come on. Let's head inside."

And with that, Stevie pushed the door all the way open, leading them into a small, dark vestibule with a narrow door on the right and, ahead, a broad archway that led into the church proper. What struck Mia first was the silence of the place. It seemed the "loudest" silence she'd ever heard, so oppressive as to be nearly claustrophobic.

"It's cold in here," Kim whispered. And it was. In fact, it felt like a freezer, so much so that their every breath clouded up more than it had out in the December air.

"Yeah, it is," Stevie remarked. "Derrick, I think we're going to need the space heater."

"Is there electricity?" Mia asked.

"No," Stevie replied. "But we have a generator in the back of the van and miles of extension cord." He nodded insistently at Derrick, who turned and went back out the still open door.

"What about lights?" Kim asked.

"I've got what we need," Lyle said, hefting a heavy-looking boxy case in one hand, while still toting his big camera in the other.

Stevie produced a flashlight and switched it on. "Let's scout out some locations."

He shone the light toward the archway.

Kim screamed and Mia jumped in surprise.

A girl stood there, just a couple of steps inside the nave. She was young, an obvious teenager, slight of build. Her long thin face was expressionless, her dark skin ashen in a way that made her look sickly—or worse.

And she wore a stained white wedding dress.

But the most disturbing things were her eyes, which had what looked like two silver dollars over them.

"Holy shit!" Lyle exclaimed, dropping his heavy case with one hand and barely managing to hold onto the camera with the other.

Stevie froze, the beam from his flashlight illuminating the girl, who didn't so much as twitch. "Lyle," he said, his voice the faintest of whispers. "Are you recording?"

"W—what?" Lyle stammered.

"Are you recording this?"

"But…it's just a girl…"

Stevie slowly turned his head to face the cameraman. His eyes were wide and almost bottomless. "I've got my flashlight on her, Lyle," he said, speaking slowly, softly, and deliberately. "Do you see a *shadow*?"

Lyle seemed to need a moment to process this. Then his eyes flicked from Stevie to the girl, who still hadn't moved. Her expression was one of slack-jawed somnambulism, but Mia could feel something else radiating off her. Awareness. Intent. Though perhaps not her *own* awareness and intent.

And a thought struck her.

This is a finger puppet.

But then another realization—both frightening and exhilarating—hammered home.

This is a fully formed apparition!

Mia had witnessed ghosts before, phantoms made of wisps of what was sometimes labeled "ectoplasm." But even the most complete of these had been spurious and intangible. This was utterly next level. This girl appeared solid, so solid that it was easier to believe she was a teenage squatter, camped out in this old church, perhaps high on heroin or fentanyl, which might explain her slack expression and her apparent disinterest in the cold.

And the coins? Well, Mia had never seen anything like that on anyone, living or dead, so she couldn't make a guess—though, of course, she grasped their significance.

But Stevie had been dead right, no pun intended. His flashlight beam was hitting this girl full in the face. Yet no shadow was thrown behind her. More than that, the circle of light appeared unbroken as it shone on the pews in the nave. It was as if the girl *and* what was behind her were somehow *both* being illuminated in equal measure.

Out of the corner of her eye, Mia saw the situation finally register on Lyle's face. With a small gasp, he lifted his camera, trying to bring it to his shoulder, trying to find the button that would start it recording this utterly unprecedented event.

But before he managed either of these things, the girl spoke. Except she didn't. Her mouth never moved. Instead, words seemed to float out of that open maw. *"The latter glory of this house shall be greater than the former, says the Lord of hosts. And in this place I will give peace, declares the Lord of hosts!"*

"Oh God!" Kim exclaimed. "Oh God! Oh God! Oh God!"

Then, as they all watched, transfixed, a hand—a man's hand—seemed to materialize out of the glare and shadow. It fell onto the girl's shoulder, at first like a father, but then more tightly, more cruelly, like a jailer.

The girl never moved.

At the same instant, a new voice spoke from behind them. "What's going on?"

They all whirled around reflexively. Derrick stood with his back to the open door, the deepening twilight behind him and a portable space heater in his hand.

"Holy shit!" Lyle exclaimed again.

When Mia looked back, the first of them to do so, both the girl and the hand were gone.

"Damn it!" Stevie cursed, seeing what she saw. "Lyle, tell me you got something… anything!"

"Sorry, boss. I didn't get the chance."

"What'd I miss?" Derrick asked anxiously.

Then Kim followed this up with, "Who…was that?"

Mia glanced around and was dismayed to find that they were all looking expectedly at her. "What?" she asked, perhaps a little defensively.

"Was that a ghost?" Kim demanded. She still held her fake microphone, but it was down by her hip, forgotten.

Mia almost dished out one of her signature lines. "That's not a word I like to use." And this was true. The term "ghost" tended to make laypeople, and even some professionals like herself, either cringe or laugh. It belittled the magnitude of the paranormal event it described, the continuing of some semblance of life beyond death, by conjuring images of figures dancing under sheets and moaning.

But inwardly she couldn't shake the image of what she'd just seen— not the girl, but the hand, which had at first touched and then grabbed her.

"That was a monster," she heard herself say.

"A monster?" Lyle asked apprehensively.

She looked at him. "A collector."

"What?" This came from Derrick.

Mia eyed the now empty archway leading into the nave. Except, of course, it *wasn't* empty, not really. This church had never been empty, far from it; she saw that now.

And it scared the living crap out of her.

"You've done the research," she said to them all. "You probably know more about Jonah Ray Barton than I do."

"We did some," Stevie said with conviction. "We always do. And you're right, Barton *was* a monster. He murdered something like thirty girls and buried their bodies in the church cellar, only to then dig them up from time to time to…do stuff with them. He was eventually confronted by the father of one of his victims, who chopped his head off with an axe. That's how his crimes were finally exposed. The cops were investigating his murder and, along the way, discovered the murders he, himself, had committed."

"It's a helluva story," Lyle remarked.

"One Camden is working very hard to forget," Stevie said. "We've been trying to get in here forever. It's the most haunted site in the state, maybe the country. But the locals keep it buttoned up tight and have for almost fifty years."

"I can…I can see why," Kim muttered. "Stevie, I don't think I want to stay here."

Lyle said, "Yeah, me neither. Boss, this is some next level shit!"

Mia, who'd been thinking those exact words while staring at the fully corporeal apparition in the archway, managed only a slight nod.

Derrick, still holding the space heater, said nothing.

"Listen, all of you," Stevie said. "I get it. What just happened shook me the fuck up, too. But we've all seen and heard stuff before. We've all been frightened by bumps in the night. And we know, from long experience, that…freaky as these investigations can sometimes get…they can't hurt us."

But, by halfway through this pep talk, both Kim and Lyle were already shaking their heads. "I'm telling you, boss," the older man replied. "This is different. *Way* different. I mean…this whole street is abandoned. There must be…like…fifty houses that no one has lived in for decades! What could cause a thing like that?"

"It's a poor town," Stevie told him. "Inner city stuff. You know how that can go."

"Uh uh, man," Lyle said. "I saw the background research. This street ain't empty because of poverty or crime…at least not *living* crime. It's empty because this church, this *place*, gets into your head. How many reports did we find of people having nightmares about Barton telling them to kill their kids and then themselves, all so they could join his 'congregation?' I'm telling you…next level, boss! We should pack it up and get out while we can."

"Dr. Lakatos," Stevie said, pleaded really. "Tell them there's nothing to worry about."

"Ordinarily, I would," she replied. "But…"

"But what?" Stevie demanded, sounding a little desperate.

Mia took a deep, steadying breath. Then she said, "I was in Germany two years ago. I was called in by a museum in Bavaria. It was the site of an eighteenth-century torture chamber, as macabre a tourist attraction as I've ever seen. There'd been stories of paranormal encounters for years. But on one particular morning, the night watchman was found dead inside an iron maiden."

"What's an iron maiden?" Kim asked.

"Isn't that a band?" Derrick added, and Mia couldn't tell if he was being facetious or not.

"It's a torture device. A large metal box with spikes lining the inside. When the victim is placed within it and the box is shut, the spikes are just long enough to pierce the flesh but still keep the occupant alive and screaming, sometimes for days. The truth is they weren't often used. But apparently this one was an exception."

"And somebody shoved this guy into it?" Lyle asked, sounding almost breathless.

Mia nodded.

"That's awful," Stevie admitted. "But couldn't it have just been straight up murder. Not everything is ghosts…right?"

"I saw the surveillance footage," Mia said, meeting his eyes. "It clearly showed the night watchmen doing his rounds when something unseen picked him up off his feet and carried him, kicking and screaming, to the iron maiden, shoved him inside and shut the door. The bottom line is that it's one of the few instances I've encountered where it seems a paranormal entity actually attacked and killed a human being. It's incredibly rare. But it does happen."

"Fuck me," Lyle muttered.

"How did it all turn out?" Kim asked Mia. "At the museum, I mean."

"The place was closed for six months. When it reopened, it was under new management, the iron maiden had been removed and destroyed, and… rumor has it…the entire building was blessed by a Catholic priest."

"And that did the trick?" Derrick asked.

Mia shrugged. "To the best of my knowledge, there have been no further paranormal incidents at the site, violent or otherwise."

"Maybe we should do that," Kim said, trying to couch it as a suggestion, though to Mia's ears it sounded more like an appeal. "We could split and come back with a priest."

For a moment, Mia thought Stevie was going to have some kind of fit. He stared at everyone, threw his hands in the air, and sort of spun in a frustrated circle. Then he tried to say something, failed, and threw his hands up again before turning his back and staring at the only other door in the vestibule. Mia didn't know where it went but, based on the exterior architecture, she guessed the belltower.

Finally, with a heavy sigh, the producer faced them all again and said, "Okay, I didn't want to tell you guys this, but I got the word from the network that they're thinking of shutting us down after this episode."

For a moment, no one spoke. Then Kim said, her voice sharp, "Excuse me?"

"Yeah, it's true. It's why I pushed so hard to get us here."

"We've had three seasons," Lyle said. "And all of a sudden they want to shut us down?"

"The numbers have been slipping lately," Stevie replied. "You know how it goes. They think we're getting stale. Our hook is our rep: that we never fake anything, that everything we show is one hundred percent real."

"Yeah," Derrick remarked. "It's why I took this job."

"And it's why I agreed to come on the show at all," Mia added, though she supposed she was probably speaking out of turn.

"It's something I've always been proud of," Stevie said. "But lately, the viewer feedback has been less supportive. They're complaining that, real or not, we rarely find *anything*. Oh sure, we've caught some solid EVPs. We even had that lamp moving in Pittsburgh. But compared to some of the other shows…the poltergeist activity, the groping of team members…we're starting to seem pretty tame."

"All that stuff's bullshit!" Lyle protested.

"Yeah," Stevie said. "I know."

"I don't believe this!" exclaimed Kim, waving her arms so vehemently that Mia had to duck to avoid being clunked by her fake microphone. "Isn't there something we can do?"

"Yeah," Stevie said again. "We can knock this last show out of the park. We can end the season with something that'll keep them talking for months. From what I understand, the final decision hasn't been made. So, we have this window, and *only* this window, if we want to save our asses." Then he looked hard at them, each in turn. "But that window closes if we lose our nerve and run away."

Mia watched them all, the cast and crew of *The Ghost Finders*, such as it was. A weathergirl-looking host, a twenty-something sound guy, a thirty-something producer/director, and a fifty-year-old veteran cameraman. As she'd noticed before, Lyle had the look of someone who considered this job just that: a job. But the others surely harbored ambitions, perhaps of using the show to launch them into bigger and better things. Mia could relate.

But this place is…wrong.

For years, she would wonder if she could have changed things by speaking up. That worry, that guilt, would haunt her dreams as surely as Jonah Ray Barton ever could. If she'd walked out right then and there, maybe—just maybe—they'd all have come with her, all still be alive. And, if they didn't, at least she could have looked in the mirror and perhaps absolved herself of at least some of the blame.

But she *didn't* speak up. She didn't say a fucking word.

"I'm in," Kim finally said.

"Me, too," Derrick added, stepping close to the blond woman, making Mia wonder for the first time if there might be something between these two—or if Derrick only wished there were.

"Lyle?" Stevie said, looking at the cameraman. "What do you say?"

Lyle made a sour face. He glanced at the archway, still empty, and then back at his young director. "Yeah," he muttered. "Okay."

Stevie grinned. "Solid!" he declared. "Let's make a show that'll knock 'em dead!"

And, while the other three all smiled and nodded in agreement, Mia thought it a very poor choice of words indeed.

CHAPTER 16
Camden, New Jersey—2017

THEY SET UP IN THE nave, which was even colder than the vestibule had been.

The space heater turned out to be pretty much for Kim, presumably to keep her teeth from chattering while she was on camera. The rest of them could only hug themselves and huddle together for warmth while Lyle recorded their host talking about St. Damien's history, its pastor, and the murders he was posthumously revealed to have committed.

Mia had to admit that Kimberly Allesbrook was good at what she did. She knew when to smile and when not to, when to add gravity to her words and when to laugh self-deprecatingly and with what Mia knew to be genuine unease.

For her own part, at least some of the Evil Eye had subsided, perhaps because all the activity kept her out of her own head and away from her psychic antenna. Kim interviewed her several times over the next hour. These little talks were always brief, maybe a minute or two at a time, exchanges that Stevie explained would be used as voice-over for archive photos and footage about Barton and the church's heyday. Mia came to welcome these little conversations, if only because they got her closer to the space heater.

Then, about ninety minutes into their efforts, Lyle started cursing.

"What's up?" Stevie asked without rancor. Apparently, his cameraman cussing like a truck driver was par for the course.

"My battery's at five percent!" Lyle groused. He crouched down with the camera beside his big black box and started fishing through it.

"Wasn't it fully charged when we parked the van?"

"Yeah. But you know how it goes."

All of them laughed, except Mia. Apparently, *The Ghost Finders* understood, as most paranormal investigators did, that paranormal activity often drained batteries.

"Sorry, kids," Lyle said. "Just give me a minute to—"

In the next instant, with the rest of them all watching, a figure seemed to melt out of the shadows directly behind him, leaning in from the pew nearest to where Lyle crouched. It took Mia a moment to register the man's sudden appearance, to really *see* his slick dark hair with its sharp widow's peak, and his angular face with its small eyes that seemed to glow red. Then it took her another moment to process his dark suit, his white clerical collar, and the straight razor in his hand.

"What the f—" Stevie began, but then the curse died in his throat.

The apparition seized Lyle from behind. The cameraman yelped in surprise as a pale, long-fingered hand clamped down on his hairline and pulled, drawing back Lyle's head and exposing his throat.

Then the razor came up.

Derrick started forward. Mia admired him for that. The rest of them seemed rooted to their respective spots about six feet from what was happening, what was *about* to happen. But the young soundman, at least, had the wherewithal to break that paralysis and rush to his colleague's aid.

When he was just a step away, however, two more figures rose up from the pews on the opposite side of the aisle, melting out of the shadows in the same way the man with the razor had. Two more coin-eyed brides, different from the one who had been in the vestibule, but equally ashen and slack-jawed.

For the first time, Mia noticed the open slits under their chins.

They were both murdered. Barton murdered them.

And now he owns them!

He owns all of them!

She would never know how she made that connection so quickly. But make it she did, and the horrible certainty of it felt like a vice around her chest, squeezing the breath from her. She tried to yell out a warning to Derrick but couldn't in the moment manage to push the words past her shock.

Instead, she watched in mute terror as the girls lashed out and seized the young man, each clutching one of his arms with what was obviously surprising strength. Derrick, who hadn't even noticed them until now, let out a frightened cry and tried to pull free. But they held him fast, closing in on either side of him and coiling their legs around him in a way that might have seemed sensual if not for their empty faces and torn throats.

All this happened in the space of a few seconds, long enough for the man in black to reach a free hand around the front of Lyle's terrified face, and run the razor across his neck, the movement quick and almost playful.

The cameraman's neck *erupted*.

Mia had only ever seen such things in movies, where the victim usually clutched at their ruined neck, stage blood squeezing between their fingers. The reality, it seemed, was much, *much* worse than that. A red fountain sprayed across the aisle, catching Derrick in the face even as he struggled wildly against the coin-eyed girls who held his arms. The moment Lyle Back's lifeblood hit him, he let out a piteous cry of revulsion. Then, as the spray moved past him and reached the two girls, both of them just seemed to wash away.

Their grip on him broken, Derrick lunged for the older man, catching him as he fell.

Lyle gurgled, his eyes fairly exploding from his skull. He clung to Derrick as a drowning man might to a life preserver. But Mia knew, as surely as he did, that there was nothing any of them could do.

The cameraman died seconds later, the light in his eyes going out.

"Little lamb," the man in black said from the pew in which he still stood. His back was ramrod straight and his voice carried a strange reverberation, as if he were speaking from inside a tunnel. The razor, red from its quick dip into Lyle's throat, remained in his pale grasp—and a satisfied smile lifted the corners of his mouth. His voice was deep and grotesquely musical. *"Little lamb. With me now. Forever."*

Then he vanished, not as the girls had, but slowly, more controlled and more deliberate.

Both Stevie and Kim started screaming. Or maybe they had been all along, and Mia simply hadn't noticed.

Well, she noticed now.

"We need to get out of here!" she exclaimed, finally finding her tongue. She knew she was in shock, and at the same time understood full well that she couldn't afford to be. The man and his coin-eyed girls were gone. But, at the same time, they *weren't*, and Mia knew it. She *knew* it!

And they had no time—*zero*—for screaming.

She grabbed Stevie by his shoulders and spun him around to face her. His eyes were wild, and spittle ran from one corner of his mouth. "Look at me!" she commanded. Then, when he didn't do so right away, she hauled off and slapped his face as hard as she could. She told herself she did this because, in the movies, it supposedly helped a panicked person to calm down. But on a deeper level, she grasped that her own fear and frustration had simply sucked every ounce of patience out of her.

"Look at me!" she demanded.

Stevie blinked. His screaming stopped, though his mouth hung open in a sick parody of the dead girls'. But then, finally, his eyes found Mia's.

"We have to get out of here!" she told him through clenched teeth. "Right now!"

For a moment, he swayed on his feet. His eyes rolled to the left, over to where Derrick was still holding Lyle's exsanguinated body. But then Mia cupped Stevie's face in her hands and pulled his attention back to her.

"Right fucking now!" she yelled.

That got him moving. He reached around and grabbed Kim by the wrist. Mia almost expected the young woman to resist, maybe even lash out violently in her panic. But she stared at Stevie as if he were Divine Salvation itself and wordlessly allowed him to pull her off the altar dais and up the nave toward the vestibule, running right past Derrick. Mia followed, the idea of the open door and the street beyond so enticing it nearly made her cry.

But then she reached Derrick a second later, and hesitated. "We...we have to go!" she told him, fighting back a sob.

He said nothing.

She crouched down and put a hand on his arm. Then she said, forcing herself to use a calmer voice, "Derrick, there's nothing you can do for him. We have to go."

He looked up at her and shook his head. "We can't just…leave him like this!"

Then, before Mia could muster a reply, no doubt some vacuous argument about Lyle not wanting Derrick to suffer his fate, the young man's eyes moved from her to something behind her. As Mia watched, his expression changed from grief to a kind of stunned horror.

She straightened and whirled around, expecting to see the man in black there, ready to do to her what he'd done to the cameraman.

What she saw instead was stranger and perhaps worse.

Lyle Back stood not three feet away.

The cameraman looked down at the two of them, an expression of sorrow on his face so profound that it nearly stole Mia's breath all over again. His thin hair was disheveled and his skin shockingly pale. A huge, ugly gash ran under his chin, nearly from ear to ear. The utter lack of blood made it almost look like a second mouth, a *smiling* mouth, and it struck Mia that the smile rather mirrored the one the man in black had worn after using his razor on Lyle's throat.

The thought made her stomach, already in knots, roll over.

Lyle's left hand was balled into a fist, not in anger but as if he were holding something. His right hand, however, remained empty and rose now to point up the aisle toward the vestibule.

The entity that had been Lyle Back said nothing. Nevertheless, Mia heard words in her head—desperate, urgent words.

"Get out!"

Derrick jumped to his feet so quickly that Mia, still clutching his forearm, was nearly knocked over. His eyes moved between the two Lyles, no doubt trying to make sense of what he was seeing.

"Get out!"

This time, when those two words were spoken and not-spoken, Derrick staggered back a step, making Mia wonder if, somehow, *he* could hear them, too.

Mia took Derrick's hand and started pulling him up the nave, away from the corpse and his ghost. And the young man followed, though it felt like she was dragging him through quicksand, every step a slow slog.

Then Lyle Back lowered his right hand, raised his left, and placed two silver coins over his eyes.

We're out of time.

"Now!" she screamed at Derrick, loud as she could, her voice ringing off the buttresses and stained-glass windows. "Now! Now!"

At last, that broke through Derrick's shock. With a cry of his own, he turned and, together, the two of them bolted up the aisle and into the vestibule—

—only to stop cold.

The door, which had been quite deliberately left open, was now closed.

Two men stood with their backs to the exit. Both had coins over their eyes. One was dressed in a Camden police uniform. He was mostly bald, his skin pasty, and his head was tilted at an impossible angle, with one ear almost resting on his shoulder. Bones, seeming to glow weirdly in the poor light, jutted from the opposite side of his thick neck. The other man was taller, leaner, dark skinned, and utterly naked. While his head was on straight, dozens of long puckered cuts peppered his forehead, his wrists appeared to have been slashed, and his feet looked like they'd been pealed—flayed— from halfway up each calf.

Both men's mouths hung open, their tongues limp inside gaping maws.

Stevie stood less than six feet away, mutely glaring at them, Kim pressed up against him, her face buried in his shoulder. As Mia and Derrick reached them, their arrival seemed to embolden the director, who suddenly shouted, "Get out of our way!"

Neither man spoke. Neither man moved.

"Derrick, take Kim."

"What?" Derrick asked.

"Take her. I'll deal with these clowns."

"Stevie," Mia said. "Don't—"

But Stevie wasn't hearing it. Gently but firmly, he extricated himself from Kim and passed her to Derrick. Stevie then turned and faced the two men, his hands balled into fists.

"We're leaving," he told them through clenched teeth. "That means you either step aside or I go *through* you. You got me?"

Mia reached for him, touching his shoulder, but he shook her off, his eyes never leaving the cop or the nudist.

"I don't know what the fuck you are! But I lost a friend today... and I'll be damned if I let you hurt anybody else. Now get out of our goddamned way!"

But instead of moving, the men spoke, both of them at the same time. Except, of course, they didn't. As before, the words—*his* words, Mia realized—emerged through their slack, open mouths.

"Bind him hand and foot and cast him into the outer darkness. In that place there will be weeping and gnashing of teeth."

"Fuck you!" Stevie screamed. Then, before anyone could even consider stopping him, he charged forward and threw his fist into the face of the bent-neck cop. For some reason, despite everything she'd seen so far, Mia expected that fist to pass right through the apparition, perhaps to slam into the hard wood of the door, breaking a few metacarpals. Instead, it hit the cop squarely in the left cheekbone, a fierce roundhouse with all of Stevie's terror, grief, and outrage behind it.

But the man didn't move. He didn't even flinch. Stevie might as well have punched a department store manikin. He stepped back, red-faced and cursing, spittle shooting from his mouth.

Then, without warning, the cop *did* move.

The dead man's hands came up together, cobra quick, and locked on either side of Stevie's head.

"No!" Mia cried, coming forward without thinking. Nobody else said anything, not even Kim, who seemed to be screamed-out, at least for the time being.

"Lay not your hands upon the Lord!" the cop's open mouth uttered.

Then the cop twisted his grip savagely, and Stevie Doyle's neck snapped in two with a sound not unlike a rifle shot.

His entire body convulsed, as if from an electric shock. Both his arms shot out and then dropped limply to his side. Then the cop, his coin-eyes unseeing and yet somehow missing nothing, let the dead director fall into a heap at his feet.

"Holy God!" Derrick exclaimed.

At this, the other man, the naked one, pointed an accusing finger at him and declared, *"Blasphemer."*

Just like that, Kim found her scream again.

Mia stared down at what was left of Stevie Doyle, then up at the guards—for that was what they were—guards, standing between her and the only known way out. But didn't a church need more than one exit? Even when this place was built, there had to have been fire codes. Besides, hadn't she read something about there being a parsonage attached.

Or would there be coin-eyed sentries that those points of egress, as well?

Maybe. Maybe not. Either way, it's worth the try!

But before she could even consider how best to act on this decision, she heard a door open to her left. Kim, in her terror, had pushed away from Derrick and run for the first escape she'd seen, the small door in the vestibule that led, not out, but elsewhere.

"Kim!" Derrick cried. "Don't!"

But the blonde woman was already gone, swallowed up in the darkness beyond that narrow threshold.

"Shit!" Derrick exclaimed. Then, before Mia could stop him, he set off after Kim, following her through the open doorway. An instant later, both of them were out of sight, and Mia found herself alone with two open-mouthed dead men.

No. Three.

Stevie stood over his own body, his eyes bulging, and his head twisted almost completely around. Even so, he was clearly aware, turning himself to look balefully down at his own broken corpse. Mia saw that his hands were balled into fists and knew with terrible certainty that one of them contained coins. It seemed that was what you got when you died in St. Damned. Two coins. Not for the ferryman, because your soul wasn't going anywhere. No, these coins were something else, something even darker.

The apparition that had been Stevie Doyle looked at her, and the sorrow on his face dug even more deeply than her terror and revulsion. He knew what had happened to him. He knew what he was now. And he knew she would soon join him if she and the others didn't get out of this hellish place.

Mia fled.

She followed Kim and Derrick through the narrow doorway, slamming the door closed at her back. The room within was small and square, the walls, floor and ceiling all white-painted wood—a fact she could only discern because Derrick had his phone out and was using its flashlight feature to take in their surroundings. Kim clung to him, his mouth moving but no sound coming out.

"I tried calling 911…" Derrick said, staring blankly at Mia. "But all I got was…"

"Was what?" she demanded. Then, without waiting for an answer, she pulled out her own cell phone and dialed emergency services. There were two rings and then a voice—a horribly *familiar* voice—said, *"Pretty little lamb, why do you run from your shepherd?"*

Cursing, Mia broke the connection and tried again. This time, instead of words or ringing, she was greeted with a high-pitched electronic shriek so loud that it sent Kim into yet another screaming fit.

No help's coming. We're on our own.

Frantically, she looked around. There were no windows in this small room, and no other doors. But there was a ladder. It led maybe twelve feet up to a trapdoor set into the ceiling.

"They still out there?" Derrick asked Mia.

She nodded.

Then he asked what struck her as a very astute question, especially given the fear he *must* be feeling. "Stevie out there, too?"

Mia swallowed. Then she nodded again.

He motioned upward. "Belltower, I figure."

"Probably," she said.

"We go up there, he's got us trapped."

"Yeah."

Derrick seemed to consider that. Then he looked at Mia and said, "It's him, isn't it? Barton."

"I think so."

"He takes anyone who comes in here."

"Yes."

"I didn't know…" he began, sounding suddenly as if he were fighting tears. "I helped Stevie research this place. You know, for the show. Just background stuff for Kim to say. I read all about the murdered girls. But it happened so long ago. I never figured there'd be anything to worry about now."

Mia didn't know how to respond to this simple, bitter monologue. So, she said nothing.

"Now Lyle and Stevie are dead," Derrick continued, stating the obvious because, well, Mia supposed right now he needed to. "And he's got us trapped. This place is like a pitcher plant, isn't it?"

Mia, a city girl, wasn't exactly sure what a pitcher plant was. But she nodded anyway.

"Why in Christ's name is this place still standing?" Derrick exclaimed, wrapping the words in a piteous, terrified wail. "Why hasn't the city just bulldozed over it all?"

"I don't know," Mia replied.

"What are we going to do?" Kim asked. They were the first words she'd spoken since Mia had followed them both in here.

Before Mia could answer her—not that she *had* an answer—a pale dead hand slipped *through* the closed door, just inches from Mia's back.

Kim shrieked, pulled herself out from under Derrick's arm, and went immediately for the ladder, an animal in full panic. At the same time, Mia spun around, her heart once again in her throat, and stared as the bent-neck cop's head seemed to melt right through the wood of the door, his coin-eyes finding her.

"Kim!" Derrick called. "Wait!"

But Mia knew full well how useless that entreaty had been. They were as trapped here as they would be in the belltower. But at least going up there might buy them a few precious minutes. And Mia found she wanted those minutes, especially since the alternative, she knew, was that cop's big hands twisting her neck as they had Stevie's.

"Go up!" she told Derrick, backpedaling into him as the cop slowly set one foot into the small room. He moved gradually, sluggishly, as if passing through solid objects were hard for him.

"Go up!" she exclaimed again.

Those two words, uttered in a high, shrill, panicked voice, would haunt her in the years to follow—no matter how many times she told herself what happened next wasn't her fault.

As Derrick reacted to her command and mounted the first rung, Kim was already at the top, twelve feet up, working the trapdoor's latch with shaking hands. The woman was sobbing openly, her makeup running, a caricature of the poised, midwestern beauty she'd been only minutes ago. Her long fingers worried at a sliding bolt that probably hadn't been moved in fifty years.

Finally, just as Derrick began to climb, Kim managed to free the latch and, with a cry of triumph that was also half a sob, she shouldered the door up and out of her way. Mia could see little of what lay above it, not leastwise because Derrick was halfway up the ladder now, bringing his cellphone-flashlight with him. Doing so slowed his ascent, but he surely thought, as Mia did, that surrendering to total darkness would be worse.

Much worse.

Then another "much worse" happened.

Kim slipped through the two-foot square opening in the ceiling with surprising agility.

Then she slammed the trapdoor shut behind her.

"Kim!" Derrick screamed. At the last second, he reached up, probably meaning to hold the door in place, keep it from closing. But, to do so, he had to use the hand with the cellphone, since his other was supporting him on one of the rungs. But he missed his target and ended up grabbing the lip of the opening—

—just as the trapdoor slammed shut on three of his fingers.

Derrick screamed.

Kim screamed.

The phone fell, tumbling past Derrick's body and landing hard on the floor by Mia's feet. For a moment, she was sure the damned thing would break, costing them their only source of light. But it didn't. Call it luck or good technological engineering, but the cellphone's flashlight kept shining, though Mia could see that the screen had been badly cracked.

Atop the ladder, Derrick was pinned by his fingertips. "Kim! Kim!" He climbed higher, until he was hunched up with his shoulder pressed against the trapdoor, trying to use the added leverage to pull his hand free. But even from down where she stood, Mia could tell he was stuck.

Slowly, fearfully, she turned around, expecting to see the bent-neck cop right there, with the naked man and perhaps even Stevie filing into the small room behind him. But, while the apparition now stood fully inside the threshold, blocking any exit with his bulk, he didn't seem inclined to advance any further—at least, not yet.

At the top of the ladder, Derrick seemed to have rallied his wits. He was now pounding the thick wooden trapdoor, calling at the top of his voice, "Kim! My hand's caught. You've got to open the door!"

"No!" the woman screamed back. She sounded close, and Mia realized with a jolt of horror that Kimberly Allesbrook was *sitting* atop the door. It was her weight that was crushing poor Derrick's fingers. Mia had heard stories of how drowning people will, in their panic, pull would-be rescuers under and stand on their shoulders, killing them, all in an effort to keep their own head above water. Maybe this wasn't so different. In Kim's mind, the ghosts were down here and she was up there, and nothing would make her open what she now saw as her only defense.

And if Derrick "drowned," metaphorically speaking, in the process— well, she'd feel awful about that later.

Mia felt a sudden, surprising jolt of righteous outrage. Not that she was in a position to do anything about it.

Derrick must have reached the same conclusion Mia had, because he suddenly yelled, "You cowardly bitch!" With most of his body bathed in shadow now that the cell phone was shining up from the base of the ladder, Derrick raised one foot and jammed it precariously against the edge the trapdoor. To do this, he needed to upend himself, so that his back pointed at the floor, while hooking his other foot around one of the ladder's top rungs. The goal was obvious: he intended to shove up on the trap door and, hopefully, raise it just enough to free his pinned fingers.

Mia felt her stomach clench. Not a premonition, just simple, human anxiety.

This is a bad idea.

Of course, given their situation, were there any "good ideas" anymore?

High above her, Derrick suddenly seemed to *coil*, like a spring, before shoving with his foot and pulling on his trapped hand at the same time.

It worked. The trapdoor moved up an inch, maybe less, but enough to make Kimberly cry out in fresh terror. In the same instant, Derrick's hand came free, and he immediately and sensibly tried to use it to grab the ladder's top rung to help stabilize himself.

Unfortunately, the hand didn't obey. Maybe the fingers were simply numb, or maybe they were quite broken. But either way, any grip he'd hoped to get on the ladder failed him, and the momentum it had required to move the trapdoor turned suddenly downward.

With a cry of alarm, Derrick fell.

Mia screamed and instinctively jumped out of the way, almost colliding with the bent-neck cop in the process.

Derrick hit the floor headfirst, his skull cracking open, spilling blood and other matter. The look of shock on his face seemed to melt away, leaving his eyes dull and his face a mangled, bloody wreck.

Mia kept screaming.

Behind her, the bent-neck cop said, *"None escape the Lord's wrath."*

For several seconds, Mia didn't move, didn't speak, barely thought. It was all she could do to look down at the poor dead boy at her feet, the body as lifeless and empty as a discarded marionette. In fact, it was hard to reconcile that he had ever *been* alive. That seemed bizarre given everything the two of them had seen and experienced together since entering his "pitcher plant." But, call it shock, that was where her mind found itself at the moment.

Of course, part of it might have been the grim certainty of what she would see next.

And she was right.

Crazily, this time she actually witnessed it happen. One instant it was just her and the body—and, of course, the bent neck cop who still hadn't made another move toward her. The next instant, Derrick stood over his own corpse. The apparition's head was a ruin, a mirror of what lay on the floor, except with awareness in the eyes behind that curtain of blood and brain matter. He stared at himself and then up at Mia. He seemed to want to say something, though not a sound passed his lips. Instead, he looked down at his left fist, which was closed, just as Lyle's and Stevie's had been.

The coins are in there, Mia thought, and she trembled at the thought.

"I'm…so sorry, Derrick," she said, the words coming out without any real deliberate effort on her part. Because it was true. She *was* sorry. She hadn't known him long, barely more than a few hours. But she'd liked him, and she was very, *very* sorry he was dead.

Derrick seemed to consider this. Then, he looked back up the ladder. The trapdoor was still shut, though Kim's screaming had evidently stopped. For a long moment, he seemed to be trying to decide something. Mia could read it in his face, damaged as it was.

Then, abruptly, he reached what decision he sought.

Because he *moved.*

Mia cried out as he came at her, throwing her hand up in front of her face as if that would make a sensible defense. But Derrick sidestepped her and went up to the bent-necked cop. The latter regarded him with utter disinterest, as if he no longer mattered now that he'd "joined the fold."

Which gave Derrick the opportunity to slam his fist into the apparition's angled face.

Mia hadn't expected this effort to yield any better results than when Stevie tried it. But Stevie had been alive at the time, trying to strike something not of this world. In this case, however, both the bent-necked cop and the newly deceased soundman were poured from the same mold—and the effect was startling.

The bent-necked cop *flew* back into the closed doorway, disappearing through it in an instant. In the *next* instant, Derrick actually opened the door, turning the knob as a living man would. Beyond it, Mia could see the cop, the nude man, and Stevie, all staring at them with their coin-eyes. Then that voice spoke again, spilling out through Stevie's slack mouth. *"What's this?*

You're mine, now! You've joined my Forever Congregation. You cannot—"

Derrick advanced one step, shoving the cop and the nudist aside in the process, and delivered a backhand blow that knocked Stevie down and cut short the voice, Barton's voice.

Then he turned and, without warning, seized Mia by the wrist.

His grip was terrifyingly, inhumanly strong, his fingers like cold marble. Mia cried out and, for a moment, tried to resist. But when he looked at her, a plea in his still coinless eyes, she nodded and followed.

He led her through the ghosts—*might as well call them what they are*—and at a full run across the vestibule and right past the closed front doors. Unguarded now, Mia wondered if they could be opened. But since Derrick wasted not a second even glancing at them, she supposed, in some way, he must know better than she.

Instead, he pulled her with him into the nave and down the center aisle.

Girls, four of them, all with coins on their eyes, stood in front of the altar, about six feet behind where Lyle's body still lay. All of them raised their hands together, their fingers like claws.

But whatever they meant to do, Mia never found out, because Derrick barrelled right through them, knocking them aside as he did so. They fell back, crashing against the altar or over the dais and into the pews. Not one of them cried out or made any other sort of sound. That is, until they did.

"You cannot do this!" Barton's voice called to them from within all four of the girls' mouths. *"You can't defy me! Not in here! Not in my church!"*

Yet, Derrick was defying him. Mia didn't understand how, couldn't even guess, but somehow, he *was*.

He pulled Mia around the altar and through a well of shadows that ended at a heavy door. As he had before, Derrick opened it by hand, a gesture that very nearly drew from Mia what would likely have been an insane laugh. Here she was being dragged along by a ghost who could, no doubt, pass right through any wall or door. Yet, he took the time to open them, simply as a courtesy to her.

Very human.

Very Casper.

"Derrick," she heard herself say, impressed by how rational she sounded. "Where are we going?"

He ignored her, yanked her through the doorway and into a glass corridor, an umbilical connecting the church with the parsonage behind it. Moonlight lit the entire length, maybe fifteen or twenty feet of it, casting a gray pall over everything.

Without allowing Mia a moment's respite, Derrick pulled her along the corridor, making for the exit on the far end.

Would the parsonage be any safer than the church had been? It was fully dark now, a fact easily seen through the floor-to-ceiling windows that flanked them on both sides. But Mia knew for a fact that her car was out there. She could see it, a dark shape parked just up the street from the abandoned bowling alley. Twenty yards away. No more.

If I could just somehow break this glass…

Derrick stopped so suddenly that Mia bumped into him and bounced painfully back as if she'd collided with a tree trunk.

In front of the parsonage door stood Lyle Back with coins on his eyes.

Derrick didn't gasp; Mia supposed he'd moved past anything as human as gasping. But he *did* stiffen, maybe with recognition, maybe with desperation.

Mia looked back the way they'd come. The four girls were there, filling the open threshold. Only now the man in black stood in their midst. Of all the apparitions, he alone wore no coins on his eyes.

Of course not. The coins are chains. He put them there.

As before, she didn't know where this realization had come from, whether the product of simple deduction or something more arcane. Either way, one thing was certain: he had them boxed in.

Derrick saw this too, looking back and forth between both closed exits.

"Lay the coins on your eyes, boy," Barton said. *"This foolishness wastes the Lord's time. Join my flock and then strangle that pretty little lamb so that she can join us as well."*

Derrick's other hand, his left hand, the one he still held in a fist, rose toward his face. The movement was hesitant, jerky, and Mia got the distinct impression that he was being *compelled* to obey.

And he was fighting it.

"Derrick!" she pleaded. "You can beat him! I know you can!"

But he couldn't. She read it on his face, his dead face, plain as day. He stared back at her, hopelessly, apologetically, and Mia understood that she was doomed.

Then the young man's face screwed up again, his eyes flashing.

With no warning, he turned in a circle, spinning her around with terrific force—

—and threw her right through one of the panes of glass.

The initial impact was like hitting a wall. Her head rang and her vision swam. But then it seemed as if the whole world shattered around her—and air, fresh air, filled her lungs.

She landed hard on the grass outside the glass corridor, the wind knocked out of her, and her flesh cut in at least a dozen places. Blinking, she looked up at Derrick, who was still in there, with *them*. For a moment, she considered calling to him, reaching for him, somehow bringing him with her. But, of course, that wasn't possible.

Derrick Porter was dead.

He gazed at her a moment longer, his expression one of utter despair.

Then his fist came up, opened, and when it lowered again, the despair was gone. Silver dollars had replaced it.

"No…" Mia whispered.

Derrick's mouth fell slack. *"You can't flee the Lord, little lamb."*

Mia found her feet. She didn't know how, but she did. And then she ran. She ran faster than ever before in her life, her legs pumping as she raced across first grass, then cracked sidewalk, then broken asphalt. She heard no footsteps following her, and yet somehow she knew they were there, right on her heels, reaching for her with clawed hands. Derrick, Lyle, Stevie, the bent-necked cop, the naked man, and all those poor dead brides.

Jonah Barton's private army.

As she reached her car, it unlocked at her approach, reading the fob that was still buried in her purse. She pulled the door open and all but threw herself behind the steering wheel, slamming down on the LOCK button and pressing the starter.

As the Lexus rumbled to life, switching on the headlights automatically,

Mia screamed.

They were all around the car. Dozens of them. They surrounded her on all sides, their faces filling every inch of every window. Slack mouths. Coins for eyes.

Mia put the car in drive and slammed her foot on the accelerator.

The Lexus leapt obediently forward, knocking aside the apparitions, sending them into telephone poles and tumbling away in every direction. Then, finally, blessedly, they were gone, and she was driving, with no other immediate destination in mind except *away from here.*

Later, they would find no less than twenty shards of glass embedded in her skin. More than forty stitches would be required.

She would carry the scars of that night for the rest of her life.

And only some of them were external.

CHAPTER 17
Camden, New Jersey—2022

MIA LOOKED UP FROM HER telling, surprised to find tears in her own eyes.

The four of them, her *new* team, were all watching her. Even Jessup appeared rapt, without a trace of the woman's trademark skepticism. Delgado had his hands pressed over his mouth, while the ever-stoic Prine wore a thoughtful, almost brooding expression.

Rene Brubaker, however, was openly crying.

Well, of course she is. I just told her exactly how her son died.

"I'm sorry, Rene," Mia said.

Brubaker nodded and turned away, visibly annoyed with herself.

"Jesus Christ…" Delgado muttered. "What happened to Ms. Allesbrook?"

Before Mia could answer him, Brubaker did. "According to the police report, first responders found her in the belltower. Her throat was cut and an old straight razor was discovered in her hand. The official story became that she killed the others and then herself."

"*She* snapped Stevie Doyle's neck?" Jessup remarked thoughtfully. "That doesn't track."

"It's unlikely," Prine admitted. "But they probably saw it as more palatable than the alternative."

Mia said, "For a while, I was so angry at her…you know, for the trapdoor. But I quickly realized that wasn't fair. She was terrified beyond all reason. Lizard brain in full fight or flight mode. In her place, I might have done the same thing. Poor Kim was simply a victim, just like the rest of Barton's 'congregation.'"

"Did you tell them what happened?" Delgado asked her. "The police, I mean. Did you tell them what *really* happened?"

"About a hundred times," Mia replied wearily. "First in the hospital after getting stitched up, and then during a succession of 'voluntary visits' to City Hall in Camden. I called in my lawyer at the time, who advised me to keep my mouth shut, if only for the sake of my reputation. But I'd seen three people die in front of me and I knew full well that Kim hadn't killed them. Well, except maybe for Derrick, but in his case it wasn't deliberate."

Brubaker stiffened at this latest mention of her son's name. But she didn't comment.

Mia continued. "Eventually, I made such a stink that the Camden County Prosecutor's Office declared me delusional and a possible public danger and their pet judge ordered me to undergo thirty days of "psychological evaluation" in a state mental health facility."

"Don't blame them," Jessup muttered, but there didn't seem to be much heat behind it.

"By the time I convinced the local shrink that I wasn't delusional… or at least not dangerous, the local press had run roughshod over me. My reputation was ruined, except with the conspiracy fringe, which didn't help anything. A major book deal fell through, and my scheduled speaking engagements were cancelled."

"All because you told the truth," Delgado said.

Mia glanced at Jessup, expecting an eye roll. There was none.

Small victories.

"After all that, Prine remarked. "I can see why you were so reluctant to return to St. Damien's." He said this so matter-of-factly, as if two plus two equalled four and that was that.

"So," Mia said, looking at them all. "I've told you my story, the first time I've told it to anyone in five years. Do you believe me?"

"Like I said," Jessup replied. "No way did Kimberly Allesbrook snap Stevie Doyle's neck. As for the rest of it…" She shrugged noncommittally.

"I got grabbed by that coin-eyed psycho," Delgado pointed out. "I remember how strong he was. Hands like blocks of stone. Yeah, I believe you."

"So, do I," Prine added. "I saw him, and I saw what happened when you used your UV light on him."

"Rene?" Mia asked, looking at Brubaker.

"I believed you before I came by your apartment, and nothing you've said has changed my mind. But I find myself trying to puzzle out the rules."

Mia blinked. "Rules?"

"This is a haunting, right?" the assistant director explained. "A deadly one, maybe even the deadliest. But still a haunting."

Mia nodded, curious about where this was going.

"Well, hauntings must be limited by *some* physical laws."

"I suppose so," Mia answered hesitantly. "But I'd be lying if I said anyone really understood them." She glanced again at Jessup, but the woman's expression remained unchanged. Thoughtful. Attentive. And, oddly, a bit sad.

"Then let's look just at this case," Brubaker suggested. "This *particular* haunting. When both Lyle Back and Stevie Doyle died, their ghosts appeared almost instantly. Isn't that right?"

"Yes," Mia said.

"But without coins on their eyes."

"Yes," Mia said again. "The coins were in their fists."

"In both cases, the men seemed to know what had happened. More than that, they seemed to not want it to happen to you and the others. So much so that they resisted Barton's influence for as long as they could. Would you agree with that assessment?"

"I would," Mia said. It was a conclusion she'd reached herself a long time ago.

"Lyle Back managed to point you toward the exit."

"He did."

"And my—" Brubaker, Derrick's mother, caught herself and amended,

"—Derrick Porter actually tried to get you out before he gave in."

Mia met the other woman's gaze and held it. "He *did* get me out."

"Forty stitches later," Delgado muttered.

"He knew he was running out of time and chose to do something drastic." It was an assessment with which Mia completely agreed. But the answer hadn't come from her.

Every head turned and looked at Karen Jessup. Her eyes were distant, her face turned slightly askance. "His will was strong," she remarked in a small voice. "Stronger than the others. Remarkable, really."

Then she glanced at Brubaker, who said nothing.

Jessup knows why Renee really came here tonight.

Clearing her throat, Mia said, "I've always believed its how Officer Mayberry made it out of the church the night he discovered Barton's body and his partner was killed. I think Officer Shaker managed to drag his unconscious partner through the nave and out the front door before Barton forced him to wear the coins."

"This Barton's a real piece of shit," Delgado muttered.

"He was a psycho," Jessup corrected. "Murdered almost thirty girls over the course of twenty-five years."

"Until John Cooley killed him," remarked Brubaker.

"I'm not familiar with the case," said Prine.

"Renee let me read the file on the drive down here," Mia told him. "One of Barton's victims, Rachel, was Cooley's daughter."

"What happened to him?" Prine asked.

"Officially?" replied Brubaker. "He hanged himself in his cell the night after his arrest."

"Officially," Jessup said thoughtfully, echoing Brubaker's word. "Makes me think that *you* think something else happened."

The assistant director didn't reply.

Mia said, "Just before his arrest, he carved a message onto Barton's tombstone, out in the graveyard."

"That's what you had me run through the crypto-analyzer," remarked Delgado.

Brubaker nodded. "And did you?"

"Sure. It's probably still running." The young man stood and crossed to the worktable, his eyes scanning the laptop's screen. Around them, around all of them, the choir loft had become quite dark, the only light coming from the equipment. Mia silently wished they had a few lamps set up, battery-powered, of course. But not only would such devices likely fail before long, the team wouldn't risk their glow leaking through the big stained-glass window.

Sitting in the dark made sense, given the circumstances. But Mia couldn't help wishing for light. St. Damien's liked the dark too much.

"Yep. Still running," Delgado reported. "Partial results are up, though."

"And?" Brubaker prompted.

"No obvious cyphers. No hidden symbology. Looks like its just words."

"What words?" Prine asked.

Mia responded, rattling off the compound sentence from memory. "All victims avenged; truth always raises demons."

"The first part's a confession," Jessup noted. "The second part…well, I don't really *get* the second part. 'Truth always raises demons.' What's that even supposed to mean?"

"Nothing at all," said a voice from the shadows.

Delgado screamed. Then he literally vaulted over the table and pressed his back against the stained-glass window. At the same time, Prine, Jessup, and Brubaker leapt to their feet and drew their weapons, training them on the figure standing at the choir loft's far end, where the meager light from Delgado's equipment didn't come close to reaching.

The figure emerged. As he did, the shadows seemed to follow him, enveloping him like a cloak.

Jonah Ray Barton, or rather the entity that had once *been* Jonah Ray Barton, wore an expression of gentle amusement that looked about as sincere as the smile on a jack-o-lantern. His hands were clasped behind his back, his eyes shining like jewels, glistening red.

Never any coins on him,

Coins are for the sheep, not the shepherd.

"Hands!" Jessup exclaimed. "Show us your hands!"

The smile widened, grew more predatory. Mia, the only one still seated, slowly found her feet. Her every instinct was to turn and run, to abandon the choir loft and everyone in it, hurry down the stairs, through the vestibule, and out the front doors into the night.

Just run blindly, the way poor Kimberly did. And look where it got her…

Besides, another part of her mind, deeper but perhaps wiser, knew it was already too late for that.

The doors would be guarded.

Barton's attention turned toward the DEA agent, and Mia saw the woman flinch and very nearly retreat a step. But then she steadied herself, replanted her feet in a shooter's stance and kept her weapon leveled.

"Are you going to shoot me, Karen?" Barton asked. The words resonated, as if spoken from some distance, with just the faintest echo to them. Yet, as strange an effect as this was, Mia knew for certain that it was Barton, himself, speaking. For one thing, his lips moved—unlike when he spoke through one of his slack-mouthed, coin-eyed minions.

No, this is him. Really him.

The devil, himself.

"You're goddamned right I am," Jessup said through clenched teeth, "unless you show me your hands right now!"

"I've never been shot at," Barton said. He made a show of being intrigued by the idea. But Mia sensed it was an act. This man, if "man" was even the right term anymore, was enjoying himself. *"I'm honestly not sure what it would do. So, please…feel free."*

"Your hands!" Karen exclaimed, very nearly shrieked. "Now!"

"Agent Jessup…" Brubaker began, a warning in her words.

Barton's grin widened. It widened hideously, impossibly, his mouth elongating until Mia was reminded, and not pleasantly, of *Pac Man*. She heard Delgado reciting the rosary behind her. To her right, Prine was motionless, his gun fixed on the shadow-bathed figure, his entire body as taut as a bowstring. To her left, Rene seemed to be trembling ever so slightly. And Jessup, there on the end—well, even in the poor light, Mia could see that the woman, despite her training, was almost red-faced with hysteria.

"Now!" she screamed again. "Do it now or I'll shoot!"

Barton showed her more teeth than any human being had ever had—ever. Then he yelled back, the word seeming to sear Mia's brain. *"Shoot!"*

"Karen, don't," Mia said. "It won't—"

Jessup fired.

The report was loud, *very* loud, reverberating off the stained-glass and echoing out over the railing and across the nave below. The bullet hit Barton in his center mass, but he didn't even flinch. Instead, the front of his black suit seemed to *ripple*, as if a stone—or a coin—had been tossed into a pond. Where the slug went after that, Mia could only guess. She didn't see it exit, but supposed it probably had, passing through the man's body like it wasn't there.

After all, in every sane way imaginable, it *wasn't.*

Mia half-expected Jessup to fire again, but she didn't. Instead, the DEA agent sort of groaned and shrank back, the pistol falling from her hands. Her eyes were glassy, and she looked like she wanted to say something, but no words came.

When Barton spoke, it was with a taunting cruelty that made Mia's insides turn to ice. *"Interesting. I wonder if it would work differently with my...valet."*

As he spoke, a second figure appeared, slipping out from amidst the shadows as if through some unseen door. It was a man, like Barton, but one that appeared considerably older, thin and balding. His hands hung at his sides, long fingers opening and closing as if in pain. Unlike the other apparitions Mia had seen in this place—Barton, himself, notwithstanding—the newcomer wore no coins over his eyes. Instead, she saw with some horror that his mouth was filled with them. Dozens of coins. They seemed to have been crammed in until their edges could be seen under his swollen cheeks and slivers of silver glistened from between black lips that couldn't quite close.

But it was the man's throat that was the most grotesque. It hadn't been slit, like with Lyle Back and the girls Mia had seen. It had been *dug out,* gouged away in a manner that suggested a savage, merciless rage. Now bloodless, the wound was like a gaping maw, so deep that Mia thought she could glimpse the white of the man's spine.

"Try it on him," Barton said to Jessup.

But Jessup didn't move. None of them did. The entire team had become as transfixed as deer in headlights, staring at this person, this victim, whose eyes bore more utter, helpless anguish than Mia had ever seen—and perhaps more than her mind could bear.

"Fabron," she heard herself say.

Barton turned to her, smirking, and raised an eyebrow. *"Ah! You know him!"*

The words came out in a kind of dry croak. "He…was…your…cook."

Barton's smirk faded. *"He was my father's cook,"* he corrected. *"And a dim-witted fool his entire life. My father, the great Joshua Barton, was a giant of a man, the latest in a long and distinguished family, a man of means and breeding who commanded respect. But he carried a bit too soft a heart when it came to the lower classes. I, however, suffer no such weakness. After he died, I did keep Fabron on to make my meals and tend to the household chores around my church. But I made sure he always knew his place. Now, as I have no need of a cook, he…tends to me in other ways, mostly as a witness."*

"To…what?" Mia heard herself ask.

"Why, to my ministrations, pretty little lamb," Barton told her. His smile was back now, as warm and welcoming as the dark side of the moon. *"Fabron gets to watch me as I sanctify my flock."* He turned and surveyed the choir loft. *"This is where I first found myself,"* he mused, sounding almost wistful. *"Officer Shaker stood just there, waving his silly gun…much like Karen here. He was afraid, so afraid. So, I brought him into my flock. He was the first lamb I took after my death. Before that miraculous moment, before two of my children seized him and cast him over the railing, I hadn't yet fully grasped how completely my will held sway in this place. It was a lesson, an awakening."*

"Where's he now?" Mia heard herself ask.

Barton smiled at her. It was a cold, predatory thing. *"He's here. He's been a good little lamb."*

"What do you want from us?" This came from Brubaker. The assistant director still had her gun trained on the figure, but Mia suspected it was more habit than hope at this point.

"I want all of you to join my Forever Congregation, of course. After the story Mia just told, I would have thought that obvious."

His use of her name, delivered with such ease, such familiarity, frightened Mia on a level deeper than she'd thought possible.

He's toying with us…the way a cat tortures a mouse.

Oh Goddess. I'm going to die here. I'm going to wear those coins!

She swallowed back another desire to bolt because—well—bolt *where*?

"And if we don't want to join your 'congregation?'" Brubaker asked, and the reasonable tone the woman affected impressed Mia enough to shore up her own courage, if only a little.

"The lost sheep may not wish to be found. They may even resent the shepherd. But the shepherd knows best."

"You're killing people!" Mia cried, the words tumbling out of her before she could stop them.

Once again, he turned his smile—*that* smile—on her. And, at the sight of it, Mia felt herself shrink back, as if from an encroaching fire. *"Everyone dies, pretty little lamb,"* he said from behind his hundred teeth. *"But, in my church, when they die, they join something greater."*

"You, I suppose," said Brubaker.

"I am the shepherd and the lord of this house." Barton spread his arms. *"Once they come to me, they are free from sin, free from any fear of Hell."*

"Free from Heaven." This came from Jessup, who looked more defeated than Mia would have believed possible.

That seemed to have some effect. Barton's smile withered. He stiffened, an odd thing to see on a shape that seemed made predominantly of shadow, and faced her.

"There is no Heaven, Karen. This is the only paradise. And I am the only God."

Jessup was openly crying now, her shoulders shaking. She looked like she wanted to say something more. But instead, she simply shook her head, closed her eyes, and turned away. Seeing this, Mia almost envied her.

How she wished *she* could turn away.

But she couldn't. She didn't dare. Seeing Jonah Ray Barton was bad enough. But knowing he was there and *not* seeing him felt infinitely worse.

Barton's glowing eyes regarded them all for several more seconds. Then he said, still without a smile, *"The night is young. I could take you all right now. But I think I'll wait a bit. I'm...curious."*

"About what?" Brubaker demanded. She took her eyes off the dead man long enough to reach over and touch Jessup's shoulder—a supportive gesture that the other woman instantly shook away.

"Why...what happens next, Renee."

Then he did an odd thing, though Mia thought she might have been the only one who noticed it. He looked directly at Prine, the only one of them who hadn't said a word since this visitation began. For a second, no more, the twisted, impossible smile was back, turning his angled face into a caricature of human expression, a circus clown without makeup but with the overwide grin splitting his face, nonetheless.

In the next second, he was gone, melted back into the shadows as if he'd never been there at all.

Except he was there and still is.

He's watching us, unseen.

Biding his time.

"Jesus, Mary and Joseph..." Delgado whispered, crossing himself again.

Brubaker holstered her weapon before turning and folding Jessup into her arms. The other woman struggled, but only for a moment. Then she surrendered to the embrace with a shuddering groan of horror and gratitude.

Prine blinked and looked at Mia, who looked helplessly back at him.

"I *do* believe in spooks," he said.

And Mia wondered if that was supposed to be funny.

CHAPTER 18
Camden, New Jersey—2022

FOR MOST OF A MINUTE, no one moved. Instead, they all looked from the place where Barton had been standing, to each other, and back again. Mia had seen enough in her career to be—perhaps—less affected by the otherworldly realities that had just been laid bare before them. Nevertheless, she struggled to find her breath, much less her tongue.

Finally though, and with no small effort, she managed to say, "We need to get out of here."

The word rang hollow in the dark and empty choir loft. Mia imagined—or did she?—that Barton was somewhere laughing.

For another most of a minute, nobody answered her. Mia, her heart hammering, scanned their faces. Prine looked ashen, his gun at his side, his breath coming in short little gasps. Delgado was visibly praying, having dropped to his knees with his eyes closed and his hands clasped in front of him. The young man's mouth moved, though no sound came out. Nevertheless, Mia could read his lips well enough, even in the poor light, to tell he was reciting the Lord's Prayer.

She hoped it would help.

Brubaker was still holding Jessup, though the DEA agent seemed to have stopped crying. Slowly, the assistant director's eyes found Mia's. She looked like she wanted to say something, thought better of it, then regrouped and declared, "This operation is aborted."

Jessup's reaction surprised them all. She stiffened and pulled out of Brubaker's embrace. "What? We can't!" she exclaimed. "Arias!"

Mia very nearly laughed. But then she caught herself and stifled it at the last second, mainly because—well, there was nothing funny about any of this.

"Arias, or one of his people, heard your shot just now, Karen. We're blown."

"You don't know that!" the other woman protested. "We might—"

But Brubaker talked over her. "Besides, given what we just witnessed, I don't think we're in any position to try to continue this surveillance effort, do you?"

Jessup stared at her. Then she stared at all of them. Finally, she said, "We…we can call for backup. I have a dozen agents on standby who could secure this place while we work. They can be here in ten minutes."

Brubaker shook her head. "Karen, listen to yourself. You want us to continue the stakeout despite your gunshot, but you figure a dozen DEA agents on site would go unnoticed?"

Jessup's retort froze on her lips. Her eyes, still red from crying, looked frantically around, as if she expected to see something that would somehow salvage this disaster. Mia watched her take several deep breaths. Then, her face pale and her expression—complicated, she finally said, "Okay. All right. We'll abort."

"He's not going to let us out," Mia told them. Each word sounded, even to her own ears, like a death nell.

Jessup whirled on her. But anything she might have planned to say died unspoken. A few minutes ago, this woman had been a hardcore skeptic, one of the most determined non-believers Mia had ever encountered. She'd clung to the absolute conviction of her beliefs like a religious zealot.

And *all of them* had just been swept away.

"I'm calling for backup," Jessup finally declared. She marched to the table and snatched her cell phone from the charging station. Then, satisfied that she had both power and signal, the DEA agent dialed a contact number and put the device on speaker.

It rang. Once. Twice. Three times. All the while, Prine and Brubaker both looked on with something close to relief.

Mia, however, knew better.

A moment later, Barton's voice declared through the phone's speaker, *"And just as it is appointed for man to die once, and after that comes judgment."*

With a string of curses the reminded Mia of Lyle, Jessup broke the connection and tried again.

Again, there were three rings, followed by a click and then a voice, *"Submit yourselves therefore to God. Resist the devil, and he will flee from you."*

"Let me try," Brubaker said. She took her own phone from its charger and initiated a call. This time, the only response was a shrill whine so piercing that it set Mia's teeth on edge and forced the assistant director to hastily break the connection.

"He's not going to let us call out," Mia told them.

Jessup looked like she might be ready to try again, but then recalled the definition of insanity and, in anger, slammed her useless phone down on the tabletop. Standing nearby, Prine shook his head without speaking, looking more lost than Mia would have imagined possible.

Brubaker turned to Delgado, "Archie, we have cameras on every exit, don't we?"

The young man, still on his knees, started at the mention of his name. "W—what?"

Brubaker looked hard at him. "We need you, Agent Delgado. Are you with us?"

Delgado nodded, licking his lips. "Yeah. Right. Cameras. I've got them on every door and in the breezeway, too."

"Check the feeds, please," Brubaker told him.

As they all watched, Archie Delgado climbed unsteadily to his feet and went to the table. When his trembling fingers tapped a few keys on the laptop, its screen, which had gone dark from disuse, suddenly lit up half the choir loft. Visibly trembling, he tapped a couple of keys. Then he froze. *"Madre Dios."*

It was the first Spanish Mia had heard the young man utter.

"What is it?" Prine asked.

Delgado didn't reply.

So, the rest of them crowded in, peering at the harshly lit laptop screen. The first camera was apparently mounted in the vestibule, with a clear view of the front doors, lit green by night vision.

Two coin-eyed men stood sentinel with their backs to the exit. The sight of them, so reminiscent of the sentries she'd encountered five years ago, shook Mia badly. For one horrible moment, she thought she was going to either faint or vomit.

One of the guards was the same bent-necked cop as before. The other was the big Hispanic man who'd attacked Delgado on the dais.

I wonder where the naked guy is.

It was a crazy thought, positively ludicrous. Yet Mia supposed she could forgive herself for thinking it. This was a night for crazy thoughts.

"That's the big dude from before," Delgado said.

"Yes," agreed Prine. "Rojas. Arias' man."

"We can get past them," Jessup declared, though Mia sensed the futility behind the words. Karen Jessup had indeed become a believer and it seemed, inside St. Damien's, that belief walked hand-in-hand with a creeping despair.

Mia understood.

"Check the other exits," Brubaker told Delgado. "Theparsonage, maybe?"

Delgado worked the laptop. The image changed to a small parlor or sitting area, again lit by the green glow of night vision. The exit was there, a simple-looking street door.

But the naked man stood in front of it.

He hadn't changed in five years. Then again, why would he? This wasn't a body, not in the flesh and blood sense. This was a vessel, a prison, in which Barton had trapped a soul and bent it to his will. It wore, as they all did, the wounds of its owner's death, in this case horrific lacerations at the forehead, wrists, and feet. This was Russel Saunders, John Cooley's friend and neighbor, who'd first discovered the body of those four girls in the church cellar back in 1972, the one who'd been crucified in his own bathtub.

And he wasn't alone.

Four blood-soaked brides stood with him in a line like soldiers in formation. All bore deep, ugly gashes under their chins—and all of them, the naked man included, had coins on their eyes.

"Shit," Jessup muttered.

"There's one more door," Delgado said. "The one that leads out into the alley. It's in the sacristy."

"Try it," Brubaker told him.

Nodding, his hands trembling, the young man touched the keyboard.

This time the image showed a down-facing view of a narrow, closed door. It had a healthy deadbolt fitted onto it and an empty peg board beside it, probably for coats and hats back when this church was still a place of the living.

"There's nobody there!" Jessup exclaimed. She sounded positively gleeful.

Standing beside her, Prine said nothing—though, from his marble expression, he didn't share the DEA agent's enthusiasm.

Neither did Mia.

Something's not right.

Brubaker said, "I don't see an alternative. Does anyone object to a careful retreat and egress?"

No one did, not even Mia, who felt all but certain this was another of Barton's games, a lure to draw them to—what? His congregation could take them here in the choir loft as easily as elsewhere. So why lead them along with false hope?

But, of course, she knew.

Fun.

The son of a bitch is having fun.

Playing with his food.

Nevertheless, she went wordlessly along when the entire team, with Brubaker in front, headed down the stairs to the nave. The assistant director had activated her phone's flashlight and was using it to guide them through the choir loft door and into the small open area behind the rearmost pews. Prine walked beside Brubaker with Mia and Delgado behind them and Jessup "watching their six," as Brubaker had put it. Both Prine and Jessup were brandishing their pistols, as if that would do any good. For Mia's part, she had her arm around Delgado, who was shaking and still whispering prayers.

Together, the five of them moved slowly down the center aisle toward the altar, doing their best to look everywhere at once. Around them, the church was graveyard quiet, the only sound their labored, anxious breaths and collective, shuffling footfalls.

Mia tried desperately to stay positive. The fact that none of St. Damned's remaining congregation was in visible evidence—not Lyle or Stevie or Derrick or Kim, assuming she was here as well, *might* be a good thing. Was it possible that those particular souls had somehow managed to escape Barton's yoke? If so, then that implied, or at least suggested, that his hold on them all might be weakening over time, despite the bravado he'd affected up in the choir loft just now.

It was an encouraging thought.

So, why don't I believe it?

A dozen feet past the altar and behind a mildewed, moth-eaten curtain that hung against the back wall of the nave, stood a small door that led into the sacristy. Mia had never been in here before and, as they stepped inside, single-file, she allowed herself a moment to evaluate her new surroundings.

There were the pegs on one wall that she'd noticed earlier. Directly below them was an old bench, likely intended for donning boots or other bad weather attire. On the opposite wall stood a modest chest of drawers and a small desk, their surfaces caked with decades of dust. In the middle of the floor was an oval carpet of some stylized pattern, now mildewed and made threadbare by time.

The sacristy had no window, only a door, the same door they'd all seen on the camera feed. And, as that feed indicated, no coin-eyed sentry blocked it.

For a moment, they all stood there, breathing hard and staring at their exit.

"Is it locked?" Brubaker asked.

Prine shook his head. "Shouldn't be. Delgado and I brought everything in through there. It's the closest door to the parking lot across the alley."

"One way to find out," Jessup said. And, with that, she marched right up and tried the knob.

The door opened with an easy, almost friendly creak.

Something's definitely not right, Mia thought again. She glanced at Brubaker and, when their eyes briefly met, Mia could tell that the other woman was thinking the same thing.

"Finally, a fucking break," Jessup declared. Then she pulled the door wide open, exposing the Camden night. Air, stinking of garbage from the nearby river, hit Mia's nose. Yet, she welcomed it. That stench meant freedom.

Then Jessup gasped.

A man filled the threshold. He was big, broad-shouldered, and barrel chested. He wore jeans, cowboy boots and a dark colored jersey of some kind. A heavy gold chain hung around his thick neck. His face was round, his features coarse and his black hair was slicked back with product. He sported a long, thin moustache.

And there were no coins on his eyes.

"What the hell…" Jessup began.

Then, in a flash, a large chrome plated pistol was in her face.

"Hello, Karen," the man said. He had a thick Columbian accent and, when he smiled, his teeth were very white. "I've been waiting a long time to meet you."

Standing beside Mia, Brubaker gasped and exclaimed, "Arias!"

Then the assistant director reached under her jacket for her own pistol, the movement smooth and quick and professional—

—only to freeze solid when another gun pressed against her temple.

Mia stared, not quite comprehending.

"I'm sorry," said Agent Matthew Prine of the FBI.

CHAPTER 19
Camden, New Jersey—2022

MEN CAME IN. SEVERAL OF them. Different sizes and builds, but all sharing the same *look*, rough, determined, pitiless. Mia was shoved out of the way almost immediately, pushed up against the wall with the clothing pegs while the agents, except Prine, were subdued, searched, and disarmed.

Brubaker looked stunned. She kept staring at Matthew Prine as if she half-expected him to pull his face off like something out of a *Mission Impossible* movie, revealing him to be someone else. She said nothing and offered little in the way of resistance.

Karen Jessup, on the other hand, was clearly pissed, her mouth a thin hard line, her eyes wide with outrage. As she was seized by men twice her size, she cursed wildly and fought with amazing pluck. But all it earned her was a savage slap that nearly knocked her off her feet.

Delgado wore an expression of dumb shock, his mouth hanging open in a way that reminded Mia of Barton's "sheep."

And Prine? Prine looked almost physically ill, especially after Arias grinned and slapped him on the back.

Nobody was tied up or handcuffed. Mia supposed there was no need. The trap had closed and the four of them were helpless, outgunned and outnumbered. She counted ten men, including Prine and Arias, all of them crowding the small sacristy.

One of them took the time to shut the door.

Her mind roiled as she tried to make sense of this terrible turn of fate. That Matthew Prine had been a plant was now obvious, this entire "stake out" or "surveillance mission" or whatever, a farce from the get-go. From the way Arias marched back and forth in front of the glowering Jessup, preening and looking supremely smug, Mia inferred some history between them. Perhaps they'd never met in person, but Arias had clearly known of Jessup as surely as she'd known of him, and he was reveling in having so thoroughly duped her.

"You look pissed, Karen," the drug czar crooned. He roughly cupped the DEA agent's chin with one calloused hand. Jessup winced from the pressure of his fingers but made no further sound. She continued to glare daggers at him. "You've been shoving your bitch nose into my business for…what's it been…eight years now? Six years since the Miami interdiction? You cost me millions that day, didn't you?" Then, when the woman still didn't respond, he slapped her and screamed directly in her face, *"Didn't you?"*

"Yes," she replied with a gasp.

Apparently satisfied, he released Jessup and stepped back, reviewing his line of prisoners. His eyes, dark and cold, settled on Mia, who flinched under that heartless gaze. This man was a psychopath; that much was clear. But there was also a charisma to him, both compelling and frightening, which had no doubt allowed him to leverage his violent tendencies into a position of leadership in the international drug trade. He probably inspired fierce loyalty from his underlings—or "employees" or "soldiers" or whatever the vernacular for hired thugs might be. And he no doubt maintained that loyalty through fear.

All of which equals one fucking dangerous individual.

These thoughts ripped through Mia's brain in the scant seconds between suffering Arias' gaze and having him step right up to her.

"You're that medium," he said.

"I'm not a medium," Mia replied.

He slapped her.

The blow came out of nowhere, landing hard enough to momentarily blind her. She fell against Delgado, who cried out so loudly that one might have thought that *he'd* been the assault victim. For a second, the two of them staggered together, and might have fallen if one of Arias' men hadn't been there to roughly force them upright.

A moment later, Arias grabbed Mia's face as he had Jessup's, forcing her to look at him. His blunt fingers dug savagely into her flesh and, while her skin was still numb from the slap, Mia knew with sickening certainty that she'd have a face full of bruises tomorrow.

Assuming, of course, that there was going to *be* a tomorrow.

"You talk when I ask a question," he said, the words coming out wrapped in an animal snarl. "Otherwise, you shut the fuck up. Now, do you understand that…medium?"

Mia tried to nod, but his hand wouldn't allow it. So instead, she swallowed and replied, "Yes."

"Better."

He released her and turned away. "Prine, where did you say you found Rojas' body?"

"The cellar," Matthew Prine replied. Mia noticed he didn't look at any of his betrayed team members as he said this.

"And he was hung?"

"I found him hanging from a joist."

Arias treated him to a long, evaluating look. "And did *you* murder him?"

"No," Prine replied without apparent rancor.

"Then who did? One of them?" Arias motioned to the line of prisoners.

"I don't see how. Delgado was the only other person in the church, and he was in the choir loft at the time."

Arias' face darkened with impatience. "Then who *did* kill one of my men?"

"Barton."

Everyone froze, mainly because this single word hadn't come from Prine but from Delgado.

"What did you say?" Arias asked. He advanced on the subdued agent, and Mia was suddenly sure he'd slap him as he had Jessup and herself, if only for the "sin" of speaking when not spoken to.

Delgado kept his head down, looking small and defeated. "Barton killed him. Then he hijacked his soul and used him to attack me."

Arias stared at the smaller man. Then he looked back at Prine and asked, sounding more confused than angry, "What the fuck is he talking about?"

Prine cleared his throat, an uncharacteristic display of nervousness. "Dr. Lakatos and I witnessed someone who looked like Rojas physically attack Agent Delgado out in the nave."

Arias' confusion pivoted instantly into sudden and terrifying anger. "Someone who looked like him? Someone who *looked* like him! Is that what you're saying?"

Mia thought Prine might cower; she sure as hell would have. But he met Arias' glare evenly. "Dr. Lakatos is convinced that Rojas' soul has been…claimed…by the former pastor of this church, a man named Jonah Ray Barton."

"Barton. That's familiar. Are you talking about Barton the serial killer?"

"Yes."

"He's in this church?"

Prine nodded. "Yes."

"And nobody thought to tell me that?"

None of his men, not even Prine, answered.

With a long-suffering sigh, he demanded, "So, where's this Barton now?"

"He's been dead for fifty years."

Arias blinked. Then he burst out laughing. After a moment, several of his men did so as well, though Mia noted how they shifted their feet and swapped surreptitious and uncomfortable glances. "A ghost possessed the body of my man and had him attack this little fellow right here?" the drug czar asked, throwing a thumb back in Delgado's direction.

"No," Prine replied. "Rojas' body is still in the cellar, as far as I'm aware. What Dr. Lakatos and I saw was a…" His words trailed off.

"A what?" Arias demanded, all laughter gone now. This man was an emotional powder keg.

"A manifestation," Prine said after a moment.

"Another ghost?"

"Yes."

Arias whirled on Mia so suddenly that she uttered an involuntary yelp of fear, one which he ignored. "And you, medium? Is that what you say?"

She swallowed dryly. It took a lot—a whole lot—to answer. "Yes."

"Ghosts can do that, can they? They can possess each other?"

It was an interesting way to look at it, Mia vaguely noted, but not inaccurate. "I've…I've never encountered one before that could. It may be unique to Barton."

For a moment, as he looked at her, Arias seemed to be fighting laughter again. But then he addressed two of his men, the ones who happened to be standing closest to the door that led from the sacristy back into the church proper. "Head down into the cellar. See if Rojas is still there."

They both nodded and left without a word.

He regarded Mia again. "You know ghosts?"

"I…study them," Mia said, wishing to the Goddess that this man would leave her alone. Her face burned terribly, and her left eye wouldn't stop tearing. Besides, every word he spoke to her felt like shark's teeth biting into her flesh. Madness and menace radiated off him like sweat.

"Can you call them?"

"No," she said.

"Why not?" he demanded, sounding impatient again.

"That's…not how it works."

"But you're sure this…Barton…killed my man and has now claimed his soul?"

"I don't know who killed the man in the cellar," Mia replied, amazed at how calm her voice sounded. "But…yes, Barton's controlling his spirit."

"Well, that's some bullshit right there!" Arias declared with another laugh. "Rojas should be safely in Hell, like the rest of us will be one fine day!"

All of his men laughed at that one. Apparently, none of them were particularly broken up about what had happened to their colleague.

"Maybe you'll join him tonight," Jessup muttered.

"Hmm?" Arias asked, theatrically placing one hand to his ear. "What did you say?"

Jessup met his eyes. "Barton got your thug, and he's going to take the rest of you."

Barton's made a true believer out of Karen, Mia thought bitterly.

Arias approached the DEA agent until he all but eclipsed her from view with his bulk. "I don't fear the dead, Karen," he said in a voice so low it reminded Mia of rolling thunder. "I don't have to. I've made too many of them. But you know that, don't you?"

"Fuck you," Jessup said.

Arias laughed. Then he turned to Brubaker, who had been watching the exchange with barely concealed alarm. "You're an assistant director of the FBI, yes?"

Brubaker nodded.

"I've never killed an FBI assistant director before."

Brubaker said nothing.

He grinned at her. Then he stepped back and grinned at them all. Finally, looking around, he declared. "It's stuffy as fuck in here. Let's all move out into the church and get more comfortable.

"You're just going to kill us," Jessup said, and Mia couldn't believe how calm she sounded. "Why bother with all these games?"

Arias shrugged. "Call it closure. Besides, you've been a dog at my heels for years, Karen. Don't you think your colleagues have the right to know why?" Then, without waiting for an answer, he motioned to his remaining men. Immediately, the four prisoners were ushered, single-file and under heavy scrutiny, through the sacristy's tiny door and out into the space behind the altar. Here, the men's flashlights splashed off the high, buttressed ceiling and stained-glass windows, sending shadows bouncing to and fro with every step.

With Arias leading the way, they all marched past the altar, off the dais, and out into the nave. There, Mia and Jessup were shoved into the first pew on the right, while Delgado and Brubaker were roughly deposited across the aisle in the left-hand pew.

None of them dared risk a word of protest, not with Arias' men positioning themselves in the pews behind them, standing and ever watchful.

Looking supremely smug, Arias moved up and down the center aisle like a warden inspecting his inmates. His attention once again settled on

Jessup, who sat at the end of the pew closest to the aisle—and seemed determined not to meet his eye. "Her name was Chelsea…I believe."

Jessup still refused to acknowledge him.

Arias, however, didn't seem to mind. Grinning again, he said. "She was seven years old, sweet little seven."

"Shut up," Jessup muttered.

Arias laughed. "She was playing in her front yard under her grandmother's watchful eye. You weren't there. Of course not. You were never there. Mommy worked very hard, didn't she?"

This time, Jessup said nothing, though Mia saw the woman's eyes fill up.

Arias must have seen it too, because he leaned over, bringing his broad face close to hers. "You weren't there when my car pulled up to the curb. You didn't see it when I rolled down my window. And you didn't do a thing to protect her when I opened fire."

Tears began rolling down both of Jessup's cheeks, something that seemed to delight Arias to no end.

"She had time to scream, that sweet little seven. Just once. Then my bullets ripped her to pieces…turned her into a bloody pile of meat on the lawn."

Mia saw Jessup's hands close into fists and, instinctively, she placed her own hands atop them. Arias *wanted* Karen Jessup to explode. Nothing would give him more pleasure than to revel in her rage and grief.

"You're a lot like him," Mia heard herself say.

Arias' smile faltered. He glanced at her. "Like who?"

"Barton."

He chuffed. "The ghost?"

Mia didn't reply.

"Why am I like some spook haunting a rundown church at the outer edge of Shithole, New Jersey?"

Mia answered as calmly as she could. "Jonah Ray Barton murdered twenty-seven teenage girls and buried their bodies in the cellar of this place. Then, from time to time, he'd dig them up and play with them. He took pleasure in the suffering and death he caused. Sounds to me like you do the same thing."

Arias straightened. "The little girl died to send a message to her mother," he said flatly. "I'd been investigated before. But Karen here was something else altogether, more dogged, more relentless than any of them. She began getting too close, costing me money. What I did was just business." Then his smile returned as he leaned down close to Jessup again. "Thing is…I didn't even shoot grandma. But they found her dead on the scene too, didn't they? Seems the old bitch's heart stopped cold in her chest." He laughed. "Two-for-one day!"

"See what I mean?" Mia said. She knew she was pushing, taking a huge risk. This man had all the power and he clearly liked hurting people. But the words just kept spilling out of her, more nervous energy than courage, she suspected. "Just like Barton."

Arias regarded her the way a bird regards a worm. Then he turned around, directing his attention to the other side of the aisle, where Brubaker and Delgado looked on in helpless silence. "By now, Assistant Director, you no doubt understand how tonight's events have been orchestrated."

Brubaker didn't reply.

Arias cocked his head and looked at her. "I find your silence rude. Answer the question."

"You didn't ask a question," Brubaker said, her face without expression.

Arias chuckled. Then, in one smooth motion, he drew his pistol and shot Renee Brubaker in the left knee. Both Brubaker and Delgado screamed. Delgado covered his face in his hands, while Brubaker clutched what had to be a shattered kneecap, blood oozing out from between her fingers.

Jessup jumped to her feet, cursing—only to be shoved back down by one of the armed men in the pew behind her.

Arias regarded his handiwork, then re-holstered the smoking pistol, took a blue bandana from his back pocket, and offered it to Brubaker. "Put pressure on it. I don't think I hit an artery, but with knees it's hard to know for sure. I wouldn't want you to bleed out…at least, not just yet." Then he turned in a circle, grinning at everyone, as if what he'd said were somehow funny.

With trembling hands, Brubaker took the bandana and tied it tightly around her knee. The woman sweated profusely, and her face had paled to a ghastly white.

She's fighting shock, Mia knew.

"Now…" Arias said with feigned patience. "Let's try again. Assistant Director, by now you must understand how I orchestrated tonight's events."

Brubaker didn't appear to be in any position to respond to him. But even in her agonized state, she grasped that silence was not an option. So, gritting her teeth and blinking her eyes rapidly, either to focus them through the pain or clear the stinging sweat, she replied, "You turned Prine."

Arias laughed, sounding pleased. "I sure as shit did! Prine, get over here!"

Matthew Prine obeyed, though Mia noticed that he did so with obvious reluctance, still studiously *not* looking at Brubaker. The man seemed—diminished—somehow, as if his act of betrayal had caused him to fold in on himself, leaving behind someone drained of confidence and self-worth.

As he came within reach, Arias threw an arm around his shoulder, pulling him close as one might a best friend. "Prine here was a real coup!" he exclaimed. "Turns out our boy likes his online casinos, and not the up-and-up ones. No, Matty here favors the dark web stuff, the big stakes and the big wins…except he did a bit more staking than winning, didn't you, Matty?" Prine didn't reply and Arias didn't seem to need him to. "He got himself in a lot of debt, the kind of debt you don't report to your bosses at the FBI, the kind that declaring bankruptcy or some shit like that won't bail you out of. Now, normally I don't get into that sort of business. I find the profit margin too low. But when Matty's name happened to cross my desk, well he was just too good an opportunity to pass up. All that was…what? A year ago?"

Prine, still not meeting anyone's eyes, nodded. He looked utterly miserable.

"I bought his debt and put him to work for me. Just quiet stuff, at first. A few heads-up when the bureau started looking where I didn't want it to. That kind of thing. But then, a couple of months back, Karen over there talked somebody in the Columbian government into backing a raid of one of my biggest manufacturing interests. Just outside of Santa Marta it was. I lost a lot of product, a lot of men, a lot of money and, most importantly, a lot of respect. You see, Assistant Director, I'd killed Karen's sweet little seven to break her…to get her to back off. Except instead, she got an even *bigger* hard-on for me. She turned from a bulldog into a bulldog with a fucking obsession. Unfortunately, she also got careful. She got herself relocated, all while still running her hunt for me. The DEA have such a program. My people couldn't find her and, good as I am, even I can't kill somebody I can't find.

"So, I called on Prine, told him what I wanted. At first, he balked. I guess a little under-the-table info was one thing, *this* was another. So, I assured him this was it. If he did this for me, his debt would be paid, and nobody would ever know a thing about our business arrangement. Keeping a secret like that carries a lot of weight. In the end, our boy here wanted to be free more than he wanted to be clean. So, Prine went to Jessup with the tip from his imaginary C.I. and, like I knew she would, she jumped at the chance to finally corner me. I didn't expect *you*, Assistant Director, and I sure as shit didn't expect a fucking medium. But life does take you by surprise sometimes, doesn't it?"

"Matt," Brubaker said. "I've known you for years. You could have come to me if you were in trouble. We'd have figured it out."

Prine managed to meet her eyes. For a moment, Mia thought he might say something, try to explain himself. But he only shook his head and looked away.

"Awkward," Arias remarked with a chuckle. "Well, never mind, Matty. I'm as good as my word. Our business arrangement is over."

Then he drew his pistol again and shot Matthew Prine between the eyes.

Arias' men moved even before the disgraced agent hit the floor. They all closed on Brubaker, Delgado and Jessup, their guns leveled. They'd obviously been told to expect this turn of events and instructed to cut off any retaliatory move.

Brubaker gasped and tried to turn on her pew, only to cry out and clutch at her ruined knee. Beside her, Delgado let out a sound halfway between a groan and a wail. Jessup, sitting next to Mia across the aisle, simply stared down at the dead man with a look of utter defeat on her already drawn face.

With a long, theatrical sigh, Arias holstered his pistol again. Then, as if recalling something, he looked around the nave. "What's taking Moreno and Leon so long?" he asked no one in particular. Then, when nobody answered him, he grunted impatiently, pointed to another of his men and commanded, "Go check on them."

The man nodded and turned up the aisle.

And froze.

Matthew Prine stood at the back of the church, illuminated by the glow of the thug's flashlight. His expression was one of profound, heart-wrenching regret, and there could be no missing the enormous red hole in his forehead. His arms hung at his sides, his right hand open, his left one in a fist as if holding something—or, more precisely—*two* somethings.

Mia hadn't been sure if Barton could claim a soul who hadn't died by his own hand or that of one of his Forever Congregation.

Apparently, he could.

"What the fuck…" the thug muttered.

Arias looked, scowled, and then did a bizarre, almost comical double-take. His eyes flitted down to the body at his feet and then up once again at the figure standing just in front of the vestibule archway.

For a moment, Prine's eyes seemed to look at everyone at once, something like a plea in his expression. Then he mouthed a single word. He didn't speak it aloud; the man no longer had vocal cords or breath to move through them if he did. But the word rang in Mia's mind nonetheless—loud and clear.

"Barbarism."

Then Prine's expression went slack, and his left fist rose to his face, momentarily obscuring his features. When the hand came down again, it was empty.

And there were coins over his eyes.

"What the hell is going on?" Arias demanded.

"Exactly that," Mia heard herself reply. "Hell *is* going on."

CHAPTER 20
Camden, New Jersey—2022

ARIAS STARTED RANTING.

"What is that? Somebody tell me what that is!"

The men around him, six by Mia's count, not including the two who'd gone down into the cellar and were almost certainly not coming back up again, all stared at Prine's ghost. So did Jessup, Delgado, and even Brubaker, insofar as her wounded leg would allow.

Everyone, except Mia.

Mia was *thinking.*

Barbarism.

That was the single word Matthew Prine had spoken—or, more accurately, *transmitted*—to her in the moment before Barton's iron yoke settled on his shoulders. It was a word that had multiple meanings, the most obvious of which described extreme cruelty or brutality. That certainly fit St. Damned, Goddess knew. But it had another definition, didn't it? A literary definition that most any writer would recognize—though she couldn't fathom Prine intending to convey *that* meaning with his *ipso facto* last word. After all, given everything that was going on and what was surely coming, some obscure grammatical vagary couldn't possibly play any part in—

Mia's thoughts churned.

She was suddenly reminded of her Doohickey. It had been confiscated by Arias' men along with the team's cell phones and guns. They were all currently in the loose pile atop the alter, dumped there when Mia and the rest had been marched in here from the sacristy.

Not that the gadget would do them much good. True, its UV setting had worked on Rojas' ghost. It might work against Prine's as well, since he was so new a spirit. But the rest of Barton's congregation wouldn't be fazed much at all.

Fazed, she considered. *Phased.*

Barbarism.

But if that's true…then what does…

And, just like that, it all clicked into place.

Message in a bottle.

And Goddess help her, Mia nearly laughed.

Still standing in the center aisle, Arias drew his pistol again, this time leveling it at the *second* Matthew Prine. Prine's coin-eyed apparition didn't move.

"What the fuck are you?" the monster—the living monster—demanded.

Prine's mouth fell open. A sound emerged, a voice that Mia instantly recognized.

"I am the Alpha and the Omega, the first and the last, the beginning and the end."

Some of his men staggered a little, as if the words had struck them like a physical blow. A few dropped their weapons and crossed themselves. Others turned their heads away, as if frightened or ashamed.

Of them all, only Arias stood his ground, his gun never wavering.

"Fuck that," he muttered. Then he fired three times. Each report sounded as loud as a cannon shot as it reverberated off the high ceiling and stained-glass windows.

Behind Prine, the archway into the vestibule suffered the impact of all three shots, spitting wooden shards into the small, shadowed space. But the coin-eyed man never moved.

Instead, figures emerged from beyond the edges of the illumination cast by the half-dozen flashlights in the nave. Some seemed to melt out of the darkness. Others rose from behind pews and stepped out from around columns as if they'd been there all along. Within seconds, there were too many to easily count—two dozen at least. Unsurprisingly, most were Barton's teenage "brides", but men were here as well: Russel Saunders the naked man, William Shaker the bent-necked cop, and Rojas, who'd died only a few hours ago in the cellar and whose ghost had subsequently attacked Delgado.

Lyle Back was here as well, standing against one wall, between two of the tall thin windows. The sight of him made Mia sick to her soul, a feeling only exacerbated when she spotted Kimberly Allesbrook—*Oh Kim, he got you, after all*—as well as Stevie Doyle and Derrick Porter.

The latter manifested from the darkness behind the altar, close to the sacristy door. He wore the same thing he'd had on when Mia had last seen him. Well, of course he did. The dead had no wardrobes; his clothes were as much a manifestation as everything else about him, including the coins on his eyes.

From across the aisle, she heard Renee Brubaker begin to sob. Apparently, Derrick's mother had seen him, too. She called his name, the longing in her voice all but heartbreaking. But if the young man heard her, he gave no sign. Like the rest, he stood ramrod straight, his arms at his sides.

"What's the matter with you all?!" Arias screamed to his men. "Shoot! Shoot!"

One of them, the thug who had been restraining Jessup and who now stood shuffling nervously within reach of Russel Saunders, hesitantly raised his gun.

An instant later, Saunders fell on him.

Bony and twisted fingers, jutting out from the ends of arms that had been sliced down to their veins and arteries—found the thug's eyes and drove deep into them, raining dark blood down his face. The thug screamed and raised his gun, firing point blank into the naked man's chest, each shot an explosion that almost drove Mia, standing one row ahead of him and no more than three feet away, to her knees.

The bullets of course did nothing but punch into the church's ceiling as the victim—Mia could no longer think of him in any other terms, toppled backward with the naked man atop him. The two of them disappeared from sight, hidden by the pew, except for an occasional flailing limb.

At the same time, *exactly* the same time, the rest of Barton's coin-eyed "parishioners" surged forward.

"Shoot!" Arias yelled again.

And they did. All of his remaining men began firing in every direction. Mia felt herself suddenly blindsided by Jessup, who tackled her to the floor between the first pew and the dais and lay atop her as bullets tore through the air above their heads. Mia heard glass shattering and knew at least some of the stained-glass windows had been hit. But she also knew that the damage wouldn't last. Barton would heal it. He had *that* much power.

But that power was predicated on something.

And that something was a secret, just as Brubaker had predicted, something so personal, so intimate, that even as openly cruel a creature as Jonah Ray Barton couldn't bare to have it revealed.

And Mia knew, or thought she knew, what it was.

"Stay down," Jessup whispered. They were close, almost face to face. But the DEA agent wasn't looking at her. Instead, her head turned to the left, her attention focusing on something under the pew.

Mia glanced that way, and instantly realized what Jessup was thinking.

"You can't…" she said.

"Watch me," Jessup replied. Then she rolled off Mia and slithered under the pew, reaching toward the thug who was still trapped, twisting and bucking, under Russel Saunder's lean body and grasping thumbs, his eyes already gone and his brain next.

But it wasn't the man himself Jessup was after. It was his pistol. It lay there on the floor of the church beside his writhing body, and the DEA agent was reaching for it with desperate fingers.

At the same time, Mia spotted something else under the pew, another thing the thug had presumably dropped in the struggle. And, almost without thinking, she went for it. Fortunately, she was smaller than the DEA agent, slighter of build, and apparently the more agile of the two. Kicking her feet, she squirmed past the other woman, straining to reach what she'd seen.

"What are you doing?" Jessup demanded, sounding more concerned than angry.

"I—" Mia began.

Then two hands seized one of Jessup's ankles and one of Mia's, pulling them both back from under the pew.

"No!" Jessup screamed, making a final, desperate grab for the fallen pistol. For her trouble, she received a savage kick to the ribs just as Mia was grabbed by the hair and pulled to her feet.

Arias' eyes were wild. Spittle hung on his chin. "You!" he screamed. "Medium! You can stop this!"

All around them, Barton's "congregation" was busy. The thug furthest up the aisle was now on his back, beset by three of the coin-eyed girls. They pinned his arms and legs with their small but impossibly strong hands, while another was shoving something deep into his mouth. It took Mia's battered mind a few moments to realize what it was. A shoe. One of the man's own shoes.

His face had gone deep purple and his eyes were wide with breathless, airless panic.

Another man, this one closer to the altar, lay on his stomach. Lyle Back and Stevie Doyle sat atop him, holding him down. Meanwhile, Kimberly Allesbrook knelt beside the victim's head, gripping it in her pale fingers, and slamming it down on the aisle floor, again and again. She did this rhythmically, like a machine, her vacant expression never changing.

The man had already stopped struggling.

One more for the fold, Mia thought with bitter certainty.

There was more going on all around her—a throat being opened with bare fingernails over there, a neck being crushed under the weight of at least three girls' feet over there.

But, so far, the FBI team remained untouched. Across the aisle, Delgado and Brubaker still sat on their pew, Brubaker because her knee wouldn't allow for anything else, and Delgado—well, either because he'd become too terrified to flee or because he wouldn't leave his boss, not even to save himself. Mia hoped it was the latter.

"Do you hear me, you little bitch!" Arias screamed, spraying spittle into her face as he did so, his hand all but ripping the hair from her head. "Make it stop!"

"I can't!" Mia wailed, staring helplessly up at him.

He shoved his gun in her face. "Then why shouldn't I kill you?"

"Because that pleasure is mine," said a voice. *"And mine alone."*

Both Arias and Mia jumped in alarm. The big man whirled around, dragging Mia along painfully in his wake, until they both faced the dais and the pulpit that stood near its right edge. There, behind the lectern and looking calmly confident, perched Jonah Ray Barton. On his face was that same patient, slightly amused smile—and, in his hand, he held the pearl-handled straight razor he'd used to kill Lyle Back five years ago.

Without a word, Arias shot him—

—or, more accurately, shot *at* him, but only ended up chipping the large cross that hung on the front wall of the nave, just above the breezeway door. Barton never moved, his shining eyes, red as blood, filled with a vicious, sadistic mirth.

"What an odd sinner you are," he said in his smooth cadence. *"I let you into my church because I wanted to see this little drama play out. I wanted to see if you are anything like the characters in those old gangster movies my father used to watch. But you're not. You're simply an animal."*

"What *are* you?" Arias screamed. He let go of Mia, who recoiled away from him, tripped over her own goddamned feet and went down hard on her back, almost but not quite knocking the wind out of herself.

"Truly, truly, I say to you, before Abraham was, I am," Barton replied.

"John…" Mia gasped, not really understanding why she was saying anything at all. "Chapter 8, Verse 58."

Barton grinned broadly and looked down at her. *"You know your scripture. Very good, Mia. You are an interesting little lamb, aren't you?"*

"Fuck off…" Mia replied, scrambling backward. Looking frantically around, she spotted Jessup, who was still curled up in a fetal position under the pew, struggling to recover from Arias' kick. For a moment, their eyes met. Then the DEA agent shifted her weight a little and showed Mia the pistol. Apparently, she'd reached it after all.

"You're killing my men!" Arias exclaimed, his useless gun still leveled at Barton's smiling face.

"They're joining my Forever Congregation. As will you."

"Fuck off!" he screamed, oblivious to the fact that Mia had just said those very words.

"Such language. I'm looking forward to making you dance for me... once you're wearing my coins."

For the first time since Mia had met the man, Andres Arias looked afraid. He licked his lips and scanned the room, as if searching for some escape. When he glanced down at Mia, there was a plea in his eyes. But Mia could only look back up at him, her heart in her throat and the sounds of screams echoing all around her.

"I'm not going to let you kill me!" Arias suddenly cried, so loudly that the words seemed to ring inside Mia's head like a bell.

"He won't!" Karen Jessup exclaimed. Then when Arias blinked and looked her way, as if he'd forgotten she was there, Jessup raised the pistol. "*I* will."

Arias was fast; Mia had to give him that. He whirled and raised his own gun, firing at the same time Jessup did, the distance between them no more than two feet. The reports came so close together that they almost sounded like a single shot.

Jessup yelled in pain, the noise swallowed up by the cacophony of violence that filled the nave.

Arias, on the other hand, offered up no sound at all. Instead, he blinked as blood flooded his eyes from the hole that had appeared in his forehead. He stared down at Jessup, the woman whose daughter he'd murdered and who had just murdered him. His mouth moved, though still no sound came out.

Then he collapsed straight down to the floor.

Barton started laughing.

"Another sinner falls. Another soul joins my blessed flock!" he extolled.

Mia did her best to ignore him, to somehow push through the paralyzing terror. Then, steeling herself, she crawled over Arias' lifeless form to where Jessup lay, the gun still in her hand and a spreading stain in her right side.

"Mia..." Jessup whispered.

"I'm here," Mia said. "Let me help you." Except she had absolutely no idea what that help might look like. Jessup needed a doctor, an ambulance, *now*. But Barton was in his full glory, his enslaved souls slaughtering the rest of Arias' men, adding them to their ranks. No way was he going to let anyone out of here. Not now. Not ever.

She took Jessup's hand.

"Don't worry, little sinner," Barton told her from his perch atop the next pew. *"You, too, will be wearing the coins very soon!"*

"No…" Jessup whispered, writhing and clutching at her side.

"Leave her alone!" Mia screamed up at the grinning, mad-eyed ghost. But that only made him laugh harder.

Jessup began to cry. "I can't! I can't become one of them! Please, Mia…help me."

But, again, she didn't know how.

"I'm sorry…" Jessup gasped, wincing as if every word cut her more deeply than the last. "I wanted you to be a fraud. I wanted you to be wrong. You see…I can't bear the thought of an afterlife. I can't bear the idea that my little girl is there by herself. I know…I know how that sounds. But since that bastard killed her, every night I dream of her in the dark alone, calling for me, begging for me. I'm sorry, Mia. I'm so sorry."

"It's okay," Mia said. But, of course, it wasn't. Nothing was okay.

"I do enjoy your antics, pretty little lamb," Barton said. *"I truly can't wait to see what you do next!"*

"Didn't I just tell you to fuck off?" Mia exclaimed. She glared at the man, the ghost, the collector—only to find the pulpit suddenly empty.

Barton had gone.

Around them, the carnage quieted. Slowly, her heart pounding, Mia climbed first to her knees and then to her feet.

She found with some surprise that the nave stood empty, except for the bodies. Human remains were scattered everywhere she looked, limbs twisted, necks slit, and faces gouged or crushed. They littered the aisle, the pews, and the dais, all of them as dead as their boss, Arias. But so far at least, there were no doppelgangers with coins on their eyes.

The entire congregation had vanished, too.

Unseen, she corrected herself. *But not gone. He's watching.*

That son of a bitch is enjoying the show.

She looked across the aisle to where Brubaker and Delgado had been sitting. But the pew was empty. Could they be hiding somewhere—or had the things in this church dragged them off and killed them. Would she see them again, this time slack-mouthed and with coins on their eyes?

The idea made her almost physically ill.

"Mia…"

She looked back down at the woman who lay at her feet. "I'm here, Karen."

"Please…don't leave me."

"I won't." She knelt down and took the woman's hand again. "Looks like it's over for now," she said. She actually tried to smile at that. But, given the circumstances, it probably came off as more of a rictus. She was watching this woman die in front of her, and it felt like her soul was drowning in the horror and grief of it.

"I don't want those coins, Mia…" Karen Jessup whispered, tears flowing freely down the sides of her face. "I can't become one of that fucker's toys."

Mia tried to respond, but she didn't know what to say. Jessup had described exactly what was going to happen and there didn't seem to be anything that anybody could do about it. Jessup might be strong, maybe even stronger than Derrick had been. But that strength could only last so long against the onslaught of Jonah Ray Barton's indominable will. Like it or not, willing or not, Karen Jessup would join his congregation.

Unless…

The idea popped unbidden into her mind, so full and complete that a part of her wondered if it was truly hers. This feeling was so strong that she found herself craning her neck and looking around the nave again, half-expecting to see someone new, someone *fresh*—maybe the Goddess, herself—sending her a silent message the way Prine had.

But there was no one, at least no one corporeal.

So, she held Jessup's hand in both of hers, leaned in close and said, with fresh conviction, "Here's what you do, Karen. When the moment comes, you think about Chelsea. Do you hear me? You call to your daughter. Because she's there. Not in here, not in this fucking church, but out there, somewhere in the ether, somewhere in the universe. And she's been waiting for you. You use her strength and her love for you to pull you away from Barton. She's your shield, Karen. She's your lifeline. Do you understand?"

Jessup looked up at her in pain and anguish, and yet with something that was almost hope. "Will…that work?"

Would it? Mia didn't know. But the feeling was *so* strong.

So, she said, "Yeah. Yeah, it will. You hold onto your little girl. You imagine in your last moments, with your last breath, taking her hand and letting her lead you out of here."

"Yes," Karen Jessup whispered—mostly, Mia thought, to herself. "Yes. Chelsea. My baby…"

It didn't take long after that. It was as if the dying woman had found a way to let go, just—let go. Her grip on Mia's hand slackened and her entire body seemed to relax. Her eyes, fixed on Mia's, glazed over, and her head fell limply to one side. A final breath passed through her parted lips, riding on a single, blessed prayer:

"Chelsea…"

And then she was gone.

Mia swallowed. As reverently as she could, she placed Karen Jessup's hands over the woman's now unbeating heart and stood up again.

She was alone.

Alone in here—with them.

The silence was perfect and profound, the air cold and thick with the smell of blood and excrement. St. Damien's wasn't a church, and hadn't been for a long, long time.

It was a charnel house.

"This way!" someone called, the sound so abrupt that Mia jumped and screamed.

Then she witnessed a sight she would never have anticipated, something that, in the moment, seemed bizarrely more remarkable than the ghosts that filled this place.

Agent Archie Delgado, technical expert for the FBI, ran out of the vestibule and down the center aisle toward the altar. As he did so, he leapt with astonishing dexterity over a half-dozen corpses, his feet navigating past each obstacle in his single-minded determination to keep moving, keep *running*.

And across his shoulders lay the limp body of Assistant Director

Renee Brubaker.

Delgado, operating on what had to be a busload of pure adrenalin, had scooped his wounded boss up into a fireman's carry and was conveying her around the church with the speed and alacrity of a panicked cat.

"They're guarding the door!" he yelled, though Mia couldn't tell if this was meant for her or just a complaint made to the world-at-large. "Maybe the sacristy?"

"No!" Mia called to him.

He blinked and looked at her, running past the pew where she still stood over Jessup's body. "What?" he gasped, as if noticing her there for the first time.

"Past the altar!" she exclaimed. "Turn left and go through the door. The breezeway. It's the way I got out last time!"

His eyes lit up, his hope much more urgent and immediate than Jessup's had been. "Right!" he cried, sounding almost jubilant. "Right! Right! Right!"

And, without even breaking stride, he vaulted up onto the dais and disappeared into the shadows.

With a final look at Karen Jessup's still form, Mia slipped out of the pew and onto the dais, where she fished through the pile of confiscated items until she found her Doohickey. The guns she left behind; they were useless. The cell phones, with their freshly charged batteries, she left as well. But not because they were useless.

No, she left them because they were *more* useful right where they sat.

If I'm right.

If...

Then she picked up one of the several fallen flashlights and followed after Delgado as quickly as her own feet could carry her.

CHAPTER 21
Camden, New Jersey—2022

THEY REACHED THE DOOR TO the breezeway without incident. Mia had to step in front of a panting Delgado to work the knob as the burden of carrying Brubaker's weight across his shoulders seemed to finally be catching up with him.

The breezeway proved to be as empty as the nave had been—or had *seemed* to be. All of the panes of glass that ran the distance between here and the parsonage door on the other end appeared to be in good condition, not a crack anywhere. The damage Derrick had caused when he'd thrown Mia to safety was completely gone. Mia couldn't even tell which window it had been. And, in her heart, she knew no glazier had been called to make the repair. The City of Camden would never have bothered.

No, Barton did it. Barton looks after his church.

And he sees everything.

"I have…" Delgado gasped. "I have…to put her down."

"Oh!" Mia exclaimed. Then she went to the young man and, with some considerable shared effort, they managed to lower Brubaker to the floor. The woman, it turned out, was conscious after all, her face pale and twisted in pain. Arias' bandana was gone. It had been replaced with a black belt that had been cinched tightly around her left thigh—a makeshift tourniquet. For the first time, Mia noticed how loose Delgado's jeans seemed, and she couldn't help but smile. Of all of them, Archie Delgado was the most out of his element, the most frightened.

And yet, more than any of them, he'd stepped up.

"Thank you, Archie," Brubaker whispered, squeezing Delgado's hand and gritting her teeth.

"What now?" he asked, glancing around and wiping at his brow with the sleeve of his shirt. "We need something to break the glass."

"No," Mia said, keeping her tone level. "Look."

She pointed through the windows at the scraggly grass and gravel that flanked them.

More than a dozen coin-eyed brides stood in regimental lines outside the windows, flanking the breezeway on both sides. All of them faced stoically inward—and Mia, though of course she couldn't actually see their eyes, somehow knew that each and every one was looking at *them*.

Delgado uttered a sound that was almost a mewl. Then he covered his face with his hands. "We're going to die in here…" he whispered.

"Where…" Brubaker said, her voice so soft that Mia had to crouch down to hear her. "Where…is Karen?"

Mia replied in as gentle a voice as she could muster, "She and Arias shot each other. They're both dead. I'm…really sorry."

"Oh, sweet Mother Mary and Joseph…" Delgado whispered, crossing himself.

"Then she's out there, isn't she?" Brubaker asked, despair in her voice. "She's one of *his* now."

"I don't know," Mia replied. "Maybe not."

Brubaker gave her a pointed, disbelieving look, as if suspecting Mia of empty platitudes. But Mia honestly wasn't sure. The advice she'd given the dying woman had come out of nowhere—and, while she had no reason to believe such a thing as she'd proposed would work, a tiny voice in the back of her mind kept insisting it might. It just might.

Delgado gave the breezeway another, helpless look around. "He's got us trapped in here," he said, his voice thick and his whole body seeming to tremble either with fear or exhaustion, maybe both. "We should have gone for the sacristy!"

"Barton has it guarded," Mia said.

"It wasn't before!"

"That's because Barton *let* Arias and his men come in. More guests for his party, or lambs for the slaughter is probably more like it. But it doesn't matter either way."

"You mean we *are* going to die!" Delgado exclaimed, his voice catching. Sitting on the floor between them, Brubaker said nothing.

But Mia shook her head. Then she showed them the cell phone she'd picked up off the floor under the pew. It had belonged to one of Arias' thugs, a nameless brute of a man who'd died at the hands—literally—of Russel Saunders. It wasn't an old flip phone like the one Prine had found on the thug in the basement, but a relatively new iPhone, and when Mia pressed the "home" button, it came to life, the screen almost blindingly bright in the dim breezeway.

"Where'd you get that?" Delgado asked.

Mia didn't bother answering. The screen demanded a four-digit password which, of course, Mia didn't know. But there might be another way into the phone. It was a trick she hadn't attempted in years, and it didn't always work. But she'd performed it at more than a few parties and had once gotten a standing ovation from two dozen drunken college kids at a mixer.

It has to work. Because, if it doesn't, then Archie's right. We'll be wearing coins over our eyes in the next few minutes.

She focused on the screen and *pushed*.

This wasn't like back in Brubaker's office, a hundred miles and a million years ago. That had been a transfer of energy, taking juice from the cell phones in the room and giving it to the desk lamp. This was far subtler than that, more delicate. It was about finesse, about having just the right *touch*.

When nothing happened, she thought again, *Please Goddess. Give us this…*

Abruptly, the iPhone's screen flickered. An instant later, the passcode request vanished, replaced by a generic background and a handful of colorful apps.

"You got in!" Delgado declared.

"Yes." Mia blew out a long sigh and said a silent thank you to whatever could hear her.

"I'm surprised…it has power," Brubaker remarked.

"It belonged to one of Arias' men," Mia told her. "So, the church hasn't had time to drain it."

"Call for backup!" Delgado exclaimed. "Tell them to hurry!"

"No. We'd just hear more twisted Bible verses."

"What?" the young man cried. "We have to try! Otherwise, we're dead!"

"I think Dr. Lakatos has something else in mind," Brubaker told him.

Mia ignored them both. She searched the phone's apps until she found the one for text messaging. Not that she intended to text anyone. She just wanted something that would let her type.

Which she did, her thumbs dancing across the iPhone's virtual keyboard. She gave the message no address, but instead showed it to Delgado, holding a finger to her lips to keep him from reading it aloud.

"What?" he asked, looking frightened and confused.

Impatiently, she put the phone in his hand. Finally, he read the words. The message was a long one and she hadn't bothered with spelling or punctuation. But he got the gist of it. For a moment, Delgado opened his mouth to reply, but Mia shook her head vehemently and tapped the screen.

He blinked. Then he nodded and started typing. When he'd finished, he handed the phone back to her, letting her read what was there.

Don't know Can try some things but will take more time than we have

Mia looked down at Brubaker, who was watching them both expectantly but wisely saying nothing. Then she typed another message into the phone and passed it once again to Delgado.

I buy you time

Delgado read these words with an expression that mixed horror and hope. Then, when Brubaker tugged insistently on his pant leg, he passed the phone down to her. The assistant director, despite her visible pain, focused on it for a moment, reading the entire unsent thread.

Then she looked up and mouthed, "You know?"

Mia nodded.

Brubaker nodded back. Then she returned the phone to Delgado and reached out her hands to them both. Mia took one and Delgado the other and, for a few powerful seconds, the three of them held one another in this way. Their heads were on the most terrible of chopping blocks and they had, by Mia's reckoning, exactly one chance. But that chance depended on Delgado and his skills, and Mia and her ability to give him the time he would need to execute them.

When the moment passed, Mia turned and faced the door leading back into the church. A few hours ago, she would have sworn that she'd never again set foot in this place, his Hellish killing ground. But now she was here and about to face down the man himself, the *thing* that used to be Jonah Ray Barton. He had an army of the dead behind him, its ever-increasing ranks enslaved to his slightest whim. And what did she have?

Well, she had John Cooley.

"Mia," Brubaker said from behind her.

Mia paused but didn't dare turn around. Doing so might drain the shallow well of courage she was currently drawing from.

"What?" she said.

"Clean house," the older woman told her.

The oblique movie reference elicited from her the smallest of smiles. But then a moment later she steeled herself and, without responding, opened the door and re-entered Barton's church.

The first thing that struck her was how dark it had become. She'd left the flashlight with Brubaker and Delgado, counting on the fact that Arias' people had brought in a half-dozen and that these had been left scattered around the nave once Barton's attack had decimated their ranks. But, in the last few minutes, since the three surviving members of her team had fled into the breezeway, most of those flashlights had either been switched off by dead fingers or, more likely, had their batteries drained dry. St. Damned was forever hungry for power, and it didn't much care where it got it.

What had been left behind was a single flashlight, its glow muted, probably because, in the carnage, it had rolled under one of the pews. Now, its illumination presented itself as a defused radiance that cast a dim gray glow over much of the nave.

And by that glow, as she stepped around the altar to the lip of the dais,

Mia saw the ghosts.

All of them were here, except the dozen girls standing sentry outside the breezeway. The rest of Barton's blooded brides—abused and dead—filled two of the righthand pews, motionless and silent. Along the far wall, flanking the archway into the vestibule, were Andres Arias and all of his men, nine of them in total. They stood silent and erect, their mouths slack and their eyes hidden by freshly applied coins. Try as she might, Mia couldn't quite manage to feel sorry for them.

That wasn't the case with some of the others.

The bent-necked cop, the ghost of Officer William Shaker of the Camden Police Department, stood beside the naked man, Russel Saunders, with his cut forehead, slashed wrists and flayed legs. With them stood Matt Prine, not far from the spot where he'd actually died.

Further down the center aisle were Stevie Doyle, Lyle Back, and Kimberly Allesbrook. They stood with others, ghosts Mia hadn't seen before, men, women, and children, all be-coined, and with a variety of terrible damage done to their chests, necks, or heads. At first, Mia didn't know who they were.

Then she *did*.

These were the souls of the residents of Bleak Street, the ones who hadn't managed to leave before Barton's cancerous influence poisoned them. Suicides. Murders. Horror and death. And all of it inspired by a man they used to trust, even revere.

Finally, glancing over her shoulder, she spotted Derrick Porter. Rene Brubaker's son was by the sacristy door, all but invisible in the poor light. His slack mouth and coin-covered eyes broke off another piece of her already splintered heart. "I'm sorry," she heard herself say to him. "And… thank you."

He didn't acknowledge her, which came as no surprise. None of these trapped souls had wills of their own anymore—or, if such wills *did* still exist, they were so completely suppressed as to be rendered meaningless.

Then she faced forward again and realized with a spark of hope that Karen Jessup wasn't in attendance.

Maybe it did *work.*

Small victories…

She half-expected Barton's army to advance on her now, closing in from all sides, sent forth to kill her as they had the others.

But so far, none of them had moved.

Besides, he wants the pleasure of killing me himself. He said so.

Well…it's time to give him his chance.

"Barton!" she called into the cavernous space, her voice echoing off the walls and distant ceiling. "Jonah Ray Barton!"

For several moments, there was no reaction. The ghosts remained stationary, watching her, despite their "coin-blindness." But then the shadows near the cellar door began to thicken, to coalesce, turning from the simple absence of light into a heavy darkness that seemed to have mass, a consistency almost like molasses. As Mia watched, fighting to keep her terror in check, resisting the urge to turn and run back to the illusionary safety of the breezeway, the molasses took on form and texture, manifesting itself into the *thing* that used to be the founder and pastor of St. Damien's.

Jonah Ray Barton slid smoothly down the center aisle. As he did, the gagged and helpless form of Fabron Avatard, took shape and fell into step behind him—ever the shackled slave. In Fabron's eyes was more anguish, more despair, than Mia had ever seen. Of all of Barton's congregation, he alone wore no coins.

Now, finally, Mia understood why.

"Hello, Mia," Barton said as he slipped smoothly past Prine and most of the crew of *The Ghost Finders*.

"Hello, Jonah," Mia replied. It took everything she had to keep her voice level. There could be no mistaking the straight razor in the apparition's hand.

"No one has used my Christian name in a long time. Your colleagues are still hiding in my breezeway, by the by, playing on that little toy of theirs."

"It's a cell phone," Mia said.

Barton considered this. *"I've heard the term. I believe the first time was when that television crew came into my church some years ago. You were there."*

"Yeah," Mia said, her throat going dry.

"You were the only one who didn't join my Forever Congregation."

"You mean I'm the only one you didn't murder."

"Death is trivial, pretty little lamb. It's simply a rite of passage between the sinful world and my loving embrace."

"You're not God, Barton," Mia heard herself say.

"In these walls, on this street, I am," he replied with what she could only describe as an easy smile. *"That's a lesson you'll learn quickly, now that you've returned to me to have your sins expunged."*

He was closer now, slowly approaching the dais. Again, Mia had to fight the urge to retreat, to turn and run away screaming. *Time*, she thought. *I need to give Archie time…"*

"I'm curious," she said, speaking more loudly than she'd intended. Still, the comment seemed to stop Barton in his tracks.

"About what, pretty little lamb?"

"What do you all do in here? Not now. Not today. But when there's no one to hunt. In the long hours and the long days and the long years, how do you occupy yourselves?"

It was one of the paranormal world's age-old questions. What did ghosts do on their time off? Of course, some hauntings were like recordings playing on a loop, events repeating over and over, without end. These, pretty much everyone in her field agreed likely went on regardless of any observer. But more sentient hauntings were a wholly different matter. One theory suggested that most ghosts lived in a perpetual delusion, a "false life," without really understanding their circumstances or that the world had moved on without them.

But that wasn't Barton's case. No, this *thing* knew exactly what it was, and it reveled in it.

"How wonderful!" Barton remarked. He looked genuinely pleased, though the slack-jawed expression of his minions never changed. *"It's been ages since someone asked me about myself. I find it…validating, and certainly worthy of an answer."* He motioned toward one of the girls, who came forward at once, moving slowly but without any apparent resistance. Resistance, Mia supposed, left them with their free will as soon as they put those coins over their eyes. She stopped next to Barton, who turned and, with

his free hand, stroked the dead girl's kinky black hair in a way that made Mia's skin crawl.

"This is Rachel," he said, speaking to Mia but keeping his full attention on the girl. *"She was a kind creature, devout and full of life. How sweet it was to lure her to me, to know her flesh, and then to slit her pretty throat. Her father found her some time later and…"* He grinned. *"…did me the favor of severing my own tether to this stifling living world. Since then, of all my sheep, Rachel has remained my favorite."*

He was talking about John Cooley. This was Cooley's daughter, the one he'd avenged by using that old axe to decapitate her murderer. But not just her, of course. Cooley had avenged them all, just as his "message in a bottle" had said.

All Victims Avenged; Truth Always Raises Demons.

Barbarism…

I'm right.

Dear Goddess, let me be right.

Barton glanced sideways at her. *"You asked how we occupy our time. Well, by playing our games, of course. I fill my hours going from girl to girl, touching, caressing, hurting, knowing. I've known them all far too many times to count. Yet still I do delight in the games. My children. My toys."* He threw Mia a wink then, the gesture so grotesque that she felt bile rise in her throat. *"Shortly, I'll know you, too."*

With that, he turned away from the girl and mounted the dais. The razor in his hand seemed to shine despite the poor lighting.

Mia opened her mouth to scream when sudden sound filled the nave.

It was an ear-splitting whine, sharp and warbling. Gasping, Mia covered her ears.

Barton's predatory smirk vanished in an instant. He whirled around, his dark eyes scanning every corner of his church. *"What is that?"* he demanded of no one in particular. *"What is that infernal racket! This is a house of the Lord. This is* my *house! I will have silence!"* And, despite everything, Mia felt a smile lift the corners of her mouth.

Archie did it.

Then: *Showtime.*

CHAPTER 22
Camden, New Jersey—2022

SECONDS OF SILENCE FOLLOWED AND then the siren returned, every bit as loud and piercing as before. Flashes of light, small but noticeable in the shadowed nave, appeared up and down the center aisle and along a couple of the pews. Others lit up the alter behind Mia, setting the marble aglow at her back.

Barton glared at it all, clearly uncomprehending, his face a mask of twisted outrage.

Meanwhile, yet another light caught Mia's peripheral vision. She risked a glance over her shoulder.

Delgado stood at the breezeway's now open threshold. With his left arm, he was supporting Brubaker, her bad leg tucked up behind her and her right arm across Delgado's shoulders. Though she grimaced in pain, her free hand was out in front of her, her thumb raised. Beside her, Delgado was holding out the cell phone Mia had left with him, the source of the light that had caught her attention.

The screen was flashing, the speaker squealing, announcing the same piercing message as the rest of the cell phones in the nave. Some had belonged to Arias' thugs and thus hadn't been in St. Damien's long enough to be fully drained. The rest had belonged to Brubaker's team and, freshly charged, were now piled on the alter.

"What is that?" Barton shrieked, turning back to Mia and pointing an

accusing finger at her. *"What are you doing to my church?"*

"It's called a Wireless Emergency Alert, or WEA for short," Mia replied. Her chest, which had felt so tight she'd feared her heart might be crushed, loosened a little with the words.

It might work. I might just make it work.

"You've probably never heard of it," she went on, speaking conversationally, as if she were lecturing at a paranormal convention. "It was established about ten years ago. It allows specific alerts to be sent to cell phones all over a given area. Only authorized agencies can use it. Fortunately, the FBI is one of them."

"What? I don't understand!"

The phones all went silent. Moments later, their screens went dark as well. A WEA repeated just once, though the alert would remain for 24 hours, or until the user dismissed it.

"Then I'll explain," Mia said.

Barton's expression surprised her. He looked almost pleading. This was an entity that had spent the last fifty years in absolute control of his environment, the god of St. Damned. Now, however, he was at a loss—and he didn't like it, not one bit.

"Then explain…explain now, pretty little lamb."

"The name," Mia said, keeping her tone level but putting as much iron as she could muster into the words, "Is *Doctor* Lakatos."

Barton glared at her, almost snarling. *"Dr. Lakatos, then,"* he said. *"Explain."*

"All Victims Avenged," Mia intoned. "Semi-colon. Truth Always Raises Demons. Period."

"What?"

"Don't you recognize that epitaph? It's on *your* gravestone."

Barton's brows knit. Around him, eerily, the brows knit on every single ghost in the nave.

"John Cooley," he finally replied. *"That was his rambling. He took all that time to etch it into my marker, but it was just nonsense. His mind had broken. I'd broken it. And within a few hours, he was dead, hanged in his cell."* Barton grinned again. Pridefully. Savagely.

"Tell me," Mia said, knowing she was going off script a little. "Did he hang himself…or did you kill him, maybe sending poor Rachel there to do the job?"

"I would have," Barton replied without rancor. *"But, as things worked out, that crazy, broken fool saved me the trouble. He took his own life."*

Mia let out a long sigh. The tragedy of it, the *courage* of it, was almost more than she could bear. "John Cooley wasn't crazy. He wasn't broken. And he certainly wasn't a fool. He may have been the bravest, cleverest, and subtlest person I've ever come across…and he was worth a hundred of *you!*"

Barton looked taken aback, his eyes widening. *"That might be the first time in a half-century that anyone has insulted me to my face."*

"I'm just getting started," Mia said.

"I should kill you right now."

Mia had to fight back a rising panic. Somehow, miraculously, she did so, though on some deep level, she suspected that strength wasn't coming from herself alone. In a steadier voice than she would have believed possible, she said, "Do that, and you'll never get your explanation. And believe me, Barton, you *want* that explanation."

Barton stood there, not six feet away. He seemed to be fuming, barely able to contain himself. Around him, behind him, his parishioners became suddenly agitated, leaning forward like dogs straining on their leashes.

Mia knew she was walking a razor's edge. She was counting on a dead man's curiosity, his *need* to be in control, to keep her alive long enough to make him understand—to make him *believe*.

And not just him. This little show is for all of them.

She said, "John knew your secret, and he committed suicide to save his wife Wanda and his two surviving children. You had told him, repeatedly, that if he revealed what he knew their lives would be forfeit. He managed to convince Wanda to leave Bleak Street. But he knew she wouldn't stay away, and the moment she and her boys returned, you'd take them. So, he made up his mind to sacrifice himself for them."

"How noble," Barton said, the words coming out almost as a growl.

Mia swallowed back a rejoinder. She didn't want to risk provoking this entity more than she already had. Instead, she just kept going, speaking quickly but reasonably, the words tumbling out of her. "But he couldn't let it be. He couldn't let what you had done go unpunished. Oh, he knew the truth of your crimes had already been revealed. But you didn't fear exposure. You reveled in the pain and death you'd caused. You considered yourself an apex predator, a *Barton*, New Jersey royalty, above the mere peasants that you trapped, tortured, raped, and murdered."

She paused then, expecting him to comment. He didn't.

Mia felt herself trembling. But she stayed rooted to her spot, her hands balled into fists, her gaze locked on the dead man's. His eyes were like ruby spears. She could almost feel them piercing her, if not her skin then her soul, draining whatever borrowed courage was pushing her forward.

"So, he conceived his 'message in a bottle.' Do you know that metaphor, Jonah?"

Barton didn't move. But his eyes changed, ever so slightly. In an instant, he'd gone from anger to uncertainty, maybe even unease.

Mia said, "It refers to a cry for help…or, in this case, a cry for understanding…that's cast out into the unknown void in the hopes that someone, somewhere will find it and read it. Well, John gave his life to send such a message. I'm only sorry that it took fifty years for someone to get it."

"I got it," Barton said, his voice low. *"I was there when he wrote it."*

"Oh, a lot of people have seen it," Mia replied. "The police. The press. Neighbors. Probably some local kids on a dare. Even the FBI and DEA. But none of them *got* it." She managed a smile, deliberately self-satisfied. "Until now."

"You?" said Barton with another sneer. *"You understood this…message?"*

"Only the first part initially. I guess you could say I was the one to pull the cork off the bottle. The punctuation. That was the first flag. A semi-colon between two independent clauses. Maybe one person in ten knows the correct ways to use a semi-colon. And a period at the end of the sentence. Now, I don't know much about the psychology of 'broken ramblings' as you put it. But it seems unlikely that such a thing would be perfectly punctuated, don't you think?"

Barton actually laughed, the sound both cruel and perhaps a bit hollow.

"That's the big secret? John Cooley was an English teacher! Is it really so much to imagine that his dying mind would cling to that in the end."

Mia shook her head. "I told you: that was just the cork. John was a subtle, brilliant, desperate man, and he used the punctuation to announce to someone, the *right* someone, that there was more here than met the eye. I'm only sorry that I wasn't the one to see the next step, to 'pull out the message' I guess you might say."

"Then who was? Quickly, Dr. Lakatos. I'm losing my patience."

Mia ignored this, or tried to. "Matthew Prine," she said. "I don't know if he figured it out before or after Arias killed him. Maybe death brings with it some greater awareness, or a newly-found or newly-remembered ability to make connections. Either way, in the moments before you forced him to wear your coins, he managed to send me a word."

"Send you? He couldn't speak!"

"He knew I was a sensitive. He knew, of all the people in the church, I was probably the only one that might hear him. So, with the last bits of his fading freewill, he took the chance."

"Fine, then," Barton said bitterly. *"What did he 'send' you?"*

"One word. 'Barbarism.' Do you know what a barbarism is, Jonah?"

"I grow weary of this lecture," Barton declared. As Mia watched in barely contained horror, he advanced on her, no more than three feet away now. Behind and around him, every single member of his congregation began a slow march toward the alter, toward *her*.

"Shit…" Mia heard Archie say from somewhere behind her.

She could run, but she had no illusions about how successful *that* would be.

So, drawing yet again from that all-but-inexplicable well of courage, she stood her ground and said, "So kill me, Jonah! But then you'll never find out about John's message in a bottle…or mine."

Barton paused again. *"Yours? What are you talking about?"*

"That sound you just heard. The WEA. It isn't just a sound. It's a message. I sent out a message to every cell phone in the county. The same message."

"What message?!" Barton exclaimed. He sounded more than uncertain

or uneasy now. He sounded alarmed.

"Why…the meaning of what John wrote on your gravestone, of course," Mia replied with a smile that belied her terror. "Barbarism has a few definitions. But in grammar, it refers to a misused word. The English language is filled with sometimes bizarre vagaries. John knew that, and deliberately used one to hide his intentions from you, to keep his family safe…but still make what he had to say accessible to someone with the education to see it. I'm ashamed to say that I didn't. But Matt did." When Barton didn't move or speak, she said, "The first half of the epitaph was a simple confession. 'All Victims Avenged.' But the second was more like an entreaty. 'Truth Always Raises Demons.'"

"It means nothing," Barton whispered, and Mia couldn't tell if he was trying to convince her or himself. *"He called me a demon. What of it?"*

"The word 'raises,' was deliberately misused," Mia told him almost gently. "The actual word is its homonym, 'razes.' Pronounced identically, but with an almost opposite meaning. To 'raise'…R-A-I-S-E is to lift up, to create. To 'raze'…R-A-Z-E is to tear down, to destroy. The actual meaning of the epitaph is therefore 'Truth Always *Destroys* Demons.' John was telling us that there was a truth that could destroy you, one that would strip away your power."

"No!" Barton exclaimed. Then, to Mia's horror, that single word was repeated by every ghost in the nave, dozens of them, men and women whose lives had been cut short and their souls hijacked by this monster, all on the strength of a single secret. Jonah Ray Barton was a known serial killer. He'd kidnapped, raped, tortured and murdered so many people. But, instead of remorse, he drew power from his crimes.

But *this* was different. This was his identity, his self-image—the lie that his entire empire had been built upon. Remove that lie, that cornerstone, and the whole thing would come crashing down.

At least, Mia *thought* it would.

Prayed it would.

Barton took a moment to compose himself. His fist, the one holding the straight razor, slowly rose. *"But what does it change, Dr. Lakatos? John Cooley merely shared with you that there was a secret. He didn't share the secret itself. He was too frightened to risk it. Rachel and I had seen to that."*

"Don't pretend Rachel had anything to do with it!" Mia told him sharply. "You'd stolen her will. That's what you do. What you call your congregation are just slaves!"

"Slaves are to be submissive to their own masters in everything; they are to be well-pleasing, not argumentative," Barton said with a sly smile.

That was from Paul's letter to Titus in the New Testament.

"You like to wield out-of-context Bible verses like weapons, Jonah," Mia said. "Well, here's *my* weapon. Here's what John Cooley's message actually said. It's the same message that I sent out just now in the WEA, the same message that the entire county already knows."

"You're going to join me now, pretty little lamb."

"Initial caps."

"What?"

"Another trick of grammar. A marketing tool. You capitalize the first word of every letter in a sentence. It adds…impact, even if it's grammatically incorrect. John knew it. John counted on someone else knowing it."

"You will be quiet now."

"I told you, Barton. It doesn't matter. It's already too late. In a way, this is *my* confession, my confession to you, informing you of what I've already revealed to the world."

"Wait…"

"All Victims Avenged; Truth Always Razes Demons."

"Shut up, you little bitch!"

"Initial caps. A. V. A. T. A. R. D."

"No!"

"I had Agent Delgado use a cell phone to search Camden's vital records. At first, we were worried they might not be digitized going that far back. But they are, and he found it. Your birth certificate."

Barton lowered the razor as if it had suddenly become too heavy. As Mia watched, he took a shaky step backward.

Mia, in turn, took a hard step forward, toward him. "Your mother, who died birthing you, was Dominique Avatard. And your father…your *real* father, was her husband, Fabron Avatard."

"Don't!" Barton exclaimed, the single word like a plea.

"The Bartons had no children. My guess is old Joshua was sterile, or maybe impotent. Either way, he couldn't father an heir. So, when his housekeeper died in childbirth, leaving behind poor, gentle, pliable Fabron, Old Joshua swept in. I don't know if there was a formal adoption, or if he simply bribed or bullied the cook into submission. But regardless, the end is the same. He wound up claiming Fabron's son as his own. All that pride he instilled in you over being a Barton, of being 'New Jersey royalty,' was a lie. And he never told you. He never told you that, in your veins, ran the blood of a servant, not a king!"

"Please!" Barton wailed. He stumbled backward and fell off the dais, the move weirdly lifelike, given that this was simply a shade, a spectre. He landed on his knees in the center aisle. The razor fell from his grasp, vanishing into nothingness before it even reached the floor. *"Please don't. Please don't tell."*

"I already have," Mia reminded him. "Even if you kill me, kill us all, it will still be out there. By morning, the press will have it. The story will run. Famed serial killer Jonah Ray Barton wasn't a Barton at all."

"Stop it!" Barton clamped his hands over his ears.

But Mia didn't stop. She didn't dare. She'd cast a charm over St. Damned, subtler perhaps but every bit as potent as anything her grandmother might have conjured. Every soul in this place, living or dead, hung on her every word. The slack mouths of Barton's 'Forever Congregation' had closed and, while the coins remained over their eyes, they'd stopped advancing and now stood still and rigid, their collective posture one of what Mia could only label "rapt attention."

All except Fabron Avatard. His eyes were shining with something like hope. And his mouth, still crammed with coins, looked like it might be trying to smile.

"That was why you killed your cook!" Mia said, standing now at the edge of the dais and pointing an accusing finger down at the man, the ghost, the *monster* that cowered below her. Barton seemed to have shriveled, diminished, sunken into hunched supplication. He didn't look up at her. He didn't move at all, making Mia wonder if he was even capable of it anymore.

"On the night John discovered your crimes and went into the parsonage to avenge his daughter's murder, you'd just done it, hadn't you? Maybe Fabron finally found out about all the girls you'd been trapping and killing. Or maybe he'd known for years but lacked the strength to do anything about it. Either way, that night he came to you and showed you the birth certificate. *Your* birth certificate. He confronted you with you *real* parentage, perhaps hoping it would stop you from hurting anyone else. Instead, you turned your rage on him, didn't you. Jonah Ray Avatard, you murdered your father because you couldn't bear that he *was* your father!"

Barton wailed. He threw back his head, his face twisted into a mask of shame and terror and screamed up to the rafters of the church. That scream seemed to reverberate off every wall and pew. It set Mia's teeth on edge, louder and more ear-piercing than even the WEA had been. In it was so much rage, so much betrayal, so much cruelty, all of it laid bare in a single instant.

And then he was gone.

Just gone.

CHAPTER 23
Camden, New Jersey—2022

THE SILENCE THAT FELL OVER St. Damien's was so complete it might have been called a magic spell.

Mia stood stock still, listening to her heartbeat, which had been thundering moments ago but was now, slowly, returning to normal. She heard tentative, shuffling footsteps at her back and turned to see Delgado, still supporting Brubaker, moving cautiously toward her from the breezeway threshold. The assistant director's face was a sheen of sweat and every step clearly pained her.

Yet, she was smiling.

"Is that it?" Delgado asked in a kind of tentative whisper.

But she couldn't answer him; she didn't know.

Was that it?

Then she looked around the nave again and realized: *No. Not yet.*

The ghosts were still there. All of them, including the brides from the breezeway. Mia didn't know when they'd joined the festivities but, sometime during the cleansing, they clearly had. Now their entire compliment, more full-form apparitions than Mia had ever *imagined* seeing, all stood perfectly still, some in the aisle, some in the pews, some against the back wall. Mia had expected them to fade when Barton's secret, which had been binding them to him, was revealed. But that, it seemed, hadn't happened.

Then one of the ghosts raised his hands to his eyes and, moving slowly, hesitantly, took the coins from them. As his hands lowered, trembling now, those same coins—those same *shackles*—dropped from his grasp. But, instead of clattering to the floor, they seemed to just melt away, vanishing in little whisps of spent psychic energy.

Derrick Porter looked up. His face was pale, his hair tousled, but his skull seemed no longer damaged. His eyes, his real eyes, looked around the church. Then they settled on Brubaker, who uttered a sound between a gasp and a sob at the sight of him.

"Mom...?" he whispered. The sound in the otherwise silent nave was like a prayer.

"Derrick?"

His mother almost started forward, reaching for him with her free hand, only to cry out in pain the moment she absently put weight on her wounded leg. Still beside her, Delgado struggled to both support and restrain her. Seeing this, Derrick's face flashed with alarm and he hurried forward, crossing the space between the sacristy door and the dais in three long strides. Hopping up with surprising agility, he took his mother's reaching hands in his and the two of them just kind of melted into one another. Delgado, with a nod from Mia, released Brubaker and stepped back, watching the reunion with wide-eyed, almost childlike fascination.

Mia, for her part, found herself momentarily blinded. Too many tears.

"Baby…" Renee Brubaker whispered, clinging to her son as if he were life itself—which was ironic, considering. Derrick was taller than she, a lanky young man who, of course, hadn't aged a day since Mia had last seen him. He held his mother to his chest while she cried openly, his eyes searching for and finding Mia's.

She wiped an impatient hand across her face to clear her vision.

Derrick smiled at her.

"You did great," he said.

Unable to speak, she simply nodded.

Finally, Derrick stepped back, supporting his mother with his strong, long-fingered hands. Brubaker gazed at him, no longer an FBI assistant director but simply a grieving mother. Her eyes raked his face as if trying to memorize its every feature. And, for most of a minute, he just stood there, smiling, and let her do it.

Then, he said, *"I'm free, Mom."*

She nodded, her eyes red from crying.

"I have to leave."

Brubaker started sobbing again. She shook her head.

"It's okay. I'll see you again. I love you."

She reached out for him, almost falling. But Delgado, bless him, was there in an instant, supporting her as he had before.

Derrick, still smiling, turned away then and seemed to step through some sort of unseen door. One moment, he was there on the dais, and the next he was gone, slipped through the veil between worlds.

"No!" Brubaker cried. Then she turned and buried her face against Delgado's chest. "No…"

Mia started toward her, intending to lend what meager comfort she could.

But then things started—*happening.*

It began with Andres Arias, who stood with his men against the back wall, presumably guarding access to the vestibule. Unlike Derrick, who seemed to turn and *step* into whatever came next, Arias was *pulled.* In one instant, he had just taken the coins from his eyes and was blinking, as if confused, and in the next something unseen seized him from behind, emerging either from the wall at his back or from some threshold that happened to have located itself there. In either case, Arias' face bore an instant's worth of terror before he was yanked backward and out of this world altogether.

In the few seconds that followed, one by one but in rapid succession, each of his men joined him.

At the same time, *The Ghost Finders* removed their coins, letting them fall absently to the floor and melt before they got there. As with Derrick, the damage their bodies had suffered was gone, erased from these manifestations of themselves. For a moment, the three of them just looked at each other, at first in bewilderment, and then in joy. Kim flew into Stevie's arms and kissed him as he held her close. Standing nearby, Lyle rolled his eyes at them, though he was smiling as he did it.

Then all three turned and stepped away, disappearing as Derrick had.

Nearby, standing amidst the pews, Matthew Prine's coins fell away. He looked at his hands for some reason, and then up at Mia, Brubaker, and Delgado. But, as Brubaker was still crying in Delgado's arms, only Mia looked back at him. For a moment, their eyes met. He was still a handsome man.

"I'm so sorry," he said. The voice was faint. He was already halfway gone.

With what she hoped was a forgiving smile, she replied, "Barbarism."

He tried to smile back but couldn't quite manage it. For an awful second, Mia feared that whatever had taken Arias and his thugs would claim this man as well. But that didn't happen. Instead, with a final sad nod, he slipped through an invisible door.

William Shaker and Russel Saunders were next, except now the bent-neck cop's neck was no longer bent and the naked man was no longer naked, his many wounds gone. As Mia watched, the two shook hands warmly. Then, together, they turned and stepped away.

In the moments that followed, the Bleak Street residents departed as well. Some of them left singly, others in small family groups. But, in every case, they went the way Shaker and Saunders had, the way *The Ghost Finders*, including Derrick, had, the way Matt Prine had—

—through a door that only they could see and into a world that Mia couldn't rightly imagine.

That left the brides.

Twenty-seven girls, the oldest no more than seventeen. Since 1972, they'd been Barton's eyes and ears, his mouth, his hands, his helpless, voiceless, assassins. Now, they were leaving, one-by-one, the coins having fallen from eyes that wept with either horror or relief, or maybe both. As Mia witnessed them disappear, like stars going out, all over the nave, some paused long enough to smile at her. A few even waved. Then they were gone, each to whatever destiny had awaited her for all these decades.

Until only one girl remained.

She stood closest to Mia, almost at the base of the dais, exactly where Barton had summoned her.

Rachel.

She looked at Mia wonderingly. Her eyes were dry, but her lower lip trembled in the way of a much younger child. She stood there for almost a full minute, until Mia was moved to say, "It's okay, sweetheart. Go home."

"Home…" Rachel whispered.

Then a third voice, a deeper voice, said, *"Home, baby."*

A man emerged seemingly out of nowhere to stand beside the shaking girl. He was a big guy, tall and broad-shouldered, his skin dark and his eyes bright with intelligence. With one hand he reached for Rachel, gently touching her shoulder. As he did, she started and looked at him, and the wonder in her face turned into something so much deeper.

"Daddy?"

He smiled. *"It's me, baby girl. Come on. Your mamma's waiting."*

She fell against him. He folded her up in his strong arms and held her fiercely. As he did, his eyes found Mia's.

"Thank you," John Cooley said.

"No, sir," Mia replied, all but crying herself now. "Thank *you.*"

He smiled a sad, long-suffering smile. Then he took his child and led her through whatever doorway he'd just come.

Rachel Cooley. Home at last.

St. Damned had become St. Damien's again, and it was now empty of the dead.

Slowly, with a shuddering sigh, Mia turned toward the only two entities left in the church. Brubaker had composed herself. While Delgado continued supporting her out of physical necessity, she'd nonetheless dried her tears and reassumed the mantle of leadership. She met Mia's gaze steadily and asked, "Ready to go?"

Mia almost laughed. "More than ready. Archie, do you need help with her?"

Delgado replied wearily, "Just help me get her off the dais. I can take it from there."

Mia did so. She wasn't strong enough to support the assistant director herself but was able to take the woman's free arm and stabilize her until Delgado managed to get her down the one step to the aisle. Brubaker grunted in pain but offered no other protest.

Then the three of them, Delgado and Brubaker in front and Mia holding up the rear, made their way up the center aisle.

It was slow going. Barton and his congregation might be gone, but the bodies they'd made this night remained. This included Prine's, and Brubaker paused just for a moment to look down at her agent, her expression unreadable.

"I'm sorry, boss," Delgado said.

Brubaker replied, "As soon as we're out of here, we'll call for backup."

"And an ambulance," he added. "For you."

"Yes. Mia?"

"I'm right behind you."

"Where's Karen? Agent Jessup?"

Mia pointed back down the aisle to the pew beneath which she and the DEA agent had hidden. "She saved my life."

"She wasn't here," Brubaker said. "She wasn't wearing those coins. I kept looking for her."

"I know."

Brubaker asked, "Why not, do you suppose?"

"I have a theory," Mia replied. "But let's wait until we're out of here, okay?"

"Yes. Good idea."

A minute or so later, the three of them slipped through the vestibule. Mia meant to circle around the other two and open the door for Brubaker, but Delgado beat her to it. With his free hand he reached eagerly for the latch, and something in his bearing made Mia think he half-expected to find it locked or otherwise impassable.

It wasn't. The big door squeaked loudly but opened obediently enough. In an instant, the vestibule filled with cool city air. Mia breathed it gratefully, closing her eyes and just enjoying the moment as Delgado led Brubaker over the threshold and out into the Camden night.

"Mia," he said, looking back. "We're going to need your help on the stoop."

"Right," Mia replied. She sighed and stepped toward the open doorway, intending to follow what was left of her team out of this hellish place.

That's when the door slammed shut with such force that, had Mia been a half-step closer, it might have taken her leg off.

"Not you, pretty little lamb!" Jonah Ray Barton declared, emerging like a coiled serpent from the shadows filling the vestibule. *"You and I have a score to settle!"*

CHAPTER 24
Camden, New Jersey—2022

MIA SCREAMED.

Barton—*No, not Barton. Avatard*—an utterly useless corner of her mind insisted, appeared different now, less corporeal. He seemed to fill half the vestibule, as much shadow as substance. But real enough. Oh yes, certainly real enough to slam the door and loom before her, as dark and unrelenting as a cresting midnight wave.

She felt herself retreat a step. Then, pushing past the shock that threatened to cripple her, Mia turned and started in the direction of the nave. She had no plan other than to find another exit. He had no congregation this time, no guards that he could station at every door. Like her now, he was alone, and that meant he couldn't be in two places at once.

At least, that was what she told herself.

But then that sweet rationalization vanished like smoke when he darted in front of her, blocking her path. She could see his face encased in the massive, undulating shadow, his eyes shining red. She could even hear his footsteps, the *clop-clop* of his shoes. But the rest of him remained fluid, indistinct.

Yet solid.

Mia slammed into him before she could stop herself, bouncing off what she'd mistaken to be a wall of shadow with enough force to knock the wind from her lungs. She landed hard on her ass on the dusty floor, her breath coming in strained gasps.

Avatard said, *"For you were straying like sheep, but have now returned to the Shepherd and Overseer of your soul."*

He was paraphrasing First Peter, quoting the Bible again, twisting it as he always had to justify his depravities, his cruelties.

"I'm not your fucking sheep!" Mia cried. Then, mustering herself, she scrambled to her feet and made for the only door still available to her. She half-expected him to dart in front of her again. *He's fast! So fast!* But she reached it without further impediment and pushed her way into the small square room at the base of the belltower.

Her plan, if panicked desperation could be called a 'plan,' was to get up to the top and pry one of the boards loose. After that—well, after that, she'd just have to see.

It was dark of course. But her eyes, she discovered, had somewhat adjusted to that. She couldn't discern colors, but then in here there were none to see. Fortunately, the walls and high ceiling all showed themselves clearly enough.

Mia hadn't been in here since her first visit, five years ago, and the room seemed even smaller than she remembered. Around her, the air was still and cold. The ladder, down which Derrick fell and died, stood before her. She spared a moment, no more, to gaze up at it—trying hard *not* to remember the way Derrick had looked when he'd hit the floor. Her courage, if not her very sanity, was hanging by a thread.

No point tugging.

She began to climb, rung by rung, moving as quickly as possible but much more slowly than she would have liked. The ladder was wooden and yet it felt like ice, each new grip biting almost painfully into her bare palms. All the while, she kept listening in the darkness, straining to hear some warning that the shadows were coming for her.

So far, there was nothing.

Mia reached the top. She expected to find the latch set, as it had been five years ago when poor, panicked Kim had been worrying at it. But it wasn't and, though the trapdoor proved heavy, by bracing her shoulder against it, she was able to lift it with relative ease. She opened it enough to allow her to climb through but didn't let it fall completely on its hinge, worried about the noise it would make.

Avatard had to know where she was. Then again, he wasn't what he'd been. The loss of his secret had cost him his slaves, his full corporeality, and had perhaps thinned the tether that connected him to this world. If so, then a door, even a simple one like that at the bottom of the ladder might flummox him.

He shut the street door easily enough.

Mia swallowed and kept moving, straightening up in the belltower and carefully closing the trapdoor. Then, with her heart in her throat, she looked around.

Another square room, no more than eight feet to a side. Much of the space was taken up by the actual bell mechanism, which consisted of a heavy wooden headstock set close to the ceiling and a four-foot diameter bell made of some kind of thick metal. There seemed to be no sheen to it, but that might have been the darkness.

There were windows on two sides of the tower, but these had been boarded up decades ago. Why Avatard had never removed these boards was a mystery she didn't have time to consider. Instead, she went to the nearest of them, her fingers running along the dusty old wood, feeling for gaps. Most were tight, hammered in with nails that had long ago rusted into place. But one in particular seemed to have some *give* to it. With a gasp, she tried to get her finger into the narrow space between it and its neighbor, painfully breaking a nail in the process.

It came loose, not much but some, granting her a flash of almost agonizing hope.

Fresh air hit her nose as it had in the vestibule right before Avatard had sprung his trap. Voices reached her from below, riding on the still night air. It sounded like Brubaker and Delgado. They were conversing urgently, all but shouting at each other.

Mia called, "I'm up here!"

The shouting stopped.

A pregnant silence followed. Then Delgado called back, "Where?"

"The belltower!"

"Mia!" Brubaker exclaimed. "Can you get out?"

"He's got me trapped. Please help me!"

"He's not blocking the cell phones anymore. So, we've called for backup. They'll be here in five minutes, ten tops."

Might as well be a thousand years, Mia thought bitterly.

"Hide!" Delgado called to her. "Wait the son of a bitch out!"

"No," Brubaker said. "Mia…you've got to finish it. You've got to clean house."

"I…don't know how!" Mia yelled back, the words choked in a sob. "Please, you have to help me!"

"We can't get in," Brubaker said with infuriating calm. "He's locked the doors. Archie tried every entrance. He even broke a window in the breezeway, but the door into the church is also locked."

That's what he's been doing all this time. He knows I can't get down from here, so he's making sure his fortress is secure.

"It's up to you, Mia," Brubaker told her. "He's a ghost, not a god. Clean house."

She heard a sound, a creak, and it almost seemed to stop her heart.

Someone—something—had just come through the door at the bottom of the ladder. Apparently, whatever Avatard was now, he needed to open doors. Forgetting the window, the loose board, and the useless conversation, Mia returned to the trapdoor and felt around it. How blessed would it be to find a latch of some kind. But no. There was no way to lock or otherwise bar the hatch from this side, and nothing handy that she could place atop it. She supposed she could sit on it as Kim had, but she had sensed his strength in the vestibule. Most likely he would throw her off and then be on her in the moment.

No, Delgado had it right.

Hiding was her only hope.

Unfortunately, there was only one place.

Mia stood, went to the center of the room and ducked under the big bell. Inside, she found a fist-sized clapper, either iron or very tarnished brass, mounted at the end of a four-foot metal arm as thick as a broom handle.

He'll find me. Of course, he will. There's nowhere else I could have gone!

Except, maybe there was. Maybe, just maybe, if Avatard was truly as diminished as she dared to hope, truly so limited by physical laws that even being made of shadows he still had to open doors to get through them, then what other limitations did he have? Mightn't he come up here, find her gone, and think she'd doubled-back on him, slipping out of the belltower to hide elsewhere in the nave while he had been busy moving around the church, locking doors?

A forlorn hope? Probably.

But it was all she had.

So, gripping the clapper shaft with both hands, and fueled by her terror, Mia hoisted herself up inside, pressing her feet against first the lip and then the waist of the bell until she was as tucked up as she could be. Here, wedged in like this, with her shoulders and back pressed against one side and the soles of her shoes against the other, she felt secure enough to free one hand. And good thing too, because a moment later, the same something that had entered through the door at the bottom of the ladder opened the hatch and climbed into the small room at the top of the belltower.

"Happy shall he be…"

Mia clamped a hand over her mouth to stifle a scream. He sounded close, *so* close, *too* close.

"…that taketh and dasheth…"

She found herself suddenly longing for the fresh air that had briefly wafted in when she'd loosened that window board just now. The air in her hiding place tasted stale from decades of rust and mold, further tainted by the faintly metallic odor of blood.

How can there be dried blood here of all places?

But then she reminded herself that this church had been bathing in blood for a long time. Blood *and* despair. Together their cancer had seeped into every crack, soaked into every board, soured every inch of surface. She'd sensed it from the moment she'd first laid eyes on the place. So why wouldn't she be sensing it now?

The Evil Eye.

"…thy little ones against the stones."

It was a cruel verse from the Book of Psalms, with each word uttered in that flat, sonorous cadence of his, ringing of malice and sadistic glee. Mia could hear his footfalls moving through the small room, striding ever closer to her hiding place—and knew with terrible certainty that, despite his heavy tread, he would leave no prints in the thick dust.

And that made her realize with a thrill of terror, that she *had!*

"Throw out the worthless slave into the outer darkness…"

Mia squeezed her eyes shut because—hell, why not? What was there to see inside this cramped little space? She couldn't have "peeked" if she'd wanted to.

But the trapdoor was still open; she felt sure of it.

Can I get to it?

If she could, and if she managed to get through and onto the ladder, then maybe—just maybe—she could pull it shut, throw the latch, and trap him up here.

Except, he was *fast*. She'd seen just how fast he could move. He'd be on her like a pouncing lion the moment she dropped to the floor.

"…in that place there will be weeping and gnashing of teeth."

That one was from the New Testament. Matthew, Chapter 25. Like the first, it had been taken out of context. No hypocrite stooped as low as one who wore a righteous man's clothes. Mia tried to remember who'd said that but couldn't.

Swallowing, she opened her eyes and peered downward.

"Behold, I will corrupt your seed, and spread dung upon your faces…"

Moments later, a shadow passed directly below her, further darkening her already dark hiding place. Mia started and clamped her hand over her mouth again, but not before a tiny gasp escaped her lips. And the minute she heard the noise, little more than a plaintive squeak, she knew she'd condemned herself.

"…even the dung of your solemn feasts; and one shall—"

He stopped mid-verse, the loud but insubstantial footsteps and roiling shadows that bore him stopping as well.

"And there is no creature hidden from His sight…"

Mia prayed furiously to the Goddess. She had to fight the urge to close her eyes again. Now that he'd found her, that was just ostrich thinking, and she'd be damned if she'd give in to it. No, if this was the end, then she'd look him in the eye when—

The entire bell *moved* around her, shoved from without.

He's playing with me!

"...but all things are open and laid bare to the eyes of Him with whom we have to do."

"No!" Mia screamed. Then, almost without thinking, she made of "V" of her fingers and pressed them against both sides of her face, just under her eyes. It was a gesture she hadn't used in five years. But it had worked then, so maybe—just maybe—it would work now. Pushing down hard, almost painfully on her cheekbones, she focused her will and shoved it out of her. Her power was a sputtering candle compared to what he could manifest. But this simple gesture, performed in this awful place, had all her terror and rage behind it, fueling it, so that it rang almost as loudly and with as much gravitas as the big old bell inside of which she hid.

She heard him stagger back several steps, more likely in surprise than alarm. But it was an opening, narrow and fleeting, but an opening, and Mia took it.

She dropped to the floor, raising a cloud of dust when she landed and all but threw herself at the open trapdoor. As she did, she could feel the shadow turn toward her, tracking her movements, reaching for her. But she didn't look at it, tried her best not to even *think* about it. Instead, she focused on the exit and the ladder beyond it, old and wooden and rickety.

If I can just be quick enough...

"No one understands; no one seeks for God!"

"Go to Hell!" Mia called back. She dove headfirst through the hatchway. It was twelve feet to the landing and, if she fell that far, she'd likely split her skull as Derrick had. But if she could be adroit enough to grab the ladder, swing herself upright, and somehow reach the trapdoor—

But that was as far as she got.

The shadow, *his* shadow—the shadow that was him—caught her around the waist. She struggled frantically. But he was strong, impossibly, irresistibly strong.

"For all have sinned and fall short of the glory of God!"

Mia screamed again as he further enveloped her, smelling of rot and decay. Out of the corner of her eye, she could see his grin. Close. Predatory. This wasn't a man, not even the ghost of a man. This was a demon, just like Cooley had said, merciless and hungry for the lives of others.

All this Mia Lakatos sensed in the space of a single heartbeat, just before she was yanked off her feet and away from the only escape there was.

"The wages of sin are death…pretty little lamb…"

He threw her across the room. She didn't hit the far wall, but instead landed hard and rolled, the wind knocked out of her for the second time in ten minutes. Frantically, she tried to turn over, her chest heaving and her eyes swimming with tears. Then she felt something, something small in the pocket of her skirt and, realizing what it had to be, scrambled to pull it out.

"I. Am. A. Barton!" Avatard screamed, his face seeming to float amidst a roiling, shadowy blackness. As he glided across the floor toward her, a portion of his shadows solidified into a pair of long pale arms. One of them ended in a fist that gripped a now familiar pearl-handled straight razor.

Mia fumbled, her fingers digging into her pocket. But she'd landed badly on her side and wasn't quite able to reach it.

It didn't help that she couldn't catch her breath.

"I will make you my own," he said in a sharp, furious exhalation. If the apparition had been able to, Mia felt sure he would have spit at her. *"I will know your flesh, little sheep. I will replace your will with mine and I will spend eternity using every inch of you."*

Mia's fingers closed around the something and she drew it out.

Damn. I'd forgotten I'd even put it in there.

Then, as Avatard came and loomed over her, his razor at his side, Mia climbed to her knees. Moving with desperate intent, she switched the Doohickey in her shaking hands to UV mode, raised it, and pressed the switch.

Nothing happened.

Nothing at all.

He's drained its battery, she thought, and a final, helpless shudder passed through her. She let the gadget fall and her hand drop to her side.

It's over.

I tried. But it's over.

Except it wasn't. It was just beginning. In moments, she'd feel that razor slit her throat wide open as it had Rachel's and Lyle's and so many others. Then she'd wear his coins and belong forever to St. Damned.

Whatever Jonah Ray Avatard was, ghost or demon or something else, he laughed at her, his red eyes gleaming. As Mia watched, transfixed, as paralyzed now as any cornered prey, he raised his razor, the blade somehow shining despite the darkness.

"Don't worry...Dr. Lakatos," he said with a triumphant grin. *"The last enemy to be destroyed is death."*

Mia closed her eyes.

When nothing happened, and then *more* nothing happened, she opened them again.

Avatard still stood over her, a thing of darkness, most of his body as amorphous as smoke. His arm remained poised, the razor still gleaming weirdly in his grasp. But where his eyes had been aglow with triumph, they were now glassy with alarm.

A pale hand was around his wrist, holding it firm.

Mia's eyes, as wide and dry as any desert, traced the slender arm attached to that hand back to its owner.

Karen Jessup, dressed in what seemed to be white light rather than the bloody attire in which she'd died, stood at Avatard's side, gripping him with preternatural strength. Her other hand, her left hand, was wrapped protectively around a child, a little girl, who huddled beside her and looked up at the shadowy figure in Jessup's grasp with fascination but not a trace of fear.

"What are you doing?" Avatard demanded. *"This is my church! You can't be here!"*

Jessup didn't reply. She simply held him in an iron grasp as he struggled and writhed to get free.

"Karen?" Mia whispered, wondering if they could even hear her.

Then both woman and child—check that, *mother and daughter—*turned her way and, together, offered her the most beatific smiles that Mia had ever seen.

"Let me go!" screamed Avatard, thrashing like a trapped animal, snarling and whipping at the air with his free and empty hand.

Then, in a flash, *that* hand was seized as well.

Another figure, taller and broader than Jessup, seemed to flicker into existence at what passed for Avatard's other shoulder. This one was a man, and he seized that flailing wrist with a strength and confidence born of something outside this world. Mia stared at him, uncomprehending, until he turned her way and winked at her— the way he used to when she'd been a little girl.

"D…dad?"

Her father, the late Alexander Lakatos, didn't waste any time. He pulled back on Avatard, firmly securing the shadowy apparition between himself and Jessup. Then they paused, neither moving, neither speaking. It seemed to Mia as if they were waiting for something.

And, moments later, that something arrived.

As it had with Arias and his men, the veil between this reality and the next *thinned* at Avatard's back. He seemed to sense this because he started screaming, shrieking in abject disbelief and terror. In the next instant, something had him from behind and was pulling him, dragging him through the veil and out and away. In the last moments of his existence, the thing that had been Jonah Ray Avatard, son of Dominique and Fabron Avatard, fixed its eyes on Mia, the expression in them desperate and pleading, as if somehow begging her for deliverance.

Mia tried to muster up some pity. She truly did.

But she failed.

Then he was gone, swallowed up by whatever had claimed him. And this time, this time for certain, he would *not* be coming back. Mia wasn't sure how she knew that, but she did.

As Karen and Chelsea Jessup lingered there a moment longer, the little girl's mother nodded to Alexander Lakatos, who solemnly returned the gesture. Then both mother and child turned and, as so many of the other innocent souls in this place had done, stepped out of the world altogether.

That left only Mia and her father.

He gazed down at her, so strong, so proud. God, how she missed him. She missed him so much it was like a lost limb.

"Daddy..." she heard herself whisper.

And he spoke. The words were faint; a part of him, she guessed, was already gone. But she heard them, and she held onto them with everything she had, everything she was.

"So proud of you, peach."

Then he blew her a kiss, turned, and was gone.

Mia knelt on the dusty floor of the belltower and wept. She wept for a long time. She wept until she heard footsteps down below and the sound of someone climbing the ladder. She was still weeping when the DEA agent, a man she didn't know, found her. He tried to talk to her, but she had nothing to say, so he just wrapped her in a blanket and, very kindly, helped her stand and make her way slowly back down to the church's main floor.

In the vestibule, she found two more agents, and heard others, maybe as many as a dozen, moving through the nave. Big flashlights, much bigger than any her team had carried, drove back the darkness and revealed the carnage that St. Damien's once again contained. Mia heard some of them cursing, others retching. Someone, presumably the Agent in Charge, was barking orders.

Her escort guided her out the now open front doors and down the stoop to the walkway that led to the street. There, lying on a gurney beside a flashing ambulance, Renee Brubaker was talking to yet another agent while a paramedic affixed an IV to her arm and tended to her wounded knee. Delgado, God love him, was still beside her, staying so close that more than once the paramedic had to ask him to get out of the way.

But he didn't.

Brubaker spotted Mia, smiled, and waved her over.

Wordlessly, her escort led her there. As he did, she pulled the blanket more tightly around herself. The night had grown chilly.

"Are you all right?" Brubaker said.

Mia nodded.

"What happened?" Delgado asked.

Mia looked at them both. She'd tell them, of course. But not yet. Not now. There'd be plenty of time for questions, questions, and more questions. She knew this dance. Most of the people she talked to wouldn't believe her answers. Most of them would chalk it up to trauma or a fugue state or some other such nonsense.

But not Renee and Archie. Renee and Archie would believe.

And maybe, just maybe, Mia would get her first good night's sleep in five years.

"'This house...'" she quoted in as strong a voice as she could muster. "'...is clean.'"

Delgado simply looked confused. But Brubaker surprised Mia by reaching out and taking hold of her hand. "Hollywood clean?" the assistant director asked, as if it were the most important question in the world. And just maybe it was. "Or *really* clean?"

So, taking the other woman's hand in both of hers and squeezing it, Mia Lakatos delivered the answer that question deserved. "Really and truly clean."

CASTLE BRIDGE MEDIA RECOMMENDS...

If you liked this book, you might also enjoy reading the following titles from Castle Bridge Media available on Amazon or by order at your favorite book store:

Animal Charmer
By Rain Nox

Austinites
By In Churl Yo

Bloodsucker City
By Jim Towns

The Burning Gem
By Don Sawyer

THE CASTLE OF HORROR ANTHOLOGY SERIES
Volume 1
Volume 2: *Holiday Horrors*
Volume 3: *Scary Summer Stories*
Volume 4: *Women Running From Houses*
Volume 5: *Thinly Veiled: The 70s*
Volume 6: *Femme Fatales**
Volume 7: *Love Gone Wrong*
Volume 8: *Thinly Veiled: The 80s*
Volume 9: *Young Adult*
Volume 10: *Thinly Veiled: Saturday Mournings*
Volume 11: *Revenge*
Edited By Jason Henderson and In Churl Yo
*Edited By P.J. Hoover

Castle of Horror Podcast Book of Great Horror: Our Favorites, Top Tens and Bizarre Pleasures
Edited By Jason Henderson

Cherry Dark
By R.L. Wilburn

Dream State
By Martin Ott

Dominic
By Lee Guzman

FRENCH DECEPTION
A Forgery in Paris
By Janice Nagourney
A Forgery in Lyon
By Janice Nagourney

FuturePast Sci-Fi Anthology
Edited by In Churl Yo

GLAZIER'S GAP
Ghosts of the Forbidden
By Leanna Renee Hieber

Hellfall
By Jay Gould

Isonation
By In Churl Yo

JAYU CITY CHRONICLES
The Hermes Protocol
By Chris M. Arnone
Necropolis Alpha
By Chris M. Arnone

Junk Film: Why Bad Movies Matter
By Katharine Coldiron

MID-LIFE CRISIS THRILLERS
18 Miles From Town
By Jason Henderson
Lost Angel
By Sam Knight
Ties That Kill
By Deven Greene

Nightwalkers: Gothic Horror Movies
By Bruce Lanier Wright

THE PATH
The Blue-Spangled Blue
By David Bowles
The Deepest Green
By David Bowles

St. Damned
By Ty Drago

SURF MYSTIC
Night of the Book Man
By Peyton Douglas
Dark of the Curl
By Peyton Douglas

The 23rd Hero
By Rebecca Anne Nguyen

Vinyl Wonderland
By Mark Rigney

Yesterday's Tomorrows: The Golden Age of Science Fiction Movies
By Bruce Lanier Wright

Please remember to leave us your reviews on Amazon and Goodreads!

THANK YOU FOR SUPPORTING INDEPENDENT PUBLISHERS AND AUTHORS!
castlebridgemedia.com